THE DARKNESS

by Jason Pinter

eISBN 978-1-947993-22-8

First published December 2009 by MIRA Books
Reissued November 2017 by Armina Press

The Darkness
a Henry Parker novel
by Jason Pinter

THE DARKNESS

Also by Jason Pinter

The Henry Parker Series
THE MARK
THE GUILTY
THE STOLEN
THE FURY
THE HUNTERS (novella)
THE DARKNESS

THE CASTLE (standalone)

Chapter 1

Paulina Cole left the office at four fifty nine p.m. Her sudden departure nearly caused a panic in the newsroom of the New York Dispatch, where she'd worked as a featured columnist and reporter for several years. Paulina was prone to late nights, though many argued whether the nights were due to a work ethic that was second to none, or simply because she was more comfortable spending her time among competitive, ambitious and bloodthirsty professionals than sitting on the couch with a glass of wine and takeout.

She had left that day after a particularly frustrating conference call with the paper's editor-in-chief, Ted Allen. Paulina had spent the better part of two years becoming the city's most notorious scribe in no small part due to her ambivalence concerning personal attacks, heated vendettas, and a complete refusal to allow anyone to get the best of her. When her instincts faltered, she called in favors. When she got scooped, she would trump the scoop by digging deeper. And she held grudges like ordinary folks held onto prized heirlooms.

Which is why, after reading a copy of that morning's New York Gazette, the paper Paulina used to work for and now wished buried under a paper landfill, she demanded to speak with Ted. She knew the man had a two o'clock tee time, but she'd seen him golf before and cell phone interruption might even improve his thirty seven handicap.

That day's Gazette featured a story about the murder of a young man named Stephen Gaines. Gaines's head had met the wrong end of a bullet recently, and in a twist of fate that Paulina could only have wished for on the most glorious of days, the prime suspect was none other than Gaines's father, James Parker. James Parker also happened to be the father of Henry Parker, the Gazette's rising young star reporter, whom Paulina had as much fondness for as her monthly cycle.

Paulina had cut her teeth at the Gazette, and had briefly worked side-by-side with Henry Parker. But after seeing what the Gazette had become--an old, tired rag, refusing to get with the program that hard news was essentially dead--she'd made it her business to put the paper out of its misery.

Nobody cared to read about the government or the economy--they only cared about what they saw right in front of them, day in and day out. It was all visceral. You bought the celebrity magazine so you could make fun of the stars' cellulite with your friends. You shook your head at the news program that exposed the foreman whose building was overrun with rats because he refused to pony up for an exterminator. You scorned the politician's wife who stood at the press conference by her cheating louse of a husband. Paulina gave those with no life something to live for.

The New York Gazette was dead. It just didn't know it yet.

So when Ted Allen suggested that Paulina write an article about vampires, she was taken aback to say the least.

"Vampires are huge," Allen had said. "There are those books that have sold like a gajillion copies. Now there are movies, television shows, soundtrack albums. Hell, newspapers are the only medium that isn't getting a piece of it. Teenage girls love them, and teenage boys want to get into the pants of teenage girls. And this all scares the living hell--no pun intended--out of their parents, so you write a piece on vampires I bet it's one of our best selling issues of the year."

"What the hell do I write about a fictional creature?" Paulina said, laughing at herself for even asking the question.

"Oh, I don't know," Allen had said, clueless as ever. "Didn't I hear about some boys and girls who go around biting people on the neck because they think they can be vampires? Go interview them. Even better, go undercover and pretend to be one of them. You know, pretend you like to bite peoples' necks and see what they tell you."

"Ted, I'm almost forty," Paulina said. "I don't think undercover will work."

"Are you kidding?" Ted said. "What's that term? Milf? The teenage boys will love you."

That's when Paulina left.

Rain beat down upon the streets steadily, with the precision of soft drumbeats. The drops splashed upward as they struck the pavement, and Paulina felt the water soaking her ankles as she exited into the gloom. A bottle of Finca Vieja Tempranillio was waiting at home. It was a good red wine, with a slight plum taste, and she could picture slipping into a warm bath with a glass in one hand and a romance novel in the other. The rest of the bottle sitting on the ledge just within reach, ready to be tilted until the last drops were consumed. Ordinarily she was not that kind of girl, but Paulina needed a night away from it all.

Paulina opened up an umbrella, and stepped into the sea of New Yorkers, entering the crowded bloodstream known as the commute home. The streets were chock full of open umbrellas, and she tried to wedge her way into the crowd without having her eye poked out by a random spoke.

As she took her first step from under the Dispatch's canopy, Paulina heard a man's voice yell, "Miss Cole! Miss Cole!"

She saw a man wearing a dapper suit and dark overcoat approaching her. He was tall, six one or two, with hair so blond it was nearly white, peeking out from underneath a billed cap. He looked to be in good shape, late thirties or early forties and for a brief moment Paulina felt her heart rate speed up. The car service company had really stepped up their recruiting.

"Miss Cole," the man said, stopping in front of her. "My name is Chester. I'm from New York Taxi and Limo service. Ted Allen called to request a ride home for you."

"Is that so," Paulina said, barely hiding her smile. She knew months ago that she had Ted by the balls. Keeping her happy and pumping out pieces was worth hundreds of thousands of dollars a year to the Dispatch, and the publicity she received raised the paper's profile more than their 'crackerjack' investigative team ever could. That Ted would extend an olive branch so quickly surprised her at first, but if she ran the company she'd want to make sure her star reporter got home safe, sound, and dry.

"Please," Chester said, "come with me."

He opened up a much larger umbrella and held it out. Paulina smiled at him, a big, bright, toothy smile, and stepped under the umbrella. He led her to a Lincoln Town car which sat double parked at the curb. Holding the umbrella to shield her from the rain, the driver opened the door. Paulina thanked him, picked up the hem of her skirt and climbed into the back seat of the car. The driver shut the door, and Paulina watched as he walked around to the front.

Two sealed bottles of water were set in a pair of cup holders, and crisp new editions of that morning's newspapers were folded in the pocket in front of her. The rain pattered against the windows, as Paulina unscrewed one of the bottles and took a long, deep sip.

The driver flicked on his blinker and pulled into traffic. He headed uptown. The only sound Paulina could hear was the rubber squeaking of the windshield wipers. The only smell that of the car's leather.

"Good day, Miss?" the driver asked.

"Better than some, worse than others," she replied. Traffic was bumper to bumper, and the car inched along. Paulina began to grow restless. As much as she hated taking the subway, she probably would have been home by now.

"You think there might be a faster route?" she asked, leaning forward slightly when the car stopped at a red light. The driver turned around, grinned.

"Let's see what we can do."

The driver made a right turn, and soon the car was heading east. When they got to First Avenue, Paulina could see signs for the FDR drive north. He pulled onto the on ramp and headed uptown. The FDR tended to get flooded during heavy rain, but Paulina didn't mind chancing that to get home quicker. She watched the cars outside, eyes widening as she saw her exit, 61st street, appear in the distance. Yet instead of slowing down and pulling left towards the exit ramp, the car sped along, bypassing the exit completely.

"Hey!" Paulina said, leaning forward again. "You should have gotten off there."

"My apologies," the driver said, "I must not have seen it."

Paulina cursed under her breath. The next exit wasn't until 96th street, and then he would have to loop all the way back downtown. Just like Ted Allen to hire a car service for her and get the one driver who didn't know North from South.

Traffic moved along steadily, and Paulina sighed as they approached the 96th street exit.

"Exit's coming up," she said, making sure to remind him.

"Got it, thanks Miss Cole.

As they approached the exit, Paulina noticed the car was not slowing down at all.

"Hey, slow down? The hell is wrong with you, you're doing to miss it!"

The car drove right by the 96th street exit without slowing down one bit.

"Where the hell are you going?" Paulina yelled. The driver did not answer. "I'm calling Ted. You're never going to work our account again."

"Put the phone down, Miss Cole." The driver's voice had lost all of its pleasantries.

"Screw you. Now I'm calling the cops. Forget our account, your ass is going to jail." She took out her cell phone and flipped open the cover.

"If you ever want to see your daughter with all her limbs intact, you'll put the phone down right now."

Paulina's mouth fell open in a silent scream. Her daughter... how? Paulina's daughter lived with her first husband, a wreck of a man named Chad Wozniak. He was a good father, an aspiring architect who never made it past the word aspiring. He was a good man, a decent man, but not a provider. That's what Paulina had wanted for her family, but in the end she had to do what Chad could not.

Abigail. She was twenty years old. A junior in college. A 3.7 average, captain of the soccer team at some all girls school up in Massachusetts. She and Paulina barely spoke. Maybe once every few months, and usually only when Abby's checking account ran low. Abby was beautiful, even if sometimes this budding young woman seemed like a stranger to her own mother.

"You're a sick monster," Paulina said, closing the phone.

"Don't be like that. We're almost there."

The driver took the FDR to the Triboro bridge, pulling off once they'd arrived in Queens. He skidded around an off ramp, took several turns in a neighborhood Paulina did not recognize, and slowly eased into an alleyway bookended by two buildings that looked like they were about to collapse. Paulina could see nobody, hear nobody. She was all alone with this man. Through the rain and desolation, nobody would hear her if she screamed.

The driver exited the car and walked around to the back seat. Paulina locked the door from the inside. She heard a click as the driver unlocked it with his remote. Before she could lock it again, he threw open the door, grabbed Paulina by her coat and spun her into the mud.

Wet slop splashed into her eyes. Paulina felt her eyes grow warm, anger rising inside of her. She launched herself at the man, her nails bared to rake at his face, but he merely grabbed her by the neck, held it for one horrible moment as he stared into her eyes.

Then Paulina felt him press something against her side, and suddenly she felt a scorching pain worse than anything she'd ever experiences. Her body twitched as she screamed. She lost control of her bladder, then dropped face down into the mud. Paulina looked up to see the man holding a taser, smiling.

"I wouldn't do that again. I can smell your piss."

Paulina could feel hot tears pouring down her face. She was on her hands and knees, caked in grime, and her body felt like it had just been plugged into an electrical socket. She slowly got to her knees, managed to stand up, her breath harsh and ragged.

"What do you want?" she cried. "Money? Sex?" She shuddered at the last word, praying he didn't, praying there was something else, something that wouldn't leave a scar. Pain she could take, but that kind of pain would never leave.

The man shook his head. Holding the taser, he reached inside his overcoat, rain beading down the dark fabric. The water spilled down his forehead into his eyes, but the man who called himself Chester hardly seemed to notice.

He removed something from his pocket and held it out to Paulina. She focused her eyes, then gasped.

It was a picture of her daughter, Abby. She was at the beach, wearing a cute pink bikini, standing in front of a massive hole she must have dug in the sand. The photo looked fairly recent, within the last year or so. Abigail's eyes were bright and cheerful, her skin a golden brown. Abby. She looked so joyful.

Her daughter. Her blood.

"Where did you get that?" Paulina yelled.

"Do you really need to ask? I had a dozen others to choose from. You really should tell her to be careful of what photos she posts on the Internet."

"You're a freak," she spat. "What the hell do you want?"

"I want you to listen to me very carefully," the man said. He stepped closer, still holding out the photograph. Water droplets landed on the photo but he didn't seem to care. "A long time ago, I fought in a war. I fought alongside men and women who were like my own blood. Then, one day, we found ourselves trapped. There was one man I fought with who was closer to me than anyone. He was like a daughter. A mother. A brother."

Paulina shivered.

"That day, we found ourselves fighting for our lives. And all of a sudden, out of nowhere, someone throws a grenade at us. I was out of harm's way, but the grenade went off right beside this man I cared about. I remember looking at him after the smoke cleared. He blinked his eyes, looked around like he was just confused. The only thing I remember more than his eyes was the splash of blood beneath him. Right where his legs had been blown clean off."

Then, in one fluid motion, he held the right side of the photo with his thumb and forefinger, tore off a piece and let it flutter to the ground. It landed in front of Paulina, speckled by rain and mud.

"This is what your daughter will look like when I cut off her legs"

Paulina felt her stomach heave, her mouth opening, her eyes burning as she cried. She reached out for the photo, but was too weak to do anything.

"Blood has its own smell. It makes you want to vomit. And imagine what happens when you see that much blood coming from someone you love."

He gripped the picture, and ripped off another piece. Again the shred fell, twisting in the rain.

"This is what your daughter will look like when I cut off her right arm."

"Please," Paulina whispered, her throat so constricted she could barely talk. She closed her eyes. "Stop. Just stop."

The man stood there, holding the mutilated picture out for Paulina to see. "Open your eyes," he said. Paulina shook her head. "Open them!"

She did.

"I have something for you," the man said. "I want you to take it home with you and I want you to read it."

"What?" she said, blinking away the tears.

"When you've read it, I want you to write an article for your newspaper based on the information contained within. Your article will run this Thursday. If it does not, for any reason whatsoever..." the man took the photo and ripped off a piece. Then he dropped the tattered photo into the mud.

"I will cut off your daughter's head and send it to you in a box."

He walked over to Paulina, and before she could react he grabbed her by the hair and thrust the taser into her side. Again Paulina shrieked, and again she fell into the mud, panting.

"If you don't do what I say, before I rip your daughter apart I will burn her in places only her mother knows about."

The man took an envelope from inside his jacket. It was sealed in plastic. He gave it to Paulina.

"This is the last you'll hear from me if you do what I say. If you tell anyone, I'll will tear Abigail apart limb by limb. If you go to the police, I will know you did and I will burn her body after I kill her. I will know. I'll burn it so thoroughly they won't be able to identify a single piece of her flesh, and the last time you will ever see your daughter whole is in photographs. I will save her severed limbs and leave them on your doorstep. " The man paused, watched the blood drain from Paulina's face. "If you live up to your end, your daughter will be able to live the rest of her life like a normal girl. She will be blissfully ignorant of what happened tonight." Chester did not find this funny. "Otherwise, she will know a pain of which you've only felt a fraction of tonight."

"Please," Paulina mewled.

Chester looked at the photograph of Abigail on the beach, her smile wide like a small child. "If not, the only bliss she'll know is whatever happens after she dies at my hands."

Paulina took the plastic, turned it over in her hands. Then she looked at him, confused.

"In there is everything you need to know. And make sure you don't lose the piece at the bottom."

Paulina looked at the bottom of the clear folder and saw what appeared to be a small, block rock, no bigger than a pebble.

Paulina sat there, crying, sniveling and drenched. Chester stared down at her, rain dripping off the tip of his nose.

"For your sake, I hope your daughter doesn't have to die. Terrible thing to lose one's family. But that's up to you."

By the time she looked up, the driver was back in his car.

Something about those words felt personal, as though Chester had experienced loss himself. Then the engine revved, and he was gone. Paulina sat in the rain, mud staining her dress brown.

She watched him go, waiting to make sure he was gone. Her body was wracked with pain, and she could barely stand. Her hands felt like they'd held a battery from both ends, and when she dialed the car service it took three tries to get the number right. When he asked where she was, Paulina had to walk ten minutes just to find a street sign.

"What the heck are you doing way out there?" the man asked.

"Just get here, fast," she said before hanging up.

It was half an hour before the car service arrived. Paulina huddled under a nearby tarp to stay dry. The driver, a short, thick man with a bushy mustache, got out. He looked her over, his lip curled up. He was as confused as she was.

"Miss," he said, "are you ok? Do you need me to take you to the hospital?"

"Just take me home," she said. "And help me up."

The driver bent down, put his arm around Paulina, and helped the shuddering reporter into the backseat of his car.

As he drove away, the man said, "Don't worry, miss. I'm taking you home. Everything's ok."

Paulina looked up at him, slimy mascara stinging her eyes. And she thought, no. It's not.

Chapter 2

Monday

New York City exists in a perpetual headwind. If you live here or work here, you can either lean into the wind and brace yourself, moving forward a step at a time, keeping pace with the other people who are doing the same. Or you can lose your balance and be blown away like a crumpled newspaper. Some people lean into the wind and try to walk faster. They press ahead; moving at greater speeds than the rest of us. But with greater reward comes greater risk, and the harder you lean the harder you might fall.

My brother fell. My idol and mentor, Jack O'Donnell fell. I was still leaning into the wind, sometimes hard enough to lose my balance. I'd lived and worked in this gusty city for several years now, and thought I was used to it. But time and time again, the city showed me just how strong its winds could be.

I got to the office at eight o'clock sharp, half an hour before I was supposed to be there, and even fifteen minutes before I'd said I'd be there. To put it mildly, this was the most excited I'd been about the job in a long time.

The last few weeks had been a maelstrom of violence and secrets. I'd recently learned that my father had had an affair thirty years ago, and that affair resulted in the birth of a boy named Stephen Gaines. My brother.

I didn't learn about Stephen until just a few weeks ago, when he showed up out of nowhere at the offices of the New York Gazette, where I worked as a reporter. Gaines was stoned and scared out of his mind that night, and for that reason I didn't give him a chance to tell his story. I didn't see the man up close until a few hours later. After I learned he'd been shot to death in his own apartment.

Not what you'd call the most enjoyable family reunion.

I'd pieced the truth together in a large part spurred on by a book written by Jack O'Donnell called Through the Darkness. In that book, he discussed the murder of a lowly drug dealer named Butch

Willingham who was possibly murdered by an elusive drug kingpin nicknamed 'The Fury.'

Yet the truth wasn't whole. If the Fury did exist, then something big was on the horizon. Butch Willingham's murder was one of a spate of drug-related murders, and if history did repeat itself that meant Stephen's murder was merely the beginning.

Coming to grips with the life and death of the brother I'd never known was difficult, if not impossible. It was something I was still struggling with. Eventually we tracked down the man who killed him, a low level drug dealer who seemed to want Gaines dead to open up the door for his own upward mobility in the New York drug trade.

But something about it still didn't sit right. It was too neat, too clean. Too many questions still lingered, an open wound that wouldn't close.

And leave it to Jack O'Donnell to throw a crowbar into the wound.

I was wearing a suit, the same one I'd worn on my very first day in the office several years ago. I remembered the day clearly. Meeting Wallace Langston, the paper's editor-in-chief, being led to my desk where I'd write the stories I was born to write. Seeing the man, Jack O'Donnell, in person for the first time.

The man was a legend of the New York newsroom, as synonymous with this city as any one of its towering monuments. But every monument has cracks, ignored by those who prefer to their gods as unfailing, monuments pristine in their foundations and men pure in their humanity. Yet while Jack raised the bar for journalism, his cracks had begun to show themselves not just to me, but to millions of people.

We all knew that Jack drank. But when you told people Jack drank, you raised your eyebrows and enunciated the word 'drank' like it was hepatitis. Jack O'Donnell drank.

Three martini lunches might have fallen out of fashion, but Jack was trying to keep the tradition going almost singlehandedly. And who else would expose the cracks in the foundation but someone who resided as low to the ground as possible.

Paulina Cole used to work with Jack at the Gazette. A few months ago, she penned a hatchet job to end all hatchet jobs, exposing Jack's drinking problem on the front page in our rival paper, the New York Dispatch. It was a colossal embarrassment to his reputation, personally and professionally.

Then Jack disappeared.

Whether he was in rehab or lying in the gutter somewhere, I figured the man needed time to figure out if he was going to be swallowed whole by his demons, or if he still had the strength to fight them off. My answer came, surprisingly, when I needed him the most.

After I learned the truth about Stephen's killer, Jack found me at my home just as my girlfriend, Amanda, and I were packing up. He told me he'd needed a 'dialysis of the soul.' He looked good. Healthy. And raring to go to answer the questions that Stephen's murder just touched upon.

Anyway, that's what I was doing here early in the morning. I wanted to get here before him. Though we'd worked in the same offices for several years, I'd never had the chance to work side by side with Jack. I was eager to prove what I'd learned, eager to prove that there was someone waiting in the wings to carry on the traditions he'd started. And what better way to show I was ready than by beating the man to his desk on his first day back in the office?

So when I got off on the ninth floor, pushed through the glass doors to the newsroom, rounded the corner to the sea of news desks, I was shocked to see Jack O'Donnell surrounded by our colleagues, looking like a kid at his own birthday party.

He was sitting on his desk, feet on his desk chair, speaking loudly and buoyantly while the other reporters and editors laughed and slapped him on the back. I hadn't seen Jack with this much energy since, well, ever. And any frustration I felt in getting here late disappeared when I saw the smile on the old man's face.

It was like a returning war hero being embraced by his countrymen. While Jack was gone, one of the things I wished I understood better was the newsroom's opinion of him. While I always held his professional career in the highest regard, there were no doubt others who looked at his departure as something of an embarrassment. Any time a paper's reporter ends up in the headlines instead of below them, it was considered an affront to the integrity of the establishment. The New York Times went through it with Jayson Blair, and the Gazette had gone through it twice in the last several years: the exposure of Jack's alcoholism by Paulina Cole at the Dispatch, and when I was accused of committing murder. And while the truth about my situation eventually came to light, the harsh reality was that every word in Paulina's story was true. Granted she handled it with the class and dignity of a five dollar hooker, but her words touched a nerve because they cut deep.

The stain on my reputation had begun to disappear over time. I didn't know if Jack's ever would.

"Henry!" Jack's voice boomed over the newsroom. He was waving me over, the reporters around his desk looking in my direction expectantly. I smiled, big and wide, and walked over.

"Jack," I said, "how's the first day back?"

"Coffee still sucks, elevator's still slow, and the receptionist still doesn't know my name. Just another day at the office, and I'm loving it."

He was wearing a suit and tie that both looked new. His beard, usually shaggy, was neat, the grey more evenly spread. The bags beneath his eyes looked to have dissolved, and his movement were sharper, livelier. It was great to see him like this, and though my smile was wide on the outside, it was nothing compared to how I felt inside.

Jonas Levinson, the paper's science editor, said, "We didn't know when we'd seen you again old boy. No note, no forwarding address. Who are you, my ex-wife?"

"I guess when you have enough of them," Jack said, "you start to inhabit their best qualities." The group laughed.

"Coffee tastes a whole lot better with a sprinkle of Beam in there," Frank Rourke said. "I got a bottle at my desk Jack, stop by if you need a taste."

The smile disappeared from Jack's face. "Hey Frank?"

"Hey Jack-O?"

"Why don't you go back to your desk and slam a drawer on your head a few times."

Rourke seemed taken aback. "Christ, it was just a joke O'Donnell."

"Just leave. Amazingly you've got less tact than brains, and that's not an easy feat. Go on, git."

Rourke walked away, fuming. Jack's face warmed again, then he turned to me. Speaking to the rest of the crew, he said, "Fellas, would you give me and Henry a minute?"

They all gave Jack a firm handshake, a pat on the back, a hug or two. I could tell Jack hadn't been hugged a whole lot. he wasn't sure where to place his hands. Once the crowd had thinned, he motioned for me to pull up a chair. I grabbed one from an empty desk a few rows away and pulled it into his cube. "Sit down," he said. I obliged.

"It's great to have you back," I said. "I wasn't sure..."

"You're late," Jack said. I checked my watch.

"It's not even ten past eight. You told me to be here at eight thirty."

"Let me ask you this. If a press conference is called for four and you show up at three thirty, you'll be sitting in the back row with the reporters from the high school newspapers."

"I get your point," I said.

Jack continued. "So far, you've made it by on talent and luck. You want to be great at this job you need to add a spoonful of brains. With the story we're going to be chasing, there's no half an hour early. Murderers don't want for you to be on time. Drug dealers don't use personal data organizers. When you catch people off guard, that's when the truth comes out. Never give someone the time to make up a lie."

"I know how important this is" I said, "I know that what my brother was killed for goes higher than the assholes who pulled the trigger."

Jack stared at me. "You don't know anything, Henry. You never go into a story' knowing' anything. A good reporter is open to every possibility. If you have on blinders, you miss the bigger picture. You might think there's a massive conspiracy, but miss the intimate picture. You may be right about Gaines. But you don't know anything yet. So let the picture paint itself for you."

"Gaines was killed because somebody thought bumping him off was the quickest route to money and power," I said. "And they wouldn't have thought that without a reason."

"You said there was a connection between Gaines and some company, right?"

"718 Enterprises," I replied. "I think it's a shell corporation. I saw a battalion of drug dealers leaving the company's midtown head-quarters, but I didn't find out what it is or who runs it. Plus my buddy at the NYPD, Curt Sheffield, told me that five people connected to 718 have been killed over the last few months. 718 is hiding something major, and for some reason its employees have shorter shelf lives than a chicken at KFC. So you think we should start by looking into 718?"

Jack put his thumb to his lip, tapped it as he thought. Then he shook his head. "You don't get a story by meeting it head on. You need to confront the big dogs with facts, not accusations. We need to poke around. Find out who and what exists at the peripherals. We..."

Just then my cell phone rang. I noticed that the red message light was blinking at the voicemail on my desk. Whoever was calling had tried to reach me at the office and was now calling my cell.

My first thought was Amanda, but she was likely on her way to the office. Taking the phone from my pocket, the number made my stomach crawl a bit. There's no way he'd be calling this early in the morning unless something had happened. Something bad.

I answered the phone. "Curt?" I said.

"Henry," Curt Sheffield said. Curt was an officer with the NYPD. A good buddy and dedicated cop. He'd helped me with numerous cases over the last few years, often giving me scoops ahead of other papers because he knew I'd do the right thing with them. A lot of other news outlets, not that I'd name names, would takes quotes out of context, make officers who stuck their necks out look bad.

The thing you learned in the news business was that the cops needed you almost as badly as you needed them. If the cops needed to swing public opinion on a certain topic, or if they needed help from the community in catching a perp, they turned to the papers and television anchors. It wasn't enough for them to come up with a sketch of an alleged rapist--they needed a medium to get the guy's face in front of millions of people. Curt understood that. He wasn't looking for fame, to see his name in the paper or the sense of rebellious pride most sources had.

"You should come down here right away," the cop said.

"Where are you?" I said. "What's going on?"

"There's been a murder. Just dredged the body up from the East River this morning," he said. And something in Curt's voice told me this wasn't just any run-of-the mill, domestic quarrel or guy jumping off the Triboro bridge death. "We've identified the body. His name was Ken Tsang. We checked his records, and Henry... the guy was Hector Guardado's roommate."

"Jesus," I said, my heart pounding. Jack's eyes were wide open, imploring me to tell him what was going on.

Hector Guardado, I believed, worked as a drug courier for 718

Enterprises. He was a colleague of the men who killed Stephen Gaines, one of the anonymous suits who delivered their drugs to buyers in their homes.

Guardado was killed just a few days ago. And now his roommate was dead as well.

"I'll be right down there," I said. "Where are you?"

"84th by the East River, on the promenade" Curt said. "You might want to bring some anti-nausea medication."

"Why?" I said. "What happened?"

"Whoever killed Ken Tsang," Curt said, "wanted his corpse to have more in common with a boneless chicken than a human being. Somebody broke every single one of his joints. Turned his toes, fingers, arms, legs and finally neck in all sorts of ways they ain't supposed to go."

Chapter 3

By the time Jack and I arrived at the East River, the smell of vomit was choking the air. The view from the promenade was breathtaking early in the morning. The sun glistened off the river, as New Yorkers jogged, walked their dogs, sat in silence admiring the beauty. Normally you would see fishing poles out. Today's catch must have driven them away.

The scene on this day, though, had the promenade at a standstill. There were no bystanders going about their business, they were all being held back by the same yellow police tape that would soon carton off my colleagues and competition.

I could see three cops who, by the look of them, were a breakfast short and still green around the gills. They'd roped off about fifty feet along the red brick walkway, and from just beyond that I could make out a white sheet covering the outline of a body. An ambulance waited twenty feet away. it's lights weren't on. They didn't need t be. There was no rush here.

"You never like to see cops this quiet," Jack said. "Most of the guys on the force, they've seen everything. Drive-by victims, people burned to death, children, everything. One thing we have in common with them, you need to learn to desensitize yourself from the horrors you see sometimes. Without that, you won't last a year on either job. It takes a lot to send a shockwave through those nervous systems."

I saw Curt Sheffield among the crowd of cops. He saw me and began to walk over. I didn't see any other reporters just yet, Curt must have given me first shot at this.

"Hey Henry," he said, nodding. He didn't offer his hand, and I didn't expect it. Even though we were friends, cops were expected to keep their distance from reporters. They were naturally distrustful of us, and as much as I hated to admit it, sometimes rightfully so. I'd seen what the media could brew without all the facts. News, like a bell, could not be unrung. Once you were accused of something, once information was given to the public, it was nearly gospel. And for cops, once your uniform was stained, fair or unfair, it never washed off.

"Hey man," I said. "Thanks for the heads up on this."

"Don't mention it," he said. Curt was a good looking guy, about six two, and filled out his uniform. As a young, black officer, he'd made high marks and was even used in some promotional materials for the department when recruiting was down. The taglines on the poster read: Good people make good cops. Good cops make a great city. Curt was a good cop, and as much as he hated to admit it a good poster child. Thankfully for him he didn't get recognized on the street much anymore. "I see a few motherchuckers in the crowd."

"You see that body," Curt said, "you're lose your last three meals, guaranteed."

"You look fine to me," I said.

"That's cause the girl I'm seeing, Denise, can't cook anything that doesn't say 'microwavable' on the box. And even then I have to remind her to take it out of the box."

"You're kidding me."

"Oh yeah? I had chicken casserole a la cardboard two nights in a row. I swear, if the girl didn't screw like a jackalope..."

"How's the leg?" I said. Talking about sex in front of Jack had the same appeal as discussing it with my parents. Curt had taken a bullet recently, the bullet nicking an artery, necessitating some time off the streets. The man went stir crazy, but considered his scar a badge.

Not to mention he liked to talk about it more than sex.

"Feels good today. Hurt like hell yesterday. Touch and go. Know the worst thing about being shot in the leg? You can't really show people the scar without causing a scene." Curt looked at Jack. I realized they'd never met.

"Sorry. Jack, this is Officer Curtis Sheffield. Curt, Jack O'Donnell."

They both nodded, familiar with the drill.

"Henry's talked a lot about you," Curt said. "I figure he must go through your garbage the way he knows you front to back. Take care of our boy, he's one of the few journos we can trust in this burg."

"I'll teach him everything I know," Jack said with a smile.

"Hey," I said, "how's Detective Makhoulian? I didn't really get to thank him for his help."

Detective Sevag Makhoulian was the officer assigned to investigating my brother's death, He'd been an invaluable asset to the investigation. Plus he had impeccable timing. Makhoulian was Armenian. Quiet and intense, as no nonsense as they came, but he'd proved his reliability and dedication. I owed him, big time.

"He's doing well. Mandatory leave for an officer involved shooting, but it's a clean cut case and he'll be back on the street any day now."

"Good. City needs more cops like you guys."

"Not going to argue with you there. I keep telling my captain that they need to clone my ass. Sure as hell save the city some money, and they need to save every penny they can these days"

Jack decided to chime in. "So according to Henry," he said, "Ken Tsang's body was beaten pretty bad?"

"Naw. The cops pushing three bills who have to play center field on our softball team get beaten pretty bad. This guy looks like somebody took a baseball bat and decided to flatten him out to the point where you can slip him inside a mail slot."

I felt a bad taste in the back of my throat.

Curt said, "Worst part is, forensics thinks at least half of the bone breaks were inflicted post mortem. Which means whoever killed Tsang didn't just want him to hurt. They wanted people to see him look more like a bean bag than a person."

"First Hector, now his roommate. Somebody is taking out drug runners in the city."

"Taking them out," Curt said, "with extreme prejudice. This isn't just about somebody cleaning up their mess, this is sending a message that if you don't watch your back, you'll find yourself dumped in the East River a whole lot more flexible than when you woke up that morning. What I want to know is, who is this message going to?"

"Officer Sheffield, where exactly was the body found?" Jack asked. He'd taken out a small notepad, uncapping a pen with his teeth. I did the same, feeling somewhat foolish. Normally when I talked to Curt it was informal. Friend talking to friend, both aware of the other's professional responsibilities. But Jack was right. The story came first. Curt looked at the pad, saw Jack was waiting for his answer.

"Garbage scow saw a big canvas bag floating in the river, a few blocks south of the garbage transfer station on 91st street."

"The body was in a bag?" I said. Curt nodded.

"Big, heavy burlap sack."

"You said it was floating," Jack said. "How would a canvas bag with a body inside float on a river without sinking?"

Curt blinked. He wasn't holding back. He just didn't know.

"Hold on a second," he said. He walked of quickly, and I could tell Curt was as curious about the answer to that question as we were.

Jack was busy scribbling in his notepad. I held back a smile. His eyes were focused, his handwriting sloppy but that didn't matter. Mine was no great shakes either, but as long as we could decipher our own it would make due. Of course recently my handwriting had taken a turn for the worse, which led to several notes from Evelyn Waterstone, the Gazette's managing editor, with helpful tips like 'Learn basic penmanship.'

"How you feeling?" I said to Jack.

"Hm?" He didn't look up from the page.

"Just wondering how you're feeling. That's all."

"Fine," he said. "Why wouldn't I be?"

I waited to see if he was going to laugh, but Jack was totally serious.

"I mean, come on, this is your first day back on the job in almost a year. You disappeared faster than Michael Moore at a Weight Watcher's convention, and nobody's heard from you. Just, you know, want to see how you're holding up."

"Just fine," Jack said with a wry smile. "If I start to slag, be sure to tell me,"

I just nodded, then saw Curt Sheffield walking towards us. There was a strange look on his face, his lip turned upwards as if processing information. He came over to where we were standing and said, "Guy was inside a bag that was tied to a buoy."

"A buoy?" Jack said, eyebrows raised.

"Yeah, the body was in a big burlap sack, but get this: whoever dropped it into the drink attached it to a freaking buoy. Not only that, but they tied a freaking balloon to the buoy so it could be spotted. A garbage scow noticed the balloon this morning and called it in."

"They're sending a message," Jack said. "Using us as the messenger."

"Us?" I said.

"This will make every newspaper. The message isn't for cops.

It's for other dealers. They read about what's happening to their friends, they keep their noses clean. So to speak."

"You could be right," Curt said.

Jack tapped the pen against his lip. "You said the bag was found by a garbage scow a few blocks from the ninety first street transfer station. Do you know if that was where the body was dumped from?"

"That isn't public knowledge yet, and I think I'll get a reprimand if I tell you guys anything else. Listen, I gotta run, but we'll release more info as it comes. Meantime, you two are smart enough to put two and two together."

"Actually I'm waiting for Jack to teach me that."

"Yeah, take is easy Henry. Mr. O'Donnell."

"Officer," Jack said. When Curt was out of earshot, Jack said to me, "hundred bucks says the body was dumped from the transfer station."

"Why?"

"This whole thing...the body pulverized, the bag attached to a buoy, I mean who does that? Once this story breaks, every low life in the city will know that Ken Tsang was mutilated in an ungodly way.

"Not to mention the garbage connotation. That he's nothing but filth."

"That too."

"But if this message is going to dealers, who's sending it?"

"The same people who killed Hector Guardado. And most likely your brother too," Jack said. "My guess is Hector might have some more info for us."

"Hey Jac, you might have missed the memo, but Guardado's dead. Kind of hard for him to be a source of new info."

"The man's got friends. Colleagues. Let's wait until the news breaks, and then tomorrow morning we see which of Hector's old friends are scared enough to talk."

Chapter 4

They could hear whispering from behind the door before they'd even knocked. The three of them walked down the hallway, the floor covered in cigarette butts and crack vials. The two men walked in front, the woman trailing them behind. She wore a jacket over a tank top, her arms loose by her side. The man on the left was blond, trim, and grinned like he'd been looking forward to this. The other wore a long coat and a scowl, and was in no mood to smile.

The men behind the door had been waiting for their arrival. The whispering was excited, impatient. So when the two lead men finally did knock on the door, it opened barely a moment later.

The bodyguard who opened it was massive. Six foot six at least, and well over three hundred pounds. There was perhaps muscle under the flab, but he was no doubt employed as much for his ability absorb bullets as much as his ability to fight. The man looked like he could stop a tank shell in that gut.

"You Mr. Malloy?" the behemoth said. The woman looked at the younger of her two accomplices, the blond man in his early forties. The blond man nodded.

"At your service."

The bodyguard stared at his sunglasses. Or more specifically, what held them up. "Man, what happened to your ear?"

The blond man ignored the question. "We're here to see Mr. Culvert."

The bodyguard looked at the woman standing behind to Malloy. She had dark skin and luminous green eyes. Her skin was the color of cinnamon, and she looked a few years older than the blond man. Her body was toned, sinewy, her breastbone visible above the curve of her tank top. The bodyguard let his gaze hover over her an extra moment, then ushered the three people inside.

The apartment was located inside a largely unoccupied building in Harlem. The man they were going to see owned the premises, and other than letting family members stay from time to time he kept it mainly for business dealings. And that's what this meeting was about. Business.

The bodyguard ushered them down a hallway into a room that was lit only by two weak floor lamps. The windows were blacked out, and there were no phones or other electronic devices present. Three couches were arranged in a semi-circle, and sitting on these couches were four men. Three of them were dressed all in black trench coats, and were just as big as the guy who opened the door. Machine guns were strapped to each of their chests. They made no efforts to hide them.

The one man who was unarmed was dressed in a simple track suit, and wore enough gold chains to bring down a hot air balloon. He was thirty two years old, and worth nearly twenty million dollars. The woman looked around the place, slightly disappointed that there was no evidence of his successful rap career in the building. No platinum albums, no framed magazine covers. For what she had in mind, those trinkets would have made the ensuing story that much more vivid.

The chains clinked together as the man twitched involuntarily. He constantly licked at his lips and rubbed his hands together. His eyes were wide, the whites almost eerie in the gloom. He smiled broadly when they entered.

"Mr. Culvert," Malloy said. "Good to see you again."

LeRoy Culvert stood up. He gripped Malloy's hand with both of his and shook them energetically. His looked warily at the two people Malloy was with. The other man he viewed with skepticism. The woman he eyed with fear.

"Mr. Culvert," the woman said. "Let's talk about the future."

"Absolutely," LeRoy Culvert said, sitting back down. The four bodyguards watched, guns at the ready. "Here, take a seat."

"That's alright," she said. "We'd prefer to keep this short."

"Whatever you say, ma'am," Culvert said with a laugh. The man was stoned out of his mind. That was clear. And the woman knew exactly what drugs he had taken.

"So?" she said. "You've clearly sampled our product. What do you think?"

LeRoy Culvert leaned back, his head tilted towards the ceiling. Then he whipped it forward.

"See, normally I'd lie to y'all. I'd tell you your 'product' is shit, and that you should feel lucky if I'd sell it to the poorest crack heads who live in the subway. See, that way I'd bargain you down, get you to sell it to me at a discount, and I'd keep the profits for my own."

"Smart business strategy," the woman said.

"But I ain't gonna do that to you. You're good people. Listen, this be the finest product I have ever tried in my whole life. Fact is, if you hadn't come on time today I'd have to get my man Buttercup to track you down and get some more down here because my stash is out."

"Buttercup?" Malloy said.

The massive, milky white bodyguard nodded. "That's what people call me."

"Intimidating," the woman said.

"Listen lady," Buttercup said, "I will break your bony ass over my knee."

"Hey, my man Cup, there's no need for that," Culvert said. "These people are our friends. They're going to double your salary, because I'm gonna be worth twice as much."

"At least," the woman said.

"So look, I want in. I'll start with a million worth of the rock. I have enough dealers on the streets that we'll probably be sold out in a month. Then we'll re-up, and go from there. Everybody makes money. You have the product, I have the distribution. Together, we'll blanket the city. Every two-bit street demon with a habit and a ten dollar bill will be aching for a taste of this."

"You do have the streets," the woman said. "And that is commendable. Very nineteen eighties. But to be honest, I'm thinking a little higher than street level."

"What you mean?" Culvert said. "Higher, where?"

"That's not important. I'm just glad you enjoyed the product."

"Enjoyed?" Culvert said. "Man, I'm gonna buy ten grand worth just for my own personal enjoyment. What do you say to that?"

Malloy shrugged. The woman did not move. The other man stayed quiet. He looked uncomfortable.

"Who is this dude?" Culvert said, nodding to the quiet man.

"This," the woman replied, "is detective Sevag Makhoulian of the NYPD. He's our liaison inside the department. He will keep us apprised of any police awareness of our operation."

"Smart bitch, you is," Culvert said. "So, let's make a deal."

"Sorry," the woman said. "No deal."

Culvert looked like he'd been punched in the stomach. "What do you mean, no deal? You gave me the product to test, I tested it, and now I want to take it to the streets. We all make money."

"We make money," she said. "You don't."

LeRoy Culvert jumped from the couch, his chains clinking, baggy pants fluttering. "Listen, bitch, I want my stash. Business or not, I got to have more of that stuff. Those rocks are life, man."

"I'm glad you're satisfied with our product," she said, "but that does not change the fact that this transaction is done."

"Man, fuck y'all," Culvert said. "You gonna be like this, I'm gonng have to take over your operation. Buttercup, gut this bitch."

Buttercup went for the gun in his waistband, but before his hand ever got there the woman ripped a blade from inside her coat and ripped it through the soft meat of Buttercup's throat. The wound yawned open a ghastly red, and Buttercup made a choking sound as he dropped to the ground, flailing. Blood poured from the severed veins. The woman wiped her hand on the couch.

LeRoy Culvert stared at the bloody mess. "What the hell are you doing?" he said. "We're partners!"

"Yes, we are," the woman said. "You're going to help us get the word out about our product. I'm just sorry that your corpse is going to be the vehicle for delivering the message."

Suddenly Malloy pulled two machine pistols from his coat, and in less than two seconds shredded Culvert's bodyguards in a hail of bullets. Blood and pillow feathers spattered the apartment, which was lit brightly by the gunfire.

When Malloy had stopped firing, he paused saw LeRoy Culvert cowering behind one of the couches. He was muttering sweet Jesus, sweet Jesus over and over again as he rubbed a gold cross hanging around his neck.

"Jesus won't save you," the woman said, walking over to the cowering man. "But give him my best."

With one thrust, she buried her knife up to the hilt just under LeRoy Culvert's jaw. He tried to open, instead aspirating a cloud of blood. When Culvert's eyes rolled back in his head, the woman pulled the knife free. Culvert's body toppled to the ground.

The woman looked at the bloody knife in her hand.

"Three days," the woman said to her associates. "Once Paulina Cole does her job, and the police tie this into it, we'll have enough product on the street to saturate the entire city in less than a week."

Malloy stood there, staring at the bodies. He made the sign of the cross. The woman turned to Malloy and put her arm across his shoulder.

"I know you're thinking about him," she said. "But I promise you, he won't have died in vain."

"Thursday" Malloy said. "I've been waiting for this day for twenty years."

"Me too," she said. "Now come on, we have some new recruits coming in. I want this room to look like something out of Stephen King's nightmares."

The woman took the knife and drew it across the wall, leaving a bloody smear. Just a few strokes later, the 'F' was visible. When she completed the rest of the word, and the apartment was sufficiently coated, they left the building and waited for Detective Sevag Makhoulian to report the crime.

Chapter 5

Amanda Davies arrived home at eight o'clock. She called it home even though it was anything but. The reality was it was the home of her friend and coworker Darcy Lapore, and Darcy was campaigning for most altruistic human being on the planet by allowing Amanda to stay there.

Living here wasn't what she'd expected after coming to New York for law school. She figured she'd graduate from NYU near the top of her class, which she did, then find a cushy job in some high profile firm and become one of those high powered career women who had brassy blond hair (hers was auburn, so this would be tricky), wear smart Hillary Clinton pantsuits, get married at thirty six, kids at thirty nine, realize by fifty that you never really spent much time with your family, sixty before you realized you were never really happy in your marriage and my didn't life go by fast.

Instead, she met a guy named Henry Parker who changed her world. Well, part of it was her own doing, choosing the not for profit sector of Legal Aid rather than one of those cushy jobs. She didn't make the money most New York lawyers did, but she was pretty sure she slept better at night.

It took a few years, but looking back Amanda realized how much of her life she'd missed. It was as if she'd taken her expected life and turned it around. Her parents had died when she was young, and after being shuttled back and forth for years she was adopted by a kind couple named Lawrence and Harriet Stein. The Steins were everything foster parents could be. Expect for real parents. Amanda went through the first twenty years of her life without knowing a real relationship of any kind, and she didn't figure that would get any better.

Then she met Henry in extraordinary circumstances, literally picking him up on the side of the road, later to find out he was wanted to murder. Thankfully he was innocent. That would have been a deal breaker.

They'd leapt into a relationship faster than either of them knew what they were doing, and for a while it was good. Really good. Then just as they met under extraordinary circumstances, so were they torn apart. Henry broke up with her for reasons that he believed were noble, but devastated them both. And after some tentative patchwork, they'd decided to give it another go. Slowly this time. They were starting like they should have from the beginning. Movies. Dinner. Holding hands while walking through Central Park, picnic lunches on the Great Lawn. She'd moved in with Henry too quickly last time. For now, Darcy would do, but every night spent in that cold guest room, with the hard mattress that was meant more for show than for use, with the artificial orchids everywhere and paint so white that it seemed to have been bleached of all personality, she couldn't wait for the day when she could feel his warmth next to her every night, where she could lean her head on his chest whenever she felt like it and listen to the beating of his heart. She craved that intimacy, that security. He needed it too, she knew it. But if it took a few extra months to build protection for the rest of their lives, she supposed she could wait. The alternative would have been unbearable.

When she used her spare key to open the apartment door, she had to fumble around in the hallway for the light switch. It wasn't by the door like it would be in a normal apartment, the hallway light was part of some intricate module by the entrance of the atrium that controlled all the lights in the house. That was one of the things she loved about Henry's previous apartments. There were no modules, and definitely no atrium.

Once she found the panel and turned on every light in the house before finding the one to her bedroom, she went inside, stripped out of her work clothes and threw on a pair of shorts and a tank top. Darcy and her husband Devin were out at their summer home in Oyster Bay. Every weekend they begged Amanda to come with them, and every weekend she declined. She hated being the third wheel, and having to do it four and a half days of every week (they usually left for Long Island early on Friday) was enough. And while sitting at the edge of a beach, dipping her toes into the luscious water of the Long Island Sound seemed like the perfect antidote to the stressful Manhattan life, it didn't mean a thing without Henry. And he wasn't the 'dip your feet in the water and laugh like a fool' kind of guy.

He had two modes: work and play. When the switch was on

'Work', Henry was as driven and ambitious as anyone she'd known. When it was on 'Play', there was nobody else in the word but the two of them. Everything faded away when he held her in his arms.

And she loved both sides of him unconditionally.

Once she had slipped on her terry cloth bathrobe, Amanda called Henry's cell. It went right to voicemail.

"Hey babe, hope you're having a good day and Jack hasn't led you off a cliff or something. Give me a call when you get a chance."

When she hung up, Amanda turned on her laptop and put Aimee Mann on high. She was a massive fan, but found she couldn't listen to her favorite song, "Wise Up," as often as she used to. The lyrics were about finding what you thought you wanted most, only to realize that once you had it it wasn't what you thought it would be. Every time she heard it, she thought about their relationship. She'd never been a goopy girl, the kind who read her horoscopes or gossiped over Cosmos while wearing outfits that cost more than the GDP of the Congo. She wasn't superstitious either, but she didn't want to think about losing what she wanted. What she had.

She figured if Aimee knew what she and Henry had been through in their few years knowing each other, she wouldn't take offense.

Kicking her shoes off, Amanda lay back on the hard bed, wanting to think about nothing until it was time to get up for work the next morning. The one thing she did like about Darcy's place was that the girl didn't spare the pillows. The guest room had no less than a dozen pillows of various shapes and sizes covering the bed. Amanda had spent her first week deciding which ones were right, and picked the right half dozen to fall asleep to. When she and Henry lived together it always drove him crazy. Mainly because he would wake up on one side of the full size bed with one nostril covered and a feather sticking out of the corner of his mouth.

Amanda groaned as she rolled off the bed, blowing a hair strand from her eye. Darcy and Devin had a fifty six inch flat screen in their bedroom, one of those cool wall mounted units that seemed to hover without wires or a bracket. It probably cost more than her education, so Amanda figured she'd make use of it.

The remote control was some digital monstrosity that took Amanda ten minutes just to turn on. She was always amused by Darcy's taste in television, so she decided to see what her friend had recorded. The DVR listed thirty two episodes of "Sex in the City", ten of "Gossip Girl," three of "Desperate Housewives"...and this morning's newscast. Amanda laughed. One of those things didn't quite fit.

She pressed 'Resume Playback' on the news program, and saw swarms of cops roaming around what appeared to be a crime scene. A reporter's voice over spoke of some horrendous murder, some young man's body found pulverized in the East River. The reporter was using her 'ultra serious' tone of voice reserved for crimes that were not just bad, but truly terrifying. Amanda felt her heart beat faster. Why the hell had Darcy taped this?

"Kenneth Tsang was survived by his mother and father and young sister. According to the police there are no suspects at the time, but sources confirm that the brutality in which the killer or killers ravaged Mr. Tsang's body was done with some sort of message in mind. And since the city medical examiner, Leon Binks, has confirmed that over one hundred of Mr. Tsang's bones were broken before the body was found in the river, that message will be heard loud and clear."

Amanda shook her head. It was still hard to fathom just how much evil there was in the world. How normal people seemed to be at risk doing leading normal lives.

And then she realized why Darcy had taped the segment.

Standing by a yellow line of police tape, talking to a uniformed officer, was Henry.

Amanda watched. Henry was just doing his job, but something about him being so close to death always unnerved her.

When the clip ended, Amanda walked back into the guest room and grabbed the cell phone. She dialed Henry's number at work. It rang through and went to voicemail. Then she tried his cell again. Right to voicemail.

"Henry...it's me. I know I just called, but I just wanted to say I love you and please be safe."

Amanda hung up the phone, threw off the robe and put on her pajamas. Then she tucked herself under the warm covers and turned off the light. Not for sleep. That wouldn't come. Not until the phone rang. Not until she knew for sure Henry was on his way home.

*   *

*

When I got home it was close to midnight. I sloughed off all the detritus from the day: wallet, keys, loose change, cell phone. The phone was off, I'd forgotten to turn it back on after Jack and I had left the crime scene. I turned it back on, saw there were two messages waiting for me.

My heart sunk when I heard Amanda's voice on both of them. In the first she seemed relaxed. The time stamp meant she'd likely sent it just after getting home from work. The second, was sent less than half an hour later, but she sounded worried, hesitant. I had no idea what could have happened in that short time frame, but the moment I erased the messages I was calling her back.

She picked up before the first ring was finished.

"Henry?" her sweet voice said.

"Hey baby, it's me."

"Are you home?"

"Sure am. Pretty exhausted, but it's been a hell of a day. I'll fill you in tomorrow."

"Are you home for good?"

"You mean tonight?"

"Yeah."

"Yes...just getting ready for bed."

"Do me a favor, make sure your door is locked."

"Is everything ok?" I didn't know where all of this was coming from. "Do you want me to come over?"

"No. Just promise me you'll stay safe."

"I promise," I said.

"Good. Thanks Henry. Now get a good night sleep. I'll talk to you tomorrow."

She hung up, but something gnawed at my gut. Like Amanda knew something I didn't.

Chapter 6

Tuesday

I was on the corner of 57th and 6th. It was seven thirty in the morning. Jack had told me to meet him at eight thirty. So unless he showed up an hour early just to prove a point, I'd be the first one there. Of course you could make the argument that I showed up an hour early just to make my own point, but that was semantics. I wanted and needed Jack to respect my work ethic. If my professional accomplishments hadn't yet convinced him, he'd just have to witness it firsthand.

I was still a little on edge from my conversation with Amanda. We'd spoken briefly this morning before she left for work, and something was definitely wrong. Again she'd told me to promise that I'd stay safe. She'd never done anything like that, at least not without cause or some psycho killer breathing down our backs. I'd see her tonight. We'd talk, and hopefully everything would be alright. They needed to be. I needed that much stability in my life right now, and I needed her to know that I was reliable.

At eight fifteen the familiar tweed jacket rounded the corner. Jack was clutching a large coffee and munching on a bagel. Cream cheese was stuck in his beard. He nodded as he drew close, said, "Henry. Way to be on time."

"I could say the same thing to you. Hey, got a little cream cheese there." I motioned to his beard. He ran his hand through it, but all that did was spread it around. I laughed, which Jack didn't take kindly to. He took a napkin and wiped himself down thoroughly, finally getting it out.

"Better, Dad?" I said.

"Better, sport."

"Good. Now that the silliness is over, let's go talk to some of these 718 guys."

"I don't know all of them," I said, "but the ones I did meet got pretty vicious. Two of them, Scott Callahan and Kyle Evans, are dead.

Two others I didn't know, Guardado and Tsang, are dead two."

"They must have a hell of a life insurance policy," Jack said.

"I don't get it," I said. "Stephen Gaines worked for these people. He ends up dead. Tsang has his boned ground to powder, and there are still people dealing for these clowns. I mean, if your colleagues are dropping like flies, why do you stay on? Why not go to the cops, spill on whoever's paying you? Seems like you have a better chance of staying alive at least."

"That's a good question, Henry, and it's one that we're going to have to answer because obviously these people disagree with your assessment."

"Survival," I said.

"Come again?" replied Jack.

"Human instinct. The number one priority is survival. If someone isn't opening up, it's because they want to survive. Ken Tsang, that wasn't just a murder. It was a message."

"I think I've seen that kind of message before."

"Yeah? Where?"

"Wrote a story once where I had to interview the foreman at a quarry. Tsang's body looked like the bad guy after Indiana Jones smushed him in that rock crusher. Said he looked like something that came out of a tube of toothpaste."

"You know, sometimes I feel I'd be better off not knowing about all your previous stories."

"Thought it might be pertinent," Jack sniffed.

"Come on, the building where 718 operates out of is over there."

We entered the building, and I wasn't shocked to find a different security guard on duty than I'd previously seen on my first visit. He was an older man, mid sixties with a tuft of gray hair parked on the top of his head like a wind ornament. He had on thick reading glasses and was reading a newspaper. We approached, and I said, "We're here for 718 Enterprises."

The man looked up. I could see a crossword puzzle on the table in front of him. Only three of the words had been filled in. And let's just say he wasn't aware the word 'nuclear' had an 'a.'

"Sorry, come again?"

"718 Enterprises," Jack said. "Can you ring them up?"

"Just a second." He pushed the newspaper away and brought out a large binder. Opening it, he began to flip through pages, studying the telephone numbers with his index finger. I watched as he scanned, unable to see the numbers for myself.

"I'm sorry, there's no company here by that name. 718 Enterprises, you said?"

"That's right. They definitely work here," I added. "I've been here before," I lied.

The guard curled his lip up, flipped through the binder again. He looked confused, frustrated. "Sorry, nothing here by that name."

"Hold on a second," I said. I took the logbook from the counter, began to look at all the people who'd signed in. Last time I was here, Scott Callahan and Kyle Evans had signed in when they visited 718 Enterprises. But to my surprise nobody was here to visit the company. Not a single name I recognized.

"Sir please give that back," he said, his voice growing impatient. "If you don't I'll have security down here right quick." Figured they'd have security, old man river here didn't look like he was hired to do much strong-arming.

"What's your name, friend?" Jack said.

"Edgar," the guard replied.

"Edgar, I'm Jack. My friend Henry here is a little impatient, for that I apologize. We were under the impression this company was located at this address...how long have you been working here?"

"It's my second day," Edgar replied.

"Really," Jack said. His voice was modulated to feign interest, but I could tell that bothered him. "Who else works this shift?"

"Nobody anymore. Building manager called the agency that was looking to place me, said they needed a new morning man five days a week, Monday through Friday. They didn't tell me about the last guy, but this is a full time job. Thank god, because in this economy heaven knows my savings and 401k aren't worth squat anymore."

"Thanks Edgar," Jack said. "Come on Henry." He didn't say my name like he were partners, but like I was his subordinate.

As we left the building, I said to Jack, "Next time you're going to do the good cop, bad cop shtick, how about letting me know ahead of time that I'm going to be the bad cop?"

Jack shook his head. "This is about the story, Henry. Not your pride or your feelings. If I need you to be my patsy to get someone to open up, that's just what I'll do. And I'd expect you to do the same with me if the situation called for it. In fact if you didn't, I'd wonder why I was letting you tag along in the first place."

"Tag along? This is my sto..." I stopped talking. This wouldn't get us anywhere. "I can tell what you're thinking."

Jack nodded. "Whoever did work here packed up and left faster than my second wife left with my collection of antique pens."

"You think it's because of Tsang?" I asked.

"No way. Tsang was killed yesterday. Edgar started a few days ago. If Tsang was connected to 718 Enterprises--and ipso facto your brother--they were long gone before they crushed his bones into oatmeal."

I don't know what we should have expected to find, but I guarantee it wasn't nothing. Not the nothing as in 'well, we got there but didn't quite find what we were looking for.' There was no trace of 718 Enterprises whatsoever. It was simply gone.

And as Jack and I stood there in the morning sunlight, I couldn't help but think about the hundreds of people who went about their day oblivious to this. Who'd walked by this building for perhaps years, unaware that it was a drug refueling station. And that all of a sudden whatever had been there had suddenly been packed up and shipped off as quickly and as easily as a parcel.

"Back to the office," Jack said. "We're not going to learn anything standing on the corner waiting for melanoma to sink in."

His hands were on his hips, a look on his face that showed he was pissed off but wouldn't stop here. I'd never seen Jack work, unless you counted watching him hunched over a keyboard sipping coffee that smelled suspiciously like something you'd find on tap at an Irish pub. I had the same gene. The 'hell if I'll stop now' gene.

I smiled inwardly as Jack rain into the street to hail a cab, moving like a man half his age. Not only did he have a story to chase, but after months spent away from the game this was the closest he'd been to fresh meat in a long time.

"There has to be a building manager," I said. "A corporation who cashes the lease payments."

"Great minds, Henry. Great minds." He told the driver to take us back to Rockefeller Plaza. I felt my cell phone vibrate, picked it up, saw Amanda had left me a text message. I opened the mail. It read 'Luv u.' I smiled. Sent her one back that read, 'u 2 babe.'

Then just before I closed the phone, I saw that I had another unopened text. This one was from Curt Sheffield. It read:

News out about Ken Tsang's murder. Undercover cops say dealers are scared shitless, holing up. Informants running like roaches.

And the text ended with one line that gave me chills.

Message delivered.

Chapter 7

Morgan Isaacs didn't want to wake up. He was lying in bed, forcing his eyelids closed, even though a few quick peeks told him it was after ten o'clock and the day had started without him. Again.

It had been just a week since Morgan had met with the real estate broker as well as his Dad's accountant (who didn't charge him, thankfully, chalking it up to years of family service). Both advised him, without a moment of hesitation, to sell his two bedroom apartment on Park Avenue. Morgan pleaded his case, said he'd be back on his feet in no time, but Morgan wasn't trying to convince the advisor as much as himself.

He'd have to give it up. All of it.

It was a sweet pad, with nearly seventeen hundred square feet, brand new appliances, a hundred fifty square foot terrace, a fifty two-inch plasma and a view that most Manhattanites would chop off their left thumb for. It was the kind of place Morgan dreamed of when he first enrolled in business school five years ago, taking on the kind of debt that would choke a third world country. Sure there were bigger apartment in NYC, but you had to start somewhere. And even with the real estate market taking a nosedive recently you couldn't find a good two bedroom for under a million three. To get the three and four bedroom pads you had to plunk down close to two mil, and even though his debts were almost all paid off he thankfully had decided to stick with the twofer until his next promotion.

But then it all crashed down faster than a load of bricks.

The rumors began to swirl about a month ago that the bank Morgan worked at as a trader was having tough times, that its liquidity was nowhere near what the CEOs were claiming. Then he read a newspaper article saying there was a chance it would be bought out by one of the company's competitors. Then, a week ago, Morgan got a call from his boss at eleven thirty on a Saturday night, telling him to be at the office at nine a.m. Sunday morning.

Morgan was there, dressed in a suit and carrying his briefcase, unsure of what to expect. When he got to the conference room he was informed, along with several dozen of his colleagues, that the firm's equity had been bought for five cents a share, that the employee stock purchase plan was essentially worthless. Oh yeah, and that they were all out of a job. They would not be permitted back to their desks, and any personal items would be mailed to their forwarding addressed.

Morgan blinked. It was all he could do. They would receive one month's severance for each year they'd been with the company. For Morgan, that was three months. Three months that would cover his mortgage and BMW payments until he could find a new job. Surely that wouldn't be hard. He had his MBA, his CFA, and graduated from Wharton in the top five percent of his class.

Whether that severance would pay for the nearly thirty three thousand dollars in credit card debt he'd racked up...he didn't even want to think about it. Uncle Sam giveth, and Morgan would be damned if he'd let Uncle Sam taketh away.

Then the next day another bank closed. And suddenly the terrifying realization hit Morgan that he would be competing for jobs in a market where opportunities had just been halved, and his competition increased by two hundred percent. In less than a month there were nearly twenty thousand young men and women just like him, many of whom were just as qualified if not more, looking for the same opportunities he was.

Suddenly those monthly payments, over eleven thousand a month, loomed like a pile of bricks about to rain down on his head.

He went out that night to a dive bar in his neighborhood, fully intent on getting stinking drunk and hooking up with whatever girl noticed the two grand in jewelry he wore. Brianna be damned, she was going to break up with him anyway. He had no illusions about why she was with him, she didn't care about cuddling or having doors opened for her. She wanted the gold. Literally.

Just like Morgan, Brianna would be getting a severance package, maybe a small diamond necklace, no more than a grand. Morgan was a big fan of "The Sopranos," and he thought Tony was brilliant for giving his jilted paramours a small token when he divested himself from them. The kind of women who dated Tony Soprano were the kind of women who dated Morgan Isaacs; they loved the money, the power (granted with Morgan it was on a slightly smaller scale). Once

Brianna learned the truth, she'd be gone and in the pocket--and pants--of some upper manager who managed to hold onto his seven figure job.

So it was morning like this, a Monday, a day where he should have already been on to his third cup of coffee and second cigarette break, that Morgan Isaacs couldn't bring himself to unwrap himself from the fifteen hundred threat count Egyptian cotton sheets.

He'd let his dirty blond hair grow too long, and whereas he used to weigh a trim hundred and eighty pounds Morgan was now threatening to blow past the two bills mark. In fact, there was a pretty good chance he'd already done so, but was too frightened to step on the scale and know for sure.

Maybe he'd fix a breakfast. Toast with peanut butter and strawberry preserves sounded good. There were some good judge shows on in the afternoons. For some reason watching brainless poor people fight with some condescending judge over twenty three dollars made Morgan feel better about his own situation.

Then he heard the chirp of his cell phone, still set to the o'Jays' "For the Love of Money." He didn't recognize the caller ID, and assumed it was a telemarketer. He was about to spin the dial to 'ignore' when he considered the faint possibility it could be one of the firms that still had his resume and had sworn to 'get back to him.'

He answered the phone with a peppy "This is Morgan," hoping to sound like a man who'd been awake all morning and not someone trying too hard to sound like he didn't still have sleep schmutz in his eyes.

"Morgan Isaacs?" the man on the other end replied.

"That's right."

"I was referred to you by a former colleague, Kenneth Tsang. I hope you don't mind my calling."

"Man, Kenneth, yeah," Morgan said. He'd seen the news about Ken's death in the paper, but it hadn't bothered him much. Ken was a good guy, went a little too crazy at the strip clubs back when he was still working at Wachovia, and even after he was laid off the guy throwing bills around like they were tissue paper. Ken was a good guy, but if you were stupid and careless eventually you'd piss off the wrong person. He felt a little guilty knowing that Ken had tried to do him a favor.

"My name is Chester. Kenneth was doing some work for my

firm and he passed your name along to us before his unfortunate passing."

"That's mighty kind of him," Morgan said, scooping some gunk from his eye. "What firm did you say you were with?"

"If you're interested in employment that will pay you quite handsomely with fair hours, meet on fifth avenue at noon. Northwest side of the street between fiftieth and fifty first. Right in front of the statue of Atlas."

"I'm sorry," Morgan said. "I don't mean to be rude, but can I have a little more information? I want to be prepared, you know, just in case."

"Noon in front of the statue," Chester said. "Ken vouched for you. He said you were reliable and that you enjoyed the lifestyle your former employment afforded you. I promise that if that's the case, you won't be sorry you came."

"Wait, how will I know who you are?" Morgan said.

His voice reached only an empty phone. Morgan sat there a moment, thinking about the call. Then he stood up, tossed off his briefs and marched right to the shower. He had just over an hour and a half. An hour and a half to get his life back.

Chapter 8

Sifting through ownership records and property deeds was nearly as much fun as it sounded. We found papers for the nearly two dozen companies who currently held leases in the building formerly housing 718 Enterprises, but for whatever reason there was no deed of ownership of the company itself. We found public listings for a brokerage firm, a jewelry store, three law offices, a psychiatrist, a pet psychiatrist, and a tantric yoga studio. Only in New York.

"Look at this," Jack said. We were sitting in a conference room, two laptop computers with several open windows each, our eyes beginning to strain from staring at various ownership deeds. I leaned over to the computer Jack was working on and looked at the screen he had pulled up. "According to tax filings, the law offices of Kaiser, Hirschtritt and Certilman occupy floors seventeen and eighteen. No other company in the building occupies more than one floor, or even appears to pay for more than one office space. If you were running a drug syndicate from an office, wouldn't you want a little more privacy than a single office would give you?"

I stared at the screen, thought about the morning I went to the building and watched a stream of young, energetic drug dealers enter and leave with briefcases full of narcotics. I had a hard time picturing them all fitting inside a row of cubicles. Plus I doubted a truck pulled up every now and then to refill their supplies. They needed space to store the drugs. Space to allow for easy pickups for dozens of couriers.

And enough lack of clutter to allow them to pack up and get the hell out of Dodge on a moment's notice.

"The building is managed by a company called Orchid Realty," I said. "According to their website, they have different managers for each property. It doesn't spell out which one is managed by who, but we can call and find out."

"Screw that," Jack said. "Why call when we can show up uninvited?"

I smiled. I liked the way Jack thought.

* * *

Orchid Realty was on the eighth floor of a stainless steel complex in midtown, not too far from many of the tony properties they managed. Jack and I walked into the lobby side by side. A pair of security guards manned a long wooden desk. They did not seem intimidated by the purposeful look in our eyes. Installed in the front of the partition were two televisions, each running infomercials for the building itself. The sets looked recently installed, and the volume was far too loud. My guess was with the economy tanking, the building had lost a bunch of leasing companies who couldn't pay their bills, and were looking for fresh blood (and fuller bank accounts) to replenish the coffers.

We stopped at the security desk, and Jack said, "We're here for Orchid Realty."

"Name of contact," the monotone voice came back.

"Mr. Orchid," Jack replied.

The guard looked up, a bored sneer on his face, like he knew Jack was screwing with him but didn't have the time or inclination to care.

"Name of contact," he repeated.

"Call the front desk," Jack said. "Tell whoever answers that we're here to talk to whoever's in charge of the 718 Enterprises account." He took out his identification, underlining the words New York Gazette with his thumb.

The guard looked at him, the apathy turning into confusion.

"This is my official ID," Jack continued. "Which means I have the official authorization to have a news crew down here in less time than it takes for you to put on that cute tie in the morning. It also means you and your friend here will have their friendly faces on our "Community Outrage" website, as impeding an official news investigation." He pointed at the phone. "One phone call. All it takes."

The guard's eyes went wide, and he picked up the phone and dialed three numbers. Jack was full of crap, but news was about information, and that was information they didn't need to know.

The guard covered the phone's mouthpiece with his hand, his eyes growing more animated as he spoke. Clearly the person on the other line wasn't too keen on us coming upstairs, but it looked like the guard wanted as much to do with our 'Community Outrage' website as

I did with bedbugs.

Finally the man hung up, pressed a button and printed out two badges from his computer kiosk. Handing them over, he said, "You promised, right? No cameras or news crew? I don't want my son to see me on the Internet."

"We'll see how things go upstairs," Jack said. "Come on."

I followed him to a bank of metal turnstiles, manned by another security guard, this one looking much less awake on the job than the guys at the front desk. We showed him our badges, and he pressed a button that swung the turnstiles. We passed through, made our way to the elevator bank and headed up to the fourth floor. Jack hummed a tune I couldn't recognize as we ascended, and I felt slightly anxious, wondering just how far this would take us. I was also somewhat concerned about pulling my weight on this story. As much as I wanted to find out just what the hell was going on with this shadow corporation, earning the respect of Jack O'Donnell was a close second.

The doors opened, and we followed a sterile beige hallway to a pair of double glass doors with the words 'Orchid Realty' stenciled on them. I opened the door for Jack, the glass swinging out effortlessly and without a sound. A heavyset woman with curly reddish hair sat behind an oak desk, a pair of old-fashioned headphones resting on her ears that looked less Bluetooth than long in the tooth. The nameplate read "Iris Mahoney."

Iris was filing her nails, pausing every few moments to blow nail dust from her hands and onto the floor.

As we approached, he eyes raised and a wide smile crossed her lips. "You must be those boys from the newspaper," she said. "Welcome to Orchid."

"Hi," I said before Jack could open his mouth. "Ms. Mahoney, if it's not too much trouble we'd like to speak to one of your property managers."

"Certainly sir, which of our managers would you like to speak with?"

"Whoever handles the building which until recently leased space to a company called 718 Enterprises."

The receptionist pursed her lips, sucked in air and squinted. "Hmm...that doesn't ring a bell. Let me check our database."

She put down the nail file and began typing. Two fingered. One finger at a time. Slow enough that I could hear Jack breathing heavier as his frustration grew. Every few moments the lady would mutter a pleasant 'no' under her breath and continue typing. After several minutes she looked up at us and said, "I'm sorry sir, we don't have any records for a 718 Enterprises. Are you sure you have the right realty corporation?"

"You do manage the building leases at sixteen twenty Avenue of the Americas, right?"

"Now that sounds familiar. If my memory serves me they have a wonderful tantric yoga studio." She blushed slightly. I pretended not to have heard anything.

"That's the building," Jack said. "Listen, hon," he continued, approaching the desk, a warm smile on his face. It was shocking to compare this to his countenance downstairs. Different folks responded to different temperaments. Jack didn't get his reputation by assuming everyone reacted the same way to everything. "We're not here to cause trouble. We're investigating a story for our newspapers, it's our job, really, and we just have a few questions about the building. If you could just let us know who manages that property, we'll be out of your hair in no time. What do you say?"

The apple-cheeked receptionist smiled, and if I didn't know any better it looked like she might have suddenly developed a small crush on the elder newsman. "Hold on one second, if you'll have a seat I'll have somebody out here to assist you right away."

"You've made my day, darlin'." Her smile widened.

We took seats in two leather chairs. I shuffled through a pile of uninteresting magazines before putting them back. Jack just sat there. He didn't need any distractions.

After thumbing through the pile of outdated magazines for a second time--in case Victorian Homes had magically been replaced by Sports Illustrated--a middle aged man with a short haircut and mustache entered the waiting room. His eyes settled on us, and I caught him taking a deep breath. He wasn't making any secret that he didn't want to be talking to us, and resented the fact that we were even here.

I stood up, assumed Jack would do the same. When he didn't, I looked at him. He didn't seem to have noticed there was someone else in the room, either that or he didn't care.

"Mr. O'Donnell?" the man said. Now Jack's eyes perked up. He didn't say a word, waited for the other man to speak. "Bill Talcott. How can I help you?'

Jack stood up. Gave Talcott a once over, sizing him up. Talcott shifted as he stood there, eyes meeting the floor. Jack was trying to make the guy nervous, take him out of any comfort zone he might have. It didn't look like Talcott had much of one when he joined us, but I guess Jack wanted to break his spirit completely.

"Thanks for finally joining us," Jack said.

"My apologies for the wait." He glanced at Iris with a condescending, apologetic smile, as though blaming her for the delay. Iris didn't look up from her desk. This did not paint Mr. Talcott in an impressive light.

"Actually Iris was quite helpful," Jack said. I noticed Iris's face look up slightly. "You have no need to embarrass her. Or yourself."

Talcott's face went pink, and he stammered, "Of course, I didn't mean to put anybody down. We're all under an enormous amount of stress these days, as you can imagine. And if I can say so, without embarrassing myself again, I'm a fan of your work Mr. O'Donnell."

Jack nodded, but did not respond to the compliment. "Should we go somewhere more private?" he said.

"Is this an issue that requires privacy?" Talcott said, confused.

"I'd say so."

Talcott nodded, said, "Right this way." We followed him down the hallway behind the reception desk. The corridor was filled with gray metal filing cabinets. A few people stood by, filing, rifling through papers with a quickness that said they'd done it for years. On the walls hung pictures of buildings. some residential, some commercial, obviously the properties Orchid Realty managed.

We passed by a small kitchen and a large conference room, and eventually were led into Talcott's office. He ushered us in and closed the door. There were two leather chairs in front of a heavy marble desk. The desk, as well as the windowsills and bookshelves, were lined with snow globes from around the world. The man had literally hundreds of them.

"I buy one in every city I set foot in," Talcott said proudly. "Three hundred and forty eight and counting.

Jack and I sat down. Talcott seemed disappointed that we weren't impressed. We took our notepads and pens as Talcott sat down.

He waited a moment to see if we might compliment his collection. When it was clear we weren't going to, he said, "So, gentlemen. What can I do for you?"

"First off, Mr. Talcott, this is my associate Henry Parker. My apologies for not introducing him earlier."

"Parker," Talcott said, "where have I heard that name before?"

"It's a pretty common surname," I replied.

"Any relation to Peter Parker?" Talcott asked.

"You mean Spider-Man?"

"Is that the character's name? I could have sworn I knew someone else named Parker. In any event, your name does ring a bell."

I looked at Jack, hoping we could move on. He seemed to get the nod.

"Mr. Talcott," he said, "do you manage the property at sixteen twenty Avenue of the Americas?"

"I do," Talcott said.

"Are you aware of a company called 718 Enterprises that, up until recently occupied space in that building?"

Talcott took a moment before responding, "No."

Jack's eyebrows raised. "You're saying there was never a company at that location with the name 718 Enterprises, or anything similar to that."

"Yes," he said.

"Yes, there was a company, or yes there was not."

"There was no company with that name at that location."

Jack turned to me, shifting his whole body. I realized Jack had never seen the sign for the company, he hadn't witnessed the young men marching in and out of the building with full bags. I was the only witness, at least the only one who was on our side.

"Mr. Talcott, do you read the news?"

"Of course I do. I'm quite fond of Mr. O'Donnell's work as I said."

"Do you read it regularly?"

"I would say so."

"Well, then do you recognize the name Stephen Gaines? Or a company called 718 Enterprises?" This time Talcott's 'no' was hesitant. There was recognition on his face, but he wasn't about to incriminate himself. "Let me give you a little backstory. Stephen Gaines was murdered a few weeks ago. Shot in the head in a dingy apartment in alphabet city. It was in the news quite a bit, especially after the primary suspect was cleared."

"That does ring a bell," Talcott said. "So much strife in the news these days, who can remember a name? But the case does sound familiar. Boy's father was accused of the crime, wasn't he?"

"That's right. Want to know something else?" I said.

Talcott seemed unsure of how to respond, so he simply said, "Sure."

"Stephen Gaines was my brother."

"I...I'm sorry to hear that. My condolences."

"See, my brother worked with those two guys, Scott Callahan and Kyle Evans. And my brother confided everything in me." This part was b.s., we'd had one conversation lasting thirty seconds and I didn't even know he was my brother at the time. "And he told me that Scott and Kyle were employed--that's a loose term--by 718 Enterprises. Who worked out of your building. Now, if you still don't remember them I can get you the documentation and you'll see it at the same time we print it." I looked at Talcott's desk. Saw a photo of him with a woman and young boy on a beach, all three beaming. "I don't know how I'd explain to my son why daddy's picture is all over the news."

Talcott turned a ghastly shade of white, and rocked back in his chair. The chair, unfortunately, did not lean back with him, and he nearly toppled over before righting himself. Talcott cleared his throat before suddenly leaning down to rummage under his desk. I felt my fingers gripping the sides of the chair--was he going for a gun?

My nerves quieted when I saw what Talcott was reaching for: a bottle of Glenfiddich single malt, aged twenty one years. Slightly less dangerous than a gun, though from the shaking of his hands my guess was that after we left Talcott would drink enough to make him sleep like he'd been shot.

He brought up a small tumbler, filled it to the brim, and downed it, closing his eyes. He looked at us, slight embarrassment on his face. Then he pushed the bottle towards us.

"No thanks," I said. "I didn't have breakfast."

Jack looked right past the bottle. I watched his reaction, but there was none.

Talcott coughed into his fist. His eyes were a little watery. I got the feeling he didn't particularly enjoy the scotch, but needed it enough to get around that small detail.

"You don't know what it's like out there," he said.

"Out where?" said Jack. "What are you talking about?"

"The economy is in the toilet. The dollar is barely worth the paper it's printed it."

"I cash my paychecks," I added. "We know this."

"But companies...they're getting hit the hardest. There aren't as many customers to go around, and the customers that they do have, well the money they pay doesn't buy what it used to."

"What's your point?"

"Sixteen twenty Ave of the Americas, we've lost a dozen tenants from that building in the last two years. Two years! And you know how many tenants have moved in? One. That's a few hundred grand that we used to be making that just disappeared in the wind."

Talcott paused, eyed the bottle.

"We needed the extra money."

"And..." I said.

"That company...718 Enterprises...they never leased the property," Talcott said. "They were never officially on our ledger. They never paid us a dime."

"Then why did you say..." I replied, but Jack cut me off.

"So what does that mean?" Jack said. "They didn't pay for the space? How did you bring in money?"

"They company itself didn't pay us," he replied, eyes looking at the bottle like it was a well-aged steak. "There was a law firm."

"Kaiser, Hirschtritt and Certilman," I said. "They occupied the floor above."

Talcott nodded, his eyes red. He bit his lower lip. Hard.

"Go on," Jack said.

"The law firm leased one floor. Eighteen. About a year after they leased it, our tenants on seventeen moved out. We needed money bad. So when Brett Kaiser came to us and made a proposition, we had no choice. The tenant that occupied that floor had left three months earlier. We couldn't afford to take another hit without recouping some of our losses."

"What was the offer?" I said.

"Somebody would occupy the seventeenth floor. Only for legal purposes, the firm would be listed as the leaser. They would take care of monthly payments for both floors. That was that. We treated it like a tenant was simply occupying two floors."

"So who was on seventeen?" I asked.

"I don't know," Talcott said. "That was part of Kaiser's deal. He said the people on seventeen would never need anything from Orchid, and we should never ever contact them for any reason. I never went to that floor, and they never even hired a cleaning crew as far as I know. One time, though one of our maid services told me she accidentally got off on the wrong floor, got lost. She said the offices were closed, and had some sort of security system she'd never seen before. Like something out of the space program, she said."

"Doesn't sound like something a law office would employ," I said to Jack. He didn't respond.

"There's something wrong with that company. I don't know what it is, but I had a feeling that some day somebody would ask me these questions. I never wanted to know what they did. But I had to lease the space as much space as possible or the building could have gone under."

"I'm sure Kaiser knew that," I said. "And knew you wouldn't ask questions as long as the checks arrived on time."

"I never needed to or wanted to ask questions," Talcott said. "There are plenty of tenants whose businesses I'm not fully acquainted with. As long as they're running a legal operation and paying on time, they have their right to privacy."

"And you have a right to know where your money is coming from," I said.

"What if," Jack said, "you had a choice between getting paid and having a tenant running a legal operation?"

"I've never had to make that choice."

"Never had to, or never wanted to think you had to," Jack replied.

Talcott said nothing, but that bottle of scotch was practically gravitating towards his hands.

"One more thing," Jack said, "do you have contact information for Brett Kaiser?"

"Sure," Talcott said. "Cell phone, home phone and email address. Will that be all?"

"Just the contact info," Jack said. "And if there's anything else you can think of, here's my card."

Jack handed it to him. Talcott stared at it like it might spontaneously burst into flame, then pocketed it.

"Not a problem." Talcott took a piece of letterhead from his printer and scribbled the information on it. His handwriting was sloppy and careless. My guess was that Iris was responsible for his 'personal' notes.

When he finished, Talcott folded the page and inserted it into an Orchid Realty envelope. Jack took it and stuffed it inside his jacket pocket.

"Pleasure meeting you," Jack said, pointing at the bottle of liquor. "Now we'll leave you two alone."

Chapter 9

Morgan Isaacs kept one hand on his Blackberry, which was nestled snugly inside his front pants pocket. To anyone on the street it looked like he might be playing a game of pocket pool, but this Chester guy was ten minutes late and Morgan didn't want to miss a phone call. He considered leaving. I mean, who in the hell meets about a job on the street? And Morgan didn't like to wait. In his previous job, people waited for him. He shared a secretary, a cute piece of ass named Charlotte he could have had at any moment. Sometimes he would send her out for coffee just because he could. Morgan didn't even drink coffee. When she came back, he wouldn't even thank her, just go into his office, pour the cup into the bottom of his fake plant, and pull out a can of Red Bull.

But this guy was late. Just a few short months ago, Morgan wouldn't wait for anybody. Some asshole wanted him to wait five minutes? Screw you, let's reschedule. Now, Morgan didn't know when he'd even find work again. And with bills piling up he needed to earn scratch no matter what the cost. So if he had to suck up his pride for a little while, so be it. A necessary evil. And whoever this jack off was who had him wait, well, if the company was good enough Morgan would be running it within a few years anyway. Then he'd be the one making people late.

He felt a sense of anger rise within him as he watched hundreds of people walking down the streets, oblivious to him, unknowing and uncaring of what he'd been through. Men, women, dressed in natty suits with the finest accoutrements, they had no idea that in the time it took to snap your fingers they could be out of a job just like him. They had no right to be so confident, so careless, while Morgan stood there, his immediate future resting in the hands of a recommendation of Ken Tsang and the charity of some guy he'd never met before.

In the cab ride over--he would have preferred the bus to save money, but Chester didn't give him a whole lot of time--Morgan wondered whether or not he'd take the position if one was offered. Then he chided himself. Now was not the time to be prideful. The bills would continue to come, the debt would continue to mount. Even a modest income would provide a stint for the bleeding, and at least he would have healthcare. Time to suck it up for a few months, Morgan had told himself. Guys with his talent and drive didn't grow on trees. And every bump road led to riches down the line.

Morgan squeezed the cell phone--thought he'd felt it vibrate.

"Mr. Isaacs?"

Morgan turned around to see where the voice came from. Standing directly behind him, almost inappropriately close, was a tall, well-built man with close-cropped blond hair. He had on a pair of rimless Cartier sunglasses, must have run at least five hundred bucks. Not too shabby. His gray suit was stretched over a lean frame, and Morgan could tell the guy had enough strength in those biceps to crush a tin can.

Morgan didn't blink. Never show weakness, never show admiration. He was never rude, but on a job interview you wanted to appear confident, not too eager. Like they would be lucky you have you work for them.

"And you are...Chester?" Morgan said.

The man smiled and took of his sunglasses, folding them and tucking the pair into his breast pocket. He held out his hand. "Nice to meet you. Thanks for coming on such short notice."

"No biggie," Morgan said. "Just had to reschedule a few things, that's all."

"Really? Such as what?"

Morgan stammered, "I, uh, meetings, you know. Banks. A bank."

"Oh, well I hope the bank understood," Chester said with complete sincerity. If this guy realized Morgan was full of shit, he wasn't letting on. "Let's walk."

Morgan followed Chester as he strolled down fifth avenue. He matched the man step for step, tried to keep his stride the same length but damn the man had long legs. Instead Morgan shortened his paces and walked faster. It was two blocks before Chester spoke again.

"How's the job hunt going?" he said.

"It is what it is. There's always room for good workers, I figure I'll take a little time, weigh my options and see what the best fit is for me."

"Really," Chester said, his voice either distant or disbelieving. "Any good leads? Anything coming down the pike?"

"Always something coming down," Morgan replied. "Just a matter of who makes me the most attractive offer."

"I understand that," Chester said. "Hold on a second."

Chester stopped at a vending cart and ordered a hot dog. He paid, then slathered ketchup, mustard and relish on it. He wolfed the dog down in the bites, still standing at the cart, then wiped his lips with a napkin and continued walking.

"Sorry, did you want one?"

"S'ok," Morgan said. "I just had breakfast an hour ago."

"Really," Chester said softly.

Morgan silently cursed himself. It was nearly twelve thirty. The fact that he had a late breakfast gave away that Morgan had woken up late. If he'd woken up late, he had nothing better to do. No job, no interview. Morgan could feel himself falling behind, and hoped Chester would let it slide.

"Your friend Ken spoke highly of you," Chester said. "It really is a shame. Always the young, talented ones who go before their time."

"I know what you mean," Morgan said. The truth was Ken was only a half-decent worker. A man with some bad habits and with maybe a quarter of the brainpower Morgan possessed. He didn't say any of this to Chester, of course, but if this guy spoke so highly of Ken Tsang he'd be simply blown away by Morgan Isaacs.

If it took this little to impress Chester, Morgan could probably have his job in less than five years.

"I know I mentioned this to you before," Chester continued, "but Kenneth did some work for our firm. He was a good man, a good soldier, and recommended you as someone who could do the same kind of work if, well, if you ever decided to pursue other opportunities."

"What kind of work did Ken do for you?" Morgan said. "Whatever it was, modesty aside, sir, I guarantee Ken doesn't know the half of what I'm capable of."

"Is that right?" Chester said, eyebrow raised.

"Yes sir."

Chester nodded. He seemed pleased.

"I don't know what kind of money you were making at your

last job," Chester said, "But I hope you'll find that if you do decide to work for us, the pay will be commensurate with what you'd expect."

Morgan was slightly surprised, considering this guy was bringing up salary before even discussing the job. It must be either crap work or a crappy salary, and Chester probably figured he wouldn't waste any time, that if Morgan didn't like the payoff, he'd walk away.

"What kind of figures are we talking about?" Morgan said.

"Well, we would have to start you out at the bottom of the ladder. I'm sure you understand. So many people competing for so few jobs these days, if you're not comfortable with that I can move on. Ken did give me a few other names."

Morgan felt his neck grow hot under his collar.

"What kind of money are we talking about."

Chester stopped walking. He reached inside his coat, pulled out a ballpoint pen. Then he walked over to a garbage can on the corner, tore a page off a loose newspaper. He scribbled something on the paper, then held it out for Morgan to see.

Morgan felt his stomach lurch, felt his hands go cold. Chester crumpled the scrap up and threw it back into the trash. Then he kept walking, Morgan unable to move for a moment, before snapping out of it and jogging to catch up. This couldn't be right. Nobody started at the bottom of any company and made that much money.

Chester was walking faster. Morgan's short legs couldn't keep up, so he found himself half walking-half jogging to keep alongside the man.

"If you're interested," Chester said, "you'll be downstairs outside of your apartment tomorrow at one p.m. You'll be dressed just like you are now. Let me make this clear. You do not have the job. Not yet. If you tell anybody about the offer, or if you're one second late, you'll never see me again."

"I'll be there," Morgan gasped.

"Good," Chester said. The man stopped walking. Out of nowhere, a black Lincoln Town Car pulled up alongside them. Chester walked over, opened the door and climbed in.

"Wait!' Morgan said. "Don't you need to know where my apartment is?"

Morgan's words faded into the roar of the exhaust as Chester's car sped away, leaving the young man confused, excited, and ready.

Chapter 10

When we arrived back at the Gazette, I followed Jack to his desk. Yet as we rounded the corner I saw Tony Valentine approaching. When Tony saw me his face lit up. Actually I couldn't tell if his face lit up, considering there was enough self-tanner on there to make John McCain look black, and his face was pumped with enough Botox to iron out a Shar-Pei. But he did have a big smile on his face, and his gait picked up when he saw me coming.

"Henry!" Tony exclaimed, jogging up and placing his arm around me. "I've been looking for you, where've you been all morning?"

"Chasing a story," I said. "Tony, have you met Jack O'Donnell?"

Tony shook his head, but took Jack's hand and did a neat little bow. "Not yet, but your reputation precedes you Mr. O'Donnell. It's a pleasure."

"Pleasure's all mine, Mr. Valentine," Jack replied. His tone surprised me. As a hard news man, I didn't think Jack would have much use for Tony Valentine. Tony had recently been brought on board at the Gazette to kickstart the paper's flailing gossip pages, which had grown stale with coverage that revolved mainly around celebrities that stopped being famous before I was born. Tony was one of the top names in the gossip field--if you could call it that--and already his columns were among the most emailed on the Gazette web site. He dressed like he was auditioning to be James Bond on a daily basis, and smiled like he was being paid to. We had nothing in common other than our employer, and I preferred to keep it that way.

"Henry," Tony said. "Glad we ran into each other. Do I have a offer for you!"

"I already have life insurance," I said.

Valentine laughed. "That's a good one. Seriously now, have you heard of Belinda Burke?"

The name sounded vaguely familiar, but I couldn't place it.

"Sounds familiar," I said, "but I'm not sure why."

"Belinda was a contestant on 'Marry my Mother-in-law. She won a million bucks by setting her mother-in-law up with the dentist who walked from Dallas to Newark stark naked."

"Oh, yeah. Right. Match made in heaven"

"Well, Belinda has quite a story to tell. So naturally she's decided to write a memoir."

"That's nice. Literature was getting a bit stale."

"I totally agree! Anyway, she was going to use this ghostwriter named Flak. Just one word, like Madonna. He ghostwrote Joe the Plumber's autobiography, did a wonderful job. Anyway, Flak came down with syphilis and I thought you might want to give it a crack. I know Belinda's agent and could get you two a meeting, no problem."

"Um...why would I want to ghostwrite the memoir of a D-list celebrity nobody's going to remember in twelve months?"

"Because there's fifty grand in it for you if you can deliver a manuscript in a month."

"Somebody thinks she's worth fifty grand?"

"Oh heck no. She got a million bucks for the book. You've get fifty k just to write it."

"She can't write it herself?"

Valentine laughed, deep and hearty.

"Henry, I don't think the woman can read. But that's not the point. Her publisher is a little worried Belinda might have a short shelf life, and they want to get the book out before the next season of 'American Idol' takes attention away from her."

"The money sounds great, but I'm just not really into that kind of thing. I never saw myself as that kind of writer." I looked at Tony. "Just out of curiosity, why come to me? What's in this for you?"

Tony grew a sly smirk. His eyes narrowed. I could tell Tony Valentine was far more calculating than he let on. "See, I knew you were a smart one. Here's the deal, Henry. If you take this job, you get the money. That's how you win. If Belinda publishes the book, she adds a few ticks on to her fifteen minutes. She wins. And because I got you the job and we work at the same paper, you feed me exclusive info from the book that I can run in my column. I win. We all win, Parker."

"Wow," I said. "It's like a whole big circle of ethics violations."

"Say what you will, but who loses here?"

"Sorry, Tony. I have to say no."

"No apologies necessary," Tony said, taking a hair pick from his suit jacket and running it through his glistening hair. That was a first. "But I hope you understand why I put it on the table."

"I do. I appreciate you looking out for me. And Belinda. And you," I said. "If you know anyone who wants me to test canned food for botulism, my Friday night is free."

"See, that rapier wit. One more thing I love about you, Henry. See you around. And it was nice to meet you, Mr. O'Donnell." Tony walked away, whistling a tune I couldn't identify but was definitely Sondheim,

"Have a good one," Jack said as Valentine rounded the corner.

"Have a good one?" I said to Jack. "It took you a month just to give me the time of day."

"You should be nicer to him," Jack said.

"You can't be serious," I replied. "Jack, he's a gossip hound. A bottom feeder. He makes a living shoveling garbage."

"And he's necessary for the survival of this newspaper," Jack said abrasively. "You can ride your high horse until it dies of thirst, but this is not a business that's growing, in case you haven't noticed. We didn't have a real gossip columnist for years. Now, people are talking about Tony. Besides, what do you think a newspaper is? Every day, we print a hundred pages, give or take, and reach over a million readers. You think every one of them wants to read about crime and corruption? Some of them need cheddar flavored potato chips in their daily routine. Something you know is crap but you enjoy it anyway. You like steak, Henry?"

"Yeah, why?"

"How do you like your cut--lean and tough, or a little more flavorful?"

"More flavor, I guess. Why?"

"You know what puts the flavor in steak? Fat. Too much fat, in case you don't keep up on healthy trends is bad for you. But it makes the steak taste like a slice of heaven. That's what gossip is. It's fat. Without it, the paper is leaner, tougher, but doesn't have as much flavor. Maybe it's the kind of flavor that increases your cholesterol or hardens your arteries, but most people live in the moment. You get what I'm saying, sport?"

"I get it," I said. "Doesn't mean I have to like it."

"You like your job, don't you?" I nodded. "Then live with it. You do your job the best you can, don't worry about everyone else."

"But don't you think, you know, that the Gazette should have a higher standard? You've been here, what, thirty years?"

"What do you think the Gazette is?" Jack said with a laugh. "Our job is to report the news for the paper, it's not the news's job to get to us. This company is the sum of what we make of it. Now, if you want to work for a company that only reports what you want, go start a blog."

"I understand what you're saying, but I don't have to like it."

"Like it, hate it. It ain't changing," Jack said. "Now here's the deal: I want you to call Brett Kaiser."

"Why me?"

"I've heard of his firm before. They handle civil litigation, among other things, including libel. Which means they know a lot about newspapers, which means, no offense kiddo, he'll be a little less threatened by a, how should I put this, wet-behind-the-ears guy like you."

"I'm not that wet behind the ears," I replied.

"Come on Henry. What was it, a year ago that you could finally rent a car without paying extra fees?"

Rather than argue (and lose), I just nodded. We went to my desk, Jack perching on the corner while I picked up the phone. I dialed the number for Kaiser, Hirschtritt and Certilman from the paper Talcott gave us. A woman picked up on the first ring.

"Kaiser, Hirschtritt and Certilman, how may I direct your call?"

"Hi, I'd like to speak with Brett Kaiser."

"And who may I ask is calling?"

I looked at Jack, knowing where this was about to go.

"My name is Henry Parker. I'm with the New York Gazette."

"Hold on," she said, wariness in her voice. "I'll put you through."

The next thing I heard was a dial tone. I placed the receiver down.

"You got hung up on," Jack correctly surmised. I nodded. "Go home."

"What?"

"It's been a long day. Get some rest. We're going to be working like dogs over the next few days, and I don't need you conking out on me."

"In case you haven't noticed, I've got almost fifty years on you."

"True, but while you were smoking from atomic bongs and doing keg stands in college, I was chasing leads. Get some rest, Parker. I'll see you here tomorrow. Nine o'clock."

"I'll see you at eight," I said.

* * *

A smell greeted me in the apartment that I did not immediately recognize. It resembled some sort of meat, maybe chicken or fish, something sweet and citrus-y--all mixed with the tangy smell of something burning. Making my way through the pungent stench to the kitchen, I found the oven on and some sort of concoction roiling and baking inside that, from the look of the sauce coating the insides of the appliance, didn't seem to be enjoying it. As I got closer a small bit of smoke escaped the oven, so I quickly shut the device off.

"Amanda?" I yelled. "Are you here?"

There was no answer, so I tried again.

"Amanda?"

I heard a squeak as the bathroom door opened. The shower was still running, and I could see Amanda's wet head poking from behind the curtain. Her hair was filled with shampoo and her eyes looked at me through a haze of steam.

"Henry?"

"Amanda, what the hell are you doing?"

"Bowling. What does it look like I'm doing?"

"You're aware that this apartment was about thirty seconds from being on the eleven o'clock news."

"What?" she said, wiping suds from her face.

"I saved your mystery meat dish just in time before it burned down the neighborhood."

"No way. The timer was supposed to go off after half an hour. I didn't hear anything."

"You are in the shower you know."

"No way, I have a keen sense of hearing."

"When you pressed half an hour," I said, "what exact buttons did you press?"

"I held the button until it read three zero minutes and zero seconds."

"Really," I said. "You're sure about that?"

"Sure. Why?"

"There's no seconds on the oven. It's just minutes and hours. You set the timer for three hours and zero minutes."

"Oh. Crap. Sorry."

"It's ok," I said. "Just...never cook again. And apologize to the fish in there."

"It was supposed to be orange chicken," she said.

"Well it's probably got the texture of volcanic rock right now. You feel like pizza?"

She offered a sheepish grin, and said, "Let me finish up in here and we'll order."

"Sure you don't want me to join you?"

"No, the toaster is on too. Would you mind checking on it?"

"The toaster? Are you ser..."

"Just kidding. Give me five minutes."

She closed the door and I collapsed on the couch. I turned on the television and clicked through a hundred a fourteen channels before deciding that there was nothing worth watching. It was just as entertaining to sit there and go through the events of the day, and prepare for the next.

Hopefully Brett Kaiser could fill in much of the information that was missing. Somebody had to be paying Kaiser's firm's share of the lease money, and with any luck that person would have intimate knowledge of just who my brother was working for and why he was killed. I still didn't buy that it was totally a power play. Stephen came to me because he was scared of something. If you work in a company and have problems with underlings, there are ways to circumvent any actions. Now when somebody above you wants you gone, that's when you have a problem. If you feel that your termination--pardon the term--is inevitable, you begin planning an exit strategy. In the workplace, maybe you look for another job, prepare a lawsuit, something so that you're not thrown from an airplane without a parachute. When

Stephen came to me that night, scared out of his mind (a mind already addled), he was looking for his exit strategy. Granted the actions you take are a little different when you led a life of crime as opposed to life in a cubicle, but the principle still stood.

What I needed to know was who set Stephen on the path to his eventual exit. Even though he didn't make it, he had something to say. A story to tell.

Amanda came out of the shower. She was wrapped in a towel, and over the towel she wore a pink bathrobe. Above this contraption she was tousling her hair with another towel. The combination of towels and thick bathrobe made Amanda look about twice as thick as she normally did, and I couldn't help but laugh.

"This is my routine," she said. "You should be used to it by now."

"I am," I said, "but that doesn't mean you don't look a little silly."

She took a seat on the couch, wrapping the towel into a turban where it sat perched a whole foot above her head. I'd bought the couch at an apartment sale for about a third of what it would cost at a department store. It was brown leather, with big cushions that I constantly rotated to change up the stains. Made me feel like it was a little less worn.

"How was your day?" she asked, absently flipping through the stack of the day's newspapers I kept on the coffee table.

"Still working on this story with Jack," I said. "It's interesting, working with him for the first time."

"In what way?"

"Jack was in pretty bad shape my first few years at the Gazette. I hate to admit it, but there was a moment or two when I wondered if this was really the same guy I grew up wanting to be. Not many kids dress up like a journalist for Halloween. It was important to me that he was who I thought he was."

"You did not dress like a journalist," Amanda said.

"You bet your ass. Had a row of pens in my shirt pocket, a camera and notepad and everything. Everyone assumed I was Clark Kent."

"I would have paid to see that," Amanda said.

"There aren't a whole lot of photo albums back in Bend. My

dad wasn't exactly the sentimental type."

"How do you feel about how things are going?" she asked. I took a seat next to her, thought for a moment.

"When I found out Stephen was dead, I felt numb. Like someone was prodding me with a stick I could see but couldn't feel. I was supposed to feel remorse, but it didn't come at first. Someone can tell you that you lost a family member, but if you didn't even know the person it's not the same. It should be, I guess. Blood is blood, but in a way it isn't. Now, it feels different. Like maybe I did lose someone who could have--should have--been closer to me." I looked at Amanda, saw she was listening to every word. "Without you, I'd have no one."

"Don't say that," she said, looking away. "That's not true."

It was true, but I didn't want to argue. I'd made mistakes during our time together. Knowing when to shut up was an important lesson.

She went back to reading the paper. Her fingers were still a little wet, and I could see the print rubbing off on them. She went to wipe her hands on the towel, then smiled and thought better of it.

"You see this?" she said, holding up a copy of that morning's Dispatch.

I shook my head. I rarely read the Dispatch. Not because I held a grudge against them--though I did--it's because they never had much I felt was worth reading. It was the kind of paper that rarely presented an even story. It was all about eliciting a reaction, stoking a fire, presenting a story so biased in one direction or the other that readers would either be incensed or infatuated. I had all the major New York City papers delivered to my door in one bundle. I could care less about the Dispatch, but it didn't cost anything more and every now and then I enjoyed reading the sports section.

"I must have missed it," I said. "What'd you see?"

"Paulina Cole," Amanda said. "Says here her column will be suspended until Thursday while she deals with a personal matter."

"Really?" I asked. That surprised me. Paulina Cole was the kind of woman who didn't take personal leaves. If my mental image of her was accurate, she stayed in her office until while darkness creeped in, waiting for some scoop to brighten her desk. And if she didn't get, it would only fuel her fire to make the next scoop even juicier.

I wondered what could be so important that she'd suspend her reporting, even just for a few days. It would take either an act of nature or a revolt by the paper's shareholders to get rid of Paulina. Which meant somewhere a storm was brewing. Not to mention I'd be lying if I didn't hope, after everything she'd done to Jack and me, that it made her life a living hell.

No doubt Paulina would come back on Thursday with a story that would open some eyes.

Chapter 11

Wednesday

Paulina Cole glanced over her shoulder. Still nobody there. The Mercedes was empty when she climbed in, empty when she started the engine, and empty when she pulled onto the FDR Drive towards I-95. She even checked the trunk--nothing--but wondered if there had been enough time for someone to climb in during the split second when she closed the trunk and climbed into the driver's seat.

The anger welling up inside Paulina was a firestorm. She was scared, and god she couldn't stand that feeling. The idea that someone controlled an aspect of her life that she did not, it was like being trapped in cement while people poked you with a stick. That night, the night that man took her, Paulina had experienced emotions she didn't think she'd ever felt. Not when her husband left her. Not when he took half of her money because his deadbeat ass barely made a dime, not she was fired from her first job as a secretary for, "Not being presentable." Of course this translated as she wouldn't wear a blouse low-cut enough that the partners could see her tits, but even then Paulina Cole didn't feel this sensation. Even then, she knew her future was in her hands. Small people thought small. She was meant for something bigger, grander, and nobody, no idiotic men--whether spouse or employer--would ever slow her down.

Until that night.

There were burn marks on her right side, just below the curve of her breast. It ached every second of every day, and she had to wear a massive bandage otherwise all the aloes she put on it would seep through her shirts. She'd never been brutalized. Not like that. She could take criticism. She could take people hating her. Hate came when you got under somebody's skin, and Paulina was nothing if not a provocateur.

But she did nothing to deserve this.

And neither did Abby.

Thinking about what that man threatened to do to her daughter made Paulina shriek inside. And when Paulina Cole got scared, she took those emotion and turned them inside out. Fear turned to rage, and rage had to be directed somewhere. She just didn't know where yet.

She arrived at Smith College at just past noon, the entire hundred and sixty mile plus drive taking just over two and a half hours. Luckily there wasn't much traffic leaving Manhattan that early in the morning. Lots of people lived outside the city and commuted in. Not a whole lot did the opposite. No sense paying New York living prices and make a non-NYC wage.

Finally Paulina found herself on College Lane, which was bracketed on the North by Elm Street. Figured, she thought, that this pagan sanctuary of a university would have an Elm Street.

The office of Admissions was a three level white-thatched cottage with a second level deck that hung over the entryway. The front door had several sun chairs on the porch, though Paulina couldn't for the life of her figure out who exactly would choose to spend a beautiful day sitting in front of the admissions office.

Paulina parked the rental on the lawn directly outside of the admissions office, purposefully ignoring the yellow sign that clearly stated "VEHICLES WITHOUT PARKING PERMITS WILL BE TOWED." Paulina knew this game. In order for her car to be towed, the admissions office would have to call the college's office of public safety. The public safety office would have to dispatch an officer to survey the vehicle. If the vehicle was, in fact, parked without a permit, the public safety officer would then have the go-ahead to call the local police department, who would then dispatch a tow truck to remove the offending vehicle. The entire process, beginning to end, would take about forty five minutes.

Paulina didn't plan to be there more than five.

She walked into the admissions office, trying to avoid eye contact with the students huddled in the foyer reading the campus paper and checking their cell phones for text messages. She went right up to the registrar, and planted her hands on the counter in front of the ruddy-faced man who looked at her like she was some vicious bear come in from the wilderness.

"Hi," Paulina said with the conviction of a woman who knew she'd get whatever information she wanted and might just tear out your spleen to get it. "I'm looking for my daughter. I was wondering if you could let me know what dorm room she's in."

"Your...daughter?" the man said, surprised. Paulina could tell from the man's demeanor that he was probably not considered any sort of threat to the student body of this all-girl school.

"Yes. My daughter. Abigail Cole." The man sat there unmoving. "Is there a problem?"

"Well no," he replied. "It's just that, well, most parents have their children's phone numbers and dorm rooms etched into their brains. You know, one of those

always know where to reach your loved ones' deals."

"Yeah, well I'm not one of those parents," Paulina said.

"No, you don't seem to be." He picked up the phone. "Would you like me to call her for you?"

"No," she said. "I'd prefer if you just told me where she lives. I'd like it to be a surprise."

"Surprise. Sure. Can I just see some ID?"

Paulina handed it over. The man took it gently between his thumb and index finger like one might handle a piece of forensic evidence. He looked at it, typed a few keys into his computer, then slid it back to her.

"Thanks Ms. Cole. Abigal lives in room three oh three of the Friedman apartments."

"Where can I find that?"

"It's the housing complex at the corner of Elm and Prospect street. But you'll need somebody to let you in--like Abigail. The doors are locked twenty four seven, and campus security is always on the lookout for people who don't necessarily look like they know what they're looking for."

"Thanks for the tip," she said, and left.

She drove over to the apartment complex and found a spot in the student lot in between a Volvo that looked sturdy enough to withstand tank fire and a Prius with a Kerry/Edwards bumper sticker lovingly forgotten on the rear bumper.

She walked across the lawn towards the middle of the three dorms, for a moment thinking back to her own time at college, wondering where it all went. She barely remembered the days that seemed to have flown by in a blur of books and late nights, staying up until four in the morning to ace the test that nobody else figured they could pass. Paulina smiled as she watched all the young women, these silly young women who probably had no idea what kind of world awaited them. Most looked like they didn't have a care in the world, and who knew, maybe they didn't. But, one thing Paulina knew for sure, it was the ones who cared too much who succeeded. The ones who refused to stay down when they were beaten down. The ones who refused to take 'no', and instead took everything. She prayed for years that her daughter was like that. Sadly, she'd resigned herself to the fact that it was not meant to be.

Approaching the dorm, Paulina stopped two young women carrying backpacks and chatting. "Excuse me," she said. "Can you tell me where I can find room three oh three?"

The thicker one who had short hair and stringy looking tassels lining it, pointed to the dorm on the left, then middle, then one. "One hundreds, two hundreds, three hundreds." She finished pointing at the dorm on the right.

"Thanks very much," Paulina said, and waited until the girls left. She walked up to the entrance, a glass door leading into a small atrium that was also locked from the outside. She took out her cell phone, pretended to send text messages while she waited. Finally a girl approached the door, looking in her purse for a key. When she found it and inserted it into the lock, Paulina stepped behind her and put the phone away. The girl opened the door, and Paulina caught it before it could close, following her into the atrium. The girl turned around, looked at Paulina.

"I'm sorry," she said, her young blond hair looking so tender, so naive. "We're not supposed to let strangers inside the dorms."

"Oh, I'm no stranger," Paulina said, laughing. "Do you know Abigail Cole?"

The girl's eyebrows lifted. "Why do you ask?"

"My daughter," Paulina said, shrugging. "Surprise visit."

Suddenly the girl turned around, enthusiasm radiating from her. It took Paulina by surprise. "No way!" the girl nearly shrieked. "I'm Pam. I've asked Abby so many times about her family and, well, I guess you know what she's like. When she decides to clam up, no crowbar in the world can get her talking."

"That's Abby," Paulina said. "So you know her?"

"Know her?" Pam asked, somewhat surprised. "Hasn't she mentioned..."

"We don't talk much."

"Oh. Because we've been...I don't know, seeing each other."

"Really," Paulina said.

Pam nodded, hesitating before she spoke. "But I guess Abby didn't tell you."

"Must have slipped her mind."

"Here," the girl said, opening the inner door and holding it for Paulina. "Sorry to keep you."

"She's in room three oh three, right?"

"She might be." "Might be?"

The girl began to look nervous. She brought a finger to his lip and began to chew. "She's kind of been hanging out at my place. Just for the last few weeks."

"Is she there now?"

"Probably. She doesn't have psych until three."

"Do you mind then?" Paulina said, pointing towards the elevator bank.

"Oh, we're on the first floor. Follow me."

The girl led Paulina down the corridor, filled with campus notices, posters and random detritus. When they arrived at room three nineteen, the girl knocked.

"Abby, are you decent?" she asked.

Before the door could open a voice from inside called, cheekily, "I don't have to be."

"Abby, open up," Pam said.

"Alright, don't get your panties knotted." Paulina heard a latch being undone from inside, and the door opened. Standing in the doorway was a girl Paulina both recognized and did not. Those green eyes, that long, equine nose she got from her father, she'd recognize those traits anywhere. But the jet black hair, the nose ring, the thick eyeliner--it nearly obscured the girl Paulina had raised all those years ago.

"Hi Abby," Paulina said.

"You've got to be fucking kidding me," came her daughter's startled reply.

Chapter 12

Morgan stood outside of his apartment, his cheeks still stinging from that morning's shave. It was a good pain, though, one that reminded him of what it felt like to wake up with a purpose, to wake up knowing that the day would take him somewhere. Shaving wasn't a big deal on the surface. Lots of people liked scruffiness, women especially these days, as though there was a magnetism to the inherent laziness of it. Morgan loved the feel of running a sharp blade over his face during a hot shower, the feel of patting his skin after drying off. He knew that whenever he felt like that, things would go his way. A big paycheck. Some honey who knew he brought home the money whereas that bearded artist who spent every penny he owed on cheap paints and canvas could not.

Cleanliness. Right next to Godliness. Perhaps somewhere in that equation was Morgan Isaacs.

He didn't dare bring a cup of coffee with him, or anything more than his wallet and keys. He had no idea what this guy Chester wanted, this guy with the hair so blond it nearly disappeared in the sunlight. He didn't look like he belonged in New York, this guy. His ear-length blond hair and lanky but strong build reminded him of a pro surfer, maybe one of those guys you saw pumping iron on Venice Beach. Someone who took care of their body for a reason. Not a gym rat like most New Yorkers, but someone whose vocation required it.

The day was crisp, the streets quiet after rush hour. Morgan wondered why Chester wanted to meet at one, such an odd time. Something about the whole deal smelled not quite right, but Ken Tsang was nothing if not a bloodhound for straight up cash, so if he ended up working with this guy there had to be money involved.

Just when he was thinking about what kind of payday could be involved, a shiny black Lincoln Town Car pulled up right in front of Morgan, the tires screeching to a halt. Morgan watched as a driver exited, an older white guy wearing one of those hats that said he'd probably been driving rich folks around most of his life, and opened the back door. When nobody came out, Morgan stepped forward. Chester was sitting inside. He was wearing a sharp grey suit and sunglasses, his blond hair a striking contrast against the black leather.

Chester tapped the seat next to him and said, "Get in.

Morgan nodded and slid into the back seat, pulling the door closed behind him. The car sped off as swiftly as it stopped. Morgan turned to see Chester staring at him, smiling.

"Glad you could make it," he said. "You ready to make some money?"

Morgan smiled right back.

The car cruised effortlessly downtown, turning left onto Fifth Avenue. Morgan felt a slight lump rise in his throat as they sped by his old office building. It wasn't right that he was gone. All his life Morgan Isaacs had dreamed of making his living in finance, working for a bank or a hedge fund, having a different, brilliant suit for every day of the week. He would have one of those massive corner offices, a bar stocked with decanters filled with the most expensive liquors money could buy. He would have a beautiful young secretary, some hot girl just out of college who had no other desires in life other than to work until the day she met someone like him, someone like Morgan, who could satisfy their every need and pay the bills so she would never have to work another day in her life. She would have dinner ready, shop (but not too much), be a doting mother and always have a good reason as to why daddy came home late.

He wouldn't be one of those absentee fathers. No, Morgan actually looked forward to having children. He wanted vacations to the Greek islands, ski trips to Telluride. He wanted a pied-à-terre in France, a vacation home in the Bahamas. He wanted to send Christmas cards and have picture frames littering his massive desk. He wanted everything. Right now, sitting in the back of this shiny black car, with a perfect stranger next to him to whom Morgan's future might well depend on, this was most definitely not the direction Morgan had expected his life to take.

This was not too much to ask, Morgan thought. Everything was going perfectly until the economy went downhill faster than an Olympic skier and soon he was out on his ass with thousands of other men just like him. Men with GPAs in the high threes, impeccable references and several internships and jobs from which they could draw experience. Even if (and this was an if the size of the Grand Canyon) a job opened up, it would be like trying to get a drink at a hot bar at one in the morning. Thousands of people pushing and shoving like barbarians to get the attention of one person. Was one resume really better than the other? It didn't matter. But Morgan had Chester. Good old Chester.

"Anything stand out to you?" Chester said as they passed through midtown.

"Um...it's a nice day?" Morgan said, not sure what Chester was getting at.

Chester smiled. "It is that. But look at the streets. Notice anything?"

"Uh, not really."

"Not really," Chester said. "Exactly what I noticed."

"Wait, what do you mean?"

"These streets, they used to teem with professionals. It's lunch hour and you can count the suits on two hands. What is the financial workforce down, ten, twenty percent?" "At least," Morgan said.

"These streets used to mean something," Chester said, his voice almost wistful, making Morgan wonder if Chester had ever held a job here. His attitude and dress were corporate all the way, but he was loose enough to hang with the boys at a steak house or strip joint. Morgan's guess was that Chester was in upper management, the kind of guy everyone else reported to who could act with a little disregard. The kind of guy Morgan couldn't be...yet.

"Did you know," Chester continued, "that over a hundred thousand people have lost their jobs in this city in the last two years? I mean Christ, think about it. Think about how many of those hundreds thousand used to work here," he said, gesturing to the towering skyscrapers that housed floors and floors of seasoned pros. "Think how many of them used to walk these streets. And now think about how many of them are sitting at home right now, watching their savings dwindle, waiting for one call that probably won't come."

Chested looked out the window as he said those last words, but Morgan could tell they were directed at him. Talking about many like him. Morgan stayed quiet. Didn't want Chester to know what he was thinking.

"Think how many of those people," Chester continued, "would

give anything for the chance to replace that income." He stopped. Looked at Morgan. "And then some. What would you do for that chance?"

Morgan's eyes met Chester's directly. Without hesitation he said, "Anything."

"We'll see."

Chapter 13

Pam said, "I uh...I think I'll go check my mail," Pam said.

Abigail looked at her and said nothing. Paulina said, "That's not a bad idea. If you wouldn't mind giving us a few minutes."

"She doesn't have to do anything she doesn't want to," Abigail said, her eyes burning a hole through her mother.

"No, she doesn't. That's why I'm asking. And," Paulina said, digging into her pocketbook and producing a twenty dollar bill, "I'll pay for her next beer run."

"Classy, mom," Abigail said. She sighed, looked at Pam. "This won't take more than fifteen minutes."

"Half an hour," Paulina said. Abigail looked at her mother as though no greater torture had ever been imposed upon man or beast. Paulina stared right back.

"Fine. Half an hour. And take the money."

"I really shouldn't..." Pam said.

Abigail continued, "Trust me. It doesn't begin to cover what she owes me."

Pam reluctantly took the money, and left the room, leaving Paulina and Abigail alone.

"Can we talk inside?" Paulina said. She peeked into the dorm room. It was a flat out mess. The floor was covered in strewn paper, dirty clothes and burnt incense sticks. Their furniture was comprised of two beanbag chairs, a twin bed with a frame that looked as stable as Paulina's ex-husband, and a ratty couch that some homeless person had probably sold to them for less than the twenty she just gave to Pam. Whatever, Paulina thought. She didn't have to live in this mess. If her daughter chose to, so be it.

"Fifteen minutes," Abigail said, checking her watch. "Then I want you out of here."

"I don't like being here anymore than you like me being here," Paulina said. "Trust me, I'll make it as quick as I can."

They nodded, and Paulina entered the room. She took a look

at the beanbag chairs, then pulled out the tiny desk chair. She eased herself onto it, and watched as her daughter launched herself into a blue beanbag chair. Abigail pulled out a cigarette and lit it, opening the window slightly to let the smoke drift out.

"When did you start smoking?" Paulina asked.

"When did you start caring?" Abigail answered.

"You're not going to make this easy, are you?"

"Is that what you want? You want me to make this easy? Sure, why not. I mean, we have all these great memories to fall back on, all these great mother and daughter moments we both cherish." She said the last words with biting sarcasm. "Why are you here mom?"

Paulina leaned forward, put her face in her hands, took a breath. "I need to ask you a few questions."

"Is this for, like, one of your newspaper articles?"

"No, it's nothing like that. Just promise me you'll answer me, and be honest. I don't care about the answers and I won't judge you. I just need to know it for safety reasons."

"Safety reasons? What the hell are you talking about?"

"There's a photo, of you. It was taken at the beach. I need to know how someone could have seen it?"

"I go to Jones Beach every weekend during the summer," Abigail said. "You'll have to be more specific."

"You're wearing a pink bikini. Yellow sunflowers on it. You look like you dug some sort of big hole, and...you look happy. And you were still a blonde."

Abigail thought for a moment. Then she smiled too. "The summer before last," she said. "I went to Jones Beach with some friends, and buried this guy named Ryan in the sand. He's dating our friend Marcia. Good times."

"How could somebody else have gotten a hold of that photo?" Paulina asked.

Abigail's scornful look disappeared, and suddenly she became concerned. "Why are you asking that? What happened?"

Paulina leaned back in the chair, the wood stiff and playing hell with her neck. "There's some guy...he's trying to get to me, to threaten me, and he said...well, and he found that photo of you somehow. I need to know where he could have gotten it."

Abigail's fright took center stage now. She cupped her hands together, started breathing into them. Paulina was unsure of what to do at first, but the sight of her only daughter terrified was too much to bear. She stood up and went over to her daughter, placing her hands on Abigail's shoulders.

"Listen, Abby, I would never let anything in the world happen to you. You might hate me, and you might have reason to hate me. But I'd sooner let my body be ripped limb from limb than let anything happen to you."

Abigail choked back a laugh. "Can't we just avoid both?"

Paulina laughed. "Hopefully."

"I posted a set of those photos to Facebook," she said. "Maybe a month ago. I was going through some old pictures. I just scanned some old albums and uploaded them."

"So who could see the photos?"

"Anyone I'm friends with online."

"How many friends do you have on Facebook?"

"Hold on, I'll check."

Abigail went over to the desk and sat in the stiff chair. She turned on the laptop, waited for it to boot, tapping her dark, polished fingernails on the desk. When the computer started, Abigail opened Internet Explorer and logged on to her Facebook account. Paulina saw that Abigail's profile photo was a close up of her face, specifically her left eye and cheek. It was so close you could see every individual pore. It looked faux artsy, the kind of thing you took with a webcam and thought it to be poignant.

"A hundred and ninety six," she said.

"Jesus," Paulina said. "A hundred and ninety six people have access to photos of you in a bikini."

"You want to judge me, mom? I've heard some stories about you."

"This isn't about me. Somebody used one of these photos. Is there any way to see who's accessed the set? Or who's printed them out?"

Abigail shook her head. "Nope. Privacy issues."

"Privacy my ass. Listen, Abby, I need you to printed out a list of all your friends on this thing, anyone who has access to those photos."

"No way mom, other people have privacy too."

"Trust me, these other people would prefer this than the alternative."

Abigail looked her mother in the eye, huffed and said. "Ok. Fine. But nobody else sees them besides you."

"You have my word. And if these 'friends' have email addresses, that would be helpful. I'm not looking to pry, I just want to be sure. I promise once I'm done it'll all be shredded."

"You gave your word," Abby said.

"One more question, then I'm done," Paulina said. "Have you recently a man around campus, tall, blond hair, about ear length? Late thirties or early forties and well-built?"

"Doesn't ring a bell. Sure he's not one of 'your' friends?" she said pointedly.

"No. He's not."

"I haven't seen anyone like that. Trust me, he'd stand out on this campus."

"Alright then."

Paulina stood up. Abigail did not. Paulina waited to see if her daughter would, to see if there was any chance at a last embrace before she left Abigail was already opening her page and scrolling through photos. Paulina leaned in closer. Abby was staring at one of her and Pam, standing in front of a gushing fountain, holding hands and smiling.

When she noticed her mother was looking, Abigail covered the screen with her hand.

"I'll scan it and email it to you," Abigail said. "You'll have it by tomorrow morning."

"Thank you," Paulina said. "You know Abby, I don't even have your cell phone number."

Paulina laughed at this. Abby did not. It took a moment, but Paulina understood why that wasn't quite so funny.

"That's not a surprise," Abigail said, "considering I hear from you once a year, I figured either you didn't have my number or you just couldn't find more than five minutes every twelve months."

"I know I could have done a better job, could have been a better friend. Consider this my attempt to make it up to you."

Abigail considered this for a moment, then said, "Fine."

Paulina took out her cell phone, plugging in the numbers as

her daughter spoke them.

“That’s it?” Paulina said.

“That’s it.”

“Thanks hon, I promise I’ll call soon.”

“Mom?” Abigail said.

“Yes Abby?”

Abigail’s face looked far more pale than it did when Paulina first entered. Eyes wider, more fearful. A pang of guilt ripped through Paulina, knowing her daughter wouldn’t have to deal with any of this if that blond bastard hadn’t needed her to promote his sick agenda. She knew many more lives were at stake than Abby’s...but this was her daughter.

“That photos set I mentioned,” Abby said. “The picture you mentioned was in that set. It was Pam’s favorite picture. She told me she loved it, and she said she wanted to keep one just for us.

“Wait,” Paulina said. “What are you saying?”

“I never posted that photo online. That guy you’re talking about...somebody else must have given it to him.”

Chapter 14

"Nothing," Jack said, slamming down the phone in disgust. "I've called his office, his cell phone, his secretary, his publicist, his wife, his alleged mistress, and nobody will connect me to Brett Kaiser. Please tell me you have something."

I shook my head, discouraged. "I've spent the entire morning trying to reach Marissa Hirschtritt and Joel Certilman. Nothing. They won't talk to me, or refer me to anybody who will. And they said that if anything is printed about their firm, their official position is 'no comment.' At least until they sue us for whatever libel they seem certain we're going to print. That firm is locked up like a vault. And the worst part is that they know we're looking into them, so they can already start preparing."

"And knowing our goodhearted Chairman, he's not going to want to pay thousands of dollars in legal fees to fight a law firm over a story that we have no backing to go on yet." Jack paused, thought for a moment. "When people aren't responding to you, there's only one way around it."

"What's that?" I asked.

Jack stood up. Picked up his briefcase. "You walk right into the enemy's camp, lay down your weapons, and ask to speak to their leader."

"You learned this, where, reporting from the jungle?"

"Vietnam, actually."

"No kidding. I knew you reported from Vietnam."

"Spent most of my time in Laos," Jack said. "Worked a lot with a great photographer named Eddie Adams. You enjoy photojournalism?"

"Back in Oregon," I said, "before I was old enough or smart enough to really understand history, I used to love flipping through them just for the photo inserts. A great picture can be a snapshot of a time or place that words could never fully describe. Jack nodded, agreeing. "I used to really admire a photographer named Hans Gustofson. I remember he took this fantastic photo of President Reagan standing next to the 'You Are Leaving' sign that had just been removed from along the Berlin Wall."

"Great eye, Gustofson. Didn't he die a few years ago?"

"Yeah," I said, shifting uncomfortably. "Badly."

Jack nodded.

"Eddie Adams," I said. "Why does that name sound familiar?"

"Nguyen Ngoc Loan," Jack said.

"Excuse me?"

"General Nguyen Ngec Loan. Chief of the National Police of the Republic of Vietnam. You say you liked historical photographs, you might remember that one. Loan was the commanding officer during the arrest of a Viet Cong political operative. The National Police mistakenly identified the prisoner as having plotted the assassination of numerous Viet Cong police officers. And so on February first, nineteen sixty eight, in the middle of a desolate street in Saigon in broad daylight, with the unarmed man's arms tied behind his back, General Loan took out a pistol, put it to the prisoner's head, and pulled the trigger. Eddie Adams was the man who took that photograph. That one snapshot, taken right as the bullet entered the innocent man's brain, was one of the catalysts that singlehandedly changed American perception of the war in Vietnam."

"I remember that picture," I said, feeling a chill, remembering the first time I'd seen it in TIME magazine. "I remember the prisoner was wearing this plaid shirt. And the look in the General's eye...like the man he just killed was nothing. Had meant nothing."

Jack nodded. Then he said, "In the background of that picture, just over the General's left shoulder. There's a man. You can't really make out his face or what he's doing, but he's there."

I looked at Jack. The lines in his face, veins in his hands, a body that had seen more than I might in two lifetimes.

"That was you," I said. "You were there that day."

"It was actually my wedding anniversary," Jack said with a slight laugh. "When my first wife asked where I was that day, I showed her the picture. Suddenly she didn't feel so bad about my not being able to spent it with her."

"Why do you still do it?" I said. "Once you've been a part of these...these...moments that change history. I mean, that's what ever reporter dreams of, right? Being there at the right time. Casting light on something that was covered in darkness. Once you've done that... how do you stay motivated?"

"I was never looking for those moments," Jack said. "If they came, they came. If not, I went right on working. But a real reporter doesn't seek out those moments. We don't judge what's happening in front of our eyes. History creates those moments. All we can do is share the truth, through our words. And if we're honest, and there's a story in that darkness, the moments come. But I never sought them out. I sought the truth. And if you keep digging for it, under ever god damn rock in this world...you'll find a few of those moments."

"If I die having had just one of those moments," I said, "I'd die a happy man."

"Maybe you already have, Henry," Jack said. "You just don't know it yet. Maybe this story is even it."

"Well if it is, Brett Kaiser sure isn't going to make it any easier."

"Well let's try the good old-fashioned ambush method."

"What do you suggest?" I said.

"I'll go to the firm's office, buy myself a big old cup of coffee, sit in the lobby and wait for Mr. Kaiser to leave. If security doesn't want a fellow such as myself loitering, I'll simply wait outside. And if they tell me to leave, I'll tell them to kiss my wrinkly old ass."

"And my job?"

"Why, you're going to wait at Mr. Kaiser's Park Avenue apartment building and do the exact same thing. You might even try sweet talking his doorman. You have no idea how much information those guys have, and what they're willing to tell you if you treat them like the human beings. Unlike Park Avenue tenants who usually treat their doormen like they're one step above pond scum."

"And what if Kaiser shows up?"

"Simple," Jack said. "You tell him what we have, and ask him for discuss it with you. Guys like this, these alpha male pricks, hate hiding behind publicists and lawyers, even if they are one. They don't like being shown up by punks like you."

"Punks like me?"

"Yes," Jack said, arching his eyebrow. "Punks like you. At least that's how he'll see you. Actually, I'm kind of hoping he does see you first. Young guy, you're less of a threat. Probably figures you write for the school newspaper. If you see Kaiser, you don't walk away with less than something we can print that doesn't rhyme with 'Woe Bomment.'"

"I think I can manage that."

"Good. Keep your cell on, I'll call you if anything happens on my end." I got up to leave. Jack put his hand on my shoulder, said, "Good luck Henry. Get this."

I nodded, went over to my desk and packed my things.

Chapter 15

I arrived at Brett Kaiser's apartment at just after two o'clock. There was a Korean deli on the corner where I bought a cup of coffee and an energy bar.

I walked over to the building, a bright Park avenue complex that by count was twenty stories high, with beautiful western views where you could see all the way down for miles. There was one doorman on duty, a man in his early forties wearing a blue uniform and the kind of top hat you only saw in movies about the 1920's. He was slightly heavyset, the beginnings of jowls on his face, a fresh razor burn under his chin.

A cab pulled up, and the doorman approached, leaning down to open the car door. A slender blonde in her forties slid out, thanked the doorman and went into the building. The doorman watched her as she entered the building, holding his gaze just long enough for me to know that had she turned around, she wouldn't have been pleased.

When the woman disappeared into the elevator, I approached.

"Afternoon," I said.

The man nodded. "Can I ring someone for you sir?" he replied.

"Not yet," I said. "Is Mr. Kaiser home?"

"I haven't seen him yet today."

"Ah, let me guess, you're on the eight a.m. to four p.m. shift. I guess that means Mr. Kaiser is up and at work early." The doorman looked at me oddly.

"Sir?"

"No sweat, just making an observation. Name's Henry," I said, extending my hand. The doorman hesitated. "I'm a reporter with the New York Gazette."

If he'd considered shaking my hand before, that idea was now gone.

"As I said sir," he replied, his voice much colder. "Mr. Kaiser is not home at the moment."

"I know, you mentioned that. I have to ask him a few questions."

"Questions?"

I had to stop myself from smiling. Here's the thing about New York City doormen: they love to talk. Your average doorman opens and closes a door for eight hours a day, but barely get more than two words from their tenants. If you stop to chat, they'll talk your ears blue. So few people actually talk to doormen, that if you gave them an inch they'd take eight miles.

And I was prepared to give this one a few feet.

"We're investigating a...I can't really talk about it yet. But hopefully Mr. Kaiser can answer all our questions thoroughly. And I promise, you won't be mentioned."

"Why would I be mentioned?" he said, that voice thawing with concern.

"You won't be," I said. "If you knew anything about Mr. Kaiser, anything suspicious, even something you thought one day and just dismissed, it would help his cause and ours. I'm looking for the truth, Mr..."

"Anderson," the man said. "Donald Anderson."

"Well, Donald..."

"You can all me Don."

"Ok, Don. Thanks for being so agreeable."

"Am I?"

"Are you what?"

"Being agreeable." Don blinked as he spoke.

"Yeah, you are. So are you friendly with Mr. Kaiser?"

"I mean, in so much as he doesn't say much, I've never gotten any complaints from him."

"No complaints. Any compliments?"

"He's not what you'd call the most talkative guy," Don said. "He tips over the holidays, kinda gives a little nod when he's on his way out of back in. Other than that he don't say much."

"You ever try talking to him?"

"You ever work as a doorman?" Don asked.

"No, I haven't."

"Every tenant's got a different personality. You got to learn how each person acts and reacts towards you, and tailor your personality towards that. I swear, my first few months on the job I felt like I was going crazy, developing one of those, whaddaya call ems, split personalities. Mrs. Delahunt, she walks her dog like clockwork at seven thirty in the morning. She always says, 'say hi Toodles!', like she's expecting the dog to talk to me. At first I couldn't figure out why she treated me like such a, pardon my french, such a bitch. Then Charles, the evening doorman, told me I had to say hello back to Toodles. So every day at seven thirty, I say hi to this little rat dog Toodles. And every year at Christmas time, Mrs. Delahunt gives me a tip twice as big as most tenants. All because I say hello to her freaking dog."

"So how does Mr. Kaiser fit in?"

"My first few months, I tried to be real polite. 'Hello Mr. Kaiser. Have a good day Mr. Kaiser. Welcome home Mr. Kaiser.' I never get more than a grunt. One day I must be thinking about something else--maybe Mrs. Delahunt's fine daughter--and I forget to say hello to him. I just open the door, not even thinking, and then I hear him say, 'Thanks Don.' I swear it was like Christmas came early that day."

"So what did you do?"

"I realized Kaiser didn't like being spoken to. Gestures were fine, but man did he think highly of himself. The most effective method is a little nod as he comes through the door. Closer to the holidays, tip time, I might give him a tip of the cap. But that's all. I don't engage in conversation, I don't say a word to the man."

"Sounds like you've got this down to a science."

"Still refining my game," Donald said. "Always room for improvement."

"So I need to ask one more question about Mr. Kaiser, Don, and I'll be out of your hair."

"Shoot. Just promise you won't tell him I spoke to you, and please don't print my name."

"This really has nothing to do with you, it's just to help me understand Mr. Kaiser. You've watched all these tenants for years, right?"

"That's right."

"Is there anything about Mr. Kaiser, either his mannerisms or something else, that strikes you as kind of strange? Something that stands out as different?"

Don laughed. "Everyone's different in their own way. There's one guy, a psychiatrist on eleven. Different prostitute every Friday night."

"Um, I don't think I needed to know that," I said. Don shrugged. "Is there anything about Brett Kaiser, though, that's different?"

Don scratched his chin. "Actually, this did seem a little strange, but I guess I got used to it. Every Tuesday night at midnight, Mrs. Kaiser leaves the apartment. And about five seconds after she leaves, this guy comes over."

"Wait, she just leaves?"

Donald said, "That's right. Goes to the twenty four seven coffee shop on the corner."

"How do you know that?"

"Every now and then she'll bring me a cup of coffee and a danish. The bags were always from that shop."

"Do you have any idea who this guy is? Business partner? Maybe a lover?"

"Hey man, I don't know that much about my tenants' private lives. But I don't think so, as far as the gay stuff goes. He was a real tall guy. Wore sunglasses a lot, even at night. Looks a little like a G.I. Joe action figure. Stands real straight, even less personable than Mr. Kaiser if that's possible, even after he'd been coming over for a few months the guy never even looked me in the eye. Got the blondest hair I've ever seen, kind of wavy. He comes out at midnight and stays for just about an hour. Then he leaves at one, and Mrs. Kaiser comes back just as he's left."

"Do you have any idea what he's doing?"

"No sir. Shows up, stays an hour, then leaves. No idea why or who he is, but he never causes trouble and always seems pleasant enough."

"What's his name?" I asked.

"Sir?"

"When you buzz him up, what name does he give you?"

"I don't buzz him up any more, by this point I know he's ok so I don't bother."

"But at the beginning," I continued, "he must have given you a name. Do you remember it?"

Don thought for a moment, then he said, "Chester. I think it was Chester."

"You sure?" I said.

"Not a hundred percent, but I think so."

"What else can you tell me about him?" I said. Suddenly Don stood up straight and took several steps back from me. He straightened his hat, then stepped forward. I turned around to see a Lincoln pulled up at the curb. Don was approaching the backseat door, which he opened, bending over slightly while holding his hat with his free hand. When the door was fully open, a man stepped out and nodded at Don.

He was about six feet tall, slightly stocky, a middle-aged man who clearly took care of himself. His black hair was slicked back into a neat coif, and his skin was evenly tanned. His watch glimmered in the late afternoon sun, and I didn't need to look closer to know it was real, and cost nearly as much as my education.

He strode up to the entrance, and I could tell from the slightly scared look in Don's eyes that this was Brett Kaiser.

"Mr. Kaiser," I said, matching his pace. Not an easy feat. "My name is Henry Parker, I'm with the New York Gazette. Can I ask you a few questions."

Kaiser turned to glare at me, barely breaking stride. "I have nothing to say to you," he sniffed.

"Can I ask you what you know about 718 Enterprises? Do you know a man named Stephen Gaines?"

Kaiser stopped, turned to face me. His eyes were cobalt blue, but there was an anger in them that went well beyond that of a businessman annoyed at a prying reporter.

"Listen here, you little prick," he said. "I don't know who the hell this Gaines fellow is, and I sure as hell am not going to talk to you about anything else. I..."

"So you know about 718 Enterprises."

"That's not what I said."

"You denied knowing Stephen Gaines, but didn't deny being aware of a company that was allegedly paying you for lease space in your office building. Why not deny that as well?"

"Like I said, I have nothing to say to you."

"One question," I said. "One question and I'll leave."

Kaiser held a moment. I could tell that this man hated being shackled by a 'no comment,' didn't believe he had to bow to anybody or pretend his nose was clean. He ran his business the way he chose, and he'd be damned if anybody else told him that he might have erred on the wrong side of the law.

"One question," he said, "and then if I ever see you again I'll have your job taken away faster than you can clean all this mud off of you."

Cute line, I thought. It never ceased to amaze me that men like Kaiser could so calmly keep potentially devastating and illegal secrets, yet somehow I was the bad guy.

"Why?" I said. "Why take their money? Your practice seems to be thriving, why take the risk?"

Kaiser opened his mouth, but just as I expected a lengthy response, a beautiful gem that would perhaps unravel the spool just a little more, his cell phone rang. When Kaiser looked at it, I could have sworn his face went pale. He shoved it back in his pocket, looked at me and said, "Good night, Mr. Parker," and walked inside the building and disappeared into the elevator.

I stood there, trembling, angry that I had felt so close to getting him. Don came up to me and said, "Sweet guy, ain't he?"

"Yeah, he's going on my Christmas list for sure." I watched at the elevator light clicked, bringing Brett Kaiser to the 20th floor. I eyed the windows facing the street, and soon saw a light turn on as Brett entered his apartment.

"Thanks Don, I appreciate the help. Keep up the good work, and thanks for being agreeable."

Don laughed. "Gotta tell my wife that one. 'Honey, a reporter told me I was agreeable.' Not sure if that will win me points at the dinner table, but it's a good conversation piece."

"The least I could do," I said. "Take it easy, Don."

I walked to the corner, thinking about my next move. I wasn't going back quite empty handed. Even in his non-answer, Brett Kaiser had confirmed that he was well aware of 718 Enterprises. I believed him when he said he didn't know about Stephen Gaines. If my brother was involved in some sort of drug trade, his work on the street was twenty floors below Brett Kaiser's penthouse.

I was about to call Jack when I felt my cell phone vibrate. Assuming it was Jack calling me, I took it out, looked at the Caller ID. I didn't recognize the number, but it was from a 646 area code. It wasn't Jack; he had a 917. Might have been somebody from Kaiser's firm calling to threaten me, could have been a wrong number. Either way it seemed like a good time to screen my calls. I didn't want to waste any time on a conversation that wasn't vital to the investigation.

When the phone stopped vibrating, I waited for the little envelope to appear that signaled I had voicemail. I called it, plugged in my security code, and listened.

And at the first word, my blood ran cold. I knew that voice. Hadn't heard it in a long time, but there was no way I'd ever forget it. I hadn't spoken to her in almost a year, when I was dragged kicking and screaming from her office after she'd tried to ruin the life of the man I admired most.

It was Paulina Cole.

"Henry, this is Paulina. You know the last name, so I won't keep you. We need to talk. Off the record. It's important. You know damn well it's important because you can bet I don't like calling you any more than you like hearing this message. But we need to talk."

She left her cell phone number and home phone number. Not her work number. I couldn't believe her audacity in calling me, but the fact that she only left her private lines clearly meant something was up. Something she didn't want her bosses at the Dispatch involved in.

And while I was making my mind up whether to call her back, Brett Kaiser's apartment exploded in a massive orange fireball that shot flaming debris half a block and cascaded smoke down upon Park Avenue

Chapter 16

"Who was that?" Morgan asked.

Chester closed the phone, putting it gently back into his coat pocket. He looked at Morgan blankly and said, "Just checking my voicemail." He then offered a smile.

"I didn't hear voicemail pick up," Morgan added.

"You one of those dogs, hear high frequency pitches and everything?" Chester asked.

The Town Car hit a bump, and Morgan gripped the armrest. "No."

"Well that's too bad. Because when dogs hear something, they don't ask questions. But if they start barking, that's when their owner is bound to get upset. You get me, Morgan?"

"I get you."

"Good," Chester said. He looked out the window. They were heading towards the Queens bound midtown tunnel. Morgan could make out the East River, Roosevelt Island.

Morgan had never considered living outside of the city. If he was going to be a power broker, a master of the universe, he had to live within the castle walls. But now the powers that be were trying to evict him, trying to get him to leave the grounds he so desperately wanted to remain on. They'd taken his job, his livelihood, his dignity. It was up to him to figure out a way to stay.

So if Chester wanted to bullshit him about who he was calling, that was fine. Morgan didn't need to know everything. As long as the paychecks cleared, that's all that mattered.

"We're almost there," Chester said. Morgan nodded, looked out the window across the river.

Somewhere in the distance, he could hear fire trucks screaming.

Chapter 17

For at least a minute, I couldn't hear a thing. The ringing in my eyes pounded like I was being pummeled by a hammer, and shutting my eyes and clasping my hands over them didn't do a thing. A dozen of us had run to the corner, under the scaffold of a construction site, to escape the brick and ash that was dropping from the sky like small mortar shells.

I looked up at the Park Avenue building, still shocked to see the gaping hole where Brett Kaiser's apartment had once been. Where just a moment ago I'd seen his light turn on. Where just a moment ago I'd questioned the man about his potentially illegal dealings with a company that may or may not have been responsible for the death of my brother.

Where a man and his wife once resided. Where at least one of them was now dead.

As the world slowly come back into focus, I could hear the sirens of police cars and fire trucks speeding to the scene. Onlookers stared at the building with masks or horror. Mouths open wide, hands covering them, tears streaming down their faces.

Then I saw Donald, my new good friend, standing across the street, his face covered in soot, his lower lip trembling as he watched flames lick at the open space where there used to be a window.

Dozens of people were pouring out of the building, screams and cries when they saw the devastation above them. Some people wondered whether it was terrorist attack, or another prop plane accidentally banking into a residential building. I wasn't sure if the truth, that Brett Kaiser had undoubtedly been murdered, would comfort them or make it worse.

When the first cop car pulled up, four officers exited and stood outside of the building looking up. One of them was barking into a walkie talkie. I watched a small piece of gray ash float down and nestle itself on his brown mustache. He didn't notice. The other cops looked at it for a moment, then turned back to the burning building.

A fire truck pulled up, and immediately nearly a dozen of New York's finest went to work hooking the hose up to a hydrant in front of the building. As they did this, I walked over to the cop car. When he noticed me coming, one of the officers turned to me.

"Sir, we're going to have to ask you to step back. We don't know how much damage there's been to the structure of the building."

"I understand that," I said, taking my wallet from my back pocket. I slid my business card out and handed it to him. "My name is Henry Parker, and I'm with the Gazette."

The rolled his eyes and prepared to hand the card back to me. "Mr. Parker, I..."

"I spoke with Mr. Kaiser. Just minutes before this happened. I don't know if I was the last person to speak with him but...I thought someone should have this in case they need to get in touch with me. If there are any questions."

The cop looked at my card, understanding. He nodded, then slipped it into his uniform. "I'll give it to the lead detective," he said.

"Thank you," I said. "And good luck."

He nodded, turning back to the gaping hole in the brick building.

I walked a few blocks away, making sure I could hear right again and was away from the commotion that would surely envelop that area for the next few days. I took out my phone, and called Jack. He picked up on the second ring.

"Hey Henry, good timing. Brett Kaiser left about twenty minutes ago, I think he's headed towards you. I didn't get much, but if you..."

"Brett Kaiser is dead," I said. There was a pause on the other end.

"Wait...what did you say?"

"I said he's dead, Jack. I caught up with him about ten minutes ago when he pulled up in front of the building. I talked to him for about thirty seconds, then he went upstairs. And less than a minute after that, somebody turned his apartment into a gigantic barbecue pit."

"Wait a damn minute," Jack said. His voice was uneven, shaky. I'd never heard Jack like this before. Scared. It put a lump in my stomach, as the enormity of it all began to sink in. "You're saying somebody killed Brett Kaiser?"

"A few times over," I said. "Somebody wanted to make sure he didn't have a chance to talk to anyone. But I do know that he knows about 718 Enterprises, and if I'd had him another minute he would have spilled everything."

"Jesus, be careful Henry. It's possible somebody saw him talking to you."

"Wait, no way, how could they..."

"Don't be stupid," Jack said. "If someone knows he was talking to you, they might think he told you something."

"But he didn't," I said, pleading my case with nobody.

"Whoever killed him doesn't know that," Jack said. "Be careful. Meet me back at the office in half an hour."

"No can do," I said, unsure of why I was going to do this but sure that I needed to.

"And why the hell not?"

I couldn't tell Jack. If he knew, it would toss our whole relationship into jeopardy. But we had the same blood, the same gene that refused to allow us a moment's breath, that refused to give us rest if there was one unanswered question. But she'd nearly ruined his career. And he couldn't know.

"I have to meet someone," I said. "A source. I'll be back in a couple hours. We'll catch up then."

"Fine, Henry. But watch your back."

"I will," I said, and then hung up to go meet the one person I was absolutely sure would never have my back. I opened the phone back up, and called Paulina Cole.

Chapter 18

The diner smelled the same as I remembered it. Diners never changed, but I had a history with this one.

Fried onions, eggs, hash browns, stale coffee. Today was only the second time I'd ever set foot in here, and once again my only companion would be Paulina Cole.

I wasn't a big fan of diner food in general, with the exception of Sunday mornings when a late breakfast consisting of a mushroom and swiss omelet with a cup of hot coffee was better than a Swedish massage.

Meeting Paulina was pretty much the opposite of all of that.

Paulina Cole was waiting for me in a back booth, a half-drank cup of coffee in front of her. There was no food, no condiments, just the coffee. She was wearing a flannel shirt over a tank top, her hair done back in a bun. Her eyes, a fierce green that normally seemed to ache for you to put up a fight, were subdued. She wore a minimum of makeup, no perfume that I could smell. This was unlike Paulina, whose switch seemed to be permanently set to 'on'.

"Thank you for coming," she said as I sat down. I nodded, unsure of how to feel.

"The last time I was this close to you," I said, "I was ready to hurl you in front of a speeding bus."

"Understandable," she replied.

"You tried to ruin his life," I said. "Jack O'Donnell has done more for this city and for this industry that you ever will. And you try to throw it all away for what? To sell a few extra copies? To put a big old smile on Ted Allen's face?"

"Henry," Paulina said.

"Don't try and justify it to me," I said. "You're a coward."

"If I was a coward," Paulina said, her voice taking on a metallic edge, cold and lifeless. "I would have hidden a drinking problem for years. I would have mortgaged the futures of my coworkers and my employer by reporting with enough liquor in me to inebriate all of

Green Bay. I wasn't the coward, Henry. Jack was. If I'm the coward for telling the truth about Jack, you have a pretty warped view of what it means to be a reporter."

"Jack wasn't news," I said, gritting my teeth. "Millions of people are losing their livelihoods. So what gets plastered on your front page? An old man and his drinking problem."

Paulina laughed, and I felt anger rising within me.

"Jack is news, Henry, and it's time you realized that. Maybe right now he's a broken down old man, but he still has a name. A reputation. And a man with that kind of reputation is beholden to the public. You just don't get it, Henry. And you'd better soon, because even if Jack is back he won't be around for much longer. And Harvey Hillerman's paper is going to need someone else to step up and be the next golden calf. And if it isn't you, like Wallace hopes it will be, than they might as well declare bankruptcy and use their papers for a grade school art class."

"You called me, and you're lucky I'm here at all. So if you want to throw mud, I'll get up and leave. I'll need a shower after this anyway.

"If you had any intention of leaving without hearing what I had to say," Paulina said, "you wouldn't have come in the first place."

I sat there, staring at her, willing my body to stand up and walk right out of the diner. But after what happened to Brett Kaiser, after the murder of my brother, I needed something I could control, something I could follow through to the end.

"Talk," I said. "Why did you call me?"

Paulina sat back, and took a long drink of her coffee. I wondered if she'd had more than one in the time it took for me to get there. Then she looked at me and said, matter-of-factly, "A few days ago, I was kidnapped."

My jaw dropped. "Wait...what? What do you mean, kidnapped?"

"Well, not kidnapped in the usual sense. It's not like there was a ransom note and the whole thing lasted about an hour in total. Somebody posing as my driver took me to Queens and..." I heard a slight choking noise come from Paulina's throat. I wondered if she was faking this, doing something to get me to sympathize with her, but deep down I knew it was real. Paulina Cole was never one to let anyone see her bleed, and the only thing worse than that would be to pretend.

She wouldn't allow herself to be seen that way. And I knew whatever had happened to her a few days ago must have scarred her deeply. "He threatened someone I care about very much. And I believed him. I still do."

"He just threatened you and left?" I said. "Did he hurt you?"

Paulina hesitated for the briefest most before saying, "No."

I didn't want to press. But I knew she was lying.

"Not me," she said. "He threatened to hurt someone close to me."

"You have someone close to you?" I smiled at the dig, but she did not. And for whatever reason, I felt somewhat guilty for it. "I'm sorry. Go on."

"My daughter," she continued. "He threatened to hurt my daughter."

"I'm sorry," I said, feeling an odd combination of guilt for making light of the situation, and surprise that Paulina had a daughter. In our brief time working next to each other, she never had any pictures. Never talked about her.

"That's ok. I didn't ask you here to sympathize with me."

"Good thing for both of us."

"I asked you here because I want to find the guy who did it."

I sat there, watching her. "And?" I said.

"And I need your help."

I laughed. "You need my help? What can I do that you can't?"

"You have friends," Paulina said. "Friends that I don't have."

"You're talking about cops," I said. She nodded. "It doesn't matter if they like you or not, this is a criminal matter and they'll investigate..."

"I can't go to them," Paulina said. "I can't go to the cops."

"Why not?"

"He told me if I did, he would know."

"You think he has an informant in the department?"

"I have to assume he does."

"How do you know he was telling the truth?" I said.

"Because if I assume the other side, and I'm wrong, my daughter is dead."

"Dead...you say he threatened to hurt her, not..."

"I was being kind. Maybe to myself, because I didn't want to think about it. But yes, he threatened to kill her."

I sat there in silence. Paulina was staring at me, a curious look on her face.

"What?" I said.

"I bet there's a part of you that's a little happy about this. You feel like I had it coming."

"I'm not like you," I said. "I don't take joy in the miseries of other."

Paulina smiled, a mischievous grin. That was the Paulina Cole I remembered. The one who pushed your buttons until they bled.

"I'm sorry for what happened to you," I said. "You and I, we'll never be friends, but I wouldn't wish that kind of thing on anyone. Not even you, whether you want to believe me or not."

"You know," she said with an odd smile, "I actually do believe you."

"Well that's peachy. But I still don't know why I'm the right person for this."

"My daughter is closer to your age than mine. You have access to the cops, and you know the world she lives in better than me. You could figure out how someone got a photograph of her."

"What do you mean?"

"My daughter, Abigail. The man showed me a photograph that my daughter said came from a set she posted online. Only this particular photo was never posted, the only one from the set that wasn't available online. This one was private, yet somebody got it."

"What's the photo of?"

Paulina shifted in her seat. She looked uncomfortable.

"It's a recent photo. Taken within the last year. Abigail wearing a pink bikini, and she's standing in front of a big hole on the beach. And she's smiling."

I took out a notepad and wrote it all down. I tried not to look at Paulina. This couldn't be easy for her.

"Don't worry," I said. "Nobody sees this but me."

Paulina nodded, but it was clear this was as enjoyable for her as an endoscopy.

"Do you know how to use MySpace? Facebook? Whatever the hell else people do to exploit themselves these days?"

"I have accounts," I said, "but I really don't use them. I had a cyberstalker once and...long story, but let's just say my girlfriend won't let me go to Staten Island anymore. Go on."

"Well, if you know how to log on you've got a leg up on me. Between that and your access to the cops, you can get information. There's bound to be a news story in this. And even though I'm still pissed about the last time you boned me over on a scoop, if you come up with a trail that leads to something printable...it's yours. And I think you're the only person I could trust to keep it a secret."

"I'm not sure if I should be flattered."

"You need to find out who the man is who got the photo," she said.

"And who he could have gotten it from."

"That's right."

"And what makes you think there's a story in this?" I asked. "Beyond what this guy did to you. How do you know he wasn't some random nutjob?"

"Because he asked me to do a favor for him too," she said. "And this favor wasn't exactly the kind of thing that a nutjob asks of you. It was something planned. It's something part of a much bigger plan."

"A plan?" I said. "What did he ask you to do?"

"It's not important," she said. "Well, it is, but important enough that I'm only going to trust you with so much."

"Are you going to do it?" I asked.

Paulina met my eyes. "You'll know in a few days."

"I assume that means you're no longer taking any personal time and that your column will be back shortly."

"Safe assumption, Sherlock."

"You're a real charmer, Paulina. You know that, right?"

"Listen, Parker. There's a story here. Trust me on this. That's all I can say. And that's the tradeoff. You find this man, you get to follow the trail to wherever it leads. We both come out ahead. And I promise you, this trail will lead somewhere."

I nodded, thought about it. If this man who kidnapped Paulina did have a photo of her daughter and did go so far as to pose as her driver, it meant the crime was planned out well in advance, weeks if not months. Nobody went through that kind of trouble unless the ends justified the means.

"Tell me about this man," I said, taking my notebook from my bag and clicking a pen. "What did he look like?"

"Tall, about six one or two," she said. "Weighed, I'd guess, between one ninety and two ten. In good shape, too. Good looking guy."

"Black? White?"

"White," she said. "He had blonde hair. Kind of wavy."

"Any tattoos or identifiable features?"

"Not that I could see. He was wearing a suit. I think his eyes were green, but I'm not sure."

"Did he walk with a limp? Anything else that could identify him in that way?"

"I don't think so," she said. "He made some sort of reference to fighting in a war. I don't know if he was telling the truth or not. He's not an old guy, so he would have had to fight in the last twenty, twenty five years. And he insinuated like he lost someone. Maybe a family member. Again I don't know if that was a lie or not."

"Is there anything else?

Paulina thought for a moment. "Chester," she said. "He said his name was Chester."

An alarm went off in my head. Chester. Blond hair. It couldn't be...could it?

"What are you thinking?" Paulina said. "You look like something just made sense."

"No, nothing," I lied. "Just thinking how I'm going to approach this."

"And I don't know if this means anything, but something he said seemed out of place. Something about losing a family member. Maybe someone close to him was killed. Look into it."

"Got it all," I said.

She nodded. "You have my cell phone. Don't call me at work."

"No problem." We both stood up. Paulina extended her hand. I looked at it for a moment before shaking it.

"Henry?" she said.

"Yeah?"

"One more thing."

"What's that?"

"Drugs," she said. "This guy...he has something to do with drugs. A lot of them."

"What do you mean."

Paulina looked down at her cup, then back up. There was a look in her eyes I hadn't seen, and I could tell that something was eating at her beyond what she was telling me.

"Just trust me," she said. "Drugs."

"I'll look into it."

"Henry?"

"What?"

"Thank you."

I shook my head, laughed. "I bet that was hard as hell for you to say."

"You'll never know. And don't expect for it to ever happen again."

I shook my head. "You don't have to thank me for anything. We haven't found him yet. And to be honest, I don't know if I could turn down this request from anyone."

Paulina smiled, but I noticed a slight smirk in there, like she found that statement funny. "That's why I love you, Henry Parker. Everyone's knight in shining armor."

"Goodbye Paulina. I'll call you when I have something."

I turned around and walked out of the diner, hoping she wouldn't notice that my palms were practically bleeding sweat. She couldn't know. Not yet.

Because I was pretty certain that the same man who threatened to kill Paulina Cole's daughter was the same man who just blew Brett Kaiser halfway to hell.

Chapter 19

It sure didn't look like a financial company. In fact, if Chester had told Morgan that they made rivets and girders, or maybe the occasional swamp creature there, he would have been more likely to bite.

They were somewhere in Queens, a borough just off the island of Manhattan but a world that couldn't have looked or felt any more different. It wasn't that Morgan hadn't traveled to the outer boroughs, but as soon as he landed his first job the rest of New York City became a foreign territory. He used to have friends in Queens, Brooklyn, Staten Island. But when you work fourteen hours a day you hardly have the energy to get out there. So he kissed that life goodbye, and hadn't thought much about it since.

For a brief moment, as they were driving up to the front gate of what looked like an abandoned factory, Morgan had second thoughts. They only lasted a moment, but they were pure, pungent. A shot of hesitation mixed with an ounce of fright, stirred with a straw of what the hell am I doing here?

Did he really know this guy, Chester? Sure he came with a recommendation from Ken Tsang, but Ken was dead so obviously his hunches didn't always pan out.

But then Morgan remembered his debts. His mortgage. That bank account that had swollen so large and was not deflating like a punctured balloon. Even if this turned out to be nothing, even if Chester was full of crap and offered him nothing more than being a three-card monte dealer in Times Square, it was worth the trip. Not like he had any plans today, and even if there was a one percent chance of paying off his mounting debts, it was worth the trip.

As the Town Car approached the gate, Morgan saw a man approach from the other side of the chain link fence. He was big, about three hundred pounds big, and Morgan couldn't be sure but what looked like a rifle or machine gun of some sort dangled from his left shoulder.

Morgan's eyes went wide, and he turned to Chester. Chester

seemed to notice this, and he smiled.

"Not to worry," he said. "That's Darryl. He's part of our private security force, and he's the best there is. We run a relatively small business, and have had to relocate our operations over the last few days, so security is at a premium. This might not exactly be what you're used to, but I'm sure you won't mind."

Morgan shook his head as though agreeing with Chester's assessment, but he couldn't help but stare at the black muzzle pointing at the ground, wondering how often, if ever it had been fired. And if so, what it had been fired at.

When the gate opened, the car drove through. Gravel crunched under the tires, and Morgan caught this armed man, Darryl, eyeing the back seat window intently as the car came to a stop. The driver got out, and Morgan went to open his door.

"Not yet," Chester said. Morgan looked at him, confused, but then the driver came around to Morgan's door and opened it for him. The driver bowed down, and Morgan slid out. Though this odd gesture in front of some sort of rundown warehouse confused him even more, Morgan did not let it show.

Chester came around to him and said, "Follow me."

The blonde man led him up the driveway to a door. It wasn't quite a front door, since this building didn't seem to have been built with traditional comings and goings in mind, but Chester punched a security code into a small black keypad and an LED light turned from red to green. Chester turned the latch, opened the door, and ushered Morgan in.

They were in a gray stairway, steps leading up and down. Chester took the path upwards, and beckoned Morgan to follow. They went up two flights of stairs. Morgan could see numerous cameras lining the stairwell, each with red lights. At the top of the third floor landing, Morgan noticed that the camera was in fact moving, panning over the entire stairwell.

"Security measures," Chester said. Morgan nodded. Again Chester punched numbers into a keypad, and Morgan heard a latch unlock. Chester smiled at him, and opened the door.

"Go on in," he said. "Take any open seat."

"Thanks," Morgan said, and stepped into the room. And if he'd been confused before, this just took it to a whole new level.

The room inside was wood paneled, as though it had been transported from some high end hotel. In the middle of the room was a long dark mahogany conference table, polished and gleaming. Track lights illuminated the entire room. But what struck Morgan more than anything was not the room's decor, but rather the dozen young men, dressed to the nines just like him, surrounding the table.

Chapter 20

Morgan didn't know what to say. The other men turned to see him when he walked in, but then turned away. They all had looks on their faces that looked startlingly like his own: confidence on the outside, but eyes that showed confusion, discomfort, and above all desperation.

Every face was cleanly shaved, every suit neatly pressed. The ties were knotted perfectly, and the room reeked of designer cologne. There were young men of every race and ethnicity. Black, White, Asian, Indian, Arab. Tall, short, fat, skinny. Some had full heads of hair, some looked to be going prematurely bald. None of the men looked to be older than their early thirties, and some looked barely old enough to have graduated college. Yet every one of them looked like a hungry dog waiting for a meaty bone.

Morgan felt Chester's hand on his back, and a soft voice said, "Sit down, Morgan." The voice had become much firmer than Morgan was used to.

There was an empty seat in between a lanky Indian man and a chubby white guy with a red face and thick shoulders who was fiddling with his cufflinks. Morgan walked over and sat down. The chairs were red leather, plush and comfortable. Morgan debated leaning back, but noticed that all the other guys were sitting straight, waiting for something, not wanting to be viewed as too aloof. Morgan guessed that they were all there for the same reason he was: money.

There was something oddly familiar about the grouping, and it didn't take Morgan long to realize what it was. Everyone at the table, their clothes, their mannerisms, their style and smell, all reminded him of men he used to work with.

Morgan looked back at the doorway, wanted to see Chester's reaction to all of this, but the blonde man had closed the door. Morgan noticed there was another small keypad on this side of the door he'd entered from. The LED light on it was red. There were all in here until someone let them out.

There were few noises. Chubby played with his cufflinks. A black guy at the opposite end seemed to have the sniffles. A young guy with red hair and a pocket square was rubbing what looked like a razor burn on his neck.

And then the door at the other end of the conference room opened. Every eye in the room turned to face it, pupils wide, breath being held.

In strode a man who stood about five foot ten. Brown hair, neatly trimmed and parted to the left. He wore a suit that Morgan guessed to be Brooks Brothers, maybe Vestimenta. There was a gold watch on his left wrist, and a thick silver wedding band as well. He had wide eyes, narrowed ever so slightly. He wore a pair of smart, stylish glasses and gave off an air of both confidence and wealth.

He stood at the doorway for a moment, his eyes traveling around the room, gazing over every single person seated. And then he walked over to the head of the table, put his palms on the wood, hunched over and stared at them.

"I know why you're here," he said. "I know why you all went to bed early last night, got up this morning, took hot showers, broke out those shave brushes and dolled yourself up like you were going to the fucking prom. I know why you did that."

He looked at the chubby kid, fingers squeezing one cufflink like a pig trying to get the hot dog out of the blanket. "Son?" the man said.

"Sorry?" Chubby replied.

"Those things aren't going to fly away. You don't need to keep touching them."

"Sorry," Chubby said. He stopped fidgeting, and placed his hands on his lap.

"Anyway," the man continued, "my name is Leonard Reeves. I'm not going to give you my last name because right now, I don't need to. But that's the only thing I'm going to keep from you today. So let's cut to the chase. Two years ago, I was making one point two million a year. I had a sweet corner office at one of the most prestigious firms on Wall Street. I had it all. When people say they had it all, they're usually bullshitting you, but man, I had it all. Beautiful wife who could've put those Swedish bikini models to shame. A penthouse spread overlooking Central Park with a terrace bigger than most peoples' homes in the

Hamptons, and a secretary that I could tell wanted to blow me every time I stepped into the office. Everyone in my life acted like I walked on water, and that's how I felt as well."

Chubby smiled. He must have liked that mental image.

"But then, just like that, I lost it all. Every cent. My company got bought by another, larger corporation. Overnight my millions in stock options were worth less than the Pope's cock. I owed three million dollars on my mortgage. When I hadn't found a new job in a month, my wife left me. For one of my best friends, who was lucky enough to be working at the same company only in a sector that didn't overlap. She divorced me on the grounds that I was emotionally distant, which, to be honest, I probably was."

Morgan heard a few muted laughs, but they were respectful rather than dismissive. They'd all been there. Or knew those who had.

"So I got thrown out of my apartment," Leonard said. "My parents offer me a place to stay, but I refuse. Stupid decision, I gotta say, because you know where I end up? On the street. Borrowing money to buy drugs that I can't pay for. One day I wake up in an alleyway on a hundred and thirty eighth street with three broken fingers and a dislocated kneecap."

He held up his left hand. Three of the fingers were held at an awkward angle. Morgan grimaced looking at them.

"I'm in the hospital, but of course I don't have insurance. Second day I'm there, a guy comes to visit me. I don't know him from the inside of my ass, but he tells me all my bills are paid for. He tells me he knows who I am, and where I've come from. His name was Stephen Gaines, and he saved my life. Want to know how Stephen saved me?" Leonard said.

The room nodded.

"He gave me my life back. More importantly, he let me become a man again. See, once I lost my job, lost my wife, lost it all, I wasn't a man anymore. I was a dickless nothing wandering the streets waiting for someone to put me out of my misery. And Stephen took me from that, and he gave me my life back."

"What did he do?" Chubby asked. Leonard smiled and walked over to Chubby, knelt down and stared at him in his bright red face.

"He let me earn again."

Chubby nodded, and suddenly Morgan realized he was doing

the same thing.

"I know each and every one of you," Leonard said. He looked at Chubby. "Franklin LoBianco. Laid off from Morgan Stanley three months ago. You're listed as owning a four bedroom apartment on Madison and thirty fourth. Nice area, Franklin, but I bet you're wishing you didn't splurge on that four bedroom now."

Franklin lowered his head.

Leonard walked around the room and stopped by a young Indian man with a slight goatee and an earring. "Nikesh Patel," Leonard said. "You were the chief financial analyst at a hedge fund that was worth 1.2 billion dollars. But then that fund blew up, and you were without a job. I bet it makes paying for your parents' home in New Delhi rather difficult."

Nikesh opened his mouth questioningly, but shut it as Leonard walked around the room some more. Morgan went rigid as Leonard stopped right by him and looked down at him.

"Morgan Isaacs," Leonard said. "A few years ago, you bought your apartment for one point eight million dollars. I'm sure at the time it seemed like a good buy. A good investment. But records show that that same apartment was listed two months ago at one point five. Then one month ago at one point two. Now, it's currently off the market. Figure between costs and renovations, you're out a million dollars minimum. And this real estate market isn't going up any time soon."

Morgan felt the eyes of the room locked on to him, but when he met their gaze he saw there was no condescension, no patronage, no disdain. Instead there was pity. And Morgan smiled when he saw his fellow brothers, knowing they were right there with him.

"In the past twenty four months," Leonard said, standing straight up and walking back to the front of the room, "I have made two point three million dollars. Twice as much as I ever made on Wall Street. And that's in the worst economy in almost eight years."

Morgan could tell his eyes were just one of a dozen pairs that went wide when hearing that sum.

Leonard continued, "And that's after taxes."

A few hushes whispers now rose through the room, including one person who said, quite audibly, "Bullshit." Leonard locked eyes with the speaker, a bald, black guy in his early thirties. "Two point three after taxes, that's, what, about a million and a quarter after Uncle

Sam takes his bit? You're telling us you went from being broke ass on the street to making seven figures after taxes in two years? In this economy?"

Leonard nodded. "Welcome to the new America," he said.

"How?' Chubby said, suddenly springing to life.

"How," Leonard said, rubbing his chin as though debating the question. "That's the key. How. And I'm guessing not just how, but how can you do it too. That's kind of a multi-part answer. And let me tell you this. If you aren't comfortable with the first part, you won't be right for the rest of it. Ready? Here goes. You will make money. You will also file a W-2. You will do everything a good taxpaying citizen of this great country does, including paying state and federal income tax... only what you will be doing to earn that money will not be legal."

"The money is illegal?" Nikesh said.

"Money itself is never illegal," Leonard said. "It's how you obtain it that determines the legality."

"So what will we be doing, exactly, that 'determines the legality," the black guy said.

"It's actually very similar to what you've all done throughout your entire adult lives," Leonard said. "What is finance? What is the stock market? It's a drug. It's gambling. It's doing something that feels so right, that can change your mood, change your mind, change your outlook on things. Just like a drug, the stock market can either expand your mind, or make you lose it. It all depends on who's doing it and how responsible they are. You're all pretty responsible guys, it's not your fault you found yourself on the sole of God's shoe. So you'll be doing exactly what you've done, and what you're good at. Selling people things that make them feel good."

"Drugs," Morgan said.

Leonard cocked his head. "That's right."

Nikesh said, "I don't understand. If you sell drugs, how can you file taxes on it?"

"That's for us to know and you not to worry about. Once you come on board you'll file your taxes just like anyone, and through our company, 718 Enterprises, you'll be just like that waitress on the corner. Nobody looks at her tax return, and nobody will give yours a second glance either."

"What do we need to do?" Nikesh said.

"Simple. Every morning, you will arrive at a predetermined location at eight o'clock a.m. You will be given different items in different quantities. You will dress the same way you did today; like a business man. You will carry on you a cell phone that will be given to you on your first day of work. Throughout your shift, you will receive calls on your cell phone, alerting you to the location of your next customer. We will also tell you what the customer requires, and how much. You will go to the customer's location, exchange money for goods just like anyone, and leave. At the end of each day, you go home. Eight hour days. None of the ten, twelve, fourteen hour crap you're used to. The next morning you'll come back, drop off all the money you received the previous day, fill up your bags and start again. The faster you are, the more runs you'll be given throughout the day, the more money you will make. Those of you who prove that they can handle a lot of runs will be promoted to later shifts. More action, more money. At the beginning you will work with a partner. This is for trust. You are your partner's eyes, and vice-versa. But you are also our watchman."

"Watchman?" Chubby asked.

"This business is built on trust," Leonard said. "Because of the sensitive nature of our business, we cannot take risks. We thoroughly check out every single person before we bring them here. We know everything about you. Your background, your families, brothers, sisters. Your son, Greg."

The black guy swallowed.

"If you do your job, you will make money. If you decide you do not want to continue, that is your prerogative provided you give us the customary two weeks notice. But if you decide that you suddenly want to, say, alert anyone outside of our employ as to your job activities, you will be reprimanded. Severely. There are no second chances, no third strikes. You are not in kindergarten. If you make your bed, you lay in it, and your first offense is a punishable one."

"Punishable by what?" Morgan asked.

Leonard stopped. Looked at Morgan. "Let's hope I never have to answer that question for you." Morgan said nothing. "If you agree to be a part of our company, you will start this Monday. You each came here with a sponsor, and that sponsor will call you Sunday night with the location where you refill and drop off your merchandise and money. Your sponsor put their reputation on the line bringing you here.

Don't embarrass them. In short time, we will be starting an initiative that has the potential to bring in even more revenue than I've already discussed. But you only get to be a part of it if you start now. So if you want to be a part of our organization," Leonard said, "stay seated. If you decide this is not right for you, I'm sorry to have wasted your time."

Nobody moved. Chubby had forgotten all about his cufflinks. Nikesh was absently rubbing his back pocket, where his wallet was surely kept. Greg looked at the table, briefly, considering the offer, then looked right back up at Leonard. His eyes said that he was in.

Morgan did not move. The money seemed too good to be true, but he knew Ken Tsang had fallen on hard times and had gotten out of it. And if things didn't work, he could always quit. But the opportunity was too good to pass up. This was Morgan's way back in the game.

Suddenly a chair squeaked. Everyone turned to the back of the room to see a short, balding man stand up. He waved his hands, as though trying to explain a crime he hadn't committed.

"I...I'm sorry," he said. "I can't do this."

Leonard tilted his head, a look on his face like a parent who's been disappointed by a child they've put so much effort into. "Jeremy, are you sure?" Leonard said.

"I, I'm sure. I can't be a part of this." He moved to the back door, still wringing his hands.

"You're disappointed us," Leonard said, motioning to the rest of the room, still riveted to their seats. "One last time, Jeremy. Stay. You heard what I said to everyone about our rules."

"I know, I...I heard you, but...I'm sorry, but I have to go. Good luck guys," Jeremy said, and he reached for the door.

"Good luck, and farewell Jeremy," Leonard said. Then, lightning quick, Leonard reached into his waistband and pulled out a gun. And before Morgan even knew what was happening, a crack echoed throughout the room, and Jeremy's head erupted in a spray of fine pink mist.

The dead man's body slid to the floor, leaving a grotesque red trail from the gaping wound in his skull.

Morgan recoiled, nearly tipping back in his seat, and when he righted himself he shivered when he realized that the conference room was dead quiet. The eyes that had bugged out of their sockets were now growing accustomed to the violence that had just taken place. The heads slowly began to swivel from the body back to Leonard.

He watched them do this, a look of apathy, a look of simple that's what happens on his face. Morgan recognized that face. He knew the emotions. He couldn't help but smile when he realized who it reminded him of. His old boss.

"There will be no dissent," Leonard said. "There will be no second guessing, and there will be no turning back. Every one of you came here for one reason, and that's to regain some of the respect you had for yourselves. Jeremy did not have this self-respect, and now he's dead. But before you start thinking to yourselves that I'm some kind of monster, let me tell you that if Jeremy had stayed, like every one of you is going to stay, you will make every penny you did at your old jobs. There will be no layoffs, no cutbacks, no downsizing. If anything, your earnings will grow at a faster rate than they ever could while you sat in some wretched cubicle or soulless office. We will be introducing a new product in the next few days that promises to help you erase all those debts. Keep making those mortgage payments. Keep driving that Lexus, keep that sweet Russian girlfriend who wants to spend five grand a month at Chanel. You'll have all of that--and enough just in case you want to throw a dime on the football games on Sunday. Now, you can either take Jeremy's way out, the coward's way out, or you can get back to work and stay the man you were supposed to be. So, men, are you in, or are you worthless?"

Morgan stood up. He felt a surge of energy through his veins, his skin felt like it was on fire. "I'm in," he said.

Within seconds, every other man in the room stood up and joined him. Leonard's eyes met each recruit as they pledged to be a part of this. Morgan looked at each one of them, silently bet himself that he would out earn each and every one of them. And he knew from the way their eyes met his that they were thinking the exact same thing.

Morgan Isaacs smiled.

Let the games begin.

"No second chances," Leonard said. "I'll see the rest of you on Monday."

Chapter 21

Amanda had just settled down with a glass of Pinot Noir, and the first sip tasted better than anything she'd eaten in weeks. She'd skipped dinner, but hell, wine had nutrients, didn't it?

It had been one of those days that never wanted to end. Her feet felt like they'd been trapped inside thimbles and she needed something to take the edge off. She'd been with a client at the office until nearly eight o'clock, and Amanda had come to the pretty secure conclusion that humans were not meant to wear high heels for twelve straights hours. So by the time she got home, weary, weak, her dogs barking like nobody's business, she wrenched that cork from the bottle faster than Pamela Anderson dropped her drawers around a rock star.

And while all those excuses were reason enough to have a drink--whether or not she continued with the bottle depended on several factors--another reason was Henry.

Things were going well. They'd endured enough rocky periods in their relationship than the next twenty couples combined, and she fully believed they'd come out stronger than ever. She never doubted his love for her. Even when that brain of his got in the way, which it often did, she knew it was only because he could be torn between the right thing to do and the smart thing to do. It still surprised her how rarely those two choices were one in the same.

Still, she'd learned a long time ago that trying to change him was not only impossible, but defeated the purpose and would undermine their entire relationship. Henry was relentless. That was the bottom line, and god did she love him for it. As much as her heart pounded during the times where he scared her half to death with his latest bit of reckless behavior, it was that full throttle stopatnothingishness that made him a great reporter and a great partner. Sure he did stupid stuff. He was a guy, that was embedded in the DNA.

For every time he brought home flowers, he would leave his underwear hanging from the bedpost. For every time he said 'I love you,' he would chew with his mouth open. But that's what made them so great. He wasn't fake and didn't pretend to be perfect. Amanda had met plenty of guys who did everything right: held the door open for her, pulled her chair out at dinner, chewed with their mouth closed. But these men were nothing but painters, carpenters, covering up holes in the frame with pretty wallpaper or a fresh coat of paint. Eventually the hole would reveal the truth, and the facade would crumble. With Henry there was none of that. He wore his holes proudly.

Still, she wondered when they might take the next step. Amanda was never one of those girls who dreamed about her wedding when she was six. She didn't name her unborn children, or buy Modern Bride magazine. If love came, she would deal with it then. For years, love to Amanda was like taxes. You only thought about it when you had to.

Yet Henry had changed that. Every so often she would think about what he would look like in a tuxedo, and thought about who would be her maid of honor. She caught herself smiling at things she once found cheesy, and more than once had felt that terror and joy-filled moment of anticipation when she thought he might pop the question.

Yet she didn't want to rush him. Or rush herself. She wasn't sure if she was ready to commit, and wanted to make that decision when the time came.

Still, it felt nice to think about it. If only once in a while.

Amanda heard someone jiggling the doorknob. She stood up, glass in hand, and watched as Henry entered the apartment. His sport jacket was rumpled, slacks dirty around the cuffs. There seemed to be some sort of dirt of substance, something gray and ashy on his lapels. He saw her and smiled, and that was enough to make her smile too.

"Hey hon," he said, dropping his briefcase on the floor and joining her. She felt his arms wrap around her, and she hugged him back. "You smell like tannins."

She held up the glass of Pinot. "Got started early. That kind of day, you know?"

"Do I know." He went into the kitchen and took out a glass. Not a wine goblet, but a regular drinking glass. Then he went over to the dining room table where she'd put a stopper in the open bottle. He wrenched out the plug, and filled his glass up nearly three quarters of the way. Then Amanda watched in both horror and admiration as he downed the entire thing in one gulp. But when he went back for a refill, that's when she stepped in and took the bottle.

"Let's talk first," she said. "That first glass was enough to knock you out."

He looked at her, then back at the bottle, debating whether it was worth arguing over. Eventually he nodded and went over to the couch, plopping down and emitting a deep sigh as he plunged his head into the soft leather.

"So," he said, his eyeballs straining to see her from his position. "Tell me about your day."

"The Morgansterns were in today. They've been trying to keep custody of their adopted daughter for the past few months. The birth mother was a crack addict, and her daughter was taken away from her after she left it in an alley wrapped in newspaper. Apparently the mother managed to clean herself up, get a job, and most importantly marry a man with enough money to make a go at challenging for custody. It's going to be long and it's going to be ugly."

"Do you think you can win?" Henry asked.

"I hope so. The adoptive parents deserve to keep the girl. The mother...she might have cleaned up, but there are certain people who you know aren't good parents. I've met her twice, and neither time did she look me in the eye. Her husband does all the talking. She stands there, hands folded across her lap, like she's almost embarrassed."

"You think he's pressuring her to try and get the daughter back."

"That's what I think."

"Do you have a shot at winning?"

Amanda smiled. Moved over to Henry, clasped his hand, leaned over and gave him a kiss on the cheek. "I always have a chance, babe."

"I know you do."

"So," Amanda said, moving back to talking distance. "How was your day? Any good stories? Jack keeping you on your toes?"

Henry looked at her, and immediately Amanda felt a sinking feeling in the pit of her stomach. Her smile disappeared. She'd seen that look before.

"There was an explosion today, on Park Avenue. An apartment..."

"Some lawyer, right?"

"That's right. Brett Kaiser."

"I saw that on the news. Terrible. The police are saying they think somebody murdered him."

Henry looked at her. "I was there."

Amanda recoiled slightly. "Wait, what?" she said, incredulous. "What do you mean you were there? Like, when the news crews came after the explosion?"

"I mean I was at the explosion. At Brett Kaiser's apartment building. Kaiser was tied into the story Jack and I have been chasing, and I was at his building trying to get some comments from him. When he left me, he went upstairs to his apartment, and a minute or two later everything just erupted."

"Oh my god," Amanda said. She held her hands to her heart, her mouth hanging open, dry. "Oh my god, Henry, are you ok?"

"I'm fine," he said. "A little ringing in my ears, but it's going away."

"You were...there?" she said. He didn't say anything. Then Amanda wiped at his lapel, her hand coming away with gray dust. "Is this..."

"Christ," Henry said, jerking up and going into the bathroom. She heard the water running, and a few minutes later Henry came back out wearing shorts and a t-shirt. Normally she'd make some sort of suggestive comment about how he looked in shorts, but her mind couldn't even fathom levity right now. "Sorry about that. I didn't even realize it."

Then Henry actually laughed a little bit. Amanda wanted to join him, but her mouth wouldn't work. "Hey, baby, you ok?"

Amanda shook her head. She felt her face grow hot, her eyes beginning to water. No, she told herself. She refused to cry. This was what their relationship was. This was what Henry was.

She couldn't protect him. Not right now. Maybe not ever. If he'd been closer to the explosion...if Kaiser had invited Henry upstairs for an interview...if a chunk of brick or concrete had come down at the right angle...he wouldn't be here right now.

Amanda stood up. She went over to the table, picked up the wine and took a swig right from the bottle. When she put it back down and wiped her mouth, she heard Henry whistle from the couch. "That must have felt good."

Amanda shook her head. “No. Not really.”

“I understand,” he said. “I didn’t mean to joke about it. I know what you must be thinking. I’m fine. Not hurt one bit. They weren’t trying to hurt me. Wrong place at the wrong time.”

“Always seems to be that way,” Amanda said, feeling the wine warming her body, her mind going fuzzy. It felt good, and she didn’t try to stop it.

“You know I don’t mean for things like this to happen,” Henry said. He walked up behind her, put his arms around her waist, leaned in close. She felt her eyes closed, breathed him in, brought her arms around his and held him tight. She felt his breath on her neck, taking her away. “I love you, and I also want to be the best at my job I can possibly be. I’m not scared of chasing stories like this. Maybe I should be, but I’m not. I’ve been through enough the past few years, a lot of it with you, to the point where I know this is what I’m meant to do.”

“I know it is,” Amanda said. “I’m not sure if I wish it wasn’t, but I know that’s what you are and what you do. And I’m proud of you. I just...you don’t know what it’s like to hear the person you love say things like that.”

“No, I don’t,” he said. “And god willing, I’ll never have to.”

“I hope not either.” She turned around. Kissed him long and hard. “So, at least tell me this. Did you get anything?”

Henry unwrapped his arms from her and went back to the couch. He sat down, and she joined him. Henry scratched his head. She could tell he’d learned something, and was troubled by it.

“I got a call today. From someone I wasn’t really expecting to hear from, like, ever.”

“Your dad,” Amanda guessed.

“No,” Henry said, somewhat relieved. “But you’re close. Paulina Cole.”

“No freaking way,” she said. “Why the hell would that bitch call you?”

“Something happened to her. Recently. Someone kidnapped her, threatened to kill her daughter.”

“Oh god,” Amanda said. “What happened?”

“The guy let her go, but asked her to do some sort of favor for him. She wouldn’t tell me what she had to do.”

“Was it,” Amanda said, grimacing, “sexual?”

"I didn't get that feeling. But she wants to find out who this guy is, but can't go to the cops. My guess is she thinks this guy is connected. And maybe he is."

"So she came to you," Amanda said.

"She told me if I found the guy, I could have whatever story there was."

"If there is one. If this guy isn't just some loon who took umbrage with one of her scorch-the-earth columns."

"I get the feeling it was more serious than that. One thing I know about Paulina Cole, she doesn't scare easily. This guy was serious, and he scared her so bad that she won't go to the cops and came to me. I have access to the cops she doesn't. And I can investigate without drawing attention, because if this guy does have a mole in the NYPD he wouldn't expect anything from my end. They're watching her. Not me."

"But if they find out that someone is asking questions about this guy, it won't matter who it comes from."

"Curt," I said. "I can trust Curt."

"Maybe," Amanda said. "But who can he trust?"

Henry didn't seem like he could answer that, so he just leaned back. "I don't know."

"Don't you think you might be putting him in danger?' Amanda said.

"When I talk to him," Henry said, "I'll tell him everything. Including that we think they might have people inside the PD. Curt is smart. If there's information to get, he can get it without drawing suspicion."

"And how do you know he'll do it?"

Henry looked at her, his eyes full of confidence. "Because Curt is like me."

"Yeah," she said. "I suppose he is. What are you going to tell Jack?"

Henry sighed. Looked back over at the table. Stared at the bottle of wine, debating pouring another glass. As much as she enjoyed watching him pass out, watching her breathe as he slept, she was kind of hoping he'd be in the mood to fool around a little.

"That's a little more complicated." He looked at her. "I can't tell him."

"About Paulina?"

Henry nodded. "I have to cue Jack in on the lead, but he finds out I got it from Paulina, that I'd even spoken to the woman who tried to ruin his career...he'd never speak to me again. Plus Jack deserves better."

"From who?" Amanda asked. "From me. I don't really know. But the bottom line is that he doesn't need to know. Not right now. If we catch this guy, it's old news. But for now...I can't do that to him."

"You know him better," Amanda said. "If you think it's the right thing to do, then trust your judgment. But at some point you need to tell him, because he'll eventually find out."

"I know and I will. But now's not that time. We're getting close on this story, and I still need to know who was really responsible for my brother's death. Somehow this all connects with the Fury."

"So you do believe this boogeyman exists."

"I think there's someone who knew about the plans to kill my brother before anyone else, and maybe even pulled the strings. Stephen was working for some sort of cartel, and in every organization, legitimate or not, there's someone at the top of the ladder."

"You think that might be this blonde guy?"

Henry shook his head. "The CEOs never get their hands dirty. They have people below them to do that for them. If this person does exist, he's been able to hide in the shadows because he didn't take stupid risks. The blonde guy is acting on this person's behalf. So even if he's not the gold at the end of the rainbow, he knows where the pot is located."

"So what are you then, some sort of freaky ass leprechaun?"

Henry laughed. "Got me the luck of the Irish."

"You're not Irish," Amanda replied.

"Yeah, but Jack is. I knew he was back for a reason."

"Come to bed. I hear leprechauns are lucky."

"Are lucky, or get lucky?"

Amanda stood up. Pulled her shirt over her head. Smiled at him as he gazed up and down her body.

"I guess we'll have to find out."

Chapter 22

The glass sat in front of him. Empty. The last remnants of the liquid sloshed in his mouth, and he finally swallowed it, his taste buds begging for more.

"Fill it up, Jack?"

Jack O'Donnell looked at the bartender, a big Irish bloke named Mickey, and said, "One more. Then I'm cutting myself off."

Mickey laughed. "If I had a nickel for every time I've heard you say that, Jacky boy."

"I mean it this time," Jack said, but something in his voice made the barman laugh. Jack had to smile. "Hit me once more."

"You got it."

Mickey took the nozzle from beneath the bar, brought it up to Jack's glass and filled it to the brim with fizzy, bubby soda.

"Here," Mickey said. He reached into a small plastic tray and removed a single maraschino cherry. Holding it by the stem, Mickey delicately placed it on top of the soda and said, "Voila. Figure since you're drinking girly drinks these days, you might as well go the full nine and have it look girly too."

"You're a saint," Jack said. He raised the glass and tipped it towards Mickey. "To never swilling a pint of that godforsaken ale again."

"You can toast to that, my friend. 'Fraid if I do the same I'll be out of a job."

"This world today you'll be out of a job in the next six months anyhow."

"Did you come here just to ruin my day, Jack?"

"I'm the black cloud hanging over every man's driveway," Jack said with a grin. He sipped the soda.

"As long as you pay your tab," Mickey said, cleaning a glass.

Jack held up the soda glass, shook it gently, the ice cubes clinking. "This stuff, what do you charge for it? Two bucks a glass?"

"Four," Mickey said, slight embarrassment in his voice.

"Four dollars," Jack said. "What does it cost to manufacture?

Three cents?"

"No idea," Mickey said. "I'll tell you one thing, it costs a whole lot more than three cents to buy the syrup."

"See, this is exactly what's wrong with this country," Jack said.

"Christ, here we go."

"No, hear me out. My paper, you can buy it on the street for fifty cents. And for that fifty cents, you get hundreds of articles written by some pretty smart people--ok, some of them are dumber than my shoes--about everything you need to know about the world. No, for this little glass of sugar piss, you could buy one of my newspapers for eight straight days."

"I thought it was more expensive on the weekends."

"Don't be a smartass," Jack continued. "Anyway, people don't value things like that anymore. When I started out in this business, you couldn't walk down the street without seeing everyone carrying a copy of the morning's paper under their arm. Now, they're doing everything but reading. iPods, Blackberries, video games, text messages, bird calls, Pictionary. It's like people go out of their way to be ignorant."

"Why are you here, Jack?" Mickey asked. Jack was surprised to see that the look on Mickey's face wasn't jovial, but serious enough to get Jack to forget about his rant. "You say you're on the wagon. Haven't had a drink in two months. I give you credit for that, my friend, and it's always good to see you back around here. But it seems kind of stupid to me for a man trying to stay off the sauce to hang out at a bar. Not exactly the best atmosphere to keep you focused, know what I mean?"

Jack nodded. He didn't have a reply for that. It just felt natural, coming back here, like a memory that haunted you but kept tugging at the edges of your subconscious. It was only in the last few years that the drinking had really become a problem. Back in the day, a lunch without three martinis was a lunch wasted. An after work cocktail wasn't an occasion, it was part of the job. You went home sauced, you woke up hung over, and everything in between was done to even it out. Now, drinks at lunch were almost passé. Expense accounts had been slashed like a murder victim, and if you ordered a second drink you might get a look.

Now, everything was moderated. People judged you. It was a few years ago when Wallace Langston pointed out that Jack's face was looking red, puffy. Wallace recommended a good dermatologist who helped cure his wife's rosacea. Jack, perplexed, took the number but never called. He lied to Wallace and told him he'd seen the doctor, though in retrospect that might not have been the wisest course of action since it made the editor-in-chief even more suspicious when the symptoms began to worsen.

He'd never wanted to leave. Never dreamed of putting down the pen until he was either good and ready, or dead and buried. And last year, he was neither. It was Paulina Cole who forced his hand, by printing a newspaper article that swung an ax at his reputation, left him alone and crying on his bedroom floor.

Jack O'Donnell refused to go out like that. Refused to go out a laughingstock.

In order to restore his reputation, he needed one last home run, one last story to remind the public just why they'd trusted him for the better part of half a century.

First, though, he needed to clean up. Funny thing, he was never in denial about his alcoholism. With every drink, Jack knew he was feeding the beast. It was easy to justify, easy to rationalize. Jack was one of the city's most respected newmen. He's earned that reputation. He'd sold nearly a million books, written god knows how many bylines.

Jack used to have an agent. Good guy named Al Zuckerberg. Tall, wispy Jew who had a company down in Union Square. For two decades, like clockwork, Al would negotiate his contracts every two or three years. And if Jack was ever late with a manuscript or running short on ideas, Al would be over with a bottle of Johnnie Walker Blue within the hour.

Jack couldn't remember the last time he'd seen Al.

Jack hadn't written a book in nearly ten years. At some point, Al must have given up. No squeezing blood from a stone. Jack had wrung himself out.

Good businessman, Al was. He realized that once Jack was tapped out, his energies would be better spent on other authors who would bring in new money. Jack still received royalty payments, but they were dwindling. They'd afford him a few nice meals a year, maybe pay off some of his mortgage. But that's all.

This story, this lead he was chasing with Henry, Jack knew this was his last chance. A big hit, and his reputation was restored. Jack still had some fight left in him, but what really stoked the coals was watching Henry work. Watching his career take off like Jack's had long ago. He was a pit bull, that young man, clutching a lead with his teeth and shaking it until the truth came loose.

Jack felt strong coming back. Felt like he had enough strength to and desire to do his best work in a long, long time.

But when that was over, Jack wasn't sure how much he'd have left. At least, he thought, the paper would be in good hands with Henry. If Jack had died, if the alcohol had overcome him, he would have died a joke. His reputation would have been reduced to a pile of smoldering ashes. Now, he could change that. Going out with a bang wasn't such a bad thing.

The glass began to grow warm in his hand. The ice cubes had begun to melt. Jack watched the soda turn from black to muddy brown as it mixed with the melting ice. He pictured, just for a moment, Mickey reaching behind the bar, picking the bottle of Jim Beam up, tilting that long neck and pouring a healthy swallow of bourbon in. He could taste it on his tongue, smiled briefly. Then he looked at the glass and set it on the table.

"Getting the urge, huh," Mickey said. He took the glass of sofa away from Jack, gently, poured it out and placed the glass behind the bar. "Maybe you should go home, Jack."

The old man laughed. He reached into his briefcase and pulled out an orange prescription tube. Mickey looked at it, confused.

"What's that?" he asked.

"Antabuse," Jack said. "My little blue pill."

"I don't get it," Mickey said. "What's that, for depression or something?"

"No, think of it as insurance. You're supposed to take one of these babies once a day. The chemicals in this tiny pill, when mixed with alcohol, make you feel like Keith Richards after a six month bender. Kind of the negative reinforcement equivalent for alcoholics of sticking your finger in an electrical socket."

"So, what, you drink and you get sick?"

"So sick you'll never want to drink again."

"Does it work?"

Jack shrugged. "Damned if I know."

"I thought you said you took a pill once a day."

"You're supposed to," Jack said, "but I haven't taken a single pill."

"Well why the hell not?"

Jack stood up. He tugged a crumpled twenty form his wallet, flattened it out and put it on the table. He then took the pill bottle and placed it on top of the money.

"Because when I decide to do something, whether it's track down a story, get a source to open up, or quit drinking," Jack said, "I don't need a damn pill to motivate me. See you around, Mickey."

Jack walked outside. He stood outside the bar for a moment, looked up and down the street. Some days he could barely recognize this city, and since his return he'd become more sensitive to what it used to be, but did not any more.

Even his old habits like drinking could not be enjoyed, replaced by something artificial that was meant to fill the void. If not for Henry, if not for the injection of new blood into his old, tired veins, Jack O'Donnell knew there was a good chance his disease would have been the end of him.

Tomorrow was a new day, and would hopefully bring new leads. He was proud of Henry for finding out information on Brett Kaiser's possible killer. That the doorman had seen this blonde man coming and going at odd hours, while Kaiser's wife left the apartment, this left him no doubt that this man held the key to many, many questions.

Tomorrow they would hopefully answer those, but he also could be certain that new questions would be asked. The key to reporting was answering the questions faster than new ones could be asked, catching up with the trail of lies while it was still warm. Give any suspect enough lead time, they would cover their tracks sufficiently, prolonging the investigating or snuffing it out altogether.

Tomorrow they'd be back on the trail. Jack felt invigorated, for the first time in years knowing he was working on something important, that his job and reputation were no longer being held hostage by the bottle.

At some point they would unravel the whole spool of thread. At some point, Jack would restore his damaged reputation.

And at some point, Jack would need to know why Henry Parker was lying to him.

Chapter 23

Thursday

"So tell me about this Mr. Joshua."

Curt Sheffield held a pad of paper in his hands and a small pen. The pen hovered above the pad as he waited for me to speak.

We were sitting on a bench next to each other in Madison Square Park. It was early morning, just after seven o'clock. The day was crisp and cool, and the park was crowded with couples walking their dogs and sipping coffee. I wasn't surprised to see a line already beginning to form outside the world famous Shake Shack. Possibly the best burgers in the city, but the kind of meal your intestines could only handle once or twice a year.

Before Curt had taken out his writing utensils, there had been a breakfast burrito that disappeared down his throat in about 1.2 seconds. His breath smelled like fried grease, but that's not the kind of thing you tell to someone you're approaching for help. Especially when they're armed.

"Mr. Joshua?" I said.

"Mr. Joshua? You know, from 'Lethal Weapon'? Played by crazy ass Gary Busey, who got his blonde ass handed to him by the man from down under at the end?"

"Oh right," I said. "I kind of stopped watching Mel Gibson movies after the whole sugartits thing."

"You know it's weird. Who would have thought that between Gary Busey and Mel Gibson that Busey would turn out to be the less crazy dude."

"So what's with the Joshua reference?"

"Well, you said this dude you're looking for is blonde, Mr. Joshua was blonde, thought I'd give him a nickname since you don't know who the hell he is."

"That's why I'm coming to you. So we can eventually call him by his real name."

"Gotcha. One more anonymous baddie, coming up. Like we

don't have enough to worry about right now."

Curt spoke these words with a little more bite than I was used to. He wasn't above bitching about his job, but there was a current underneath this that caught my attention.

"You ok buddy?" I asked.

"Yeah, just, you know."

"No, I don't know. What do you mean?"

Curt shifted, blew into his hands and rubbed them together. "Department has been hit hard lately. The city's budget's been slashed beyond belief so the Mayor could make his budget targets, and we're taking it in the ass just like everyone else."

"In what way?"

"Well, frankly, the city has no money."

"Yeah, I remember the Governor's press conference where he made it seem like we were some sort of third world country outpost."

"You wouldn't think it, you know? That a city where they can charge fifteen bucks for a hamburger would go broke?"

"Tourists," I said. "The dollar is so weak that people from pretty much all over the world can come here and buy anything basically half off. They pay it because they can, and we get stuck with the inflated prices because we have no choice."

"The rich get richer and...you know how the rest goes," Curt said. "But right now there are parts of the city with less cops. And less cops means less supervision, means the bad guys get emboldened."

"But the NYPD?" I said, confused. "Isn't that one area they don't have a choice but to keep fully loaded?"

"They're trying," Curt said. "Louis Carruthers, the Chief of Department, said the brass is looking into more funding, but it might take a little while. At the state and city level right now, they have less money than Michael Jackson. A lack of money means the city is cutting back on pretty much everything that the government picks up the tab on. Overtime, patrol routes, even new recruits. Starting pay for a first year police officer is just below your average hot dog vendor."

"Which is just above that of a journalist," I said with a smile.

"Yeah, at least you get those fancy suit jackets with elbow pads."

"I've never heard anybody claim to be jealous over those."

"You can never guess where fashion trends go. If tomorrow

Kanye shows up with one of those tweed jackets, five million kids will show up at Diesel begging for them."

"So what do you got for me on this guy besides hair color?" Curt said.

"First off, you need to know that anything you do could come back and bite you in the ass."

"Isn't that why we're friends?" Curt said. "I don't have enough problems at work or at home, so I come to you to satisfy my daily craving for emotional and physical trauma."

"Your breath is terrible," I said.

"Point proven," Curt said.

"Seriously. It smells like you ate a hot dog, then burped up that hot dog, then fried the burped up hot dog, ate it, and burped it up again."

Curt stared at me. "I think my stomach just threw up inside of itself."

"Then my job here is done."

"You're a laugh riot. Go on. Tell me what you know about this dude.

"I was outside of Brett Kaiser's building right before it turned into something out of Dante's Inferno. The doorman told me a guy with blonde hair came and went at freaky hours."

"You told me this. That's not a hell of a lot to go on."

"I'm not done. You know Paulina Cole, right?"

"Of course. Hot piece of MILF ass who works at that dirt rag and has no love lost for you. Am I close?"

"Enough for a shave."

"I don't know her personally, but I've heard some of the guys talking about her. She doesn't have a lot of friends in the department. Ever since she wrote that article accusing NYPD recruits of being underqualified and unmotivated. Things like that tend to rub cops the wrong way. Rumor has it they won't give her scoops any more because of the crap she's written, so she has her lackeys covering the crime beat act as spies for her."

"Yeah, well, that's part of the problem. Turns out she was kidnapped a few days ago, and I'm ninety nine percent sure the guy who did it is the same one who charbroiled Brett Kaiser. Her description of him matched the same one I was given by Kaiser's doorman to a T.

Blond, late thirties or early forties, muscular."

"Does she know the same guy is a suspect in the Kaiser murder?" Curt said.

"No. You're the only person I've told."

"So I'm looking for blonde guy, about six one or six two, two hundred ten pounds or so if he's well built."

"Sounds like a ballpark to work in."

"Right. That ballpark narrow it down to about ten thousand men in New York."

"There's one more thing," I said. "Paulina said he's involved in drugs."

"Drugs."

"Yeah."

"Care to elaborate on that?"

"That's all I know. Let's just say she was a little secretive on that part.

"So we have a blonde guy. Somewhere between six feet and six foot two, two hundred and ten pounds, who for all we know has smoked weed some time in his life."

"Chester," I said. "She said he introduced himself as Chester. And she said he might have lost a family member, and it didn't sound as though it was as a result of natural causes."

"Sounds to me like Paulina could be cooking up a stew of major league bullshit to me."

"I don't think so," I said. "Paulina is a lot of things, but she had to swallow some major pride to ask me to help her. And she's not a woman who's to keen on losing face. Especially to me. And this guy threatened her daughter. Paulina's low, but not low enough to make up something like that. She wants this guy caught. All between the physical description and the alias, it should give you enough to at least do some digging."

"Plus if this is the same guy who turned Brett Kaiser into burnt toast," Curt said. "it wouldn't surprise me if this guy has some sort of explosives or military background."

"That's gotta narrow your ten thousand down a bit."

"Maybe so."

"Be careful," I said. "Paulina's pretty sure this Chester has eyes in the NYPD. Can you do some digging without anyone seeing your shovel?"

"That sounds sexy," Curt said.

"Come on, Curt."

"I'll grow eyes in the back of my head," Curt said. "Digging, I can do. But if we find out who this guy is, I'm going to need to bring Paulina in to ID him so we can charge him."

"I hear you. But wait until you know who he is for certain before we make a move. And make sure you only tell people you can trust."

"Yeah, and if you need help typing or proofreading, I'll give you a hand. Come on, I know how to do my job, Henry," Curt said.

"Just looking out for you buddy."

"Appreciate it."

"How are things, you know, with the job?"

"Strange times, Parker," Curt said.

"Care to elaborate?" I said, smiling. Curt did not return the pleasantry.

"This city, you know, just a different vibe right now. People see cops now, they look at us differently. Like they really need us. Not that they ever didn't, but it's like the city is waiting for another shoe to drop. You know that dude who lost fifty billion dollars in a Ponzi scheme?"

"Madoff" I said.

"You know the city spent more money protecting that scumbag than it does Joe Six Pack? People just don't trust any more. You know the saying, but it's true. People expect things are gonna get worse before they get better."

"The city needs cops like you," I said. "Protect and serve, right?"

"Yeah, I appreciate that man. Anyway," Curt said, standing up. "Lunch break's over. Gotta get back to protecting the rest of this overcrowded sardine can." He breathed into his hands, then held it up to his nose. "My breath really that bad?"

"Makes me toes curl just talking to you," I said.

"That's the way I like it. This way I don't ever have to pull my gun."

He held out his hand, and I shook it.

"Later, Henry."

Curt walked off. I stretched my legs, felt the cup of coffee I'd inhaled half an hour ago take hold. Amanda was probably still in bed, still asleep thanks to her friend the snooze button.

Right as I was about to head towards to subway, my cell phone rang. It was Jack. I knew the man's mind was always working, but it was not normal for him to be calling me before breakfast, especially when we had no meetings planned.

I answered the phone. "Hey Jack. Either you're up early or you're up really late."

"Why the hell aren't you here yet?" Jack said.

"At the Gazette? It's barely seven, and I was meeting Curt Sheffield to give him more details about the Kaiser investigation."

"That's old news," Jack said. "Wallace and Harvey Hillerman are about to bite our nuts off, so get your ass over here right away."

"Why? What happened?"

"Have you seen the cover of today's Dispatch?" Jack said.

"No, figured I could wait until getting in before reading about which celebrities were caught in the Dominican Republic sunbathing in the nude with their boy toys."

"Laugh all you want, but Henry...we got scooped."

"Yeah right. By who? We have every inch of this town covered, so unless I've been working in a different city...by the way, who scooped us?"

"Paulina Cole," Jack said. "She's got an exclusive that'll make your eyes pop out."

Chapter 24

I hailed a cab, which slowed to a crawl once we hit midtown. I got out at fifty first and Lexington, threw the driver a good tip, and sprinted the few blocks over to Rockefeller Center. I was nearly disemboweled pushing through the security turnstile when my ID failed to work, and got off on the eleventh floor out of breath and with probably internal bleeding.

I entered the newsroom, and as I walked through the sea of desks my heart dropped when I saw Tony Valentine approaching.

"Henry," he said, huffing as he jogged over. "Do you have a minute?"

"Actually I don't. Not right now," I said.

"Come on Parker, you've been avoiding me since I got here. At some point you'll need to open that hard heart of yours for a get-to-know-you session."

"Listen, Tony, I appreciate that, and at some point we will. But right now I have a situation to deal with."

"A situation? That sounds juicy. Do tell."

"Like I said, Tony, not right now."

"If I didn't know any better," Tony said, his eyes narrowing, offset by a strangely playful smile, "I'd think you were avoiding me."

"Listen man, I'd be lying if I didn't think our two types of... reporting didn't really overlap. But today there actually is something going on. No joke."

He looked me over, trying to determine if I was telling the truth or lying just to get out of a conversation. I certainly wasn't above doing that, at least not with Tony. That I didn't have much respect for the profession of gossip columnist was no secret to anyone who'd ever had a conversation with me about the job. I ranked its important on the Journalism Scale of Importance somewhere between the people who filled up tubes of White-Out and telemarketers.

"Fine," he said. "I'll take a rain check for today. But at some point I'm going to cash in all my checks and you're going to have lunch with me."

I offered a non-committal nod/shake, and Tony walked away, In the meantime, I had one person who might actually skin me alive if I didn't answer to him soon.

I arrived at Jack's desk only to find it vacant. It didn't take me long to figure out where he'd gone.

The shouting coming from Wallace Langston's office could be heard throughout the entire newsroom, and reporters who tended to make more noise than the average airbus on takeoff sat dead silent listening to the barrage.

Wallace tended to be a fairly mellow guy. In fact, in my few years at the Gazette I'd rarely heard him chew a reporter out, rarely saw him get pissed at the Copy Desk (if he had, Evelyn Waterstone might have impaled him on one of the flagpoles outside). What really burned Wallace was losing a story to the competition. And since Jack was the newsroom's elder statesman, he surely took the brunt of it. And since I was partnering with Jack, he no doubt wanted me there to take some of the small arms fire.

I walked past Wallace's secretary. She was usually kind to me, always with a good word, but today she looked at me like I was marching right into the sights of a firing squad. I could have sworn she gave me one of those please, don't go in there looks usually reserved for the girlfriend in horror movies who pleads with her man not to go into the basement where the killer is waiting with a machete the size of a guitar.

Sadly, I could not heed her advice, and knocked on Wallace's door.

"Who is it?" he yelled from inside.

"It's Henry," I said.

"Get the hell in here."

I gripped the doorknob, took a breath, and hoped Wallace's machete was dull.

I opened the door to see Jack seated in front of Wallace's desk. Wallace was not seated behind it, as per usual. Instead he was pacing around the room while Jack's head swiveled trying to keep pace.

Wallace looked like he'd come in to work properly dressed, hair combed, clothes ironed. But now his graying hair was askew, glasses crooked on his nose. And the pads on his elbows looked like they were being worn away.

"Where the hell have you been?" Wallace said.

"Meeting with a cop about the Kaiser investigation," I said. "He's going to find out what he can about the guy who might be responsible."

"That's dandy," Wallace said. "While you were out pussyfooting with your boys in blue, did you happen to see this?'

He walked over to his desk and picked up a copy of that morning's New York Dispatch. Wallace stomped over to me, holding the paper with as much as you would a bag of dog poop. I looked at Jack, wanted to see if he had anything to say, but the old man sat there, head down.

Wallace handed me the paper. "Read it," he said.

I looked at the front page. Immediately my stomach lurched up to my throat, frustration and anger welling up inside me.

I turned to where the front page article continued, and read the whole thing. Slowly. Word by word. Then I closed the paper and threw it across the room, cursing loud enough that Wallace's secretary would probably have to apologize to whoever she was on the phone with.

"How the hell did she..." I said.

"Don't you dare ask that question," Wallace said. "It's your job to know what goes on in this city. You handle the crime beat. It is your duty to know every nook and cranny of this island, from the mayor's office to the bums who live beneath the subway. For something like this to get past you...you must have been asleep at the wheel." He looked at Jack, waited for a response. "Either that or the two of you have become so narrow-minded with this Kaiser murder and Gaines follow up that you can't sniff what's under your nose."

"I didn't know anything about this," I said. "Paulina...I don't know where she got it. And I don't know which cops she spoke to, but if you look at the article they all spoke on conditions of anonymity. I just met with my man in the NYPD, and he's as clued in as anyone. He didn't mention a word of this, and he doesn't keep things from me. Not like this. Something about this piece doesn't pass the smell test, Wallace."

Wallace picked the newspaper back up. He held the cover out for us both to see.

On the front page of the New York Dispatch was an enlarged

picture of what looked like a small stone, possible a piece of gravel, pitch black in color with a rough texture.

The headline next to the photo read 'The Darkness.'

The subtitle said, 'The Drug That's About to Take Manhattan Back to the Stone Age."

Chapter 25

Darkness Rising
As a deadly new drug hits the streets, police and citizens silently fear a return of chaos a quarter century old

Most New Yorkers did not know Kenneth Tsang. The son of Chinese immigrants who passed away before he graduated high school, Tsang received his MBA from Wharton and spent most of his twenties raking in the dough while working at two prestigious investment firms. Most New Yorkers did not know that, despite his income, Tsang owed nearly half a million dollars in taxes and mortgage payments, and that he burned through his money nearly as fast as it came in.

Most New Yorkers know that Tsang was found dead this week, his body pulverized and found floating in the East River. What they do not know is that a balloon marker was tied to the buoy that Tsang's body was tethered to. They do not know that inside that balloon were half a dozen small, black rocks, left by Tsang's killer. These rocks were no bigger than a piece of gravel, but each contain enough destructive power to clinch a plastic bag around the head of a city already gasping for air.

Now, come with me for a moment. I have a brief history lesson to impart upon you.

For those of us who lived through New York in the 1980's much of the information within this article will ring horrifyingly familiar. Let's backtrack for a minute, about twenty five years ago to 1984. George Orwell would have been proud. Or terrified.

New York as we know it today did not exist. Following the oil shortage of the 1970's, the Son of Sam murders, and an economy on the verge of chaos, the plumbing system that was New York was about to get hit with a cherry bomb that nearly destroyed it totally.

That cherry bomb was a new drug known to scientists as methylbenzoylecgonine. Or as it is more commonly known, Crack.

Crack first appeared on our shores in 1984. Before that, the drug of choice was cocaine. But as cocaine became more plentiful, prices dropped and dealers began to lose much of their profit margin.

Poor them.

So to get back the money they were losing on coke, they came up with a new way to profit. In a nutshell, they used baking soda or other bases to cut the cocaine. This increased the volume of their product while retaining the same toxicity of the drug. It was the equivalent of taking a dollar bill, mixing it with a few pennies, and turning it into two dollars.

By 1986, just two years after crack hit the streets, over fifty five thousand people were admitted to emergency rooms around the country with crack related injuries (most often this was either from overdosing, or violence which was a result of the drug trade).

For those of you who lived in New York during that time, as I did, the effects of the crack epidemic were as visible as a street lamp. Crime in this city hit highs never before seen. Murder and rape rates rose dramatically. Cases of aggravated assault skyrocketed from just over 60,000 in 1980 to over 91,000 by the end of the decade. Burglaries. Larceny. Vehicle theft.

New York began to resemble less of a modern, cosmopolitan city than an outpost of Beirut.

Thankfully, this trend reversed itself in the 1990's, and through the new millennium New York has enjoyed its lowest crime rates per capita since the 1960's. New York was known as one of the safest big cities in the country, and if you live here or came to visit, you could walk down the street feeling safe.

After the atrocities of 9/11, New Yorkers banded together to create a safer city. One that reclaimed its place among the grandest in the world. The virus that infected us twenty five years ago had long been forgotten.

To my horror, though recent developments have proven that this virus was not extinguished, but had rather been laying dormant, in remission, waiting for a catalyst to revitalize its poisons.

That catalyst has finally found us. And it is not a terrorist, or a crooked financial institution. It exists in the tiniest form possible: a small black rock.

Though the human eye might not register this tiny specimen as anything more than a pebble, a piece of gravel, something that might even pave a driveway, the properties that exist within it threaten the very sanctity of the city we have fought so bravely to protect.

The culprit? A simple black rock that dissolves on your tongue as fast as a breath strip.

Nobody is quite sure where the Darkness came from, who manufactures it, or whether this drug has spread to other states. Crack began in primarily metropolitan cities. New York. California. Washington, D.C. Cities with large urban populations. Cities where there was enough poverty to turn the need of a cheap hit into gold for the men and women whose lack of humanity drove them to produce it.

As of press time, the police had no leads on who deals the drug. A high ranking member inside the NYPD did comment, off the record, stating "We are fully preparing for another epidemic similar to the rise of crack cocaine we saw in the 1980's. Though privately, we're worried that this one will be much, much worse and have a potentially more devastating impact considering that our infrastructure is already damaged."

So what's the harm in a little black rock, you might ask? Why should I care about some idiots getting high?

Because increases in drug production and consumption lead to increases in crime. But here's where this drug differs: whereas a normal crack user will find successive hits of the drug granting decreasing effects. The hits, as they are, are not as potent.

With the Darkness, however, some insane chemical genius has figured out a way around this.

The human brain produces a certain amount of dopamine, a neurotransmitter often associated with pleasure. Dopamine is released through many pleasurable experiences, including food, exercise, sex and, of course, drugs. Simple crack cocaine releases a larger amount of dopamine than the brain is accustomed to, so when the user takes a second hit before the brain can replenish dopamine, a lesser amount is released.

Yet the Darkness circumvents this by causing the brain to produce more dopamine. This means that each successive hit will have the exact same impact as the one proceeding it, making it more addictive than nearly every drug on the market.

It's no wonder the cops are nervous. They're facing streets about to be teeming with a drug that's cheaper, more plentiful, and delivers, pardon the expression, the best hit money can buy.

God help us all.

Chapter 26

Friday

The call came close to midnight. Morgan wondered what the hell had taken them so long.

He didn't recognize the voice on the other line. It wasn't Chester, and he didn't think it was Leonard. Not that it mattered much, he assumed there had to be more to the operation than the two guys he'd met. There were twelve other men in that room--well, eleven after the accident with Jeremy--and they'd all been recruited like him.

Leonard had said that they'd each been recruited by a different person, as Leonard had been brought in by this guy Stephen Gaines. If each new recruit was brought in by a different guy, a la Chester, that meant at least eleven people on Chester's level.

Morgan wondered just how many people were a part of this organization. Then he wondered how long it might take before he could be promoted, and how much money he'd have to bring in. Didn't matter. He'd do it.

In his mind's eye, Morgan could see Jeremy's lifeless body sliding down the wall, clumps of his blood like egg yolk on the wallpaper behind him. Morgan wished he felt remorseful, wished he felt some sort of sympathy for Jeremy, but as hard as he tried he simply could not.

When Leonard described what the job entailed, it was a zero sum equation: either you had the sack for it or you didn't.

Jeremy didn't.

It was clear from the moment the mission was explained. Morgan had seen that look before. He found it a little funny, considering he'd gone so far in business because of his ability to spot men like Jeremy. Men who wouldn't take the extra step, who worried so much about teetering on the diving board that they couldn't even see the riches hidden beneath the water's surface.

Morgan saw it all. He had a knack for it, could see deals before they materialized. That was the rule of thumb: first one in, last one out.

See the profits before everyone else did, and stay longer than everyone else who got cold feet.

That look in Leonard's eye said it all. New product.

That's when Morgan knew he had to jump in.

When you introduced a new product to the marketplace, you didn't trust it to people who couldn't sell it, who couldn't get the job done. A new product has a extremely narrow window of opportunity to work, and while that door is cracked open, you needed to wedge everything but the kitchen sink in there because once that sucker closed up, it wasn't cracking open again.

Morgan sold to people. Plan and simple. He sold them investments in their future. He sold them the belief that if they did not trust him than they were putting their family's stability at risk.

Was this any different?

Morgan had done a few lines in his day. A night out at the strip joint with his buddies, a bump or two in the bathroom to make those lights flicker just a little faster. He didn't quite have the taste for it, though, felt if you needed an external force to get high you were simply doing the wrong drugs.

Not that he judged them. Most people were simply not born with the same drive and instincts Morgan had been. His parents were blue collar all the way, but had good enough credit to get him a decent financial aid package. Morgan knew a lot of kids from his hometown that weren't so lucky.

They were the ones who filled up his tank at the gas station. They were the ones who sprayed perfume on his mother when she went to the mall. They were the ones who needed something to take the edge off the real world, because if they spent too much time with their own life and their own thoughts eventually it would occur to them what they had never become.

So this new product, Morgan guessed, was just one more thing to take the edge off. And that was fine. He trusted these guys. Jeremy was a message. Like no limit hold 'em, you're either all in or you fold.

Jeremy folded. Morgan's stack of chips wasn't as high as it used to be, but what was that great line from "Rounders"?

Kid's got alligator blood.

Morgan liked the sound of that.

When the caller told him the address, Morgan was a little surprised at first. He'd actually been there once before, a few years back when he'd first started dating this French model named Claudia who was in town for some photo shoot where she was supposed to pose in a pink tutu atop the Brooklyn Bridge

Morgan never really understood art.

She'd insisted that they go to the Kitten Club, the rationale being more along the lines of it being a trendy hotspot rather than a place where actual enjoyment could be had.

Morgan remembered that the music was deafening, the light show transfixing, and the drinks ridiculously overpriced.

And then that rich diva Athena Paradis got killed there, and somehow the Kitten Club became even more popular.

Now why Morgan was supposed to be there at seven o'clock in the morning, a good sixteen hours before the club even opened its doors, was beyond him. But it was his first day. And Morgan knew well enough not to ask questions.

He took the subway downtown, then walked to the meatpacking district where the Kitten Club, and its brethren, served generous amounts of alcohol to hip, young New Yorkers seven days a week. At midnight, you couldn't walk down the block without having to cut through any one of a number of long lines dedicated to keeping impatient drinkers outside until the Lord of the Velvet Rope decided it was time to allow them entry.

The Kitten Club used to have one of those large neon signs above the awning, this one depicting a feline in naughty attire sipping from some sort of pink cocktail. The lights were arranged so that it looked like the cat was tipping the drink back. As the glass hit the cat's lips, the drink actually appeared to disappear down its furry throat.

If you had enough money, you could get anyone to make you anything.

As Morgan approached the entrance, the front door opened up. He immediately recognized the man who held it open.

"Morgan, good to see you," Chester said. "Feels good to be up bright and early, doesn't it?"

Chester said this with the slightest air of contempt, as though he knew that Morgan hadn't needed to wake up before noon any time in recent memory. Though he felt his cheeks flush slightly red, he did feel a bit of pride in rejoining the workforce.

"If it's worth getting up for, there's no such thing as too early."

"Words to live by," Chester replied. "Come on it."

Chester held the door ajar, and Morgan slipped inside. He couldn't help but find it funny that for the first time he hadn't needed to wait on line to enter a club. Maybe he needed to go clubbing as seven in the morning more often.

Chester led Morgan through the club, the early morning sun peeking through black tinted windows, casting an eerie glow on a floor than seemed ghostlike without the cavalcade of dancing, drinking bodies. The first floor of the Kitten Club was essentially one large open space, nearly the length of a football field.

At either end was a bar, about thirty feet long, that housed four different bartenders in order to make sure drinks were served promptly, and that every penny was squeezed out of every patron.

Large bird cages hung above the floor, with doors big enough to fit the dancers who gyrated inside them all night. Morgan could see a pulley system keeping them high, attached to a chain that could be lowered. Still, the dancers had to keep going all night. Made you think twice before entering a giant bird cage.

Chester led Morgan across the first floor, towards a sign marked 'restrooms.' Morgan followed, but slowed down when Chester turned towards the door to the women's bathroom.

"Um, dude, you can't go in there."

Chester turned around, looked at Morgan like he'd sprouted another head.

"You're really going to question me? Now?"

Morgan felt a chill travel down his spine. He simply shook his head, and whispered, "Sorry."

Stupid, Morgan thought. His gut reaction, of course, was to question why the hell they were going into the ladies bathroom in a nightclub at seven in the morning. On the surface, not the most egregious question to be asking. But Morgan should have known better.

So when Chester pushed open the door to the women's room, Morgan followed obediently behind.

The women's room was cleaner than most clubs, especially considering it was known for being a veritable petrie dish of chemical indulgences. There was an irony in that the club was owned by Shawn Kensbrook, who was as clean as they came. Hell, the guy became a regular on the 'Today Show' after Athena Paradis died. One of those celebrities, like Puff Daddy or P. Diddy or whatever the hell his name was now who skyrocketed to fame after the death of someone close. And when fame came knocking, the mourning period lasted all of about two more seconds before the checks started rolling in.

Kensbrook himself was clean, but the Kitten Club itself was as dirty as a public restroom. And like a public restroom, Morgan held his nose when he took one whiff of the foul odor that permeated this particular restroom.

He couldn't tell where it was coming from, but got an idea when Chester walked over to a closed stall door clearly marked 'Out of Order.'

Morgan followed, peeking over Chester's shoulder as he pushed the stall door open.

Yup, that was it. No doubt whatever had died had done so in this stall.

The toilet seat itself was covered in a brown foulness that nearly made Morgan retch. The wall behind it was chipping, the plaster coming loose. The metal toilet paper holder was rusted and gross, and the floor tiles had hints of yellow that reminded Morgan of writing his name without hands on snow days in his youth.

Without hesitation, Chester stepped through the rusted door and stood over the toilet.

"Dude," Morgan said, "that's pretty nasty. I'm sure there's a working one in here that doesn't look like something out of 'Trainspotting.'"

Chester appeared to ignore him, instead leaning forward. Morgan couldn't make it out, but Chester was apparently doing something against the wall, either scratching it with his fingernails, pushing on something, he couldn't tell what.

Suddenly Chester stepped back, and Morgan heard a brief clicking noise before the entire compartment--the toilet and the wall behind it--simply slid backwards, revealing a walkway behind it.

"You've gotta be kidding me," Morgan said. "Who are you, James Bond?"

"Guess I got the blond hair right," Chester said. "Come on."

Morgan stepped into the passageway. It was a long narrow hallway, metal on both sides, no deviations. At the end of the hallway stood a simple metal door. There was no doorknob, no metal slats. Nothing except two video cameras perched above the doorway, each pointed down to capture whoever was about to enter.

"Who's back there?" Morgan said.

"What did I tell you about questions?"

"Not to ask them."

"You're a quick learner."

Chester kept walking until he was standing directly in front of the door. He looked up at the cameras. Smiled.

Morgan was about to ask if whoever was back there could see him, but remembered the previous conversation. "The cameras don't work," Chester said.

"Huh?"

"That's what you were about to ask. Do you see any wires? Any outlets?"

Morgan eyes the cameras. "Nope. But there's a red light on."

"Runs on a battery," Chester said. "Fakes out most burglars and trespassers. You can buy these things at Radio Shack for sixty bucks."

"So then how do they..."

"Trust me, security is a lot tighter than a simple camera. Just don't bring any of your friends here. They'll be dead before they count to five."

"What..."

Before Morgan could finish his question (something he was thankful for), the metal door slid open. Standing there was Leonard.

He was wearing black jeans and a green turtleneck. He held a clipboard in one hand, and gripped the door's handle with his other.

"Hey," he said to Chester. Then he looked at Morgan. "Glad you could make it. You guys are late."

"Traffic," Chester said.

"Of course." Leonard took a pen from the clipboard, checked something on it, and went back into the room.

"Come on," Chester said, and Morgan followed him inside.

The room was fairly small, and resembled an atrium of some sort. There was another door off to the side, and that was all. The only light was overhead track lighting, and Morgan noticed a dozen cameras pointed at different parts of the room.

Unlike the ones outside,

The first thing he saw was Nikesh. The Indian boy was standing in the center of the room. He was wearing a black pinstripe suit, with a red tie and wingtip loafers. His hair was freshly cut, and Morgan noticed a small shaving nick under his chin.

Nikesh turned around. He nodded when he saw Morgan.

"Hey," he said.

"Hey," Morgan replied, wittily.

Then Nikesh turned around, and Morgan saw that he had a large briefcase slung over his shoulders. The bag was full, but not overstuffed. There was a combination lock on the front, and the clasp was done.

"Patel, you're finished here. Flanagan?"

The chubby white kid from the conference room ambled out of the side room. He was also clutching a briefcase, this one stuffed even more. Though the bag looked ready to burst, Chubby--aka Flanagan--seemed to have no trouble carrying it. Obviously whatever was inside didn't weigh much.

"You two have your orders," Leonard told them. "And you remember everything I told you."

Patel and Flanagan both nodded. They looked confident. Whatever Leonard had told them, they remembered it.

Leonard clicked something in his ear, nodded, then motioned for the duo to follow him. He slid the door open, revealing the corridor. When they'd stepped outside, Leonard pulled the door back into place.

"Your turn," Leonard said. "Time for orientation."

Leonard walked over to the side door. This one looked fairly standard, with a doorknob and everything. Leonard simply turned the knob, pulled it open, and beckoned Morgan to follow him.

Tentatively Morgan came forward, surprised at first that the door wasn't guarded by some super electromagnet or something else similarly complicated.

As he approached the door, another young man stepped out. Morgan recognized him from the conference room. He was black, about five foot ten. Stocky but not fat, with a neatly shaved head. He wore a cream colored suit and a blue tie, a pocket square neatly tucked into his jacket.

"Theodore W. Goggins," Leonard said. "This is Morgan Isaacs."

Morgan extended his hand. Theodore shook it. His grip was tight.

"Call me Theo."

"Call me Morgan," he replied. "So 'W' huh? Like George W. Bush?"

"Do I look like I was born in Texas?" Theo said. "The 'W' is for Willingham, my uncle's last name."

"Keeping it all in the family," Morgan said. "Nice."

Theo laughed. "You keep up, brother, you and me are gonna get along just fine."

"Get along?" Morgan said.

"You two are partners, for the time being," Leonard said. "You ever use the buddy system on school trips?"

Neither of the young men answered, but they both knew what he was talking about.

"Same principle. Theo, you're responsible for Morgan. Morgan, you're responsible for Theo. Either of you get into any trouble, it's up to the other one to help out."

"No problem," Morgan said.

"That's a pretty sweet tie," Morgan said, admiring the silk.

"Only kind I wear," Theo said. "Red is too loud. Says you're trying too hard. Lighter colors--yellow, green--those are pansy ass colors. Black, white, hell, you're not even trying. Blue is the perfect in between. It's bold, but it doesn't say that. It's like a backrub. Sounds pretty innocent, but it's going to get your panties off before the night is over."

"I'm not wearing any panties. So I guess you already won."

"Enough, girls, Leonard said. His voice grew stern, and he moved forward until his face was just inches from Morgan's. "Theo is also your insurance policy, Isaacs, and Isaacs is yours Goggins. If you ever try anything funny, ever do anything to place yourself or your partner in danger...well, there's a quarter million dollar bonus in it for your partner if he turns you in."

"Wait, what?" Morgan said. "He gets two hundred and fifty grand for ratting on me?"

"Yes and no," Leonard continued. "I already explained this to Theo, but you need to know it as well. If your partner does anything--talks to the cops, tells his friends, tells his family, tells his fucking Shih Tzu--if you inform us you get quarter million dollar bonus. Tax free."

Morgan could tell Theo was eyeballing him. He didn't like it. "But," Leonard said, "if one of you lies just to get the money, you won't need money where you're going. So before you decide to play games, ask yourself if the risk is really worth the reward. You can either continue to make money--good money--working for us. Or you can get cute, try to get rich quick, and end up like Ken Tsang."

Morgan's stomach felt like someone had just poured acid inside of it.

Leonard and his people couldn't have been responsible for Ken's death--could they?

"Hopefully you'll never need to know what it feels like to be able to touch your knee to the small of your back," Leonard said. "Or for your arms to suddenly grow another joint. Because Ken sure did."

Theo didn't move. Did not react. Morgan stared at Leonard. He was scared, and Leonard seemed to recognize this.

"Now, don't get ahead of yourself thinking all doom and gloom. Ken was stupid," Leonard said. "I'm hoping you're smart. Because if you are, it's nothing but gravy for all of us. Theo here is your guardian angel, and the bomb collar strapped to your neck. He will protect you at all costs, but if you try and remove him in any way whatsoever--he'll still be around long after the bomb goes off. Do you get this? Both of you?"

Theo nodded. He didn't seem to care, didn't seem affected in the least. if was as though he knew he would never turn. Never lie to these people. He was there for the money. And as long as he did what he was told, that green would pour in.

"I get it," Morgan finally said. The acid had gone. The look on Theo's face had made it dry up. This was Morgan's chance to get his life back. He would never do what Ken did. And he knew Theo would never turn on him.

They both had too much to lose.

"Great. Now that we're clear on the rules, let's go over everything. But first, let's give you a look at your merchandise."

Leonard opened the door up wider. Theo went back inside, and Morgan followed. And when he saw what was inside, it was all he could do not to gasp.

"How much..." he said.

"Doesn't matter," Leonard said.

Morgan looked around. In a dozen neat piles, each about twenty feet wide and five feet tall, were small, individual bags. Each of these bags contained what looked like a different kind of narcotic.

Cocaine. Ecstasy. Weed. Pills. Things Morgan didn't recognize in the slightest.

And then, in the back corner, he saw something that piqued his curiosity.

Bags filled with what looked like small pieces of black gravel. Rocks so small and so insignificant that they looked like they could have been taken from his grandmother's driveway.

"What's that?" Morgan said.

"That," replied Leonard. "Is going to revolutionize our business."

Morgan stared at it. Theo's eyes were wide open.

"We call it 'The Darkness.' And in one week's time," Leonard said, "you'll be so busy selling those bags you won't have time to spend all the money you make." Then Leonard smiled. "But I imagine you'll find the time."

Chapter 27

"Nobody knows anything."

Even though I was holding a telephone to my ear, I wanted to wrap my hands around the piece of plastic and choke the life out of it.

"You can't be serious," I said.

"I'm telling you Henry," Curt said. "Nobody here knows a damn thing about Paulina Cole's article. Nobody knows who gave her those quotes, nobody knows where she got her information, and if it makes you feel any better nobody here has even heard of this so-called magic drug, Darkness or whatever. It's like she pulled the whole thing out of thin air."

My head hurt. Both from the chewing out by Wallace, the frustration in having been scooped by Paulina Cole, and the feeling that Curt was telling the truth. Curt had his finger pretty well placed on the pulse of the NYPD, and whenever a bombshell was about to drop, even if he didn't clue me in ahead of time he was rarely surprised. Right now, though, he spoke as if he was as pissed off as I was. It sounded like Curt felt he'd been scooped by Paulina as well.

"This whole thing doesn't make any sense," I said. "And the details about the rocks inside the balloon--you didn't mention that."

"I didn't even know about that until I saw the article," Curt said, frustration growing in his voice. "Listen Henry. I know the rank and file. I know the guys who work narcotics detail, the guys sweeping the street corners for dealers, the ones who confiscate this crap, and even the ones who log it in to evidence. None of them, let me repeat none of them, have any idea what the hell she's talking about or where she got the info from."

"Either she pulled enough information from her ass to make her walk funny for a month, somebody in your department has loose lips, or something is being kept a pretty big secret from all of us."

"I don't know about you, but I think her article is half bull."

"And the other half?"

Curt was silent for a moment. I could feel my heart pounding in my chest. I knew his answer before he said it. Bull or not, there was a lining of truth in Paulina's article.

"The other half," he said, "I'm just praying she's wrong about. I grew up in this city in the eighties, Henry. I had a cousin who got hooked on junk. He stole two twenties from some junkie's wallet because he needed money to cook more of that poison on a spoon. He ended up taking eight bullets. From a six shooter. Which meant the junkie who killed him reloaded and then shot him two more times. I know what crack did to this city. I watched saw it man. I'm not comparing apples to oranges, belts to syringes. I'm just saying that if there is any truth to Cole's story, and this stuff is already in the marketplace, it's a faucet that's gonna be real tough to shut off."

"If this thing is as big as Paulina claims it is," I said, "won't it be easy to track down?"

"You'd think so, but I know a dozen narco officers who have eyes and ears and informants up the ying yang with access to all kinds of dope. They know everyone from the absolute bottom of the totem pole to the people at the top. And not one of them has heard a single peep about Darkness."

"I just don't see Paulina making this up. I mean, she presses every button there is, but she's not an all out liar. Even when she torpedoed Jack, everything she said was true. It was a pretty despicable takedown, but she wasn't lying."

"Listen Henry, I hear you, but this isn't my beat. I can only go by what the guys in Narcotics are telling me. And if I hear anything I'll let you know. But right now there's nothing."

"Thanks Curt. Good luck out there. For your sake, I hope Paulina had a sudden case of the truthful yips."

"Truthful yips. Sounds like a good name for a band."

"Yeah. I'll let you know when I form it. You can play base."

"Always saw myself as more of a saxophone man. You know, Charlie Parker. Sure you don't have a black uncle?"

"Hey man, you know how my father plays hide-and-seek with the truth. It wouldn't shock me. But as far as I know I don't."

"Gotcha. Take it easy Henry."

"Later Curt."

I hung up the phone. I noticed Jack had come over, and was standing next to my desk.

"Was that your buddy Sheffield?"

I nodded, leaned back in my chair and stretched.

"I don't get it. Curt knows this stuff, and he said nobody in the department has heard word one about this new drug."

"Is it possible his ear is just a little too far from the juice?"

"It's possible, but Curt's been pretty reliable when it comes to big stories."

"Well until we hear otherwise, we have to assume that the Wicked Witch of the West Side scooped us fair and square."

"I don't think that's going to make Wallace like us any more."

"No. He'll bitch and moan for a day or two, until we break something big and Ted Allen at the Dispatch has to eat a nice big turd sandwich."

"He has to deal with Paulina every day. That's gotta be enough punishment for one man."

Jack laughed. It felt strange, though, as though he was laughing more to gauge my reaction than out of actual emotion. Then he stayed silent for a minute, just thinking.

"So where are we at?" he said. "It seems like our number one lead got himself a one-way ticket to the big adios."

"Well, my gut says for certain that Kaiser knew exactly what I was talking about when I asked him about 718 Enterprises. Of course he was killed before I could get any deeper."

"So think about this, sport," Jack said. "I'm guessing Kaiser's demise was not due to a leak in his gas stove. He was killed. So who benefits from Kaiser being out of the picture? And why kill him now?"

"It was probably no secret that we were looking at him, so whoever killed him was worried he would talk."

"Did he seem like a talker to you?"

"Are you kidding? If he'd given me another thirty seconds he would have told me what his wife was like in bed."

"So someone ices him before he can talk. Who?"

"I'm pretty sure it's this blond guy the doorman saw coming at odd hours. He clearly had business with Kaiser that couldn't take place during the light of day."

"Didn't you say his wife left when he came over?"

"Yeah," I said. "Mrs. Kaiser left and went to a coffee shop on the corner. She let this guy and Brett do their thing, then she'd just come back like she'd gone to the beauty salon. Nothing strange about her attitudes, according to the doorman."

"So you know who we have to talk to now?" Jack said.

"Victoria Kaiser."

"Wonderful. Nothing I need more than bothering a grieving widow."

"You're too mushy, Parker. If I was a grieving widow..."

"You'd be a pretty widow," I said. Jack ignored me.

"If I was a grieving widow, I'd sure as hell want to find the bastards who killed my husband."

"Isn't that the job of the NYPD?"

"Yeah. And they did a real bang up job investigating your brother's death. Since Stephen Gaines is connected to 718--per your estimation--I have a funny feeling the NYPD might be taking this whole thing a little lightly."

"Why would they do that?" I said.

"Easy," Jack said. "For whatever reason, somebody over there thinks it's in their best interests to let this story slide. And that's where we come in, little buddy."

"O.K. Gramps. Let's see if we can get in touch with Mrs. Kaiser."

Jack stood up. I noticed a bulge in his pants pocket.

"What the hell do you have in there?" I asked, slightly worried and a little grossed out at the same time.

"This? Just a soda." He took the can out of his pocket.

"You walk around carrying soda cans in your pants."

"Just in the office. Need a little sugar rush from time to time."

I acted as though that made perfect sense.

"How's the...are you still on the wagon?" I asked. I wasn't sure how Jack would take my asking. He could have been offended, he could have told me it was none of my business, and I wasn't sure if it was. But as long as I was working with him, as long as I was trusting him, I needed to know he was all there.

That wasn't the only reason of course. If I found out Jack was back on the sauce, to be honest it would have devastated me. I needed to see Jack the way he'd been during his prime. Even if he'd lost a few miles off his fastball, I needed to see the Jack O'Donnell who'd earned the reputation of being one of the best newsmen in the city's history.

Though I wasn't sure if I needed it more for Jack's sake, or for mine.

"Six months," Jack said. There was sincerity on his face, and it made me breathe easier.

"I'm glad to hear that, I..."

"It's not easy," Jack said. "I'm not going to lie to you Henry. You do something every day for almost fifty years, it's not like a switch you can just turn off. It's almost a part of you. And when you don't to it--drink, I mean--it's like there 's a space that needs to be filled."

"Hence the soda," I said.

"Sometimes the space is literal," he said, patting his stomach. "Not the exact same, but it helps."

"Like a nicotine patch,"

"Kind of like that, only that doesn't rot your teeth."

"If you need any help," I said, "physical, emotional..."

"Sexual?" Jack grinned at me.

"I'm not into necrophilia, old man."

This time Jack closed his eyes when he laughed.

"Come on Parker, let's go. Victoria Kaiser is probably being held by the cops for questioning and protection. I have a man at One Police Plaza who can put us in touch with her."

"Sounds like a plan," I said. "I'll meet you outside. Just gotta make a quick call."

"To who?" Jack asked.

"Amanda," I lied.

"What about?"

"We're planning a vacation, just wanted to see if she booked it yet."

"That's nice. You could use a little time away. I'll be waiting in the lobby. Don't take so long that I'll need to sit down."

"I'll be right there."

Jack left. When I saw him enter the elevator vestibule, and the doors closed on him, I picked up my phone. I took out my cell phone, scrolled down to the number I'd just recently entered and filed under Ray's Pizza. Didn't need anyone knowing the truth right now.

I dialed the number, and chewed a fingernail as it rang. Finally a voice answered.

"I recognize the prefix," Paulina Cole said. "There had better be a reason somebody's calling me from the Gazette."

"It's Henry Parker," I said.

"Oh. Parker. What do you want?"

"What do I want? The article you wrote today, what's the deal?"

"I don't know what you mean," she said, defiance and annoyance battling for supremacy in her voice.

"The cops don't have any idea what you're talking about. And nobody has seen this drug. Not to mention you didn't even mention it when we spoke."

"What, I ask a favor of you and suddenly I need to tell you everything I'm working on?"

"No, but I..."

"I told you there was a quid pro quo."

"Wait...the guy who threatened your daughter...did he make you write that story?" I waited for Paulina to answer. "Hello? You still there?"

"I told you there was a quid pro quo," Paulina said. "That's all you need to know. Goodbye Parker. Thanks again."

She hung up.

I sat there, shaking.

Paulina Cole was no pushover. I'd believed her when we spoke, but for her to do this kind of favor, to write a story that might have had no factual basis, it went beyond morally wrong into ethically wrong. Paulina was a good reporter; too good sometimes. She might have had a nose for the tabloidy, for the melodramatic, but she almost never got her facts wrong. So why the heck would somebody want her to print that? Why invent a drug if it didn't exist? Why falsely quote a cop if the story was grounded in a lie? For her to print this, it either meant she'd fabricated a hell of a story with somebody else's help...or that the story was true. And whoever wanted the story written wanted it seen by millions of people for a reason.

Did that blond guy who killed Brett Kaiser also blackmail Paulina Cole into writing that article? What the hell did he have to do with this new drug? And if he had something to do with it, no doubt Brett Kaiser did too. I could only hope Victoria Kaiser could shed a little light on this, because just like the drug, this story felt dangerous as hell and getting darker.

Chapter 28

Morgan held the metal bar as the train sped uptown. He was standing next to Theo Goggins, the two of them carrying briefcases with enough narcotics to last Scarface until the sequel.

Theo was dressed in a gray suit, and his blue tie was bold and bright.

"You were right about the tie," Morgan said. "It works."

"You think I'd lie about something as important as that? I started off making cold calls. First time I got a fish to bite on a stock, I was wearing a blue tie. First time I closed an account--blue tie."

"First time you sold stuff that would get you jail time."

Theo smiled. "Blue tie. But I ain't never going to jail. Only way I go to jail is if you rat on me, and I ain't never going to give you cause to do that. So you make up a story, it's your ass they find broken into itty bitty pieces floating in the East River."

"Same to you, my friend."

"See," Theo said, smiling. "we're going to get along just fine."

Morgan's palms were sweaty. His legs shook from time to time, as he waited for somebody to come up to him--maybe a cop or one of those transit workers--grab him by the collar, rip open the briefcase spilling pills and dope all over the dirty car floor.

But that didn't happen.

Nobody batted an eye at them.

It was about eight thirty in the morning, and Morgan and Theo were on their way to meet their first customer of the day. Morgan wondered who ordered drugs along with their morning cup of Joe, but he figured there were enough people in this city who either worked from home or were unemployed that there was a twenty four seven market for their wares.

Theo was whistling something softly. Morgan couldn't tell what it was, but he figured trying to guess would keep his mind off the legal ramifications of being caught with his goods.

Guessing the tune was impossible. First of all, Theo didn't

seem like a particularly good whistler. Instead of a clean, high-pitched noise coming from his lips, it was more like a low rattle punctuated by occasional bursts of spit.

Theo paused to wipe his mouth, then he said to Morgan, "You need something?" Morgan hadn't realized that he'd likely been staring at his partner for nearly five minutes.

"Just wondered what you're whistling," he said. "A little Jay-Z."

"Cool."

Theo resumed his 'whistling.' Morgan held the rails, his mind beginning to wander.

"So what's your story?" Theo said, snapping Morgan out of it.

"My story?"

"Yeah. How'd you end up in the basement of some nightclub loading up on this stuff. Not exactly the kind of job you find on Monster dot com."

"I got laid off," Morgan said. "A few months ago."

"How much you owe?"

"Excuse me?"

"Come on," Theo said, smiling. "You wouldn't be here if you didn't have debts pouring out your eyeballs. So how much?"

"In total?"

"No, itemize it for me asshole."

Morgan smiled back. He liked Theo.

"All in all? A little over nine hundred thousand."

Theo whistled. For whatever reason, this time the sound came through clean.

"Let me guess, most of that tied up in your pad."

"Most of it. Still have almost a million on my mortgage."

"You try to sell it?"

"Yeah. No takers. What about you?"

"Same shit. Only I got laid off a year ago."

"How much do you owe?" Morgan asked.

"Three million."

"You're kidding me."

"Uh uh," Theo said. "I bought up half a dozen properties in the city. Made the down payments, figured I could rent them out, have other people pay my carrying costs and then I'd just sell them down the road and make a killing."

"Man, talk about bad timing."

"Yeah, tell me about it. My credit is shot. I couldn't get a loan for a pack of gum right now."

"So who'd you know that got you in?" Morgan asked.

"My uncle," he said. "Used to use. Never dealt, but got friendly with one of his dealers. I used to be a major pothead, and I started buying from his guy after my uncle quit. Pretty soon I couldn't afford to buy, so my man asked if I was going through tough times. I told him what had happened, and he offered to make an introduction for me. I'm not above this. To me, it's all the same whether you're selling junk, real estate or stocks. In the end you're giving something to somebody that they think will make them happier. And whether it's financial, emotional or chemical happiness, who the hell are we to judge. Are the people who get strung out on dope any worse than people like me who lose everything on some bad bets? I figure if I can do something to get myself out of this mess and make some coin, why not?"

"I know what you mean," Morgan said.

"I bet you do."

* * *

Theo and Morgan got off the train at twenty third and Park and headed east. The Manhattan neighborhood of Gramercy tended to be full of young professionals who enjoyed the area's local bars (both dive and trendy). Morgan used to come here often for the movie theater at Kips Bay, and noticed that over the last few years the population appeared to grow a little more affluent, likely due to doctors working at Bellevue and small business owners who moved into vacated storefronts.

They walked side by side, matching briefcases slung over their shoulders. If anybody looked at them, it was only because they might have been slightly jealous that two younger guys had weathered the economic storm, as that could be the only explanation for their attire and accessories.

Morgan took out the cell phone from his coat pocket. It was old, nearly an antique, and he was amazed that this piece of junk still even worked. Still, Leonard had given it to them for a reason.

Right after they'd packed up their briefcases with specific quantities of various drugs, Leonard had given them each a cell phone. And this was how it worked.

Before they left the warehouse/club, they'd be given an address. The address was of their first customer of the day. The customer had called somebody, probably some sort of switchboard at another location, and placed an order. That order was relayed to one of the courier teams, who were then dispatched to the location. The customer would also have placed an order and they were also quoted a price. Once arriving at the location, Leonard said, they would make the transaction with the customer.

Once leaving the customer's address, they would call the number programmed in the cell phone as 'Home'. After confirming the deal, they would be sent a text message with the address of their next transaction, as well as the price quoted to the customer for whatever they'd requested.

Obviously there would be a little flexibility, as sometimes the customer would buy more than they'd initially requested. And sometimes, of course, they would buy less, often because the customer didn't have enough money to pay for the goods.

It was a regular business, Leonard said.

All orders would be kept track of, and Leonard's people also knew the exact quantities of drugs given to the couriers as well as their value. At the end of the day, Leonard said, just like any other business they would make sure the goods matched the receipts, and confirm that all the money was handed over.

Assuming Theo and Morgan were honest, they would have no problems. If there were ever any payment issues, or they'd taken in more (or less) money than expected, all they had to do was relay the information.

The quicker they worked the more money they made, the more stops they'd be able to hit during the day. You wanted to take a two hour lunch? Your take would suffer. Get caught in traffic? Tough shit.

The only people who moved up in this world were the ones who fully dedicated themselves. You want vacation days? You got 'em. Only your creditors don't really think of them that way.

The first stop was on nineteenth and third, off the corner of the avenue, a brownstone wedged between a cellular phone store and a diner. Morgan walked up and pressed the buzzer for 5A, taking a quick look around them to see if anyone was watching.

"You need to relax, man," Theo said. "Ain't nobody thinking twice about us."

"Who is it?" came the scratchy voice.

"Delivery," Morgan said.

"I didn't order...oh wait, yeah, come right up."

Another buzzer went off and the door unlatched. They entered the lobby and went over to the elevator. It was not a particularly nice brownstone. The floor tiles were chipping, and it looked like with just minimum force he could have pried open any mailbox he chose.

The elevator arrived and they took it to the fifth floor in silence. Morgan held his briefcase, feeling the plastic crinkle through the leather. Theo watched him do this but said nothing.

When the door opened, they turned left (A-D) and rang the doorbell for 5A.

"Who is it?" the familiar voice said.

"Delivery," Morgan said.

"Oh yeah, right, come on in."

The door opened, revealing a tall, thin guy in his mid thirties wearing pajama bottoms, a loose t-shirt and slippers. The apartment behind him was sparingly furnished. There was a cot covered in faded blankets, an old twenty four inch television, and a bookshelf with textbooks. Morgan looked closer. The textbooks had odd titles like 'Principles of Economics' and 'Financial Management: Theory and Practice.' The books looked well used.

The man had a three day beard growth and his hair looked like it hadn't been combed since the last time he'd shaved. His eyes were red-rimmed, and his breathing was quick. Morgan had no doubt the man had a serious coke problem. He supposed that's why they were there.

The man moved out of the way and ushered them inside, waving his hand like he was shooing away an unpleasant smell

"Two of you," he said, looking at Theo. "Is he like your bodyguard?"

Theo simply replied, "One eight ball. That right?"

The man nodded his head vigorously and reached out his

hand.

Theo placed his briefcase on a small wooden coffee table, stained with circular rings and other substances that couldn't even be guessed. Theo undid the lock and rummaged through the case, eventually coming up with a small plastic pouch containing white powder. Marked on the outside were the numbers 1/8, for an eighth of an ounce.

The man's eyes went wide.

"That's a hundred and fifty," Theo said.

The man reached into his pockets (it didn't occur to Morgan that they made pajama bottoms that had pockets) and pulled out seven crumpled twenties and two fives. He handed them over to Theo like he was getting rid of Toxic material. He put out his hand eagerly and Theo dropped the pouch into it.

"Pleasure doing business with you," Theo said.

"Hey man, one sec," the guy said, his eyes rimmed with red. "I heard about this new drug, dark something."

"Darkness," Theo said.

"Yeah. Supposedly it'll mess you up right. You ever tried it?"

Morgan shook his head. Theo said, "No."

The guy stammered, almost embarrassed. "You wouldn't happen to have any, would you?"

"Matter of fact," Theo said, "we do. How much do you want?"

"I'm not sure," the guy said. "How much is enough for a few good hits? I don't want to love the stuff and have to call you right back."

"Three rocks," Theo said. "We have an introductory offer, and it's enough for a few hits."

"And how much is this introductory offer?"

"Three rocks? That'll run you fifty bucks for the first purchase. Call it a beginner's discount. After that it's twenty five a pop."

"S'not bad," the guy said. "Can I try the intro offer?"

"Let me see the money."

"Yeah, money, hold on one sec."

The guy walked out of the living room and into a side room. Morgan heard him rummaging around and cursing. Then he came out with five neatly folded tens.

"My old lady'll kill me if she knows I used this. Supposed to be for emergencies and stuff. Ever since we both lost our jobs, money's hard to come by."

"Don't I know it," Morgan said. Theo shot him a look.

"Fifty for three," Theo said. He took another small plastic pouch from the briefcase, containing three small black rocks.

"How do you...do it?" the guy asked.

"Two ways, either a pipe--same way you'd smoke weed--or you can crush it up, cook it and inhale like that. They're both pretty potent."

"Gotcha." He handed Theo the bills, and Theo dropped the pouch on top of the cocaine.

"That it?"

"That's it until my unemployment check comes at the end of the week. Thanks fellas."

Theo didn't say a word. Morgan followed him out the door. When the elevator door had closed behind them, Morgan said, "That was impressive. Not sure if I would have remembered all of that."

"For your sake I hope you do. I'm not gonna be doing all the talking at every stop."

The elevator began to go down, but then there was a screeching noise and the car ground to a halt. Morgan looked up at the display. The light had stopped between the second and third floors. They were stuck.

"Just perfect," Morgan said.

"No," Theo said softly, an undercurrent of anger in his voice. "No! God damnit, come on!"

"Hey man, take it easy. I'm sure we'll get going in no time."

Theo kicked the elevator door hard, leaving a small dent in the metal. "Let's move this crate!" He jammed his thumb against the 'emergency' button. When he released it, he jammed it in again.

"I think they heard us," Morgan said.

"Are you kidding? Roach motel like this, I bet the super doesn't even live on the premises. We could be stuck here all day."

Morgan looked at the roof of the car, hoping there might be some easily opened hatch where they could boost each other out onto the roof, then find a ladder or escape hatch that would lead them to freedom. Sadly, Morgan realized, those kind of things only existed in 'Die Hard' films, and the roof of this car was one solid piece of metal.

"Ok," he said. "Maybe we can pry the doors open." Theo kicked the door again, widening his boot imprint. "I don't think that's helping."

"Listen asshole," Theo said. "Every second we're stuck in here, there are other folks selling product. And when they come back at the end of the day with higher receipts than us, you tell me then to calm down. I'm not in this to lose, Morgan."

Morgan stood there, nodded, figuring anything he said would only enrage Theo more.

Five minutes went by. Ten. Theo stopped kicking. He tried his cell phone, but they didn't get reception in the elevator.

Theo was shaking. His hands were trembling, knees knocking against one another. A sheen of moisture appeared on the young man's lip, and he licked it away, his eyes darting around the car looking for some way out.

"Theo, you ok?"

"Shut up, I'm trying to figure out how we can get out of here."

"I don't think..."

"I said shut the hell up."

Morgan moved into the corner of the elevator, looked at his watch and hoped for a miracle.

Finally, after fifteen minutes, Morgan felt a jolt and the elevator began to move.

"Oh thank God," Theo said.

Morgan held his breath until they reached the first floor, then as soon as the doors opened the pair bolted into the lobby before the elevator could change its mind.

"Holy crap man," Theo said. His hands were shaking, and his brow was covered with sweat. "I was worried we'd be stuck in there until the cleaning crew came by or the thing just detached from its cables."

"Well, we're out now," Morgan said. "We can get back to business."

"Next stop," Theo said, still breathing heavy, "you handle all the talking."

"No problem. I'm a fast learner."

"You might be a fast learner, but I've already learned." Theo looked at Morgan with a cocky smile, letting him know that they weren't just partners, but competitors. Theo wanted to move up the ranks just as much as Morgan did, and the longer it took Morgan to catch up the farther ahead Theo would pull. His reaction inside the elevator only proved it. Theo didn't want to waste a single second not making money.

They exited the building into the early sunlight, Morgan squinting as he took out the cell phone to wait for the location of their next customer.

"That went easy," Theo said.

"Yeah. Hope they're all like that."

"I'm sure some of these freaks will be a little more strung out than our man up there but just remember that all they want in the end is the stuff. They don't want to haggle and they don't want a lot of fuss. Some of these guys might have coke muscles, but if in the end they think you're going to hold out on them, they'll bend faster than an elbow."

"I hear you."

"So what's the next stop?" Theo asked.

Morgan looked at his cell phone, reception returning after the elevator fiasco. He had one new text message.

Morgan pressed the 'Retrieve Messages' button, and an address appeared on the screen.

"That can't be right," Morgan said.

"What? Where is it?"

Morgan checked the time and date it was sent. The time stamp was dated just minutes ago, while they were stuck in the elevator.

"Hold on, I need to confirm this."

Morgan went to the address book and dialed the number marked 'Home.' A strange, deep, robotic voice answered. It was clearly being masked by some sort of voice-altering technology.

"Yes?" the voice said.

"Hi, uh, this is Isaacs and Goggins, we just wanted to confirm the address just sent to us."

"Three forty east nineteenth. Apartment five A," the voice said.

"Yeah, um, that's where we just left."

"And that's where you're going back to."

"Uh, ok."

The voice explained the situation to Morgan, who stood there, eyes widening. He understood everything that was being relayed, but couldn't understand why it was happening so quick.

He didn't know what was in those little black rocks, but it must have thrown pajama dude in 5A for a loop.

The other line went dead. Morgan closed the phone and put it back in his pocket.

"What was that?" Theo said.

"We're going right back upstairs," Morgan said. "That guy we just sold to, he took one hit of the Darkness and put in an order for half a dozen more rocks at the standard price. Guy said it was the best high he's ever experienced."

"Good for him, good for us," Theo said.

"And," Morgan continued, "after we're done here they're sending over another address where the customer wants another ten. Home base said to expect a lot of Darkness deliveries today."

"Another hundred and fifty bucks for five minutes work," Theo said. He tried to whistle, but again it came out more like an aborted attempt at a raspberry. "Let's not keep the man waiting."

"Agreed," Morgan said. He felt a strange sensation, and for a moment couldn't place it. Then, as they were about to reenter the brownstone, it occurred to Morgan the last time he'd felt that singular feeling of joy, confidence and ambition.

The day he got his first paycheck at his old job. That was the first day he truly felt like he was going to conquer the world.

"Let's hurry it up," Morgan said. "But this time let's take the stairs."

Chapter 29

"Always makes me smile a little," Jack said.

"What does?"

"Tourists. They spend thousands of dollars to see this city, but they really know nothing about it. You don't get a sense of Manhattan by taking pictures or sitting on a double decker bus."

"Not everyone has had the fortune of being at gunpoint in Vietnam," I said. "For some people this is as close as they can get."

"I suppose," Jack said, "but sometimes I wonder if I even understand the city after all these years."

"Are you still thinking about Paulina's article?" I asked.

"A little. I never used to get scooped, Henry. Every time I went out for lunch, I could feel a dozen eyes on me, hating me. They were other reporters, and they were staring daggers through me because they knew I was working on stories that they'd never get. They'd be working mop up duty on yesterday's page seven while I was breaking news. It's a great feeling to be hated for doing your job well. And right now, I hate Paulina Cole. Not because she tried to ruin my life, but because she got a story that I didn't. So not only do I hate her, but I hate her for making me hate her."

"That's a lot of hate to be carrying around," I said. "But what we're working on could squash that."

"You aren't going to know that until we follow the bread crumb trail to the end. Maybe we find something, maybe we don't."

"I know there's something at the end," I said. "My brother didn't die for nothing. Somebody had him killed. And I know whoever had him killed knows what 718 Enterprises is."

"You told me your brother was a courier," Jack said. "Right?"

"I think so. He was somewhere on the drug ladder, and not at the bottom."

"You think it's a coincidence your brother gets killed--you claim by someone higher up on the food chain than he was--and then such a short time later this story breaks?"

"I don't know," I said.

"I think you have a feeling, the same one I do. You talked to Butch Willingham, you know my reporting on the Fury."

"I know you didn't have enough to go on to report more than you did," I said. "And that wasn't much. If the Fury even exists."

Jack stared me down, backed me down, knowing what we both full well believed.

"Twenty years ago," Jack said, "I thought I was certain that there was some sort of kingpin, some sort of Wizard of Oz named the Fury. And for whatever reason, that person was eliminating mid level drug dealers."

"Yeah, so?"

"Paulina might have beaten us to the story, but I don't think she got the full story. Not even close. If the Fury exists, he came to power in the eighties, right around the time the crack epidemic was strangling the life out of New York. I don't think that's a coincidence."

"Go on," I said. I felt that familiar rush.

"Twenty years later, your brother is killed. Then this guy Ken Tsang is killed. Both around the same age, both likely somewhere on the totem pole in the drug game. And then Paulina's article about this new drug, the Darkness gets printed. Two dealers killed. A new drug hitting the streets. I think this person was instrumental during the eighties, and is now taking it to a whole new level."

"History repeats itself," I said. "But this isn't the same city as it was twenty years ago. I mean, between Giuliani and 9/11, you can't argue that we're not more secure."

"Security is all relative," Jack said. "When the economy takes a turn for the worse, especially when it nosedives like it has, it breeds crime and corruption. They're both sides of the same coin, you get one you get the other. You know the expression, 'seeing the forest from the trees', right?"

"Of course."

"Right now, this city is staring at the forest. It's looking at the big picture. Terrorism, biohazards, all nobles things to be watching out for. In the eighties and nineties, we didn't have to worry about things like that. So guys like Giuliani, Ray Kelly and Bill Bratton could look at it from the street level. There's a reason Forty Second street looks like Walt Disney threw up all over it and not like hooker paradise anymore.

Twenty years ago, the cops could look at the city through a microscope. Nowadays, they need to look at it via satellite. And when you look at things from a macro perspective, when you're looking at rooftops and airplanes, you miss the rat holes. Beneath our noses, there's something big brewing. And whoever's behind it is smart enough to know that this is the right time, and that we might be defenseless."

"Paulina's story," I said, "all it's going to do is create demand for the product."

"Without a doubt. Nothing gets people motivated like being told they shouldn't do something. Word of mouth takes a match to ignite it. For all of Paulina's moxie in getting this story, I worry that she's going to inadvertently do the exact opposite of alarming the public: she's going to make them want it even more."

I suddenly felt nauseous. When I'd met with Paulina, she told me there was a 'quid pro quo' with the man who kidnapped her and threatened her daughter. She would have to do something for him in order to keep her daughter safe.

Now I knew what that quid pro quo was. And why it was asked.

The blond man, the same one who'd killed Brett Kaiser, had told her to write the article. He'd gotten her all the information she needed, perhaps even fabricated a few quotes, and those were her 'unnamed sources.'

I'd never seen Paulina scared, and I'd never seen her lie. In the last few days I'd seen both. And they scared the hell out of me.

Whoever the man was that asked her to write the article knew that it would create an automatic demand for the product it featured. Paulina's weapon was words, and he'd given her ammunition to forge something dangerous and potentially deadly.

I had to tell Jack. This was getting too big. This man had scope and vision and knew exactly what getting to Paulina would do. Jack needed to know.

And he was staring right at me. Knew full well I was thinking something.

But to my surprise, the look on Jack's face wasn't full of wonder at what I was thinking...it was one of disappointment because he knew I was hiding something.

"Time to spill it Henry," he said. Jack's face turned to stone.

This was a look I hadn't seen before, and immediately I felt awful, lying to the man I'd idolized for so long. The man who'd been my partner on this story, who was motivated to come back to work because of what I'd uncovered.

I left that man in the dust, but now he'd caught up to me.

"After the explosion at Brett Kaiser's apartment," I said, trying hard to look at Jack but finding it hard. Finally I met his eyes. "I got a call."

"From who?" Jack said. He said it as much just to get me to admit it as he did to find out the answer.

"Paulina Cole."

If Jack's face had been stone, this caused it to crack a bit. His eyes opened wider, mouth opened just enough to show the surprise on his face.

"Paulina," he said. "Why in God's name..."

"She was kidnapped," I said, the dam bursting. But truth be told, it felt good.

"Kidnapped? By who? And why the hell would she call you?"

I could see Jack's eyes reddening, but his anger at learning the truth was now tempered by his desire to know the full story. And he'd get it.

"She doesn't know," I said. "But the man who did it threatened to kill her daughter."

"You know I always kind of assumed Paulina was some sort of devil spawn, I'm moderately surprised to learn that she has a reproductive system."

"She thinks the guy who did it has connections in the NYPD, he said if she went to the cops he'd know."

"So she goes to you because you know cops you can trust."

"Partly, yeah."

"So what does she want from you?"

"To help her find the man who did it."

"And in return, let me guess, you get the story."

I nodded. "That's right."

"Jesus, Henry," Jack said, tilting his head back, wiping his forehead with the tips of his fingers. "The story she wrote this morning, did you know it was going to run?"

"No, I swear I didn't."

"But?" Jack said.

"But she told me she had to do something for him. That was the deal for him not to harm her daughter. My guess is the story this morning was what she promised, what he made her do."

"That would explain why the cops don't know anything and why nobody would go on the record. Strange that for an article about a potential drug epidemic nobody from the narcotics division was quoted, or even knew about it."

"Or why the cops patrolling the streets haven't heard about it."

"Today," Jack said, taking a breath, "was the coming out party for this drug. Paulina's story was the spark to get the Darkness into the mainstream. A cover story in a major New York newspaper will be read by over two million people, and another few million will see the headline and remember it."

"Word of mouth," I said. "Best marketing in the world, and they got it for free."

Jack lowered his head. "They used us."

"There's more," I said. "I'm ninety nine percent sure that the guy who kidnapped Paulina is the same guy who killed Brett Kaiser. Physical descriptions matched. Curt Sheffield is helping me track him down, going off the physical info plus access to explosives and drugs."

"Do you think this guy," Jack said, "could be the Fury?"

"I don't think so," I said. "The descriptions from both Paulina and Kaiser's doorman peg the suspect in his late thirties or early forties. It's not impossible but I suspect twenty years ago he would have been a little too young to run a drug empire."

"So then he must be working for somebody," Jack said. "Somebody smart enough to go after Paulina, and somebody powerful enough to have their fingers dug into the NYPD."

"So how the hell do we find out who this guy is?" I said. "Sheffield is looking into it, but if Paulina is right then most of my contacts in the department are useless."

"Paulina," I said. "She said this guy showed her a picture of her daughter that was taken from a social networking site. The way these things work is that the only people who have access to the pictures you post are the people you accept as friends."

"You're saying this guy would be stupid enough to be her friend online?"

"No," I said. "But I think he found someone who was. Paulina gave me a list of everyone her daughter is friends with. Jack, I know you're used to typewriters and ink quills, but this is going to take some electronic leg work."

"I can use the Google," Jack said.

"Yeah...I was afraid you'd say that. The list is upstairs. Forget about Victoria Kaiser for now. What we need to do is cross check everyone on that list with Abigail Cole, if need be call everyone she's friends with online."

"She's in college, right? That could be hundreds of people."

"Good thing you don't have any children, you won't go into it knowing how damn difficult it is to talk to someone in their late teens or early twenties."

"You're not that far from that age, Henry," Jack said.

"Yeah, I know. Why do you think I know they're all nightmares?"

Jack laughed. "Ok sport, let's go. Just one thing."

"What's that?"

"I accidentally spilled coffee on my keyboard. Can you ask the help desk for a new one? This would be my fourth and I don't think they'll give me another one."

"Sure," I said. "Come on George Jetson, let's go find Mr. Joshua."

Chapter 30

I forgot what it was like to be a college student.

Abigail Cole had one hundred and ninety seven friends on Facebook. Many of them had public profiles, and from that I was able to glean phone numbers and sometimes email addresses. To those who had email addresses, I sent them notes asking to speak to them in a matter pertaining to an ongoing investigation. I clearly identified myself.

The rest I called. At least four of them picked up their cell phone during class. I could tell this because in the background someone in the background said quite audibly that if the phone wasn't turned off post haste, F would be merely the first of four letters on that student's papers.

When I was in college, one of my dreams was to have a beeper some day. As young as I was, sometimes I felt pretty old.

Frustration began to seep in after I'd contacted nearly thirty of Abigail's friends and made no leeway. I wasn't even sure how many of these people she was still close to, or whether or not they were real friends or just random friends-of-friends-of-friends.

There had to be an easier way to do this. And just when I was about to brainstorm what those were, Jack came walking over.

He had a big smile on his face, the kind of smile that you didn't often see on a man approaching seventy. This was more along the lines of a young child who'd accidentally discovered a hidden Christmas present that they didn't expect to be there. Jack almost looked embarrassed to be happy.

"What's got you so toothy?" I said.

"I think I found it," he said.

"Found what?"

Jack took a chair from an empty cubicle and pulled it over to my desk. He laid a series of printouts in front of me. They looked to be from some sort of websites. They were chock from of random ruminations, thoughts and pictures.

"What is this?" I said.

"Well," Jack continued, the pride in his voice unmistakable. "I took the list of all of Abigail Cole's online friends. I did every kind of search imaginable--Google, Yahoo, Lexis Nexis, you name it--and cross-referenced her name along with websites that contained photos. I figured if somebody had access to personal photos, they might have had access even earlier than when Paulina was first taken."

"Why would you assume that?" I said.

"Whoever took Paulina wanted her to write that article to help publicize the Darkness. Which means these plans have been in the works for a lot longer than the little time gone by since her abduction. This blond guy needed to know how to get to Paulina well before he actually did it, meaning he needed to be sure of who had access to her daughter's photos ahead of time. So when I did all that...I found something."

"A website," I said.

"A blog," Jack continued. "Not active anymore, but get this: it was deleted just three days after Paulina was abducted. Coincidence, right?"

"Could be," I said. "What makes you think it has anything to do with this story?"

"The blog was deleted, but a few cached pages were still available to see. Other websites had linked to it, that's part of the reason I was able to find it."

"And?"

"And the blog's creator is a girl named Pamela Ruffalo," Jack said. "I know you haven't had time to read all of these pages I printed out yet, but I'll save you the detective work. Pam Ruffalo either was, or, more likely, still is Abigail Cole's girlfriend."

"You're kidding me. Her girlfriend posted pictures of her on the blog?"

"No sir, Henry. Take a look for yourself."

I picked the half a dozen pages up, began to shuffle through them.

There were about fifteen blog entries on the pages. They were dated starting about three months ago, and continued up until the last few days when the account was deleted.

The posts were fairly specific about their relationship. According to the second entry, Pamela had met Abigail in college during a job recruitment fair. They'd both been on line to hear more about an environmental consulting firm, got to talking, and had dinner at a campus eatery that night.

Their first official date was that weekend. 'Weekend at Bernie's,' which Pam had rented on Netflix. She marveled at how they both had an appreciation for bad movies. And since that first date had gone so well, Pam had ordered 'Showgirls,' 'Battlefield Earth' and 'Mother Dearest' for her new romantic interest.

As the relationship progressed, Pam began to post pictures of the couple on the page. Some of the pictures were innocuous. The couple out at a party. Watching a field hockey game together. Sitting under a tree reading.

Some of the pictures, though, were far more intimate.

The first one that caught my attention was the two girls lying in bed, sheets up to their chins, bare shoulders visible. The photo must have been a self-portrait taken by one of the two girls, as a finger smudge obscured part of the right side of the shot.

In another photo, the girls were dressed up in bustiers and garter belts. It looked like they were about to go to some sort of party.

And in another shot, the two girls were snapped kissing passionately. I'd say one thing, but they were kind of cute together.

"These all came off the blog?" I said.

"Every one."

"Were there any photos of Abigail Cole in a bikini? Or on the beach at all?"

"Listen, I know she's a good looking girl but I'm not about to..."

"No, that's not why I'm asking. Paulina said when the guy took her, he showed her a photo of her daughter wearing a bikini on the beach. There are no photos like that on this website."

"Paulina told me the photo the guy used was private. She said Abigail never posted it online, and she was clear about that. So where did the photo come from?"

"I think I know," Jack said. "But I need two things to confirm it."

"What are they?"

"First off, I need you to find out one thing for me online. I don't have access to it, but either you do or know someone who does."

"What do I..."

"And the second thing," Jack said, looking me dead in the eyes, "is that I need to talk to Paulina Cole."

Chapter 31

I stood in the middle of Rockefeller Center with my hands in my pockets, watching people go about their day. The sun was bright and there was just a wisp of breeze.

A tour group passed us by, clinking and clanking as the binoculars and cameras jangled about their necks. There was lots of tour groups always walking about this area, and they would often look at me in my work clothes like I was some sort of alien species. These people didn't seem to believe that anyone actually lived or worked in Manhattan, that we all just bused in day after day and wandered about star struck, wondering when we might run into Derek Jeter or Sarah Jessica Parker on the street. I think they believed only celebrities and homeless people lived in the city.

I watched the corner of fifty first street, knowing that's the direction she'd be coming from. Paulina wasn't too keen on meeting me up by the Gazette, partly because she didn't like to move for anybody and partly because when she left the paper she was thought of just about as fondly as Mussolini.

"Parker?" Paulina Cole said. She had just rounded the corner and was staring at me like I'd just thrown a pie at her from across a crowded room. She was wearing black leather boots and a knee-length skirt. Her hair was recently done, and I hated to admit it but she looked pretty good. "You'd better have a damn good reason for calling me up to the Hard Rock Cafe."

I'd heard Paulina refer to Rockefeller Center by that moniker that before. And she didn't mean it as a compliment. To her, this neighborhood was a tourists mecca, drastically overpriced, and as close to 'real' New York as the Hard Rock was to being the 'real' Arnold Schwarzenegger. "I expense my cell phone bill and cab rides, and if you keep calling me I'll have some explaining to do when the finance department reviews it."

"Nice to talk to you too Paulina," I said. "Thanks for coming."

"Don't thank me. I came because you said you had more information about my daughter."

"Yeah...you might want to sit down."

"What, you think whatever you have to tell me is going to make me suddenly pass out in your arms or something? Get over yourself, Henry. Nothing surprises me anymore."

"Well, I don't want to tell you what to do. But there is news."

"Did you find the man?" Paulina said. She said it like she'd expected us to do so all along. There was no appreciation in her voice. Whatever, that wasn't quite her style.

"No. But we know where the photo came from. The one of your daughter at the beach."

"How did you find it? Where did it come from?"

"Well, I'll let the person who figured it out tell you all about it. Hey Jack."

Paulina whipped around to see Jack O'Donnell standing right behind her. He had a massive smile on his face, and he was standing close enough to her that he could almost tickle her nose with his beard.

"Hey Cole," Jack said. "Long time. How's the ex-husband and your kid?"

"You've got to be kidding me."

The surprise in Paulina's voice proved that Jack O'Donnell was the last person she expected--and wanted--to see.

The reporter stood there, looking like she wanted to kill Jack, kill me, then tear our bodies to pieces.

Instead she merely said, "You've got to be fucking kidding me."

"I am neither kidding nor fucking you," Jack said. "But I am going to help you."

Paulina's face contorted, as she sneered at Jack. I stood there wondering if this was a good idea. But Jack insisted that this meeting take place. He said it wasn't a vendetta, and it wasn't because he needed to get even with the woman who nearly ruined his career. He said it was because it was the right thing to do.

"What the hell do you want you dried up old mummy?"

I wondered if Jack still felt like it was the right thing to do.

"You know the old saying, people only call you names if they really care about you? Well between your sweet nothings and that big kiss of an article you wrote about me, I'm willing to bet most New York psychiatrists would testify that you're head over heels in love with me."

"What the hell is this O'Donnell? Parker, you'd better have a reason for this that goes well beyond morbid curiosity."

"Jack asked me to set this up," I said. I didn't have to worry about throwing Jack under the bus here, he told me he wanted it full known that this was his decision. "But I knew you'd want to hear what he has to say."

"I only want to hear one of two things come out of your mouth," Paulina said. "One, that you know who threatened my daughter. Or two, you're leaving this business and wanted to thank me for showing this city what a washed up, drunk old hack you really are."

I saw Jack flinch at that, but he stood his ground. Paulina was staring daggers into Jack's eyes, but he didn't waver.

"I can't say either of those," Jack said.

"Then why the hell am I here? Serves me right for trusting you, Parker."

"You trusted me for a reason," I said. "Now hear him out."

Paulina looked at Jack, shook her head. "I'm surprised you had the balls to poke your head out from whatever rock you've been under the last few months."

"Balls have never been my problem," Jack said. "It's knowing when to think with my head instead of my balls that's gotten me into trouble."

Had Jack been thirty years younger, I could see these two having the best enemy sex in history.

"Seems like that's a problem a lot of male journalists have. Even Henry, here. Right, Parker? No reporter's had his life threatened more times in a few years than your protégé, Jack. These balls? How would you feel if one day Henry gets too close to the fire and gets burned to a crisp?"

"Shut the hell up," I said. Paulina smiled.

"There are those balls I talked about," she said. "You're a reporter, Henry, not a soldier. You're not supposed to have emotion or take sides. And you're not supposed to come this close to getting yourself killed on every story you report."

"I do what I need to in order to get to the truth," I said.

"You don't seem to care much about the truth in the story I wrote about Jack," she said. "You might hate me for it, but every word in that was true. And you don't judge him the way you're judging me right now."

"You see, that's where you and I aren't alike," I said. "I don't look at life as one big story to report. There's a big difference between blood and ink. It's a shame you never learned that."

"Enough of this crap," Jack said. "Do you want to hear what we found or not?"

"Fine," Paulina said, folding her arms across her chest. I could tell this was a practiced look, sternness crossed with just a hint of pouty sexuality. She was used to pressing just hard enough to elicit a reaction, but not hard enough to drive people away. Jack had information she needed, but she wouldn't stay quiet without letting him know what she thought. And it was then that I realized Paulina didn't write that article just to get publicity, she did it because she truly loathed Jack.

"Does a girl named Pamela Ruffalo ring a bell?" Jack said.

Paulina didn't give any indication that she recognized the name. "No, who the hell is that?"

"She's a student at Smith college," Jack said. "A junior, I believe, according to her Facebook page."

As Jack spoke, I could see the blank look on Paulina's face changing. She recognized the name from somewhere.

"What does Pam have to do with any of this?" she said in an argumentative tone, hoping Jack would answer her in a way that would vindicate Pam. Not only did Paulina know Pam Ruffalo, but for some reason whatever Jack was going to say was going to hit her--hard.

"A few months ago, Pam Ruffalo began posting to a personal blog. She talked about a lot of things on the site, one of which was her relationship with her new girlfriend. A girl named Abigail Cole."

Paulina watched, and I could have sworn she didn't blink for a minute straight.

"Keep talking," she said.

"She posted a lot of photos on the site. But she never posted any photos like the one you described the blond man having that night."

"So if she didn't post those photos," Paulina said, "why do you think she was involved?"

"Pam shut the blog down, according to records, just a few days after you were abducted. In the days leading up to the cancellation, there was nothing to suggest that there was anything wrong in her life.

Did you ever tell your daughter what happened to you?" Jack said.

I was surprised, looking at Jack, to see a hint of sympathy in his face. He had no love for Paulina Cole as a reporter, but considering her as a human and a mother outweighed that.

"Yes," she said. "A few days after it happened. I went up to Smith and told her about it. Only to keep her safe."

"Do you think it's fair to assume," Jack said, "that Abigail told her girlfriend what you told her? That she told Pam?"

Paulina stood there, then wiped at her eyes which were reddening. For some reason I felt ashamed watching this.

"It's possible," Paulina said. Jack nodded slowly.

"Henry was able to log on to Facebook and contact a few of Abigail's friends. Through them, he found the photos you referred to, the beach shots. They were taken by a girl named Samantha Isringhausen, who then uploaded them to her account."

"I called Samantha," I said, "in her dorm room. When I asked her about the photos, specifically the one of Abigail in front of the hole, she told me that when Pam saw it she immediately asked for the only copy. She loved that picture so much that she never wanted it to be seen by anyone other than her. Samantha agreed, and said she after sending the file to Pamela and uploading the rest, she deleted them from her digital camera."

"So the only person who had that photo," Jack said, "was your daughter's girlfriend."

"Wait," Paulina said, tears starting to run freely now. "Are you saying..."

"I'm saying that the man who attacked you that night," Jack said, "got the photo from Pamela Ruffalo, your daughter's girlfriend. She sold your daughter out."

Chapter 32

Paulina didn't move. Her entire upper body trembled as she looked from Jack to me and back again. Then she stared at me long and hard, without taking her eyes away. I couldn't understand why at first, but then I realized that she trusted me more than she trusted Jack.

Paulina was hoping I would tell her than none of this was true.

Instead I walked up to Paulina, and I'll be damned if I know why I did this, but I took the woman's hand in mine and held it.

"It's true," I said. "We haven't spoken to Pam or Abigail yet."

"Why not?" she said.

Jack replied, "Because you're Abigail's mother. And you're a reporter too. Because this part of the story needs to be reported by you."

"How can I..." Paulina said, trailing off. "My daughter, she'll be..."

"She'll hate you," I said, "for a while. But eventually she'll know the truth. And she'll respect you for it."

Paulina laughed bitterly. "My daughter hasn't respected me in a long time."

"Well if she doesn't respect you," I said, "she'll sure as hell love you for it."

"What about you two? What happens next?"

Jack said, "We'll be waiting for your call. Your promise to Henry still stands. We did our part and will continue to."

Paulina nodded. Then she looked at her watch.

"I can be there in a few hours," she said.

"So go," I said.

"Yeah. Right." She looked at her hand, still held in mine, and pulled it back. Then she ran it through her hair, and straightened her jacket. "I'll call you once it's done."

As Paulina turned to walk away, Jack called, "Don't we get a thank you?"

She turned back, glared at Jack. "I'll thank you once that blond bastard is either behind bars or in the ground."

Then Paulina Cole walked away.

"I think that's the closest she's ever come to a real thank you," Jack said. "I had a wager with myself, fifty fifty odds that she slapped me before she left."

"You might have just saved her daughter's life," I said. "I think that's at least enough to avoid a slap."

"Eh, women like Paulina don't always need a reason. Especially when they feel like they've lost some sense of power or authority, they get it back by lashing out. It's a gimmick for sure. In a way, I respect her more for that. She's so confident, she didn't even feel the need to slap me."

"If you're disappointed, I can take her place. I have a mean right hook."

"I think I'll pass," Jack said, "though at least you wouldn't have nails. Those things leave scars."

As we watched Paulina leave, my cell phone began to vibrate. Jack heard it took, said, "Your lady friend?"

I checked the ID, recognized it as Curt Sheffield.

"Hey Curt," I said. "How's my favorite boy in blue?"

"Been better," he said.

"Dunkin decided to discontinue their donuts?"

"That's a terrible stereotype perpetuated by the media, just like you."

"My bad, man. What's up?"

"It's been a hell of a day," he said. "I'll give you the heads up because I didn't know about Paulina's story until too late...but it's true."

"What's true?" I asked, feeling my heart begin to beat a little faster. It was a strange sensation. The excitement of another thread unspooling mixed with the dread that came with Curt's apprehension.

"Homicide down in Chelsea," Curt said. "Gruesome stuff. I just left the scene, and...it's bad, man. Real bad."

"What happened?"

Jack's composure from talking to Paulina was gone, as he watched the conversation trying to decipher my reaction. I tried to keep a straight face, but when Curt told me the details I felt my whole body drain of blood.

"We got the call about an hour ago," he said, "a tenant on the floor above. A girl comes home to find her husband passed out on the floor. He'd been laid off a month ago, and took every spare cent they had and spent it on drugs. When she found out, she told him she was going to leave him, then divorce him and take all their savings. And that's when he took a knife from the kitchen and sliced her head nearly clean off."

"That's horrible," I said, "who'd you hear this from?"

"The killer himself," Curt said. "The guy confessed to everything, right before his brain nearly switched clean off. He'd spent every cent they had around the house on what he said was some new drug, something called Darkness he said. Said it was the best high he'd ever had, and he wasn't going to give that up for anything, including his bitch of a wife."

"So Paulina's story was true," I said.

"We've had half a dozen calls today, from robbery to assault to this, and all of them have one thing in common: all the perpetrators ingested these little black rocks."

"That'll be all over the news tomorrow," I said. "Not just the Dispatch, but we'll have to cover it too."

"Best publicity you can get," Curt said. "But man, I hope Paulina's wrong about one thing, because if this drug blows up we're gonna have major problems in this city."

"What do you mean?"

"Hell, the NYPD's lost a thousand jobs since last year. The Narcotics division is strapped thin as it is, and our men and women on the street haven't caught a wink of this thing. If the Darkness is being sold, it's not being sold through traditional dealers."

I heard a siren in the distance, and I lost my focus. Then I heard Curt's voice again.

"Henry, Henry you there man?"

"Yeah, sorry Curt. Just thinking about all of this."

"Yeah, us too. But listen, Henry, the main reason I called, I wanted to tell you about one more thing."

"What, this stuff isn't enough? I got enough material here for a week's worth of stories."

"Yeah, well, try this on for size and tell me if you want to drop it. I think I found your man. The blond guy who kidnapped Paulina."

"No shit," I said. "Who is he?"

"I haven't told anyone else yet because, hell, after what you told me and Paulina's story quoting non-existent members of the department, I'm officially a member of the church of paranoia."

"I've belonged there for a while," I said. "So what did you find?"

I heard Curt take a deep breath and say, "You gotta swear to me this doesn't come back with my name on it until you figured out what the hell is going on. Cause this stuff is scaring even me."

"You know you have my word."

"I think you're going to want to sit down for this one."

And when he told me who and what this man was, I felt my knees go weak, Jack came over and we both sat down on a bench in Rockefeller Plaza. I thought I was through with stories like this, stories where the fire was so close it could burn me. I looked at Jack, wondered how many times he'd been through the kind of hell I'd gone through. And knowing it all, feeling the scars beneath my clothing, I knew there was a chance it could get bloody again.

"What is it Henry?" Jack said.

The fact that he didn't call me sport or kiddo or any one of those nicknames scared me even more.

"Curt," I said. "He found our man."

"Who is it?" Jack asked.

"You know how Paulina wrote, in that article, about how close this city was to burning down twenty years ago?"

"Yeah," Jack said, his voice soft, monotone. "I lived through it."

"Well, I think someone's turned the gas tank back on and is getting ready to light this place up all over again."

Chapter 33

Morgan threw open his apartment door, tossed his coat onto a chair and plopped down onto his couch with an audible thump. He could feel his pulse racing as he clenched and unclenched his fists.

He couldn't sit there, not with this kind of energy, this kind of juice flowing through him.

Standing back up, Morgan walked to the refrigerator and to his delight saw that there were two more tall boys resting inside, nice and cold. He popped the top on the first one and guzzled it down in one long messy gulp, then wiped his mouth on his sleeve. He took the second beer back to the couch and sat back down, buzzing, feeling alive for the first time in months.

When he and Theo finally parted ways at five o'clock, Morgan could scarcely believe how the day had unfolded. At first he was unsure about this new opportunity. Sure Morgan had done some blow in his day, never one to throw a good party off its axis. But he never knew just how high the demand was for product right now, and he never realized just how many poor saps there were sitting in their apartments without a job, without hope, all their joy coming in the form of some fine white powder...or a small black rock.

Morgan had no idea what the stuff did beyond what Theo told him. According to his partner, this stuff, the Darkness, was the most potent and addictive substance to hit the populace since opium. It was cheap, it was strong, and it gave you a rush every single time.

Morgan had no desire to try the stuff. Theo didn't seem to care either. When you had a good thing going, like they did, you didn't gum up the works by losing your head.

At the end of their first day on the job, Morgan and Theo had sold nearly ten thousand dollars worth of product.

Over a full year, that amounted to well over three million dollars.

And they were just one team out of god knows how many.

And they were working, according to that Leonard guy, the slow shift. If all his calculations were correct, and this enterprise had as many teams as Morgan supposed they did--then this was a billion dollar industry.

To be a part of something like that, with potential for rapid growth, you didn't take any chances.

It was unbelievable to think that Ken Tsang, who was a relatively smart guy as far as Morgan was concerned, would be stupid enough to rat out his partner. At first, when Morgan found out he was dead, there was a fleeting moment of remorse, of sadness. Now, he thought of Ken Tsang like a homeless person you saw on the street. Nothing more than pity, nothing less than scorn because whatever predicament they were it, it was most certainly of their own doing.

Morgan's tongue tasted nothing, and he laughed, realizing he'd finished his beer several minutes ago.

For the last few months, Morgan Isaacs spent his nights on the couch, sitting alone, tipping back beers and watching basketball games with teams he didn't give a rats ass about. The nights usually did not end until around three o'clock in the morning, when, tired of infomercials and out of snacks, Morgan would pass out on his sofa, covered in a thin blanket, where he would sleep until the sun woke him up mid day.

It was a sad, dreary existence, but Morgan felt to some extent that this was his penance, a punishment for not living up to the promise he'd seen in himself.

How could he be a confident boyfriend--or lover at all--with no income? How could he buy a girl a drink knowing that he was three months behind on his credit card payments? How could he buy his buddies a round when there was a chance the card would be declined?

Not of that existed any more.

Morgan's first paycheck would give him more than financial breathing room. It would give him his life back.

Morgan picked up his cell phone, scrolled through his address book until he found her name. And then Morgan smiled. Svetlana. When in doubt, go with the Russian model.

Svetlana was beautiful and nearly six feet in heels, with jet black hair, legs that were longer than a New York City lamp post, and a body that would make Putin himself kneel and beg for mercy.

She was a tough one, her father was a doctor, and he'd been killed recently or something, and Svetlana refused to ever discuss it. Not that Morgan minded, if anything he preferred that they keep their relationship as uncomplicated as possible.

The sex was freaking mind-blowing, and damned if he didn't miss that the most. And now that he could treat her again like he did in the old days (well, at least he was getting there), he felt that sizzle, that confidence that had been robbed from him all coming back.

He dialed the number and held it to his ear, praying that she wasn't somewhere without service or, god help him, another man. If she was, Morgan might have just had to kill him.

"Who is this?" the female voice said on the other end. It wasn't said with any sort of real curiosity, but with anger because she knew exactly who was calling.

"It's me, babe," Morgan said. "What are you doing right now?"

"What am I doing?" she said. God, he loved that accent. "I am sitting on my ass because my worthless friend Sabina decided to go on a date with some lawyer. So I was about to open a bottle of wine when you called. Why the hell are you calling, Morgan?"

"What are you wearing?" he said.

"What am I wearing? What the hell is wrong with you? Why does that matter?"

"Because I want you to pick out your hottest outfit right this minute, put it on and meet me at the Kitten Club in half an hour."

"And why would I do that?" she asked, her hesitancy melting.

"Because I'm back, sweetheart, and I'm going to get us both wasted and then I'm going to make you thank god you were born a woman."

"Morgan?" she said.

"Yeah?"

"I'll be there in fifteen."

Chapter 34

She didn't remember the drive taking this long. Maybe because last time was of the essence. Or maybe last time there was an excitement about seeing her daughter for the first time in months.

As the yellow lines sped past in a blur, as the trees on I-95 merged into one long emerald line, Paulina thought about those days nearly twenty years ago when she first held Abigail in her arms. She was so tiny, so fragile, and Paulina remembered breast feeding her, thinking that this small person was dependent on her for love, for life. And though she'd never wanted that feeling to die, it had done just that a long time ago.

Paulina had never wanted to be one of those corporate mothers who took a week off for maternity leave, was back in the office like nothing had ever happened while her child was raised and cared for by nannies with calloused hands and heaving bosoms. She never wanted her daughter to grow up hearing somebody else's voice read her bedtime stories, never wanted her daughter to feel the same sense of loneliness that Paulina had as a little girl.

Abby would be her daughter forever, and she would not let her daughter grow up without a true mother.

Of course, life didn't work out that way. As soon as they wanted her to take on bigger stories, she jumped at the chance. Paulina told herself that it was only for a short period of time, that she would make money and make a name for herself so that when she finally stepped back from the job, she would have created a better life for Abigail.

But Paulina never stepped back.

The stories got bigger and bigger, and the chase became intoxicating. And when her name didn't grow at the pace she wanted it to, she left the Gazette and took a job at their rival. And now, finally, after so long in the trenches of this industry, Paulina was a name, a brand, making the kind of money that she always hoped to.

Some people said newspapers were a dying industry, but if you wrote what people wanted to read, they'd never bury you. There was always a medium.

And then one day, Paulina looked back and realized that Abby was gone. A grown woman, a college student, with her own hopes and dreams and desires and loves.

And Paulina had not been there for any of it.

Which is why this drive felt like the longest hours of Paulina's life. Because just as she'd reentered Abby's life the other day, today she was going to pull the shade over a part of Abigail's life that Paulina had been too busy to realize had even felt sunshine.

She arrived at the dorm as the sun was setting, casting a beautiful orange hue over the tree tops and green grass. The red brick of the dorms look radiant in the glow, and for a moment Paulina had to stand and watch them.

Then as shadows began to creep across the grounds, Paulina locked the car door and prepared herself.

She walked up to the front door and dialed Abby's cell. She had no idea what her daughter's schedule was, whether she had evening class, what time she went to dinner, if she had plans to see a movie tonight.

It didn't matter. She'd wait at the door all night if she had to.

Fortunately Abby picked up right away.

"Hello?" she said.

"Hey, Abby, it's your mother."

"Oh, hey mom." Abby laughed and continued, "You know when you said you'd try to call more I didn't think you meant it."

"Oh I meant it," Paulina said. "In fact, would you mind buzzing me in? I'm downstairs."

"You're what?"

"I'm downstairs. In front of your dorm."

"Why are you..."

"Just let me in, it's important."

"Alright, fine, hold on a second."

The buzzer rang, and Paulina entered. She made her way to Abby's dorm room and knocked on the door. Abigail answered, wearing a green tank top and shorts. A bowl of popcorn was on the coffee table and the television was on. The menu of a DVD was on the screen. And sitting on the couch was Pam Ruffalo.

Her brown hair was done up in a ponytail, and she was wearing socks without shoes. Her legs were crossed underneath her on the couch. She munched popcorn, then swallowed it when she saw Paulina standing there.

She coughed out a kernel and said, "Hi Ms. Cole."

Paulina looked at her. Her eyes widened, and she turned to her daughter, pleading.

"We need to talk alone."

"You don't even say hello back, mom?"

"Hi Pam. Can you ask her to give us a few minutes?"

"Why? What the hell is going on now?"

"Please, Abby, don't ask me to..."

"You asked Pam to leave the first time you came here," Abigail said, "and I agreed. I don't answer to you and I never have, so whatever you say to me you can say to her."

"Abby, she really shouldn't..."

"Mom, I love her. She has a right to know whatever you have to say to me."

Paulina stepped back, her breath caught in her throat for a moment. She looked over at Pamela, a massive grin on the young girl's face at that statement. Abby had a look of pride, both at her love for this girl and her confidence in telling her mother off.

"Fine, Abby, if you want to do this by your rules, so be it. But remember I asked for privacy."

"I'll remember to tell that to the judge," Abby said. Pam laughed. Paulina had to struggle not to shoot the girl a dirty look.

And then she looked at her daughter, her young, beautiful vibrant daughter, who might never speak to her again after today.

"I found out more about that...issue I talked to you about the other day."

Abigail placed her hand against the door frame. It was clear she'd tried to put it out of her mind, and from the change in her stance it looked like she'd succeeded until now.

"What did you find out?" Abby asked, almost perfunctorily.

Paulina looked at Pam again, then back at her daughter. "Last chance," she said.

"Spill it mom."

"Ok then. I had some friends look into the photo and the album it came from. Did you know Pam here had a blog?"

Abigail smiled, turned to her girlfriend. "Of course I did. She showed me every posting before it went up."

Pamela blushed and said, "At first I wanted to make sure Abby was ok with it. Then she just trusted me."

"How sweet," Paulina said, her voice emotionless. "Do you know a girl named Samantha Isringhausen?"

Abigail squinted, trying to figure her mother out. "You're talking to me like a reporter," Abigail said. "Asking me all these questions like you're going after a story. 'Do you know this person. Have you heard of such and such.' Be an adult, mom, and tell me what the hell is going on."

"Fine," Paulina said, "but if I'm going to talk to you like an adult, you're going to have to act like one when I'm done."

"I'm sure that won't be a problem."

"Your words," Paulina said. Then she nodded at Pam. "Your girlfriend there sold you out."

"What?" came the confused cry from both girls.

"You heard me," she said.

"Mom, I swear to god, you and me have never really gotten along, but if you ever want to talk to me again you'd better have a damn good explanation for this."

"I do," she said, "and take a second to look at your 'girlfriend.' She doesn't seem that angry."

They both turned to Pamela. the girl's mouth was wide open, but it was more out of protest than surprise. "I don't know what the heck she's talking about," Pam said.

"Samantha Isringhausen," Paulina said, "took those photos at the beach. You then posted the album online. All except for one photo. The photo that man showed me the night he threatened your life and burned me to drive his point home."

"Burned you?" Abigail said. "What are you talking about?"

Paulina lifted her shirt to reveal a deep red burn mark, several inches long. Abigail and Pam both sucked in their breath.

"Mom..." she said.

"That doesn't matter now," Paulina said. "You told me you didn't post that photo, it doesn't go public, and yet somehow Pam ends up with a copy."

"What the hell is she talking about?" Abigail said to Pam.

Pamela stuttered. "Ok, I wanted a copy for myself. So what? You looked gorgeous, Abby. I thought it was kind of romantic."

"And then Sam deleted the memory card, right?" Paulina said.

"I saw her do it," Abigail said. "She had a set of her ex-boyfriend on there and erased the entire memory card."

"So if you two are the only ones who had a copy of the photo," Paulina said, "can you explain to me why a man who threatened my daughter's life had one too?"

Abby stared at Pamela, the girl's mouth flopping open and closed.

"I..." Pamela said.

"Pam," Abigail said, her voice trembling. "Pam, did you do something?"

Tears began to flow down Abigail Cole's cheeks, and Paulina felt her heart ache at the sight of this. She knew exactly how this was going to play out, but there was nothing that could steel her for the sight of her daughter crying.

"How much did he give you?" Paulina said.

"What?" Pam said. Not that she didn't hear, but that she wasn't expecting the question.

"Or did he threaten you too."

"Pam?" Abigail said. "Pam, please tell me..."

Pamela looked at Abigail, then back at Paulina. She composed herself, uncrossed her legs and set them on the floor.

"He came up to me one day, after Econ," Pam said, her eyes on Abigail. "At first he was really nice and kind, saying he was a friend of your mom's. Then he told me he wanted a picture of you. A picture nobody else had. Something private that when Abby saw it, she'd be scared. He told me with a private photo, you'd both know how serious he was. I still don't know how he knew we were together..."

"Your blog," Paulina said. "He knew he could get to me through Abigail, and he could get to Abigail through you. You made it all public for him. You made it easy."

"He offered me ten thousand dollars!" Pamela screamed. "I'm on financial aid. I'm going to have six figures in debt by the time I leave this stupid place. He told me he was going to give it to you as a present. I thought, I don't know, that he was your boyfriend or something."

"Are you stupid," Abigail said, wiping at her nose, "or just ignorant?"

Pam stared daggers at her, then softened. "I never thought it would hurt you."

"You didn't think about her," Paulina said. "Only you and that money. So don't give us the 'I never thought it would hurt you' bull. You just pocketed the dough and crossed your fingers."

"Pam?" Abigail said. Her face was a wreck, tears flowing down in rivulets, eyes red and devastated. Paulina closed her eyes for a moment, and hated herself for what she'd done.

"What Abby?"

"Pam, did you...did you give him that picture?"

"Abby, please, I..."

Abigail screamed, "Did you give him that picture or not?"

Pam looked at her girlfriend, nodded once, and that was all she had to do.

"I want you to leave," Abigail said, looking at Pam.

"Pam, I..."

"Right now. Or I call the cops."

Pam began to sob too, but surprisingly Abigail's tears had stopped running.

"I love you," Pam said.

"No you don't," came Abigail's reply. "Just leave."

Pam stood up. Before leaving, she stared down Paulina who returned the gaze.

"Don't you even think about staring me down you little bitch. You do this to my family and you want to hate me? Get the hell away from here and don't ever speak to Abigail again."

Pam looked like she'd been slapped. Before she left, she took out her cell phone and turned back to Paulina.

"What's your phone number?" she said.

"What the hell are you talking about?"

"I need your cell phone number."

"I'm not giving you any..."

"I took a picture of him. With my phone camera. When he was walking away, I took a picture of him. I don't know why I did it, maybe I wanted to remember what he looked like. I just wanted to send it to you. Maybe it'll help you find him."

Paulina's anger multiplied, and every part of her wanted to

curse this girl out and tell her to leave. But that photo could come in handy. So she gave Pamela the number.

The girl plugged it in to her cell phone, and a moment later Paulina's phone chirped. She opened the message, and found a grainy photo on the screen.

It was him. No doubt about it. Paulina shivered, remembering the man's face as he tore the picture of Abby to shreds, threatening to end her daughter's life as easily as he defaced her image.

The picture was a profile of the man, from his left side. She recognized the wavy blond hair, the eyes. She had to give Pam a little credit for being smart enough to take it, but it was far too little and way too late.

"Now go," Abigail said. So Pam turned and left.

"Baby, I'm so sorry," Paulina said. "I know this must have been hard for you, but I'm going to get this guy."

"I want you to leave too."

Paulina stood there for a moment. stunned.

"What did you say?'

"You heard me mom. I want you to leave too. And I don't want to speak to you again. Not for a long time."

"Abby, baby, I came here to help you. You needed to know the truth."

"And now I do. So you can leave."

Abigail went to the small fridge/microwave combination and pulled a beer out. She twisted the cap, grimacing as the top dug into her palm.

"This was for your own good. I'm just trying to help. Abby, please, let me stay."

"You did what you came here to do. I bet when all this is over you'll have a hell of a story, and I can tell all my friends what a great reporter my mom is. But I don't want to see you right now. So please, please leave. Don't make me ask again. I don't want to cry any more."

Paulina felt her face grow hot, her eyes beginning to water as she stared at her daughter, hating every word she'd said but deep down, in some way, understanding it too. She knew the night would come to this, that these revelations would destroy her daughter's relationship. It had to be done, Paulina knew, and she'd have to deal with being the messenger.

She would take the misplaced anger, and she would let her daughter cool down over time even though it would kill her every second she thought about what might have happened.

And that, Paulina thought, walking out the door, dabbing at her eyes with a tailored sleeve, was what she supposed being a mother was all about.

Chapter 35

"Major Chester A. Malloy," Jack said. He was holding in his hand a printout of all the information we could find regarding Malloy. And it didn't make us feel any better.

Jack's eyes were wide as he read, scanning the print. I wondered if he was as nervous as I was.

"According to his file," Jack said, "Chester A. Malloy was a member of the Special Operations Task Force assembled in 1989 to overthrow Manuel Noriega's control of Panama. Along with ten other members of his unit, Operational Detachment Bravo, Major Malloy encountered a brigade of the Panama Defense Force, where several members of their squad were killed. The rest of the squad was returned to the U.S. after Noriega's capture, and that's where the trail ends."

"So what the hell is a goddamn Special Forces major doing kidnapping New York journalists for?" I said.

"Look at this," Jack said. We huddled over his computer, where nearly a dozen internet searches were pulled up. Jack pointed to one, a photograph of eleven young men and women, identified in a military photo as the Bravo unit. I read the names.

Franklin K. Loughlin.
Andros I. Browning.
Roy Winnick.
Eve S. Ramos.
Chester A. Malloy.
Rex M. Malloy.
Wendy C. DiBonaventura.
Harrison L. Daughterty.
Shonda P. Williamson.
Emmett R. Douglas.
Bill E. Hollinsworth.

Chester A. Malloy, along with the rest of his team, was wearing his Special Forces uniform. Green sport jacket over white shirt. Black tie. Nameplate on the right of his chest. All the uniforms were decorated with various medals and pins, and they all wore their Green Beret caps raised to the left, the signature of their division of the Special Forces.

Standing to the left of Chester Malloy was a man named Rex Malloy. According to the documents, Rex Malloy was Chester's younger brother by three years. They were both members of Special Forces, both Green Berets.

And both had looks on their faces as serious and deadly as a man who threatens to kill a teenage girl.

I pointed at Chester Malloy.

"Nice and blond" I said. "That's our man."

"Hey Mr. cottontail," Jack said, smiling.

Just then I felt my cell phone vibrate in my pocket. I pulled it out, saw I had a new message. Not a voicemail, but a text message. It was from Paulina, and it contained an attachment.

I opened the note. It said:

Taken one month ago by Pam Ruffalo. This is our guy.

"I'll be a monkey's uncle," Jack said.

"Wow. I haven't heard anyone say that since the sixties."

"Oldie but a goodie."

"That one either. Hold on, I'll enlarge it."

I plugged the phone into my computer and waited for the image to download. When it finished, I opened it up and enlarged the shot.

It was a grainy image, taken with some sort of low-res camera or cell phone. The man could be seen from his left side. Only the left side of his body and face were visible. What was visible, though, was that shock of wavy blond hair.

"Holy crap," Jack said, "look at this."

He pointed to the photo of Chester Malloy in the army photograph.

"That's not the same guy as in this photo," Jack said. "Look at his ear."

"I don't see it," I said. "What, is there an old earring hole or something?"

"Didn't you ever wrestle?" Jack said.

"Uh, no. I watched a little WWF when I was growing up."

"That's as close to real wrestling as Harvey Hillerman's hair plugs are to the real deal. No, look closely at Chester Malloy's ear in the earlier photo, and then compare it to the ear in this new one."

I did, and while I couldn't be sure, it looked like the ear in the recent shot was slightly puffy, slightly deformed.

"That's called cauliflower ear," Jack said. "Wrestlers get it all the time. It's when fluid collects in the ear, causing the cartilage to die and harden. The result ain't pretty, but it's kind of a badge of honor for a lot of wrestlers. Unless you treat it right away, drain the fluid, it's not going away. Chester Malloy doesn't have cauliflower ear in this new photo. But look who does in the earlier one."

I stared intently at the military shot, and clear as day was the left ear of Rex Malloy. It was deformed, puffy, just like the ear in the later shot.

"This means that the person in this recent photo wasn't Chester Malloy," Jack said, "but his brother Rex. My guess is Rex was a wrestler before joining the army, and he had the bad ear when this photo was taken."

"And notice something else?" I said.

"And look at Chester's hair in this photo" Jack replied. "It's not blond."

"That'd be a fine shade of black," I said. "And it's straight, not wavy at all."

"That means that it wasn't Chester Malloy who kidnapped Paulina," Jack said. "It was Rex, all dolled up to look like his brother."

"So if that's Rex Malloy in the picture, and it was Rex who took Paulina, where is Chester Malloy?"

"That's the million dollar question, sport."

"So we're back to this again," I said.

"Until further notice," Jack replied. "So Rex Malloy grew out his hair, dyed it blond, gave himself a nice perm and is now going by his brother's name."

"Come on, who doesn't do that?"

"I have a brother. Name is Roy. Man's got a head balder than an eight ball and smells worse than Oscar the Grouch. If I ever dressed like him, you'd have permission to throw me off the nearest suspension bridge."

"That would make sense. Paulina told me the man who kidnapped her insinuated that he'd lost someone. Maybe he was referring to his brother," I said. "It looks like he's purposefully dressing just like his brother, Chester. And if the guy in Paulina's photo isn't Chester, but Rex, why call himself Chester? Why not make up some other completely random alias?"

"Some sort of psychotic tribute perhaps," Jack said. "Now look at the rest of this squad. Eleven men and women. The Department of Justice should have records on the rest of them. We need to know where the rest of this squad is, and get any more information about Malloy that we can. Maybe somebody who knew him can explain why a Green Beret seems to be armpit deep in some new drug epidemic."

"Noriega was a massive drug trafficker," I said. "If this Bravo squad was flown in to help depose Noriega, they obviously had some part to play in the Panama drug war."

"Maybe," Jack said. "But the question remains: whose side were they on?"

We split up the list, Jack taking five names and myself taking six. Our job was to track down the remaining members of Rex Malloy's Detachment Bravo team and contact them to find out whatever information we could about the family Malloy.

The DOJ had every member of the squad on file, but to my surprise only three of my six were still alive.

And one of those was not Chester Malloy.

The surviving members on my list were Rex Malloy, Eve Ramos and Frank Loughlin. There were no records of employment or housing for either Ramos or Loughlin, and according to the DOJ, Frank Loughlin was serving twenty years for the murder of a homeless man on the streets of Atlanta.

Researching the newspaper records, Loughlin had pled insanity, his lawyer making the case that Loughlin still suffered from Post Traumatic Stress Disorder from his time in the military, and that his client was better served under psychiatric supervision than under our federal prison system.

Loughlin has been returning home from a movie when a homeless man approached him on the street. After asking for change and being denied, the man placed his hand on Loughlin's shoulder. The ex-Special Forces agent then threw the man to the ground and pressed his boot against the man's neck until his larynx was crushed under the force.

Police testified that when they arrived on the scene, Loughlin was sitting on the curb by the body, crying.

Nevertheless, the judge disagreed that Frank was missing his marbles, and now the man who once fought for the United States was rotting in one of its very own jail cells.

Not the kind of irony that brings a smile to your face.

Seeing as how Frank Loughlin couldn't be involved in this unless he somehow gained the ability to walk through walls, cross state borders and look like one of his former squadmates (a possibility considering the amount of drastic plastic surgery you see in New York), I went to find Jack to see if he had any more luck.

I found him at his desk, on the phone, writing on a notepad.

He didn't pay me any attention, just kept nodding as though the person on the other line could be persuaded by his nonverbal approval. I took that moment to glance around Jack's desk.

He'd been back for such a short amount of time, and since then he'd done nothing to make his desk more personal, nothing to show that a human being actually worked, breathed and dwelled there.

I wasn't the most sensitive guy in the world and I had no need to plaster my workspace with pictures of every living relative, every birthday party and a child from every conceivable camera angle, but you could walk by my desk and know that somebody took the time to make it more habitable.

There was a photo of Amanda and I taken a few years ago at a concert at Jones Beach. I had a clipping of the first article I ever published in the Gazette, and the first piece I ever published in the Bend Bulletin from back in the day when I was cutting my teeth.

Those articles were steps to me. Chapters in a life and career. I wasn't sure what the next clipping would be. I supposed I would only know when, well, I knew.

Finally Jack hung up the phone and turned to me.

"Whaddaya got?"

"Very little," I said. "Three of my six are still alive. One of them is in prison, one has no records of pretty much anything, and Rex Malloy hasn't been heard from in almost fifteen years. The kicker, though, is that Chester Malloy is dead."

"I had a feeling," Jack said.

"Turns out the older brother was killed in action in Panama. He was in a transport vehicle with his brother Rex, Eve Ramos and William Hollinsworth when they made a wrong turn and ended up on a street not far from Noriega's headquarters. They were approached by members of the PDF who tried to detain them, but when the squad resisted they opened fire. As far as I can tell Chester Malloy was the only casualty, but according to news reports all four members of the team were seriously injured."

Jack stroked his beard, thinking. Either that or he was ignoring me. But since I doubted that, he just continued to stroke his beard.

"That give you good luck?" I asked.

"Been doing this my whole adult life. So depending on your perspective, probably not."

"What did you find out?"

"Well not as much as you, but between the two of us I think we know exactly where to go."

"What did you find?"

"Of my five squad members, four are dead. The only living Bravo Detachment member is Bill Hollinsworth. Hollinsworth was deployed as a Special Reconnaissance officer, his job was to gather intelligence on the enemy and their tactics.

"This is the guy who was in the car with the Malloys when they came under fire."

"Exactly right. And get this: Hollinsworth is a professor of American History, post World War II at Columbia."

"What you learn in war you teach to future generations," I said.

"If he was in Panama, he probably knows Rex Malloy. I called over there, Hollinsworth has office hours today until six."

"We should meet with him right away," I said.

"No worries, Henry. I already called the History Department and they said he never leaves until six on the dot. And apparently he's not the easiest guy to get along with, because the lady who answered the phone seemed rather shocked that we wanted to meet with him. She said students steer clear of Hollinsworth like you do from matching clothes."

"Or you from denture cream," I said.

"Go screw yourself," Jack said. "Come on, let's see why this guy's friend is poisoning our city."

Chapter 36

As soon as Morgan Isaacs got off the subway to head home, his cell phone rang. He didn't recognize the number, but picked it up anyway, figuring after all the money he and Theo made that day everything in his life was taking a turn for the better.

He couldn't believe how well this new drug, these small black rocks called the Darkness were selling. It seemed every customers had either bought recently and needed a refill, or heard about it from a friend and wanted a go. It thrilled Morgan to no end that he was carrying a product that was so desired. It made him feel powerful, again, for the first time since everything was snatched from him so unfairly.

To Morgan, he wouldn't trade that feeling away for anything. And he would do anything to make sure it never left him.

The sun was beginning to descend, and the Manhattan skyline looked a gorgeous dark blue in the evening sky. For months, Morgan wondered how long he would be able to look at that view, if his lack of employment would force him to relocate, take some job outside the city where he'd be a nobody, a nothing, working for a company that the Wall Street Journal barely knew existed, a company whose CEO wore a cowboy hat rather than a three piece suit. Where the offices were decorated with shag carpeting and the secretaries were all fifty and overweight.

That was a world Morgan refused to live in.

So he took in the crisp air, and remembered why he fell in love with this city in the first place. And he thanked his benefactors for giving him the chance to stay.

"Hello?" he said.

"Morgan, it's Chester."

"Oh, hey, what's up?"

"Just wanted to let you know I talked to Leonard, and he told me you and Goggins cleared almost twenty grand today. That's quite a haul."

Morgan smiled. He was well aware of how much money they

were bringing in, but he'd learned one thing in business and that was never to brag to your boss about how well you were doing. At the end of the month, when all the receipts were tallied up, you'd get all the praise you needed. Braggarts were so nineties.

So to hear this from Chester during his first week of work, to Morgan that was all the praise he'd need for a month.

"I know you haven't received a paycheck yet," Chester said, "but you deserve a bonus."

Morgan's jaw dropped. He stopped walking and leaned up against a mailbox. Then he had to move when a man asked him to move so he could deposit a letter.

"I...I don't know what to say...thanks, I guess."

"You've earned it," Chester said. "But you will need to do one thing for me."

"Anything."

"I'm glad to hear that. And if you do this for me, you'll get a hundred grand on the spot. I'll need you to sign one piece of paper, for tax purposes, but you'll have six figures to play with by the time you're hungry for dinner tonight."

"You're kidding me, right?"

"Yes, I'm kidding you. In fact, we never want to see you again. Goodbye Morgan."

"Wait! I was kidding too!"

"I know, stupid. Be on the corner of thirteenth and avenue A in half an hour."

"I'll be there."

"One more thing, Morgan."

"What's up?"

"Do you like the suit you're wearing?"

"I guess so. It was one of the first ones I bought when I got my job in banking."

"Too bad. Because you're never going to wear it again after today."

Chapter 37

"Beautiful, isn't it?" Jack said. He was staring out the window of our cab as we sped uptown to meet William Hollinsworth.

Rather than responding, I studied Jack's face. For some reason it made me think about his clean desk, how for some reason there was something holding him back from returning fully to a normal life.

We'd never had a chance to have a real talk about Paulina's article and what it had done to him, and it was probably for the better. When a man's reputation, and maybe his soul, is nearly destroyed, the last thing he wants to do is revisit it. But it was clear that Jack hadn't quite gotten past it, that he was still between two worlds.

The wistful look on his face confirmed my thoughts. It was not the look of a face simply admiring the beauty of a city, but the look of a man who wasn't sure if he'd ever see these sights again.

Sixth Avenue was crowded, full of taxis, livery cabs and black company cars carrying executives and blue collar workers alike home from a long day's work. Traffic in the city had actually gotten better over the last few months, but it was a wolf wrapped in sheep's clothing.

The decrease in traffic was primarily due to a cutback in both taxis and hired car services, but also a massive drop in truck deliveries that ordinarily clogged up New York's arteries during the early morning. With so many stores and restaurants closing due to massive revenue drops, there was natural belt tightening in the quantity and frequency of transports it took to ship in new supplies.

Nevertheless, traveling through the city during the seemingly endless rush hour times was still a harrowing proposition, and the fact that it took forty five minutes rather than an hour to go from midtown to upper Manhattan was a small victory at best.

We eked past taxis crawling slower than they needed to, trying to squeeze out a few extra pennies from their charges. Businessmen who would normally be glued to their Blackberries in the backseat, blissfully unaware of this common practice, now stared at the rising fare ready to berate the driver for taking his sweet time.

Prior to leaving, I left Curt Sheffield a message filling him in on where we were headed. He needed to know what was going on. Like Paulina said I didn't know who to trust, but I wanted to leave a trail just in case. I could trust Curt to follow it if something bad happened.

We merged onto Central Park West, and several minutes later arrived at the Columbia campus. Jack paid the driver and tucked the receipt into his wallet. We got out, checking our pockets to make sure all our belongings had arrived with us.

A few months back, I'd forgotten my wallet in a taxi, and was dismayed to think I'd have to spend the whole day on line at the DMV while explaining the situation to my credit card companies and, worst of all, Wallace Langston, who would need to order me a new corporate card. Yet just half an hour after realizing the gaffe, I received an email from a Mr. Alex Kolodej, the kindly driver who'd found my wallet in the back seat of his cab, put two and two together between my driver's license and business card, and even drove by my office to drop the wallet off.

He refused any sort of reward, and drove off with the plain smile of a good samaritan.

Amanda, on the other hand, had forgotten her purse at a bar just a few weeks ago, and returned home later that night to find no less than twenty five hundred dollars in charges racked up. Ironically they were not at jewelry or electronic stores, the bastion of people looking to make a quick splurge with a stolen card, but rather from places like Home Depot and Ace Hardware. A sign that whoever had taken her bag was way behind on their home renovations.

A small thing perhaps, but I considered it a sign of the times. For years, after the mayor and cops had cleaned the city up, New York was known as one of the safest big cities in the world. Like any city, of course you needed a modicum of common sense, the knowledge that despite this change if you wandered into the wrong neighborhood at the wrong time you were playing Russian Roulette.

But now, New York didn't feel quite as safe. There was a constant tension, a thickness in the air, that something combustible could ignite at any moment. There were too many people out of work, too many people unable to afford their homes, too many businesses hanging on for dear life.

And when a city is being stretched like a piece of taffy, just the slightest bit of tension will cause it to snap.

The Columbia University department of history was located in a building called Fayerweather hall. It looked like a building transported from Victorian England, red brick and laced with intricate scrollwork. It felt as out of place in Manhattan as I did several years ago.

We entered the building and the receptionist, a middle-aged women whose nameplate read Carolyn, directed us to William Hollinsworth's office on the first floor. The door to William Hollinsworth's office was wide open. I entered first, Jack following me.

Hollinsworth was about forty years old, with a severe crew cut and intense green eyes. His hair was specked with gray, and he wore a pair of square-rimmed reading glasses that sat on the tip of his nose. He wore a well cut gray suit jacket that did little to hide the taut frame underneath.

I'd met many athletes, cops and military personnel over the years, and they fell into one of two categories. Either they continued their fitness routines to a 'T' after leaving their vocation, or let themselves go entirely. Bill Hollinsworth clearly had not let his post military career become a detriment to his fitness.

"Professor Hollinsworth?" I said.

He stood up, removed his glasses.

Hollinsworth was not a tall man, maybe five ten or eleven, but he stood up straight as an arrow and held his shoulders back like he was expecting a salute.

"You must be Parker," he said. Jack had followed behind me, and peeked his head out. "And Jack O'Donnell."

"It's a pleasure, sir." Jack extended his hand. Hollinsworth took it, shook it, then motioned for us to sit down. Jack took his seat, and I noticed him rubbing his hand and grimacing.

I closed the door to the professor's office, took a seat as well, and glanced around the room.

The former Special Forces officer kept his office as clean and free from excess debris as he kept his body. The bookshelves were all neatly aligned, every paper neatly arranged. Even his in and outboxes, which were full, somehow managed to be perfect examples of immaculate care. There were no picture frames, no trinkets, no souvenirs, posters, awards or plaques. Nothing that led you to believe that William Hollinsworth had anything in his life but his work.

If the sign of a sick mind was a clean desk, then William Hollinsworth was Hannibal Lecter.

The professor sat back down, folded his hands and crossed his legs.

"Mr. Parker. Mr. O'Donnell. What can I do for you sirs?"

"Professor Hollinsworth," I said.

"Bill," he said with a smile. "I ask my students to call me Professor Hollinsworth, so unless you've just applied here to be an undergraduate I don't expect the same formalities from you, Mr. Parker."

"Alright then, Bill, as we told your secretary we're here from the New York Gazette."

"Carolyn did mention that to me, yes. What can I do for you?"

"Twenty years ago, you were a member of a Special Forces unit in Panama. Is that correct?"

Hollinsworth shifted in his chair. He clearly wasn't expecting this line of questioning.

"That's right," he said. "I was there for a little over a year."

"You were with Operational Detachment Bravo, along with ten other men and women. Correct?"

"That's correct," he said, a hint of agitation dipping into his voice. "Did you just come here to confirm things we both already know?"

"Sorry to waste your time," I said, "but Mr. O'Donnell and I did some background research on you and your squad before we came here. But we both know that what you read in the newspapers and what you experience in actual life can differ greatly."

"That's true. Fair enough."

"According to military records, you and three other members of your squad were attacked by members of Manuel Noriega's military deployment, the PDF, on January 6th 1990. Is that right?"

Hollinsworth's eyes narrowed. He was no longer shifting but staring straight at me. I couldn't tell if he was angry that I was dredging up old memories, glad that his near-death experience was still a topic of discussion, or furious to the point where he might rip my head off with his bare hands.

"That's right."

"One man was killed that day. Chester Malloy." Hollinsworth nodded slowly, as his eyes softened.

"Were you close with officer Malloy?" Jack said suddenly. I turned to face him, but he was looking at Hollinsworth.

"I was," the man said. "Our whole unit, Bravo, we trained together, fought together. I would have died for any one of them. And I wish I had been able to. But..." then Hollinsworth trailed off.

"But what?" Jack said.

"I have no problem giving my life for my country, or for one of my countrymen. But that day, we shouldn't have been a position for anyone to lose their life."

"Why not?" Jack said.

"We knew not to mess around with the PDF," Hollinsworth said. "A few weeks earlier, Second Lieutenant Robert Paz was coming out of a restaurant in Panama City. He came across a PDF squad. He was alone. Now, any smart man or woman would have had the common sense to know when the right time is to fight, and that was most certainly the wrong time. We never got an official number, but civilian reports said that Lieutenant Paz was outnumbered at least eight to one."

"He decided to fight," I said.

"Not fight," Hollinsworth said. "See Paz was a member of a special unit nicknamed the 'Hard Chargers.' Their job was to actively provoke the PDF, to incite them either to violence against American troops or Panamanian civilians."

"Why would they do that?" I asked.

"Because until then, we had no reason to go after Noriega. Nothing official, anyway. Lots of innuendo, and we knew for certain he was trafficking in enough drugs to fill the Grand Canyon fifty times over. But you can't overthrow every dictator that's dabbling in illegal goods. If that was the case we'd be at war with half the known world. No, we needed something more tangible. Something we could sell to citizens back home."

"That's where Paz came in."

Hollinsworth nodded slowly.

"It wasn't supposed to go like that, though. Hard Chargers were never supposed to travel alone. Paz just happened to be in the wrong place at the wrong time, and they recognized him."

"So they killed him," I said.

"Not immediately. Paz quickly realized that things were going to get out of hand, so he tried to run. But because the PDF had set up a legitimate roadblock, they felt they were justified in killing him. That's the way Noriega spun it. Have you heard of Franz Ferdinand?"

"Of course," Jack said. "His assassination in Sarajevo was the primary catalyst for World War I."

"That's right. Well, Robert Paz was our Archduke Ferdinand. Until December 16th, 1989, no members of the United States military had been killed by Panamanian forces. When Lieutenant Paz was killed, suddenly we had all the cause in the world. And on December 20th, the floodgates opened. We went into Panama with a vengeance, and we took Noriega out of power and that bastard has been rotting in prison ever since."

"So how does this all play into Chester Malloy getting killed?"

Hollinsworth said, "Why are you so interested in this? All of this happened almost twenty years ago and suddenly you want to know about it? I'm not buying it. What else are you looking for, Mr. Parker?"

I looked at Jack. He said to Hollinsworth, "We finish our interview, you can start interviewing us."

He pursed his lips, said, "Fair enough."

Chapter 38

Morgan couldn't believe how fast his heart was pounding. Even when he used to snort a few lines at a club then dance until his blood felt like lava, he couldn't remember ever feeling quite like this. Those nights when he was high, there was always a sense of floating above the world, that the Morgan who was doing those things, saying those things, would wake up the next morning a different person.

The world didn't really count when you were out of it. Everything you did could be explained. This, though, there was no explaining it. No justifying it. If he accepted what was being proposed right now, he would wake up tomorrow the same Morgan Isaacs, remembering every detail and never be able to wash it away.

Which is, perhaps, to his great surprise, the reason he didn't feel the slightest hesitation.

The gun was heavier than he expected it to be. You always saw movies where guys swung guns around like they were made of tissue paper, aiming them sideways and backwards and doing cool tricks. Not this gun, though. He held it in his hand, and it felt just fine.

"This is a Glock 36, .45 caliber handgun," Chester said. He was looking at Morgan with dead seriousness in his face. Chester had been nice to him during the short time he'd known the man. A good conversationalist, even jokey at times, but right now Morgan got the feeling that if he even cracked a smile Chester would throw him out of the car.

They were driving uptown, passing by the glistening Time Warner center, the natural beauty of Central Park on the right as they drove up Central Park West. Morgan never spent a whole lot of time in the Park, or in any sort of nature. When he wasn't behind a desk, he was at home with a beer or at a club throwing back martinis like they were iced tea. At first the idea of traveling all over the city to hawk his wares worried him. What if he didn't like it? What if he couldn't take all the time on the subway, didn't want to deal with the asshole who often paid with crinkled twenties and smelled like dirty socks?

But when that money started rolling in, when he saw the smile on Chester's face, Morgan knew he could hack it, and hack it quite easily.

"You sure you can do this," Chester said. His eyes betrayed no sympathy; he was simply making sure that Morgan was up to the task.

"Yes," he said emphatically. "I am."

"Well alright then. Once we pull up to the building, the office is number A17. You're going to walk straight past the receptionist. If she gives you a hard time, just tell her you're going to the bathroom. Her name is Carolyn. Don't look at her, just walk right past and say, 'Just going to the bathroom Carolyn, thanks.'"

"Got it."

"Once you enter the hallway past her desk, make a quick left, and it's the third office on your right. You know who your target is."

"I do. Why..."

"No whys," Chester said. "Once it's done, you run as fast as you can back here. The car will be idling in front of the entrance. The door will be open. You just climb in, hand me the gun, and we're gone. The gun will be disposed of before the police arrive on the scene. And we want you to wear this," he said.

Chester handed Morgan a baseball cap, underneath which and sewn in to the cap was a blond wig. Morgan put it on his head, and Chester adjusted it so that none of Morgan's black hair could be seen.

"Anything to throw them off a little bit. Carolyn will be the only witness, and she's an old lady. They'll be looking for a young blond guy wearing a baseball cap."

"Ok."

"We'll drop you off near the subway after we ditch the car. Call your girlfriend. Have her come over, get her good and drunk and screw the shit out of her. She'll be another layer of protection, so to speak. Then wake up tomorrow, come to work and act like this never happened."

Chester handed Morgan a folded piece of paper. The young man opened it. It was a money order for $50,000, made out to him.

"Just in case anyone asks, you've been doing some contracting work on the side," he said with a grin. "You'll get the second half once it's done. And Morgan?"

"Yeah?"

"Make sure nobody asks."

Morgan nodded, then folded the slip back up and slipped it into the inside of his coat pocket. It felt good to have it there, and it would feel even better tomorrow when he deposited a hundred thousand dollars into his bank account.

Those debts, the ones that had nearly crippled him for so long, would be wiped clean by the end of the month.

"You ready?" Chester said.

"Ready?" Morgan said with a smile. "I'm bored. Let's do this."

Chapter 39

"Go on," I said.

"Our troops invaded Panama because of Paz's death, but because he ran from a PDF blockade the Panamanian government claimed they did nothing wrong. So folks back home in the States began to feel the same way, especially when more people started dying on both sides of the conflict. Two weeks after Paz's death, a marine unit was supposed to infiltrate a Noriega drug lab, but instead they found themselves trapped in an alleyway where they were ambushed by the PDF. They all managed to get out alive, but there were some on our side that wondered if they were given the wrong directions on purpose."

I said, "That they were led into a trap in the hopes they'd be killed to strengthen the cause for the invasion."

"Exactly," Hollinsworth said. "Nobody knew for sure."

"That day in January," Jack said. "When your squad was attacked...the same thing happened, didn't it?"

I could see Hollinsworth struggling to remain passive, remain calm, but there was something behind those eyes that he was unable to hide. It wasn't grief or sadness, it was rage.

"I know we were set up," Hollinsworth said. "We were scheduled to join up with a Ranger regiment. I was given directions, instructions on when and where we'd meet. But by the time we got there, it was just us and the armed guard. By the time the survivors got back to the base, Chester was dead. And the Rangers had no idea what the hell I was talking about. The military discharged me a month after that, and I went back to school to get my masters degree. I never saw anyone else from our squad again."

"So Chester Malloy was killed that day," Jack said, "but Rex Malloy and Eve Ramos lived."

"Rex, Chester and Eve were close," Hollinsworth continued. "The whole squad was like a family, but those three were the tightest. When Chester died, it hit Rex and Eve hard. Some of us thought Chester and Eve might have been seeing each other behind closed doors, but we never knew for sure."

I felt something then, a twinge, a faint bell going off. I decided to go after it. I had a feeling we were close to the truth.

I pulled my cell phone from my pocket, searched through my email inbox and found the message. Clicking on it, I opened the attachment. When it finished loading, I handed it to Williams Hollinsworth.

"Do you recognize that person?" I said.

Hollinsworth squinted, adjusting his glasses to view the grainy shot better.

"It's hard to tell, with the angle and the picture quality being, well, substandard. But if I had to guess...no....it couldn't be." He looked at me. "Chester Malloy?"

"Close," I said. "You knew both Malloy brothers. Look at the ear."

Hollinsworth took another glance, then nodded. "I remember Rex's ear. We used to call him Potato Head because his ear looked like a mashed potato. But everything else is wrong. The hair. Rex's hair wasn't blond."

"You're right there," I said. "Rex's wasn't. Chester's was. Rex Malloy is alive, and he's taken on his brother's look, his dress, even coloring and styling his hair like Chester used to."

"Ok," the professor said, "so you say. But so what? I haven't seen Rex Malloy in almost twenty years."

"About a week ago," Jack said, "Rex Malloy kidnapped a woman and threatened to kill her daughter."

Hollinsworth's head snapped up, his eyes wide open.

"He did what?"

"You heard me," Jack said.

"Jesus, how do you know this?"

"Because the girl who took that photo was paid ten thousand dollars by Malloy to help him."

"I don't understand," Hollinsworth said. "Why would he do such a terrible thing?"

"The woman he kidnapped was a reporter," I said. "Like us. He blackmailed her into writing an article for her newspaper."

"I don't read the papers," he said.

"So I gather. I just happened to bring a copy with me."

I took out the copy of the New York Gazette with Paulina's

article and slid it across the table to Hollinsworth. He picked it up.

And as soon as he read the headline, I knew the whole story was about to unravel.

"That's...that's impossible," he said.

Hollinsworth ripped open the paper to Paulina's story and read the entire piece. We sat there, watching his face, studying it, transfixed by the multitude of emotions that ran through it.

When he finished, the professor dropped the paper to the floor. The man's shoulders were slumped, his eyes nearly closed. He stared at the floor.

Then finally he said, his voice barely above a whisper, "I never thought they'd do it."

"Do what?" I said.

"Darkness...Ramos...Rex and Eve were always talking about some new drug Noriega's people were developing, something that if synthesized properly would be twice as potent but half the cost. But the way they were talking about it...it wasn't kosher. I always got the feeling that if we didn't keep tabs on them they could..."

Then, before William Hollinsworth could say nother word, the door to his office banged open. Standing in the doorway was a young man wearing a suit along with a baseball cap. His hair was blond, but I noticed a tuft of black hair beneath it. He was wearing a wig.

And I knew what he was going to do even before he pulled the gun out.

Suddenly the world became a blur, and before I could get out of my seat the young man was holding a small, black gun and pointing it at William Hollinsworth.

The professor's eyes went wide and I heard him scream No!

Then there were three deafening blasts, and three gouts of blood erupted from the former special forces agent's chest.

I couldn't breathe, couldn't think, watching helplessly as Hollinsworth toppled backwards in his chair, a horrific spray of blood covering the back wall of his office, decorating the space with grisly red where the professor himself had declined to hang any decorations.

The shooter's eyes met mine, and to my surprise there was not anger or malice in them, but pure and simple fear.

His head shook as our eyes met, and suddenly he turned and ran away.

"Jack, call 911!" I shouted, jumping from my seat and racing into the hallway.

Peeking out from the doorway to make sure there wasn't a muzzle waiting for me, I saw the coattail of the man rounding the corner and heading for the lobby.

I ran after him, screaming and shouting echoing in the halls behind me. I couldn't sense anything else, my world narrowed to a tunnel.

Turning the corner at the end of the hall, I heard some sort of commotion and a loud crash. Again I leaned out from the corner, only to see that the shooter had tripped over Carolyn's desk and was gathering himself up.

Carolyn was screaming, holding her head in her hands and she stared at the man with terror etched on her face.

Then I saw it. The gun. It had fallen from his grasp and was sitting mere feet away.

I had one chance.

Without thinking, I sprinted forward and threw my weight into the man's back.

I heard a humph as his breath was driven from his, as we both fell forward onto the ugly brown carpeting.

The man swung his elbow around at my head, but I was able to duck it. As he did so, the ball cap and wig fell off, revealing the man's hair and face.

His hair was short, black, and he was breathing heavy, sweating. One thing was for sure, that this man was far from any sort of professional.

The suit. Something snapped together in my mind, and I knew why this man was here.

Then I heard him pleading with me.

"Let me go! Please!"

What kind of killer said 'please'?

I held on tighter, tried to get a better grip to immobilize the man. I needed to hold him down long enough for someone to help me incapacitate him until the cops arrived.

"Get off him!" I heard somebody scream. I turned around slightly to see Carolyn hovering over us holding her desk lamp. It was a big thing, brass colored, metal and a foot and a half long. We both looked, and then she swung the pole at us.

Then I felt a massive crunch on the back of my neck, and for a moment the world went black. I could feel the man getting out from under me, so I blindly grabbed at him. I managed to catch my fingers inside some sort of pocket, which tore away as he escaped.

When the darkness cleared, I looked up to see Carolyn standing over me. Her hand was covering her mouth as she stammered.

"Oh my god! I'm so sorry, I was trying to hit him! Are you ok?"

I nodded, but felt exactly like I'd been hit with a metal pole on the back of my neck. Carolyn dropped the lamp and went over to help me up.

When I got to my feet I looked around. My stomach lurched when I realized that he was gone. Not only that, but the gun was gone too.

I ran/stumbled out into the street, hoping to see a flash of suit jacket, something. But the street was empty. Business as usual. If anybody had seen where the shooter had gone, they weren't letting on.

I turned around jogged back inside where Carolyn was still blubbering. That's when I saw Jack enter the lobby.

His shirt was covered in blood, and his face was a terrible crimson mask. He looked at me, his lower lip trembling.

"Hollinsworth," I said.

"He's gone," Jack replied.

"Goddamn it!" I yelled. "Who the hell knew we were coming here?"

Jack came over to me and held out his hand. I thought he was going to hug me, so I said, "Not now, Jack."

Instead he walked right past me, leaned down and picked something up off the floor.

"What is that?"

Jack stood back up and showed me. It was a piece of black cloth from the pocket I'd ripped during the struggle. Beneath it was a folded piece of paper. Jack opened it.

"What the hell..." I said.

In Jack's hand was a money order. It was made out for fifty thousand dollars to a Morgan Isaacs.

"I bet this guy knows," Jack said.

The payee on the order was a man named Leonard Reeves.

Chapter 40

"Oh my god, oh my god, oh my god, oh my god," Morgan said.

That his heart hadn't exploded yet was shocking, but every pore in his body seemed to be leaking sweat, every nerve ending on fire.

Once he was able to get away from the guy who'd tackled him, Morgan found the car waiting for him just like Chester had said it would. The door was open, and somehow Morgan managed to dive into the car a split second before it went speeding off.

Once inside, he found Chester waiting for him, a huge smile on his face.

"The gun," Chester said.

Morgan handed it to him, his hand shaking like a lead in a hurricane. Chester took the revolver and put it into a valise on the floor below him.

"You ok?" he said.

"I don't know," Morgan replied. "He's dead. Oh man, he's really, really dead."

"How many times did you shoot him?"

"Three."

"Did all the bullets hit?"

"I think so. I was pretty close, but everything...man, everything just went crazy after that."

"It's a good thing you got away," Chester said. "You're a resourceful man, Morgan."

"Thanks," he said. Morgan's heart rate was finally beginning to slow down.

The car sped down Broadway, and Morgan was pleasantly surprised to see that nobody was following them.

"No cops," Morgan said. "Nobody, they..."

"Don't worry about that," Chester said. "I'm just glad you're alright. You did a great job, Morgan. I knew we could trust you."

Morgan beamed inside. "You always can, sir."

"Yes," Chester said, "I know that now."

Chester leaned over and put his arm around Morgan. It was an odd gesture, but for some reason Morgan felt strangely comforted.

"Hey, uh, can I get the second part of the payment now? Just don't want to forget."

"The money, of course. I knew you wouldn't forget."

Then Morgan felt something sharp pierce his neck, and then a terrible burning sensation began to creep its way into his bloodstream.

He jerked backwards, and Chester moved away. "What the hell was that?" he cried.

Then he saw the syringe in Chester's hand, and Morgan knew exactly what the man had done.

"Sleep," Chester said.

Morgan tried to reach for the man, but suddenly his entire body felt weak. His arms hung limply at his sides, as Morgan felt his body begin to slump down in the seat.

"Why..." he said. "I...I would have done anything for you..."

"I know that," Chester said. Morgan caught the slightest hint of remorse in the man's face. "And you gave as much as you possibly could have."

"My mom..." Morgan groaned, barely able to make out the words.

"She'll never see you again."

"I..."

"We're here," another voice said from the front seat. It was the driver. Morgan hadn't had time to see him when he jumped into the car.

The driver turned around briefly to talk to Chester. That's when Morgan saw who was driving the car.

Theodore Goggins.

"Sorry man," Theo said. "No hard feelings."

"Tell them to chop the car and burn the body," Chester said. Then he looked back at Morgan. Morgan's eyelids were falling, he could feel his heart slowing down, draining him. It was all he could do to retain a small sliver of light to see the man who'd killed him.

"Goodnight, Morgan. I hope wherever you're going you find all the money you can possibly dream of."

And then Morgan Isaacs died.

Chapter 41

I told the cops everything I knew, which wasn't much, even though it was apparently too much. I didn't recognize the shooter, didn't know where he'd come from, who hired him, or why he wanted William Hollinsworth dead.

Well, that wasn't entirely true.

There was no doubt in my mind that Hollinsworth was killed because somebody was frightened of what he was going to tell me. And for good reason. Hollinsworth had confirmed several things before his death, and every one of them scared me to death.

I sat in a coffee shop with Jack, the two of us frazzled beyond belief. I'd called Amanda and told her what happened. Her voice told me that she was deathly afraid for me, but I couldn't come home just yet. We were so close, after all this time so many of the pieces were coming together.

What still itched at me was the police response to Hollinsworth's murder. I'd been around death before, had seen it up close. I'd seen death as personal as it got. And regardless of who was killed, whether it be the most respected cop or the lowliest drug dealer, there was always a police response.

But when Hollinsworth was killed, the response was a simple blue and white patrol car and a small forensics team.

It was more like a motel cleaning crew than a homicide investigation.

I'd asked the officer in charge, a round, pleasant man in his early forties named Hanrahan, if they were expecting more on the scene. He laughed, but not in a condescending way, a way that told me I shouldn't expect more.

"The department is stretched thin as a dollar bill," said Hanrahan. "If we're the only ones here it's because there's nobody else who responded."

It felt like a cloud had descended over this city, something far more menacing than Jack or I knew. I thought about my brother, the now prophetic words he'd spoken just hours before he was gunned down in a dingy apartment building, alone and unloved.

This city's gonna burn.

If this city was going to burn, I could already smell the smoke.

Jack sipped a cup of coffee. Black, he grimaced as he drank it. I had a soda in front of me. Caffeine would have been a mistake. I didn't need it. The way I felt right now I wasn't sure my blood pressure would ever return to normal.

"Somebody knew we were going to speak to Hollinsworth," I said. "And they knew early enough to be able to send someone to kill him."

"It doesn't make sense," Jack said. "We didn't decide to go up there until about an hour before we got there. Who knew?"

"The only person I told," I said, an icy chill making its way down my spine when I said it, "was Curt Sheffield."

Jack stared at me, the mug resting against his lip. He put it down, cupped it with his hands.

"Is there a chance..."

"Not in a million years," I said. "I know Curt. And more than that, I know people. I know how they act. I've talked to Curt about this a dozen times since my brother was killed. I would have known if he was involved. I would have seen it in his eyes, I would have heard it in his voice. He couldn't have known."

""He couldn't be involved," Jack said, "or you don't want him to be involved?"

"Both," I said without hesitation.

"Until we know for sure," Jack said, "you don't say a word to Curt Sheffield or anyone else."

"You either," I said. Not that I needed to tell Jack. I trusted him, but I wanted to level the field, let him know that my contacts were trustworthy ones.

"Even Amanda," Jack said. "You don't know who has access to her, and information you give her."

"Jack, come on..."

"It's us or nothing now, Henry," he said. "I don't trust anyone in this city and I won't until we know what the hell is going on."

I heard my cell phone beep. I took it out, saw I had a text message. It was from Curt Sheffield.

Three people dead in midtown hi-rise. Looks like a double murder-suicide. Bags of the Darkness found all over the place. One of the victims was Lil' Warren.

I snapped the phone shut. "This is not good," I said.

"What happened?"

"According to Curt, they found four bodies, one of whom was LeRoy Culvert, also known as the rapper Lil' Leroy."

"No crap," Jack said. "He's famous enough that even I've heard of him."

"He was with three other people, and they're all dead, drawn and quartered. I mean the place looks like a bloody Rorschach test. And apparently the cops found drugs at the scene. Darkness."

Jack lowered his head.

"There's something else..." I said. "Somebody wrote 'Fury' on one of the walls. In blood."

"Just like Butch Willingham. This is how the bloodshed begins. This is how it starts. Things will only get worse."

"This will be all over the papers tomorrow," I said. "Front page stuff, probably, and it will go national. The Fury only killed dealers. And once people know what kind of drugs Culvert was killed over..."

"People all over the country will want it. "

"Guy had to be worth millions," I said. "Always saw him drinking expensive champagne and hanging out on yachts. Guy like that only indulges in the good stuff. Killing him creates instant demand. This is the best marketing money could buy."

"I've never seen anything like this," Jack said. "Even crack...it took a while to seep in. This drug sounds like it's already swimming in the city's bloodstream, polluting it from the inside out."

"And people are literally dying to get their own taste," I said. Then I went into my wallet and pulled out a piece of paper.

Jack's eyes widened. "You didn't give that to the cops?" he said.

I opened the money order made out to Morgan Isaacs, looked at it.

"Like you said, I don't trust anybody either now. This is our only lead. And even though I trust Curt, I don't trust the whole department. We lose this, it might never be seen again."

"Henry, this is dangerous," Jack said. "You could get in trouble for that."

"I don't care," I said. "This isn't about a story any more. It's about stopping whatever the hell is happening to this city.

"Leonard Reeves," Jack said. "Who the hell is he?"

"Let's find out. His name is on this order. He has to live and work in the city. And I'll bet he has some connection to 718 Enterprises. And maybe to my brother."

"So, what, you think we can just dial four one one and the operator will connect us?" Jack said.

"No, but guy like this has to be connected. He has to have access to a large amount of money, or at least people who can get it. I want to use my LexisNexis account, see what we can find."

"Great, let's go to the office."

"No way," I said. "Like you said, trust no one. We're doing this from my apartment."

"Your apartment? Won't your ladyfriend mind?"

"Her name is Amanda," I said, slightly annoyed. "You've met her. You know that."

Jack nodded. "You're right. I'm sorry. You guys doing well?"

"Just fine," I said.

"Glad to hear it."

I laughed. "Come on Jack. We both know it wasn't too long ago you told me to dump her in so many words. And I stupidly listened to you, and it almost ruined my life to do it. I trust your relationship advice as much as I trust your recommendations on after shave."

"You do what you want," Jack said. "I'm in no position to judge anyone. I do seem to remember you standing over me in a puddle of my own puke."

"Glad you remember that," I said. "Not exactly either of our finer moments."

"Not something I'll want brought up in my eulogy. Come on, let's see what we can find out."

"You'll behave yourself?" I said.

"What do you think I am?" Jack said, finishing the last of his coffee and dropping a few singles on the table. He wiped at his shirt where a few drops of black liquid had stained it. "Uncouth?"

Chapter 42

I turned the key in the lock. Amanda was staying at my place tonight. Odds were she was asleep and I didn't want to wake her.

But when I turned the knob and opened the door, Amanda was sitting on the couch, a beer in her hand, staring at the door like she'd been patiently waiting for a toaster to go off.

The room smelled like flowers, and a could tell she'd been burning one of her scented candles. A copy of a Nora Roberts book lied dog-eared on the table, and a spoon covered in chocolate lay next to it.

She wasn't one of those girls who did that kind of thing often. She didn't eat ice cream when she was depressed, didn't have a weakness for chick flicks or romance novels. At least not for the same reasons as most people.

Amanda only did those things when she was nervous, when taking her mind far away from the real world. When reality was too frightening a place to be in.

When she saw me, Amanda slowly stood up, came over, and threw her arms around me. I felt a cold splash of beer drip down my back, but I didn't care. I closed my eyes and hugged her back.

"I'm going to have to install a GPS device on you," she said. I laughed. Then she pulled her head from the crook of my neck and kissed me hard. I pressed my lips against her, held her tight.

I felt her hand travel down my lower back until she was cupping my butt. It felt great, and for a moment I totally forgot that I hadn't come home alone.

Then Amanda saw him and shrieked.

"Mr. O'Donnell?" Amanda said, her arms still around me, but her hand jerking away like she'd touched a hot stove.

"Sorry to intrude Ms. Davies," he said. "Your boyfriend and I have been through a lot today, and we unfortunately have to take up a little more of your time."

"Henry?' she said. "What's going on?"

"We found something at the scene," I said. "A document that we hope will connect the guy who killed Hollinsworth to 718 Enterprises. We just need to find out who he is."

"And then what?" she said. "You're going to call the cops?"

I looked at Jack. He shrugged, as if to say this is all yours.

I turned back to Amanda. Her arms had slipped from my shoulders. I took her hand, held it, but she was reluctant to hold on.

"Not yet," I said.

"Why not?"

"Somebody knew we were meeting Hollinsworth. I don't know how they found out, but until we know who did it we're going to play this pretty close to the vest."

She nodded, understanding it though it was clear she wasn't happy about it.

Then she looked at Jack, said, "How are you? Feeling better?"

Jack smiled. "I am. Thank you for asking."

"So get on with it," Amanda said. "If you don't mind I have half a bottle of wine and I stopped reading in the middle of a really good sex scene. Have you ever heard the term 'purple-headed warrior?"

"Uh, no," I said. "but whatever floats your boat."

"I think the warrior in this book does float," she said, "at least according to the narrator, it sounds big enough to sail down the Amazon. Anyway, good luck guys."

Amanda went back to the sofa, lay down, kicked her feet up and dove back into the book.

"She's a pistol," Jack said.

"Sure is. Here, we can sit at the table."

Jack took a seat at our meager dining room table as I hooked up my laptop. Once I powered it on, I accessed LexisNexis and did a search for 'Leonard Reeves.'

Half a dozen hits came up. I opened the first one.

It was from The Daily Princetonian, the student newspaper at Princeton University. we searched through the highlighted article and finally came across the name Leonard Reeves. The passage read:

The Princeton Economy department, spearheaded by Professor Sheila DeWitt, has seen its fair number of notable professionals in the fields of finance and economics.

The article was accompanied by a photo of a middle-aged black woman who must have been Professor DeWitt. She was standing at the front of a small classroom. Two students were visible in the front row. One was a girl, early twenties, with a ponytail and wearing a skirt and blouse. The man was dressed in slacks and a button down shirt, his hair short, and he wore glasses. The caption read:

Rachel Vine '93 and Leonard Reeves '94 are captivated by the renowned Professor.

"Is that him?" Jack said.

"I don't know. Let's see the next article."

I pulled up the next search result. It was from Crain's Business Daily. The article was from 1998, and the headline was 'Economic boom sees rise in dot com investors.'

We found Leonard Reeves's name halfway through the piece. It read:

Flush with cash, many young men and women who have prospered during unparalleled growth are putting their money into what many consider to be risky investments--namely websites and internet domains. Leonard Reeves, a graduate of the Princeton economic department and executive at Morgan Stanley, admits to finding thrill in such a venture.

"You don't get into this industry to watch from the sidelines," said Reeves. "The people who take the biggest risks reap the biggest rewards."

Reeves, who already owns three apartments in New York City, says he plans to take his earnings from internet ventures and invest even further in the housing market.

"Man, that can't have worked out too well for him," Jack said.

"Holy crap," I said.

"What?"

"Look, there." I pointed to the next article. The headline said it all.

The piece was from 2001, and was published in the Wall Street

Journal. It read 'Reeves named as liaison to New York City Department of Finance.'

The article was also accompanied by a photograph. It was definitely the same guy from the Princetonian article.

"He worked for the government?" Jack said. "You've got to be kidding me."

I sat there, stunned. How was that possible? Could this have been the same guy?

The other articles were not dated any later than 2004, and all references Reeves's job with the DoF. There were no other hits for the name, nothing else came up.

"It has to be him," I said. "But I don't get it. If this is the same Reeves as on the order made out to Morgan Isaacs, what the hell is someone who worked for the government and who worked for one of the biggest brokerage firms in the world doing associated with 718 Enterprises? I mean, these people are drug dealers, plain and simple, and the crap they're producing is killing people. How did someone like Reeves get connected to that?"

Jack sat there, thinking. Not listening to me, but lost in his own thoughts. Then I heard Amanda's voice from the couch.

"What if Reeves didn't just used to work for the government?" she said. "I mean, what if he still does?"

"That's crazy," I said. "Obviously Reeves fell on hard times somehow and ended up selling his soul for a pile of black rocks."

"Not necessarily," Jack said.

"What do you mean?"

"Have you ever heard of the name Gary Webb?"

"It rings a bell, but I'm not sure why."

"Ok, well have you heard of the Dark Alliance?"

"That's a little more familiar," I replied. "Something about Nicaragua, right?"

"Something like that," Jack said. "In the eighties, Gary Webb was a reporter for the San Jose Mercury News."

"Now it rings a bell," I said.

"What does he have to do with this?" Amanda said.

"In nineteen ninety six, Webb published a three-part series of articles in the Mercury News called 'Dark Alliance.' See in the eighties, President Reagan was embroiled in the Iran-Contra affair where it was determined that the U.S, government had supplied a group of Nicaraguan Contras with financial aid through the sale of weapons to Iran, in part thanks to our buddy Oliver North. Our government was supporting the Contras as part of the Reagan doctrine, which supported organizations that opposed communistic and socialistic regimes. The Nicaraguan government in the eighties, let's just say, fit the bill."

"Webb claimed in his articles," Jack continued, "that not only did we supply the Contras with funds through the sale of weapons, but through the sale of drugs as well."

"That's ridiculous. We weren't selling drugs," Amanda said.

"We weren't," Jack said. "But the Contras were reaping millions of dollars through the sale of drugs within the United States. Crack cocaine spread like wildfire through urban areas in the eighties, and much of the money from those sales went directly into funding the Contras. Webb claimed that members of the NSC, or National Security Council, were aware that money from drug sales in the U.S. was being funneled to the Contras. Webb found out that not only was our government aware of this, but members of the NSC purposefully withheld that information from the Drug Enforcement Agency. They felt that by curtailing drug sales and cracking down on shipments, we would effectively stem the flow of money to the Contras and in turn hurt their efforts to overthrow Nicaragua's communist FSLN government."

"So in essence," I said, "they were selling drugs in our cities, killing our citizens and choking the national crime rates. And we turned a blind eye because we felt it pushed our agenda in another country."

"Pretty much," Jack said. "When Webb published these articles, he caused a firestorm unlike many seen in journalism. It was without a doubt one of the most controversial articles of the past twenty five years. So what happened to Webb? Well, he was completely discredited by the government which issued denials faster that meter maids issue parking tickets. He was eventually pushed out of the Mercury News, and after years in which he failed to get another job at a major newspaper Webb put a gun to his head and pulled the trigger."

"Damn," Amanda said.

"Twice," Jack added.

"Twice? How does someone shoot themselves in the head twice?"

"Don't get your panties in a bunch," Jack said. I glared at him. "Apologies, Ms. Davies. Sometimes I forget that I'm around a lady."

"This lady thinks she could kick your old ass," Amanda said.

"Now that's my kind of lady," Jack said. "Hold onto this firebrand, Henry. Anyway, common thought was that Webb had been bumped off. But it turns out Webb was genuinely depressed and had written despondent letters to his family. And an autopsy and gun residue test proved that the man really did shoot himself twice. It doesn't happen often, but it does happen if the suicidal person happens to have lousy aim."

"So, what, you think the sale of drugs in New York City is being funneled to, who, some shady overseas organization? Some anti-Taliban fighting squad?"

"Not at all," Jack said. "If what I'm thinking is correct at all, and if this guy Reeves is connected the way I suspect he is, then the sale of drugs in this city isn't going abroad. It isn't being diverted to an anti-terrorism foreign legion. What I'm saying is that money gained through the sale of drugs like the Darkness is going directly to the city itself. I'm saying that not only is our government turning a blind eye, but it's taking a cut of the profits."

"The layoffs, the deficits," I said. "You're saying they're trying to make up for budget shortfalls by taking a cut of drug payoffs?"

"Words to live by, especially in politics. If something worked twenty years ago, it'll probably work again now."

Just then I heard my cell phone ring. I went over to pick it up, but when I saw the caller ID I stopped. Looked at Jack.

"Who is it?" he said.

I shook my head, confused

"It's Curt Sheffield," I said.

"Curt," Jack said, taken aback. "Well, pick it up!"

I answered the phone. Tried to play it cool.

"Hey man, what's up?"

Then I listened as Curt explained to me what was going to happen in just a few minutes.

When I hung up, I looked at Jack and said, "You need to leave."

Needless to say this was not exactly what he was expecting to hear.

"What the hell are you talking about Henry?"

"In less than half an hour, somebody is going to come here to sell me drugs. And unless you want to try and pass off as my pot-addicted uncle or something, we can't have any trace of you in this apartment."

Chapter 43

Curt Sheffield had only been working for the NYPD for five years, but the past two days made it feel like a lifetime.

Two days. Twelve dead. All deaths related to this new drug, the Darkness.

For years, New York was considered one of the safest big cities in the world. Crime existed was relegated to back alleys and dingy apartments. Upstanding citizens had little to fear as long as they used common sense.

The drug dealers were easy to smoke out. They were usually junkies themselves. They sold because that's all they had, all they knew. They were uneducated, unloved, and an honest day's work for an honest day's pay was a foreign concept.

And that's why dealers were so easy to break.

In real life, those dealers in their teens and twenties didn't have any sort of real loyalty to the drug lords. It wasn't like television. There was no 'game' and no loyalty beyond a wad of cash. Your employer was simply whoever could pay that day.

When a man making seventeen thousand dollars a year selling crack is forced to choose between turning in a man he barely knows or spending five years behind bars, the decision was always easy.

That's why people on the top never lasted long. They could never offer the people below them a life worth risking on the streets. Every moment was fleeting, but when push came to shove a fistful of crumpled twenties wasn't enough to keep someone from saving their own ass.

This drug, though, was different. The Narcotics division was sweeping all those back alleys, talking to all their sources, offering all their informants good, hard cash for one tip that could loosen the first thread.

So far, they'd come up empty handed.

And it wasn't because the informants had suddenly grown balls or a sense of loyalty. It's that they didn't know.

However this product was being moved, it was being done away from the streets, away from the bottom feeders, away from the men and women who sold the very same drugs they ingested.

This was different. And that's what scared Curt the most.

This city had the best police force in the world, but now that force was being slashed like an unfortunately located forest. A thousand cops, vanished from the streets, victims of a mayor legally beholden to a budget that had come in four billion dollars in the red.

Curt stopped to pick up a pizza on the way home. Half mushroom, half pepperoni. He had no bigger plans than to throw on his Rutgers sweatshirt, lounge on the couch with a few slices and a few beers and flip between games and late night Cinemax.

As he approached his apartment building, he noticed a man hanging on the street corner. He was wearing a t-shirt and sweatpants, and did not have any socks on. Ordinarily such a thing wouldn't catch his eye, but this guy was swaying slightly, looking like every few seconds he had to remind himself not to topple over. It was a chilly night, and clearly the man had either gone out knowingly underdressed or was so zoned out that he hadn't noticed.

Suddenly he found himself walking over to the man, balancing the pizza in one hand while checking his gun to make sure it was at the ready. Curt had never been forced to use his gun off-duty, but something about this man made him tense up. It was the jittery movements, how he looked like he might fall asleep one moment and then suddenly jerk awake the next. He looked like a classic user, and Curt had learned long ago that someone high could only be trusted as much as the drugs allowed them to be.

Curt approached slowly. His hand was getting warm from the bottom of the pizza box. As he got closer, he called out, "Hey, man, you ok?"

The man didn't respond, just kept swaying. His right arm shot out and caught a lamp post to steady himself.

"I said, you ok man?"

Then the guy whipped around, and the look in his eyes made Curt glad his gun was so close. His eyes were bloodshot, but they were wide out, crazy-like, and he stared at Curt with a mixture of confusion and apprehension, like an animal cornered who might bare its fangs out of pure panic.

Curt slowly knelt down and laid the pizza on the sidewalk. He hoped this guy was just drunk, and that he could throw him in a cab, be done with it and retreat to his pepperoni. But getting closer, he knew it wouldn't be that simple.

"Hey man," Curt called out. "You're not looking so hot. Why don't you head home. Sleep it off."

The man shook his head. Slowly at first, but then more rapidly until Curt was worried he might hurt himself.

"Whoa, slow down there. I'm a cop. See?" Curt took out his badge, showed it to the guy. "My name's Officer Sheffield. I'm here to help."

"No," the man moaned. "No. No. No. Nooooooo.."

"It's ok. We've all had bad days. Why don't I call a cab..."

"It's all gone," he said, his body swaying faster than the breeze.

"What's gone?"

"All of it," he said. "All of it. It's gone."

"I don't know what you're talking about, but I'm sure you have some in your fridge."

"No. I can't get any more."

Curt kept playing along. "Why not?"

"Money," he said, his voice like tar pulled through a pasta strainer. "I need it to buy more."

"More what?"

"Darkness," the man said, his eyes fixated on Curt.

Sheffield felt his body tense up. The drug was too early in its life for cops to fully know how users reacted to it, how their bodies responded. Each drug did different things to people who took it, and as a cop you learned how to deal with each of them. You had to be supple with your voice, malleable with your body language. The wrong tone or stilted reaction could set someone off, putting you or others at risk.

Curt didn't know how to deal with people who used this new drug. They were unpredictable, but if anything the last few days had proven without a doubt is that they were uncompromisingly violent. They'd been trained on how to deal with addicts of various substances, but this seemed to go well beyond the training manual.

"Why do you want more, man? What say we get you somewhere safe. St. Luke's hospital isn't too far from here. We'll get you a nice bed, get you cleaned up..."

"I don't want to be cleaned up!" the man yelled. Curt stepped back, the look in the man's eyes giving him pause. He thought about calling for an ambulance, figuring whether he liked it or not this guy could use a night in detox. The only worry was whether in the time it took for an ambulance to come, if this man was intent on hurting Curt or someone else.

"Hey, I hear you. That stuff is good. But being able to think clearly, ain't nothing you buy can replicate that feeling."

"You're wrong," the man slurred, his eyes closed as he smiled. "I feel...alive. I feel...fine." Then his mood turned sour, the smile disappearing. "There's no more money. No more money. It's gone. I can't have any more."

"It's ok, we can just..."

"I can't have any more!" he shouted.

"Come on, buddy, that stuff isn't going to do anything for you. Let's talk."

Then the man reached into his pocket and pulled out a cell phone. "They won't take my calls any more," he said. "The last guy who came, Vinnie, he told me unless I had cold hard cash he wouldn't sell me anything." The man held up the phone like it was a soiled diaper, and dropped it into the trash can. "Where am I going to get more money? I can't find anybody to trade with me."

"Trade with you? What the hell are you talking about? Listen to yourself man. You don't need more, you need help."

Curt took out his phone and dialed 911. When the operator picked up, he said, "This is officer Curt Sheffield, currently off duty, I have a ten sixty nine in progress. Adult male, mid thirties, high on I believe this new drug, Darkness. Guy looks pretty out of it and potentially dangerous. Send a unit and an ambulance to eighty eighty and Amsterdam."

"Ten four Officer Sheffield. Ambulance will be en route. Might have to wait for a squad car, busy night tonight. Can you watch him until the EMTs get there?"

Curt sighed. Always short handed.

"I'll do my best." He hung up.

The man's body was draped across the lamp post now, as he barely looked able to stand. Curt took a few steps closer, put his hand in his jacket pocket where he felt the comfort of his holster.

"Listen, buddy. I got a few friends coming. They're going to take care of you. They..."

"My wife," the man said.

"What's you say?"

"My wife is dead," the man said in a guttural rasp. "She died."

"I'm so sorry...how did she die?"

"I killed her."

Curt stopped moving. His fingers went from tickling the gun to gripping the pistol.

His eyes darted back and forth as he spoke.

"I wanted to sell her wedding ring. She told me I couldn't. I could have bought so much with it, but she said no. I didn't know what to do. I needed it so badly. So I took a knife and I cut it off of her.

"Oh, Jesus..."

The man looked down, reached into his pocket.

"Ok, my friend, I'm going to come over there. I have a gun on me. Please, don't move any more and take your hand out of your pocket."

Without warning the man yanked his hand from his pocket. It took Curt a second to realize what he was holding.

In the man's hand was a severed finger. A glittering diamond ring still attached to it.

"I don't know what to do!"

Suddenly the man dropped the finger, turned around and ran out into the middle of the street.

"Stop!" Curt shouted, sprinting forward.

Half a dozen cars were speeding up Amsterdam, headlights blazing in the dark blue sky. Their horns started blaring as the man weaved in and out of the way of thousands of pounds of metal passing him by at upwards of forty miles an hour.

Suddenly there was a flash of metal, sparks, and a terrible crunching sound as Curt stopped dead in his tracks. Curt saw the man's body go flying, literally lifted into the air, where it spun end over end until landing in a heap by the curb.

The car, a dark sedan, came screeching to a halt. The driver leapt out of the car, hands holding his head in disbelief. Cars ground to a stop all around the sedan, whose hood was dented, grill smashed inwards. A slick of blood pooling around the hood ornament.

And just below the front of the car was a sight that would never leave Curt Sheffield as long as he lived.

Resting on the asphalt, in a perfect row as if placed there gently, was a pair of slippers.

"Oh my god," he said. The man looked at Curt, his mouth wide open. "You...you saw that. He ran out in front of me. He...oh, sweet jesus..."

Curt ran over to the body, knelt down next to it. The man's face looked like it had been bludgeoned with a sledgehammer, and his limbs were twisted in a way that god had most certainly not intended.

He ripped his phone from his pocket, dialed 911. "Ten fifty three," Curt said, his mouth dry, the words tumbling out. "Officer needs assistance. We have a motor vehicle accident. One civilian is down and hurt, potentially fatal. He's not breathing."

Curt put his fingers to the man's neck, searched for a pulse.

He felt nothing.

Picking up the man's wrist, he tried again. Still nothing.

No use. He was long gone.

"I think I lost him," Curt said into the phone.

When he was assured an ambulance was en route, Curt stood up, took in the scene unfolding in front of him.

Cars were lining up down the street, drivers getting out at first to see what was causing the traffic holdup. Then when they saw what was going on, phones came out as they called 911. Onlookers began to crowd the sidewalks. A few people started heading towards the body. Some looked concerned, fearful, but a few had a glint in their eyes that Curt didn't like. He knew that not everybody was concerned for this guy's well being.

Curt stood up, pulled out his badge. Let his arm hang loose to his jacket opened up a bit, revealing the gun and holster inside.

"NYPD!" he shouted. The surge stopped. A few people slipped back into the crowds and disappeared, disappointed they didn't have a chance to search the man for jewelry or money. "An ambulance is on the way. I'm going to need everyone to back away and clear room."

He walked towards the crowd, and they stepped back, obeying. Then Curt remembered something.

He turned and jogged back to the street corner where he'd seen the man. Reaching into the garbage can, he managed to find the man's cell phone he'd dropped inside. He wiped off the crud and liquid, relieved to see the machine was still working.

He clicked it on.

The home page blinked on, and an LCD screen read 'Gil's Phone.'

Gil. That was the dead man's name.

Then Curt scrolled through the numerous functions until he found a button marked 'Recent Calls.'

He clicked on it, and saw Gil's call log from the last twelve hours. Incoming calls marked with an orange 'down' arrow, outgoing with a red 'up' arrow.

Then Curt felt his breath catch in his throat.

There was one phone number that stood out. Gil had called it no less than ten times in the last three hours.

And the number had a 718 prefix.

Without hesitating, Curt called the number from Gil's phone.

It rang twice, and then was picked up.

"Mr. Meadows, we've already explained to you the situation. Until you have legal tender available, we cannot serve you. Goodbye."

Then person on the other end hung up.

And as soon as they hung up, Curt called one more number. A number he never thought he'd be calling to help him do his job.

Curt had never gone undercover. He wasn't sure he could pull this off.

But he knew, without a doubt, that Henry Parker could.

Chapter 44

"You're insane," Amanda said, watching as I went about straightening up the apartment. I had already cleaned up my dirty socks, stacked the magazines into a neat pile, organized the DVD collection and even cleaned the stove top.

"They should be here in less than fifteen minutes," I said.

"Who the hell are you expecting? Martha Stewart? It's a freaking drug dealer, Henry. They're not going to care if your floor is clean enough to eat off of. In fact, they'll probably be a little suspicious if the place doesn't look like, oh, I don't know, somewhere a junkie might live."

"I don't have to be a junkie," I said. "Just a guy who wants a late night hit to calm my nerves." I smiled at her. "It has been a long week."

She was right, of course. I was cleaning more out of nerves than anything.

I didn't know what to expect. Curt's call had come out of the blue, something about getting a lead on 718 Enterprises. He had a plan, he said, but to me it sounded like a plan he'd hashed up in about thirty seconds.

Not that it mattered.

To this point, all of the investigating I'd done on 718 Enterprises, this shadowy person known only as the Fury and this new drug called Darkness had been done in just that: darkness. I hadn't written a single word of copy for the Gazette, and as far as I knew the police had no leads and didn't seem to be banging down a whole lot of doors to get them.

With Curt in the game, at least I knew whatever we found would get sent up the ladder. If I could trust him.

Not that I had much choice. And if Curt was somehow in on all of this, there were far easier ways to get to me. To get to people close to me. But deep down I didn't believe there was any chance he would turn. Curt was a good cop, respected the badge. Hell, he'd even taken a bullet because of me. You couldn't buy that kind of loyalty. At least as far as I knew.

And Jack took it surprisingly well. I fully expected him to put up a fight, to tell me that he'd put as much effort and risked as much of his reputation on this story--if not more so--than I had. And that gave him every right to be present. I expected him to suggest hiding in the closet, in the bathroom, or to actually pose as my pothead uncle or something. And I would have to let him down, gently, and tell him that if whoever came got even a whiff of Jack's presence, he would not only be putting our careers on the line but perhaps something much, much more.

But Jack just left.

He made sure I had his cell phone number, and made me promise to call him when I knew more. I told him I would, and I meant it. But right now it was all Curt and myself. I could tell from Curt's call he was having the same doubts I was. Wondering who to trust, feeling like his world had been closed off. Something had happened, and I wasn't sure what yet, but Curt had decided that he was going to trust me with this. And it was all I could do to not let him down.

As I picked up around the apartment, Amanda followed me dirtying it up. Finally I gave up and realized she was right. Better off looking like an apartment two people actually lived in rather than a set up. Or an apartment in which the tenants could actually afford to hire a cleaning person.

Ten minutes later, we were both sitting on the couch, finishing the last of the wine.

"Are you sure wine is ok?" I said. "Not too high class? He won't think we're some sort of rich couple?"

"That bottle of red cost twelve ninety nine. I think we're safe."

We sat there, waiting, my stomach fluttering. And then the buzzer rang and the nerves went away.

I pushed the call button and said, "Who is it?"

"It's Vinnie."

"Come on up."

Unlocking the front door, I looked at Amanda. Her face was a mask, no nerves either. She wanted me to crack this story too. I smiled at her, knowing how much she was risking for this.

I waited by the door, shifting back and forth. When it rang, I waited three seconds before opening it. You know, so the guy wouldn't know I was actually waiting by the door.

Opening the door, I saw a man standing there. He was about five foot ten, black, a bit chunky but barely winded from walking the three flights up to our apartment.

He was wearing a suit, pinstriped, slightly rumpled, and his striking blue tie was loosened just slightly.

"Hey," I said, again wondering if that was the right way to start the conversation.

"Can I come in?"

"Yeah, of course."

'Vinnie' stepped inside and let the door close behind him. He walked over to the dining table and set his briefcase on it. I tried not to stare, but remember that it wasn't too long ago when another drug-filled briefcase sat on my table.

And a man had died because of that.

I pushed it from my mind, but couldn't help but realize I'd never actually spoken to a real dealer before. Not that I'd had no experiences with illicit substances--it was college, and unlike former presidents I did inhale--but whenever drugs were present they seemingly appeared out of nowhere in little plastic bags. I assumed some of my friends had connections, but down the road I realized I was just blissfully ignorant. I didn't want to have to involve myself, didn't want to think of myself as trading money for it.

Now there was no choice.

"Hey," the guy responded. "You called for Vinnie, right?"

"That's right. But you don't look like a Vinnie."

"You don't look like an asshole, so don't be one."

"Sorry, just making conversation. How's your night going?"

"What are you, a fucking reporter? Shut up and let's do this."

I decided less talking was better.

"So what can I get you?" he said.

"This new thing...Darkness, right? What will fifty get me?"

"Fifty will get you three tabs. That's an introductory offer. After that, it's twenty five a pop."

I took out my wallet, counted out fifty, and handed it over. He counted quickly, then unlocked his briefcase and pulled open the flap. He rummaged around inside as I tried not to stare. I looked over at Amanda on the couch. She was sitting there reading a magazine and sipping her wine, acting like this was a totally normal evening occurrence. Monday we go to the movies, Tuesdays are date nights, Wednesday we invite over our dealer. Just like all normal city kids.

'Vinnie' took out a small bag with three tiny black rocks inside. They looked like pebbles, the exact same rock that was featured in Paulina's article.

He handed me the drugs and closed up the briefcase.

"Pleasure doing business with you. One quick thing. If you're going to reorder tonight, make sure you have cash on hand. We've had, um, troubles with people who ordered and then didn't have the money to pay."

"People really reorder this stuff the same night? Is it that good?"

'Vinnie' laughed.

"If we don't hear from you within the next few days, it's cause you ran out of money or you're dead. So let's just say I'm hoping to see you again real soon."

As Vinnie turned to leave, I looked at Amanda. She peeked up from her wine. I rubbed my pointer finger and thumb together and mouthed Tip?

She looked at me like I was insane and gave her head a quick 'no' shake.

Vinnie opened the door, nodded, and left.

I ran over and put my ear to the door. Vinnie was a big guy, and his footsteps were easily heard as he clomped down the stairs.

I waited ten seconds and then called Curt Sheffield.

"Henry, I saw him go in. Did he leave?"

"He should be leaving the building any second now."

"Got it. You know the plan, right?"

"You're going to follow him on foot, I take your car and wait for you to contact me. Then I meet you with the car and we tail him to wherever he refills on dope."

"You got it hoss. Keys are in the tire well, wait until you can't see our friend any more before you come down. Last thing we need is this guy think you're following him."

"Got it. I've done this before."

"But don't wait too long, I don't want to chance somebody stealing my ride. You don't exactly live in the safest neighborhood, bro."

"Hey Curt?"

"Yeah Parker?"

"Are you sure about this? Am I really the guy you want tagging along with you tonight?"

Curt was silent for a moment on the other end.

"I hear what you're saying, fact is I don't know who to trust right now. Just the other day I got tip on some fired banker who might have been running drugs, cat named Morgan Isaacs. We were just about to put a tail on him when the guy disappears into thin air. Nobody knows where he is, not even his parents have seen him in weeks. Doesn't add up."

"Morgan Isaacs," I said. "The man who killed William Hollinsworth had a money order on him made out to Morgan Isaacs. If that was Isaacs, he was hired to kill Hollinsoworth."

"Which means he's no longer in this country, or no longer of this earth," Curt said.

"I got that feeling. So right now, you're the only man I trust. I know why you're in this, Henry. You want to know the truth about Stephen Gaines, and I want to get rid of this crap that's turning our city into Beirut. Two paths, same destination my friend."

"Then I'll meet you there."

"See you soon Parker. Oh wait, here he comes. Later."

"Good luck Curt."

We both hung up.

I looked out the window and could see Vinnie exiting our building. As soon as he stepped outside, he put his cell phone to his ear. Then he nodded a few times, clicked it off, put it in his pocket and headed east. The subway was in that direction.

When Vinnie rounded the corner, I saw Curt Sheffield trailing him, walking briskly but without enough distance that hopefully our mark wouldn't notice. I silently wished Curt luck again.

"That wasn't so bad," I said to Amanda. She'd put down the magazine and wine. Standing up, she went over to the table and picked up the baggie with three rocks of the Darkness.

"Amanda, you're not going to..."

Before I could say another word, she walked over to the bathroom, opened the bag, and dumped the rocks into the toilet. Then she flushed it. Once she was sure the rocks were on their way to some sewage treatment plant, Amanda came over to me and planted a massive kiss right on my lips.

"That's the closest I ever want that stuff to us," she said, her arms warm around my neck.

"Same here. You know the reason I'm doing this is to stop whatever this stuff is from getting out there more than it already is."

"I know that. And I hope you do. But given a choice between that and you staying safe...just come home to me, Henry. That's all I want."

"I will," I said. "And hopefully I won't have to say this too many times, but don't wait up for me."

She sighed. "I won't wait up for you, but that doesn't mean I won't be thinking about you."

"I'd never tell you to stop doing that," I said.

She kissed me again and said, "Now go help Curt."

I nodded, grabbed my coat from the closet, gave her one last look and headed outside.

Chapter 45

Curt drove a Ford Fusion. The key was in the tire well just like he said. As I climbed into the car and adjusted the seat, I couldn't help but think Curt was a pretty conscientious guy to own a hybrid. I started the car and put my cell phone in the cup holder by the arm rest, just to be sure I wouldn't miss it if he called.

For the next few hours, most likely, Curt would be on his own. He wasn't supposed to call me unless there was an emergency, as anything that could lead the dealer to know he was being followed was curtailed until we met up later.

So all I had to do now was wait.

I picked through the CDs. Some good stuff. Jay-Z, Lil Wayne, T-Pain. Then, underneath all of them, I found a Barry Manilow CD and I cracked up. When this was over, Curt would surely have to explain himself on that one.

An hour in, I ran to the corner deli and got a big, steaming cup of coffee and a muffin. So far this was the lamest stakeout ever. I wasn't even staking anything out, I was just sitting in a car on the side of the street, waiting for a call so I could then follow someone. I couldn't complain, though. It wasn't too long ago I did just what Curt was doing, following one of these dealers, trying to find out just where their stash was hidden.

And then I found it, but when we went back it was gone. They obviously hadn't given up, but had simply moved to a new location.

Tonight we were going to find out where 718 Enterprises was hoarding their stash. Then Curt would take it down with his fellow boys in blue, Jack and I would get the exclusive, eyewitness story, and everyone would go home happy.

At least that's how it all played out in my mind. What happened next was something, far, far different.

Two hours into my stakeout of, well, nothing, my cell phone rang. It was Curt.

I picked up it, said, "Hey. Where are you?"

"One hundred twelfth and Amsterdam," Curt said. "I'm pretty sure our boy is going home for the night. He just took off his tie, and he's swinging that briefcase like it's full of air, not powdered substances. Start making your way over here, I'll call you when I get a more precise location."

"On my way," I said.

"See you soon, Dick Tracy."

Starting the car, I pulled onto the street, turned my beams on and began the drive over to 112th and Amsterdam, just on the Western edge of Morningside Heights.

It was a foggy night, a fine mist surrounding the yellow street lamps, casting an eerie glow over New York. Most cars had their windshield wipers on. Mine made a rapid snick snick every thirty seconds, wiping the condensation away in a perfect arc.

The streets uptown weren't particularly crowded for a Saturday night, most of the Columbia University crew either in bed or already at the bar and beginning their long trek to drunkenness. Meanwhile I was in a car, heading to meet my cop friend, hoping to finally put to bed once and for all who had killed my brother. And who was poisoning the city.

This neighborhood was familiar. I'd met a guy up here named Clarence Willingham, the son of a small-time dealer who'd been killed by the Fury twenty years ago. Clarence was still trying to come to grips with his father's murder, and it was only then when I learned the truth about how close he was to my own family. Secrets. Sometimes I wondered if more secrets were kept from us in the light of day as opposed to the dark of night.

I idled on the corner of a hundred and tenth, right where Columbus Avenue turned into Morningside Drive. I'd just put the car in park when I was jolted by a rapping on the passenger side window. Whipping around, I saw Curt Sheffield's face peering in at me, his eyes squinting as rain began to fall harder around him.

He mouthed the words open up and I unlocked the door.

As he slid inside, Curt ran his hands through his hair, spraying a layer of rain onto the seats. He was wearing jeans and a brown coat, sneakers and a t-shirt. He looked like a normal guy.

"If that's your undercover look, I gotta say it works."

Curt ignored me. "His name is Theodore Goggins."

"How'd you get that info?"

"He stopped into a Starbucks. I waited outside, but saw him pay with a credit card. After he left, I waited a minute and went inside and told them I found his ATM card. And I needed his name in case I couldn't catch up with him. He lives just down the block. Definitely not his building, because he had to buzz up. But the guy who lived there said 'come on up Theo' as he buzzed him in."

"He worked in finance," I said.

"How do you know?"

"All these guys do. When I was looking into Stephen's murder, Scott Callahan told me all of it. Tens of thousands of young professionals out of work in this city, most of whom lived a few miles beyond their means. Then they get laid off when the economy goes in the crapper, and they're left with huge mortgages and bills on toys and apartments. That's where 718 comes in. They offer to pay these out of work go-getters to go house to house. They make good money. It's a win win. They can still afford the lifestyle they're accustomed to."

Curt sat back, put his hand on his forehead. He looked trouble.

"That's why," he said.

"Why what?"

"The Narcotics division. They haven't been able to find out where this drug, Darkness, where it's coming from or who's selling it. But they're looking in the wrong place. They're so busy turning over logs and monitoring alleys that they're not noticing the business assholes."

"Nobody looks at a guy in a suit and thinks he's guilty of anything more than maybe then white collar stuff. Fraud and all that jazz."

"Ken Tsang," Curt said. "That's where we got a lead on Morgan Isaacs. They worked at the same bank, both got laid off on the same day and Ken's coworkers said they were friendly. We cross checked his phone records and found half a dozen calls a day to the same 718 number I found on a dead man's cell phone. Ken was working for these creeps. I'm willing to bet on it."

"And you found him with less bone density than the Pillsbury Doughboy," I said. "That probably doesn't bode well when it comes to finding Morgan Isaacs in one piece."

Curt just sat there, rain dripping from his hair into his lap as we watched cars zip down the street, the errant noises of a night unaware of its own shadow. We could see Theodore Goggin's awning from the car, and we kept the windshield on fast enough where we wouldn't miss any activity.

And so we waited. Sat in the car until the morning. When Theodore Goggins would leave his apartment and head towards wherever it was that the refills were being kept.

All we could do was keep each other awake through our silences, and the knowledge that something foul was lurking just beneath the streets of our city. But it wasn't until the next day when we realized just how deep those sewers ran.

Chapter 46

Saturday

It was six thirty in the morning, and we were both awake. My brain was fogged over with that thick haze that comes from a night spent ingesting too much coffee while thinking too much about terrible things that would keep you up under normal circumstances.

Curt's eyes were open too, but they were more aware, less troubled. He seemed less like someone running on fumes, like I was, and more like a hawk poised to strike. Waiting for that moment when his prey poked its head from the shadows. And at six thirty, that's when our prey, Theodore Goggins, poked his head out from his uptown apartment. "Right there," I said.

"I see him." Curt quickly combed his hair, opened the mirror above the windshield to get rid of the whole 'I stayed up all night in a car' look. Whether that kind of makeover could be done without trained professionals and Heidi Klum, I wasn't sure.

"Same drill," Curt said. "I follow our man to his destination, then I call you. We're not going to have a ton of time because I have no idea where this guy is headed. Just be on alert."

"I'm going to head over to the West Side Highway," I said. "Better to have access to a faster road. Just in case."

"Good thinking Parker. I'll call you when Goggins takes me... wherever," Curt said. "And Henry?"

"Yeah Curt?"

"Be careful. I don't know how this day is going to unwind."

I nodded, didn't need to say anything. Curt knew I was game.

"Ok, let's get this party started."

"Some party. Six in the morning."

"Can it buddy. Stay focused."

"Good luck, Curt."

He exited the car, walked over to a sidewalk newspaper salesman and bought a copy of the Gazette. At least he was supporting my paper.

Theodore Goggins left his apartment wearing a different suit, this one straight black, with shiny shoes and another sparkling blue tie. He headed south on Columbus, right towards where Curt was standing reading the paper.

When Goggins passed him, Curt waited thirty seconds before starting his tail. After they'd both disappeared, I started the car and headed west on a hundred and tenth street. The morning sun was rising above the trees as I drove on the south side of Morningside Park. The lush green foliage such a stark contrast to the brick and stone just south across the street.

Suddenly I realized that the West Side Highway had just two entrances near my location: one on a hundred and twenty fifth street and the other on ninety sixth. They were a mile and a half apart from each other, and given Manhattan traffic it could be fifteen minutes easily from one exit to the other. If I chose the wrong one, I could miss Curt and Goggins entirely.

I slowed down briefly approaching Riverside drive, then made a decision and turned south towards ninety sixth. I figured Goggins went south, best guess was that his pick up point was south of our location.

I pulled the car over on ninety sixth and waited for Curt to call.

Thankfully, I didn't have to wait long.

My phone rang less than fifteen minutes later. It was Curt. He was breathless, panting.

"I almost lost him," Curt said. "Stupid Metrocard was out of cash. Anyway, get your ass downtown to the Meatpacking district."

"On the way," I said, putting the car into drive and easing onto the Henry Hudson Parkway. "Where to?"

"You know the Kitten Club?"

"Um...yeah. Unfortunately. Why?"

"Our friend Theodore Goggins just walked inside."

"You're kidding me," I said. "I knew Shawn Kensbrook was dirty, but he's got his hands full in the mud."

"You think this is the new depot where the lackeys get their refills?"

"It would make sense," I said. "I've been to the Kitten Club and that place has more unexplored territory than the Jonas Brothers. Plus it doesn't fill up until late at night, so nobody's there during the day to watch it."

"Given the history of this place," Curt said, "it wouldn't surprise me in the least."

"What do you mean?"

"I'll explain when you get down here. Meet me on the southeast corner of Washington and Little West 12th street."

"Will do. I'll be down there right away."

I exited my spot and pulled Curt's car onto the Hudson River drive south. The traffic wasn't bad, rush hour still an hour or so from reaching its apex. The sun cast a brilliant glow on the water, the shores of New Jersey visible, the highway directly across Port Imperial Marina.

I took the fourteenth street exit and made my way south on tenth avenue towards the Kitten Club. There were plenty of spots available, so I pulled up on the corner of Washington and 12th and rang Curt's cell phone. He didn't answer, but then I saw him walking towards me. Hanging up the phone, I unlocked the passenger side door. Curt slipped in and stretched out.

There were massive bags under his eyes, and his clothes were rumpled. Plus he smelled kind of funky. Not the Curt Sheffield I was used to hanging out with.

"How was your night?" I said.

"Let's not go there. For a chunky guy, Goggins has a motor that would make Jeff Gordon piss his pants."

Across the street, we could both see the entrance to the Kitten Club. I'd been there twice. Once to cover a murder, the second to rescue Amanda when I felt she might be in danger. I was getting a little tired of this place.

"You said something about the club not surprising you," I said. "What did you mean by that?'

"You're not a native New Yorker," Curt said, "so you wouldn't remember. For about ten years during the mid seventies and eighties, the space the Kitten Club currently occupies was a different club called Mineshaft."

"Sounds hot."

"You have no idea. While it was open, Mineshaft was one of the most popular gay bars in the city. They had dungeons, cages, S and

M, bondage, you name it. Then the city shut the club down in eighty five, claiming that all the rampant sexual activity was helping to spread the AIDS virus."

"Holy crap, are you serious?"

"Yessir. Apparently Mineshaft--and a number of other clubs--had back rooms and basements where club goers could partake in, let's just say, activities that did not require clothing. Rumors had it that the club was actually Mafia owned and operated. The mob started losing money hand over fist, and the lunkheads figured people just weren't spending money, but the sad truth is they were losing a lot of their clientele to the virus. After it was shut down, the club was a ghost lot for almost twenty years and was basically nothing more than an abandoned warehouse. It was supposed to be torn down until somebody--guess who--bought the lot."

"Shawn Kensbrook."

"Bingo. This place is all sorts of bad news. It wouldn't surprise me in the least if an entrepreneur like Kensbrook was padding his wallet by giving some of those hidden rooms to 718 Enterprises."

As we watched the club, a young man wearing a suit turned the corner and entered the front door.

"You saw that?" I said.

"Sure did."

"So what do we do now?" I said. "You want to call for backup?"

"Not yet. Right now we have no probable cause. I didn't see Goggins enter with any drugs and we haven't seen anybody leave with them. We go charging in now without a warrant, the whole thing gets thrown out."

"Come on Curt, we have to do someth..."

And then I stopped talking.

"There," I said, pointing out the object of my curiosity to Sheffield. "We follow that."

Curt focused his eyes on what I was staring at. It was a shipping truck, and it was parked around the back entrance of the Kitten Club. On the side of the side were written the words "Sam's Fresh Fish!". The slogan was accompanied by a cute illustration of a live fish standing on a plate smiling while holding a sign that read, "I'm Fresh!"

And standing behind the truck were two men, unloading boxes and carrying them inside the club.

"This place serves dinner," Curt said. "And those little hors d'oeuvres with salmon on toast points. It's a fine attempt Parker, but you're reaching."

I turned to Curt. "Fish isn't delivered on Sundays."

He cocked his had. "What are you talking about?"

"The markets are closed on Sundays. That's why you when you order fish on a Sunday, you're getting food that's been on ice over the weekend."

"You're kidding."

"No sir. I did a piece on the South Street Seaport a few months ago. Took seven showers to wash that smell off me. And one thing I learned is that there are no fish deliveries on Sundays in this city. "

"So if that truck isn't delivering fish," Curt said, "then..."

"Then we follow the truck."

"The truck?"

"This place is a refilling station. My guess is they don't keep more than a few days supply in here. Wherever the Darkness is coming from, it's not here. But I have a feeling Sam the fisherman might have an idea."

"Lead the way."

But I couldn't lead the way. That was up to the employees of Sam's, or whatever front the Sam's truck was used for, and they took their sweet time. The men unloaded at least a dozen large boxes, which they carefully brought inside the Kitten Club. Curt and I sat there and watched in silence, trying to figure out just how much the merchandise inside those boxes were worth, where they came from, and where it was being manufactured.

Finally, at about eight thirty, just as the New York streets were beginning to clog up with rush hour traffic, one of the men climbed into the driver's side and churned the ignition. He slowly pulled away from the club, turning south onto ninth avenue and then right on fourteenth street heading east.

Fourteenth was one of the major Manhattan arteries, so going crosstown took some time. The driver of the truck didn't seem in a particular hurry, never honking or making any maneuvers that would have gotten him noticed.

When we got to third avenue, the truck headed north, and then a right at thirty sixth.

"Is he headed to the tunnel?" Curt said.

The truck seemed to answer that question for us as it merged left on thirty sixth into the Midtown tunnel, heading out towards Queens.

"What the hell is in Queens?" Curt asked again.

"I hope you're just thinking out loud and not expecting me to answer," I said, "because I'm as confused as you are."

Once through the tunnel, the truck stayed on 495-East, not going a single mile over the speed limit. After about seven miles, the truck merged onto the Grand Central Expressway, then took the Van Wyck south. I was not thoroughly confused, and I could tell from Curt's expression he was too.

As we neared the Briarwood section of Queens, the truck abruptly turned off of the Van Wyck, still keeping legal speed, and continued south until it began to slow. As this point I slowed the car as well, traffic easing up, making us more noticeable. We were still two cars behind the truck, and I was hoping that driving a big rig made it a little harder for the driver to spot us.

Then, a mile down the road, the truck made another right and disappeared.

"This isn't good," I said, slowing down and pulling over to the side of the road.

Running at least half a mile was a fence made of chicken wire, the top lined with sharp barbs. We were a good few miles from any sort of body of water. "My guess is they don't ship fish here," I said. "What do we do now?"

Curt sat there, shaking his head. "We don't have PC," he said.

"Screw probable cause Curt, we go in there I'll be my father's eyes we'll find it within thirty seconds."

"I don't know," he said. "We don't even know what we'd be walking into."

"You're a cop and I'm a reporter at one of the biggest papers in the city," I said. "They can't just kill us."

As I said that, suddenly we whipped around as something rapped at the passenger side door. There was a man standing then leaning over, gently knocking his knuckles against the window.

I felt a lump rise in my throat. What the hell was he doing here? Curt immediately lowered his window and said, "Detective

Makhoulian, I...how did you get here?"

Detective Sevi Makhoulian, wearing a light brown jacket that fluttered in the wind, nodded, gesturing across the front seat towards my window.

We turned around to find another man there. This one I'd never met before, but I knew him right away. He was in his early forties, with wavy blonde hair and an ear that looked like a bad science experiment.

It was Rex Malloy, and he was smiling as he aimed a gun at my head.

Chapter 47

Rex Malloy opened up the backseat door and slid in, keeping his gun trailed on the back of Curt's head. Detective Makhoulian was walking in front of us, leading us towards the path that the Sam's fish truck had pulled into.

"Weapon, please," Malloy said to Curt.

"I'm not packing."

"And I'm Tiger Woods. Weapon. Please."

I closed my eyes as I felt the muzzle of the gun pressed against my head. Curt reached down and unstrapped a gun from his ankle, then handed it over.

"Thank you," Malloy said. "Was that so hard?"

I could see Malloy through the rearview mirror. His gun was held level, steady, and there was even the slightest hint of a grin on his face.

Curt looked straight ahead. He was quiet, but I could sense that he was seething inside. As a cop, I could imagine it was a massive blow to your ego to be ambushed like this. But it wasn't Curt's fault. At least now we knew who the mole was inside the NYPD. And it was the very man who'd helped 'investigate' my brother's murder.

"How long has Makhoulian been working for you?" I asked. Up ahead we approached a gate, which opened for us.

Malloy tilted his head just slightly. "Now come on Henry. There'll be plenty of time to ask questions. And please call him 'Detective.'"

"He's no more a detective than you are a soldier," I spat.

Malloy squinted his eyes just slightly, and the hint of a grin became a full blown smile.

"You know, I wasn't sure how much Bill Hollinsworth was able to get out before we quieted that rat," Malloy said.

"He told us everything," I said. "I know about Panama, about the Hard Chargers. I know that your brother was killed and you've decided to emulate him in some sick game, you whack job."

"Emulate?" Malloy said. "My friend, I am a living tribute to my brother."

"Shame you didn't both get plugged over there," Curt said. "Save us all a lot of time."

"Even if I did," Malloy said, "it wouldn't have changed anything except my post-military career. You two just happened to be caught up in the current, and lucky enough for you, you'll actually get to know the truth before you die. Well, at least all the truth that's fit to print."

"What the hell's that supposed to mean?" I said.

"Just sit tight," Malloy said. "We're almost there."

I followed Makhoulian down a long dirt road, both sides bracketed by fencing topped with razor wire. The forest was thick behind the fence, blocking our path from view. The road snaked and twisted for over a mile, before it opened into a large open field, surrounding by more fencing and still closed off from the rest of the world.

There was a large brown warehouse in the middle, some sort of facility. As we approached the facility, two men carrying machine guns came out to meet us. The stopped on either side of the car and waited.

"Get out," Malloy said.

"Or what?" Curt replied.

"Or I'll kill your friend Parker. And if Parker doesn't get out, I'll kill you. And if you both refuse to get out, I'll kill every member of your family."

Hatred burning through me, I opened the door and stepped out. Curt did the same.

As we stepped out, I was shoved up against the car and searched by the man with the machine gun. The man on the other side did the same to Curt.

From me they confiscated a Bic pen, and from Curt a Swiss army knife that was attached to his keychain. Then they took the whole keychain as well.

I was sweating terribly, my mind and heart racing. As I stood back up, I was finally able to get a full glimpse of our surroundings. Parked around the side of the warehouse was the fish truck, the rear backed in to what looked like a loading dock. And if there was a loading dock here, I had no doubt that this was where they shipped the Darkness.

"Come on," Malloy said, "she's waiting for you."

"Who the hell is waiting for us?" Curt said. Then he turned to Detective Makhoulian. "And you, you fucking rat. If I don't leave here alive, I swear to God you're coming with me."

Makhoulian just stood there and said, "I'm sorry Curtis. You're a good man, but you're out of your league."

"What the hell does that mean? And who is this 'she' you're talking about?"

"Eve Ramos," I said. "She was one of the survivors of the attack in Panama. She's the Fury." Curt looked at me, confused, this his eyes widened as the totality of our situation sank in. "She's the one who wanted my brother killed."

"Henry," he said.

"I know."

Malloy said, "Follow me."

As if we'd had second thoughts, the two gunmen proceeded to follow us as Malloy led us up to the warehouse. He entered a code on a side door, opened it and ushered us in.

We were in a long, narrow stairwell, painted a dull gray. Cameras were positioned at several spots at every landing. Malloy walked in front of us, taking us up two flights of stairs before we stopped in front of a door with another keypad. I counted three cameras, red lights glowing steadily.

"You come with me," Malloy said, looking at Curt. "You're staying here."

"I'm not going anywhere," Curt said.

Malloy ripped the gun from his waistband and jammed it under Curt's jaw, hard enough to make the man wince. "You're going to come with me, right now."

Malloy signaled to the two gunmen, and they kept their muzzles trained on me as Malloy led Curt somewhere upstairs. When he was out of sight, one of the men turned to me and said, "You're going to wait in here."

He jabbed a code in with a calloused finger, and when the LED light turned green he pushed it open.

To my surprise, the door opened into a medium sized conference room, complete with varnished wood table and comfortable leather chairs. There was even a speakerphone hooked up and sitting on the middle of the table, like a cadre of suits was about to walk through the door and talk shop while scarfing down bagels and coffee.

"What the hell..." I was able to say before I was pushed inside, the door slamming shut behind me.

The first thing I did when the door clicked shut was run to the table and turn on the speaker phone. I wasn't shocked to find that there was no dial tone.

"Shit!" I yelled at the top of my lungs. It wasn't quite a substitute for 'Help' but nobody could hear me anyway.

I walked around the room, looking for anything I could use. There was nothing. I debated unscrewing one of wheels from the chairs to brandish as a weapon, but in a warehouse filled with people armed to the gills it was more apt to get me killed quicker.

They wanted me here for a reason, or they would have killed me already. Besides, this room was too pretty to commit murder in.

At least, that's what I thought until I saw the light red stain on the carpet by the door I'd come in through. It had clearly been scrubbed numerous times, but damned if blood was just too difficult a liquid to get out.

"His name was Jeremy Robertson," a voice said. "And he didn't listen."

I whirled around to find a woman standing at the other end of the room. From the lines and age in her face I made her out to be in her early to mid forties, but the tone and muscle definition was striking beneath her black tank top. She had long black hair that I could see spread out behind her waist and her green eyes looked at me with a strange kind of calmness that would have given me chills if I wasn't scared to death.

"Jeremy killed himself," she said. "We only bring in men who have something to lose. Unfortunately, as we learned later, Jeremy had nothing."

"Eve Ramos," I said. "You're the Fury."

Ramos laughed, her voice high pitched, full of delight. "The Fury," she said. "I always found such enjoyment in that name. And to think how many people trembled at the very sound of a person who might not even exist. I suppose it works the same way with Satan and even Jesus. Beholden to deities we will never know exist until the day we die." Eve Ramos looked up at the ceiling. "I bet Jeremy Robertson knows whether there is a devil."

"You manufacture this poison," I said. "I'm pretty sure that if there is a devil, that puts you on even keel with him."

"Oh, Mr. Parker," Eve said as she crossed the room to where I was standing. Then, moving faster then I knew possible, she had gripped my throat in her hand and said, "Who's to say the devil is a man?"

She then pushed me backwards. I coughed once, but stared her down.

"You killed my brother," I said. "Just like you're responsible for about a dozen more deaths from this drug."

"A dozen?" Ramos said. "Henry, you don't know the half of it."

"So what do you want?" I said. "And where's my friend?"

"Officer Sheffield is fine," she said. "Unfortunately as a police officer, we cannot simply dispose of your friend until we can be certain it is done in a way that is, shall we say, less than incriminating."

"And me. Why am I here?"

"Henry, you came to us, remember?"

"Why am I alive?"

"You're alive because you have use to me. Before you die, you have a chance to do one last noble deed. And then when the time comes to meet your maker, you can be sure it will be the right one."

"I don't understand," I said.

"Please," Ramos said. "Sit."

I didn't move.

"Fine. You'll be sitting enough anyway." She went to the head of the table, pulled out a leather chair and lay back, propping her feet up on the table. She was wearing dark boots, dirty and worn. This was not a woman who preferred high heels. "You are a newspaper man. I take it you know much about our product from the reporting of Ms. Paulina Cole."

"I read her article," I said. "And I know how you got her to write it."

"See," she said, smiling. "I knew you were a bright young man. There's no way Ms. Cole could have had access to that information without anybody else knowing about it. Yes, we fed it to Ms. Cole. And now you are going to write another article for your newspaper. And once that is done, you can leave this world in peace, knowing you've kept your loved ones from harm's way."

"My loved ones?"

Eve took her feet down, leaned forward. "You came to my attention right after your brother, Mr. Gaines, was killed. How fortunate for us that another man was accused of his murder, that was an unexpected bonus. But when you figured out who pulled the trigger, needed a way to keep you in check. It is part of my job to learn about people. Their families, backgrounds, careers, loved ones. I know you have barely seen your parents in ten years. I know you have little family or friends. But you do have a woman who holds your heart. So piercing her would piece you." She smiled. "So to speak."

"My brother," I said. "You were behind it. You killed him."

"Guilty," she said. "When you run an organization, the buck stops with you. When your brother learned about our plans to diversify our product, and he objected. In my line of business you cannot have employees questioning decisions, or threatening to divulge company secrets. He came to you, and that's when I decided he had to be dealt with."

"Dealt with," I said. "That's a pleasant term for cold blooded murder."

"Nothing around here happens without my say so," Ramos said. "And if you do not write this for me, I will take your woman, Amanda, and I will make her scream so loud that even if you do make it to heaven, Henry, her cries will pierce the ears of God himself. I will grind her bones to paste, and coat the walls of this room with her blood. And I will make sure you are alive when all of it takes place. And only when you have no screams left to offer will you join her."

I sat there, my whole body cold. Amanda.

"You see when I kill a person, their death must not be in vain. It must represent something. Your brother's death was a sign that even our highest-earning lieutenants were not invulnerable. Kenneth Tsang's death was a warning to new employees as to what could happen if you weren't trustworthy. Brett Kaiser's death showed that we can reach anybody, anywhere. To me, blood and bone are like paint and a brush. With the right artistry, one can create a work of art that speaks to people. Your family, Henry, would be a message that our reach does not stop within our organization, but that we can touch even the smallest, most insignificant lives."

"You wouldn't..."

"I wouldn't?" Ramos said. "Your mother and father live in Bend, Oregon on a sunny little street called Eastview drive. I can have a man there tonight. Your parents could be dead before the evening news. Your parents are insignificant, which is why their deaths would be all the more glorious."

"You're a monster."

"I'm only a monster because this involves you, Henry. How many monsters do you see, day in and day out, in your line of work? Proximity heightens emotions. Things could be different. You could have been down on your luck, penniless, and come to work for me. And then, like so many of these young men, you would have understood."

"I don't know anything besides what Paulina wrote," I said. "There's nothing more to the story."

"That's not true," she said. "You've been quite an explorer. Tell me what you know."

I looked up at her, and if looks could kill Eve Ramos would have been dead several times over. "I know that you and Rex Malloy were in Panama together, and that your troop was attacked and Chester Malloy was killed. I also know that it was in Panama that you learned how to synthesize Darkness, and you managed to smuggle it back to America. I know that all your drug mules are young men, and you're using their debts to get them to work for you."

"Great thing about those young men," Eve said, "is that they have something to lose. You see, when a man has pride, he will do things he knows are wrong to prove his worth. These men were born with nothing, but worked their way into high paying jobs. When those lives were taken away, that ambition, that pride left a gaping hole. I simple offer to fill that hole. I will not use men from the slums, poor urban souls who have nothing to lose. Dealers are nothing more than hungry animals. You feed them, throw them an extra bone here or there, they'll do anything for you."

"Even die for you."

"Not by choice, but yes."

"Why 718 Enterprises?" I asked.

"Ha! That's simple, Henry. I was born in Queens."

"That's it?"

"That's it."

There was a knock at the door behind Ramos. She went and opened it. A man stood there. He was wearing a suit, brown hair neatly combed. And he was holding a legal pad and pen.

"Leonard, come in," she said. "Meet Henry Parker."

"Mr. Parker, it's a pleasure." He didn't offer a hand. Just as well.

"Leonard Reeves," I said. He looked at Ramos with discomfort evident.

"How much does he know?"

Eve chuckled softly. "Apparently more than I thought."

"Leonard Reeves," I said again, "Graduated from Princeton in 1993. Former executive at Morgan Stanley, and liaison to the Department of Finance."

I watched as Reeves's eyes widened, rage drumming up inside of his.

"How do you..."

"Which leads me to this question," I said. "How much is Eve Ramos paying you to sell out our government?"

Now it was Ramos who couldn't contain herself, laughing hysterically. Reeves looked at her. His rage seemed to subside as he saw how unperturbed she was by my knowledge.

"Henry, you have this all wrong," she said. "We're not selling out the government. Hell, we're working for them."

Chapter 48

"Working for them," I said. "You mean the city is making money off of you. That's why I found a money order made out to Morgan Isaacs for fifty grand from Leonard Reeves. Reeves works for 718. You set your drug cartel set up as a legit business, and the government is making millions of dollars in taxes off of dead people and blood money."

"Millions right now, maybe. Soon it'll be hundreds of millions," Ramos said. "And once the Darkness spreads to other metropolitan areas--Los Angeles, Boston, Chicago--it'll be in the billions."

"How can they let this happen?" I said. "Don't they know these drugs are killing people? Don't they know who you are?"

"Know who I am?" Eve said. "Not only do they know who I am...they're the reason I'm here."

"Panama," I said. "The Hard Chargers--you were one of them?"

"Yes and no. I certainly did my share of hell raising down there. Nothing helps sell a war than violence against our troops. But those bastards weren't supposed to kill me. And it's their fault Chester died."

"Hollinsworth said you found a way to synthesize Darkness," I said. "So why would the government still work with you if you stole this from Noriega?"

"Oh they didn't know," she said. "In fact, they trusted me so much that when the CIA-backed cartels in the eighties got out of hand, guess who they put in charge to oversee things?"

"That's why you're the Fury," I said. "They installed you as a watchdog because their money was at stake. With you there, they could make sure the money was going to fund the Contras."

"Yeah, but that stopped being fun after a while. Why be a watchdog when you can be the top dog? Those cartels made billions, but the leadership had more balls than they had brains. They were more than happy to let someone take over who could handle distribution on a nationwide basis. Unfortunately word got out and that reporter Webb found out about it, and the CIA tried to pull the plug. But when you're running a covert operation, pulling the plug doesn't mean ending things so much as pretending they never happened."

I said, "So they left you in charge of the largest drug cartel in North America."

"Your tax dollars at work. And Mr. Reeves here was kind enough to set up a deal where not only could we work in peace, but we'd benefit the city of New York as well. Thousands of Federal employees laid off due to a lack of funds, and that's exactly what we're giving them back."

"Makhoulian," I said. "He was the mole in the NYPD. He knew everything we were doing."

"More or less. I am a little surprised by how persistent you are Henry."

"So why this?" I said. "Why now?"

"Well, the truth is we weren't able to perfect the mixture until recently. But if you believe in fate--like I do--than everything came together for a reason. Look at this city, Henry. It's infrastructure is crumbling. It's billions of dollars in debt. Millions of people have lost everything, and the people who pump the most money into this economy--the rich--are losing their jobs. The pipes have been rotting for years. With the Darkness, I managed to build the greatest cherry bomb the city has ever seen, and dropping it into those pipes now will cause the whole system to come crashing down. Cities burn from the ground up, not the top down."

"All because you think you were sent to die in Panama. This isn't about money. It's about payback."

"Call it what you want. Truth is, I'm doing this city a favor. New York will have a chance to bring itself back from the wreckage. Twenty years ago this city teetered on the edge, and it was brought back. When a city comes so close for a second time, it needs a little push. That's where I come in."

"No matter how many people die in the process."

"I read somewhere that over a hundred billion people have died since the earth was created. Am I really supposed to shed a tear for a few more?"

"You're settling a grudge," I said. "You feel you were sent to die, so you're taking revenge."

"Not to mention a handsome profit," she said. "If there is a better feeling than seeing the same fat, stupid men who sent you to die line your pockets, I don't know what it is."

Reeves came over and placed the pad and pen in front of me. Then he stepped back and folded his arms behind his back. I could tell he wasn't happy about this, wasn't happy I knew the depth of his involvement. But Ramos kept him fed. And that was good enough.

"You write your article, including the facts I've told you. Once it is written, Leonard and I will go over it to make sure it doesn't contain anything that we don't approve of. After that we will email it to your boss, Mr. Langston."

"And then what?"

"And when it runs, we can assure you that Amanda Davies will live a long, happy life. Well, a long life at least."

"And me?"

"Having saved a life, you can go to your grave with the nobility many men do not."

"And you get to promote the Darkness even more."

"The New York Dispatch is only read by half the city," she said. "With your paper we'll get the other half too."

I eyed the pen, wondering if there was a way I could use it. Not that I'd been trained in any Bourne-esque dojo where they taught you how to kill two people with a single pen.

"Mr. Reeves here will watch you. I don't expect your finest work, Henry. Time is of the essence."

I didn't know what to do. Amanda's life versus thousands of people who would read about this drug and be tempted to buy it. I pictured Amanda, sitting at home, while the city burned around her. Then I pictured her grieving at my funeral, not knowing I'd given my life for her. What the hell could I do?

Before I could do or say anything, there was another knock at the door behind Eve Ramos. It startled her very briefly, and I took a step forward.

She opened it, and standing there was Rex Malloy.

"Eve," he said. "We've got a problem."

"What kind of problem."

"Sheffield and Parker," he said. "They didn't come alone."

Ramos stood there, unsure what to make of what Malloy had

said. We had come alone. What the hell was Malloy talking about?

Suddenly I heard a loud noise come from outside the compound. A second explosion, then a third, rattling the floor, reverberating. Somebody was shooting at the warehouse from outside. Eve Ramos's eyes narrowed as she stared at me. I had no answers.

They didn't come alone.

Had somebody followed us?

"Get up Parker," Ramos said, her voice gone to steel. She marched over and grabbed me by the hair, pulling me up. I stood, wrenched away.

"Get off of me."

Then I realized where the gunfire had come from. We weren't being shot at from outside. Somebody inside the compound was firing at someone outside.

Then it dawned on me.

We had been followed. By Jack O'Donnell.

Chapter 49

The first volley of gunfire drove them to dive behind the police cars, bullets strafing the metal, punching quarter-sized holes in every car. Jack O'Donnell felt a pain in his arm as he hit the ground, dirt kicking up around him.

He was surrounded by two dozen of New York's finest, and now that the level of violence had escalated there was sure to be SWAT and helicopter backup. But for now it was just this ragged old journalist and a bunch of cops who'd walked into a buzzsaw.

"Is this normal?" Jack shouted when the gunfire stopped.

Chief of Department Louis Carruthers, his back pressed up against a blue and white, shook his head. "Not in the least. It only means one thing, so you'd better keep your head down."

"What's that?"

"It means they're not planning to be arrested."

Jack slowly picked himself, peeked over the hood of a car, just in time for another round to rip up the car and force him back to the ground.

His heart was beating a million miles a minute, but something besides fear coursed through the old lion. Neither Henry or Curt knew Jack had followed them all the way from Parker's apartment, and it gave Jack a slight bit of pride to know he still had a little left in the old oil can. But when he saw the two men force Henry and Curt to follow them at gunpoint, he knew the time for hide and seek was over.

It was less than ten minutes before the cavalry arrived, and it took less than one to tear open the gated entrance and force themselves inside. Jack didn't know what to expect, but when he saw the massive warehouse and the sentry guards, the fence barricading the area from both trespassers and onlookers, he had a feeling they'd stumbled onto the very heart of where the Darkness was produced.

"Do we just wait until they run out of bullets then?" Jack yelled above the storm.

Carruthers looked at him and shook his head.

Then he yelled to the rest of the cops perched outside, "There are two innocents in there, including one of our own. Let's get them the hell out of there!"

Then a barrage of gunfire strafed the outside of the warehouse, shattering glasses, shredding brick, smoke and dust pouring from everywhere.

Jack covered his ears, felt dirt and gravel raining down around him, stinging his face and neck. And below the pain in his arm, the rapid pace of his heart that scared the hell out of him, Jack had a feeling this was just the beginning.

Chapter 50

When the gunfire first erupted, Eve Ramos went into the hallway to find out what was going on. I could see she and Rex Malloy talking. Malloy was animated, pointing somewhere I couldn't see, gesturing like mad as Ramos stood there impassively, processing it all. Behind them, still in the room with me, was Leonard Reeves. And unlike his two comrades, Reeves eyes betrayed him. He looked nervous, the kind of man who might dish out violence but never expected it to come back to him.

Whatever Rex Malloy was saying, it as frightening Leonard Reeves something bad.

While they were preoccupied, I picked up the pen and quietly walked over to where Reeves was standing. He was not an especially large man, about five foot ten, not fat but without much discernible muscle definition. Sometimes you could take one look at a person, they way they carried themselves, and know how brave they were. What kind of fight they would put up. In Leonard Reeves, I got the sense of a man who talked a big game but once cornered, would piss his pants faster than an eight year old with a tiny bladder.

So with little time to decide my course of action, I took a chance that could lead either to my freedom, or my death.

Gripping the pen in my first, the point sticking out two inches, I wrapped my left arm around the front of Reeves's neck and jammed the pen right under his jawline on his carotid artery, hard enough to that I felt the tip threaten to pierce skin. Reeves was surprised and struggled, crying out, but I whispered into his ear, "Move once more and you'll see your blood all over Malloy's nice blond hair."

Reeves relaxed. His hand was still on the arm that held his neck in place, but there was no strength in it.

I could feel the gun against my hip, and holding the pen I quickly grabbed it and swapped the writing utensil for the pistol. Not a bad choice. I flicked the safety off. I'd only held a gun once before, and even then it was out of self defense. I didn't want to fire it.

Right now, though, I was certain that if need be I would use it. I wasn't sure who was more frightened: me knowing I could be forced to end a man's life, or Reeves knowing his life was in the hands of a man who had nothing to lose.

I led Reeves into the stairwell where Ramos and Malloy were standing. Windows opened onto the front of the compound, but Ramos and Malloy were blocking my view. I couldn't see who or what was out there. Whoever it was clearly had their attention.

Eve Ramos turned around. Rex Malloy did as well. They both stared at me, Malloy seeming more pissed off while Ramos smiled at me like I'd just built a nice big house of cards.

"Take me to Sheffield," I said. "As soon as we're outside, I let Reeves go. If not, he's a dead man."

"Henry," Ramos said, cocking her head to the side, that smile still spread on her face. "I give you credit for keeping your balls intact. But you have gravely overestimated Mr. Reeves's worth to me. Especially in light of his less than stellar reflexes."

With that, Eve Ramos pulled a gun from her waistband and put a bullet right in Leonard Reeves's head.

He dropped to the floor, his body becoming dead weight in less than a second. I felt sticky blood on my hands. I looked at Ramos. She seemed oddly disappointed.

"Sometimes," she said, "you don't have time to paint a picture."

I held Reeves's gun out, pointed it at Ramos.

"Let us of here," I said.

"Or what? You shoot me and end up looking like something the butcher threw away? Put the gun down, Henry, before you get hurt."

And just like that, the window behind Ramos shattered, gunfire riddling the stairwell. Sparks cascaded all around us at the bullets ricocheted off the metal bars. Whoever was outside was now firing back.

We all ducked, covering out heads as glass came pouring down around us. Ramos knelt on the floor below the window, her back against the wall. She held a hand up to her cheek. It came away slick with blood where she'd been cut by an arrant shard. Malloy was on his stomach, and crawled over to see if she was alright. And right there I saw my one chance to live.

While they were distracted, I rushed forward and shoved Malloy as hard as I could. His body, already off balance, went toppling down the stairs. He landed with a thud two floors below, screamed in pain and clutching his leg.

Before Ramos had a chance to recover, I leapt back into the stairwell and began to climb. They'd taken Curt somewhere upstairs, and I could only hope to find him before the entire warehouse was shredded.

As I ascended, relief spread through me as I saw that Ramos was still pinned down in the stairwell below me. I tried the door one flight above but it was locked from the inside. There was no keypad I could see, no way inside. So I kept going up, hunched over, trying not to get shot or sliced.

One more flight up and I'd reached the top level of the warehouse. Peering over the railing, my breath caught in my throat when I saw that neither Ramos or Malloy were still there. They weren't on the stairwell though, so I had a small window to figure out what the hell to do.

The stairwell here had one door, and this had an electronic keypad. I tried several combinations, including 718, but none of them worked. But just as I was about to give up and turn to my non-existent plan B, I heard the doorknob turn from the other side.

Stepping back to allow the door to open, the handle turned and into the hall walked another man. He big, with a gleaming bald head, numerous tattoos running down his arms. And, oh yeah, he was also holding a big, black assault rifle.

I was hidden between the door and the wall, my gun held out in defense, but the man didn't see me as he raced down the stairs. When he'd gone down several steps, I spun around the closing door, stuck the gun muzzle into the crack, threw it open and pulled the door shut behind me just as I heard a startled 'Hey!' from below.

Turning around, I found myself in a narrow hallway. It was painted stark white. There were two doors at the other end, and I could see an LED light blinking red on the farthest one.

Curt.

I ran as fast as I could to the other end and banged on the door.

"Curt!" I shouted. "You in there?"

It took a moment, but then I heard someone say, "Henry?"

"Yeah! How do I open this thing?"

"Four eight two one nine," he said. "I saw the guy enter it when he put me in here."

I pressed the numbers on the keypad, and the light turned green.

I yanked the handle and pulled the door open, just as the door as the other end flew open revealing the guy with the rifle. He yelled some sort of curse, but I dove inside Curt's room and pulled the door closed just as a spatter of bullets his the metal. I held my foot against the door, keeping it open just slightly to make sure we didn't get locked inside.

"Holy shit," Curt said, "you ok?"

"Yeah, fine," I said, noticing a trickle of blood on my arm where glass had cut me. "No big deal."

"How'd the hell you get away?"

"No time. Here," I said, handing Curt the gun. "You're probably better with this than I am."

Another round of gunfire hit the door, and we parted on either side. Dimples punched out on our side of the door every time a round hit it.

"That's an M16," Curt said. "A4, I believe. Thirty round magazine. And he's fired twenty three of them."

Another burst of gunfire shelled the door. Curt looked at the dimples, said, "Seven. Get your shit together Parker, here we go."

Curt turned the handle and kicked the door open, training the gun on the rifleman just as he was popping out the old magazine.

"You move and I take your head off," Curt said. The man stood there, unsure of what to do, the magazine clattering to the ground. "Take your hand out of your pocket."

He did so, holding a fresh mag.

"Drop it," Curt said. The bald man looked at him, trying to size Curt up. Then, instead of putting down the magazine, he snapped it into place and raised it to fire.

Three loud reports exploded in the hallway, and the rifleman was driven backwards, three fresh holes in his chest. As he fell he looked at Curt, surprised that he'd actually pulled the trigger.

Without a moment of hesitation, Curt went over to the fallen gunman and picked up the rifle. He checked the new magazine, then came back over to me and held out the gun, butt first.

"You've used one of these before, right?"

"Um, not on purpose."

"It's easy. Safety's already off. Aim with two hands and squeeze. None of this holding the gun sideways or upside down or any of that stupid gangster, Angelina Jolie crap in the movies. You hold it straight, two hands, squeeze hard for each round and take kickback into account. Aim for the chest. Think you can handle that?"

"If I say yes will it matter?"

"Not really, but we don't have a choice. Come on Parker."

Curt led the way, rifle snug against his shoulder, as we crouched outside the door to the opposite stairwell from where I'd come from. This was where they'd brought him from, and somewhere below was the way out. And we had to get out fast, because the gunfire from both sides was turning this place into swiss cheese.

We stood on either side of the door, both of our guns at the ready. Curt reached over and pulled it open, and as he did I swung the gun into the opening, ready for anything.

It was empty.

Curt joined me, using the rifle as a sight to confirm that we were the only people there. I could hear Curt breathing hard, but his eyes were focused. He nodded down.

I'd lead, he'd cover me.

He mouthed age before beauty. I gave him the finger, and slowly crept into the stairwell.

If I remembered correctly, the entrance was three flights below us. But looking down, I saw that the stairwell continued below that one to a basement. Four levels in total.

The noise in the stairwell was deafening, the gunfire echoing all around us. I made my way down the stairs, sensing Curt's muzzle right above me.

The landing below us was empty. Curt stood one step above me, then flicked the muzzle once. Two more flights.

My heart pounding, the gun shaking ever so slightly in my hands, I moved down to the next level, the third floor. Nobody there. One more to go.

Between the blood roaring in my veins and the deafening noise surrounding us, even if there was someone below us hiding, we wouldn't know. Only one way to find out.

No time for creeping around. I leapt down the next flight, to the second floor, recognizing the same door they'd brought us through, the same cameras recording everything. Curt steped onto the landing as well, the rifle still aimed forward. He nodded at the door. I reached for it, turned the knob. Felt it go. One step from freedom.

But then I looked below me, saw the landing of the next floor below us, and knew there was one more thing to do. To know.

Below us, on the basement landing, was a small pile of black rocks. It was Darkness, the drug, the cherry bomb Ramos was using to tear down the city. And I knew what that basement was used for, and that I couldn't leave without knowing for sure.

I nodded to Curt. He rolled his eyes, said, come on. And he was on board to see what lay below us. To see what kind of evil Eve Ramos had been waiting to unleash upon this city.

Chapter 51

The door below us opened with the same combination as Curt's holding cell. And as soon as that smell hit our nostrils, we know what we'd found. It was only when we entered the room that we saw the extent of it.

The basement of the warehouse was nearly the length of a football field, and nearly every inch of it was piled high with pills, rocks and powders of different sizes and concentrations. There were bags of powder stacked fifteen feet high, piles of black rocks that you could literally dive into.

I lowered my gun, the blood draining from my face.

"Holy shit," Curt said beside me. "Are they supplying the whole country?"

"That's the idea," I said. "First New York, then anywhere that needs a fix. And I don't see any mixing agents or supplies here, so my guess is it's brought in across our borders somehow."

"This is incredible," I said. "But we can't let it survive this."

"What do you mean?"

"Makhoulian," I said. "Who knows if he's the only cop in on it? We let this stuff go into evidence, what are the odds it leaks out? Seventy five? Ninety?"

"So what do we do?" Curt said.

"I don't know, but this place has to burn."

As I said that, a hail of gunfire drilled the wall behind us, sending us running for cover. It had come from inside somewhere.

"I know you're in here asshole," the voice yelled. It was Rex Malloy. "Let's make this easy."

Another round let loose, this time grinding up a pile of black rocks beside me, the dark suit raining into the air, burning my eyes. I sure as hell hoped Curt was counting this guy's round too.

Curt was crouched behind a steel beam. He tried to lean out to look, but gunfire drove him back behind it.

Asshole.

Only one asshole. That was my chance. Malloy thought there was only one of us.

I ran around the side of one pile, then crouched down, holding the gun in front of me. I tried to listen for footsteps, but heard nothing. Then more gunfire sounded, aimed as Curt's hiding spot. It was a matter of seconds before he got close enough to get a good shot.

I rounded the pile, gun outstretched, and saw two boot heels pass me. Rex Malloy. He was closing on Sheffield.

As he passed, I stepped out behind him and raised my gun to his chest level. As Malloy raised his gun to fire, I could see the side of Curt's face. And if I could see it, Malloy could hit it. Once shot. That's all I had.

So I pulled the trigger.

The force of the gunshot drove my hands upwards, but I didn't stumble. Rex Malloy grunted as he fell forward, his rifle clattering to the floor as he fell. And then he lay there, still.

"Oh my god," I said, stepping over the body. "Oh my god. Curt? You there?"

Sheffield came out from behind the beam. "Nice shooting, Tex."

I looked at him, then felt like I was going to vomit. Then something stirred, and I felt something crack the side of my head.

I fell down, shook it off, and turned to see Rex Malloy standing up. There was no blood, nothing. Then I saw the hole in his vest. He rapped it once with his knuckle. "Was a nice shot," he said. Then as he raised the rifle towards me, a gunshot rang out and Malloy fell to one knee, blood spurting from his leg. Curt ran up to us, aimed at Malloy's head, but the man struck out lightning quick and knocked the gun from Curt's hand. Then he punched Curt in the throat.

Sheffield, wheezing, tried to catch his breath, but Malloy was on top of him. He wrapped his hands around Curt's throat and began to squeeze. My head throbbing, I picked up Malloy's dropped rifle, ran over, and drilled the butt into Malloy's head. He went down, but was simply shaken.

As he tried to get up, Curt stomped on Malloy's hand, a sickening crunch as his fingers broke. Malloy cried out. Curt placed his knee on Malloy's left shoulder, pinning him. I ran over and grabbed his other arm, trying to neutralize the man's strength. Then Curt reached over and grabbed a handful of the black gravel and shoved it into Malloy's throat.

The former Special Forces operative hacked and coughed, but Curt drove him backward with a vicious headbutt, and I could hear Malloy swallow the rocks. Then Curt raised his fist and brought it right onto Malloy's windpipe. Once, twice, until there was another sickening crack as his windpipe broke.

Malloy tried to claw at his throat, but we held him fast. Finally the man stopped struggling, his eyes glazing over. Curt felt the man's pulse, looked at me, nodded. We were both breathing hard, and the side of my head felt wet.

"Let's get the hell out of here," I said.

"Good plan. Come on."

We ran back to the stairwell and up one flight, bursting through the door into the late morning sun. The sudden glare caused us to cover our eyes, but when we opened them we saw a phalanx of cops outside the warehouse, guns trained on us.

"Don't shoot!" a voice yelled. "He's a cop!"

"And he's a reporter!" yelled another.

Jack. I laughed, never happier to hear the old man's voice.

Three cops ran over to us, guns trained, and led us back to the group. We were dirty, bleeding, but didn't feel any of it.

The shooting had stopped. All guns were still trained on the warehouse, but the area had gone silent. The calm after the storm.

Then I felt a pair of arms squeezing me to death, and I looked up to see Jack O'Donnell.

"Jesus Christ kid, what are you, a method journalist? You don't need to kill yourself to get the story."

I laughed, hugged the man right back. "You followed us," I said.

"Damn right. I have to admit it was a little selfish. Didn't want you and your cop buddy learning the truth without me."

A man came over to us. He said, "Louis Carruthers, Chief of Department. Who's left in there?"

"I don't know. At least three are dead. Leonard Reeves, another gunman and Rex Malloy."

"We've taken out another three, but we don't know how many were there to begin with. Are there any other innocents? Do we need to go back in?"

"Back in? Why would you do that?"

"Look," Jack said.

I turned around to see orange flames licking at the windows of the warehouse, thick black smoke pouring from inside.

"How'd it catch on fire?" I said.

"Don't know," Carruthers said. "But that smoke isn't from fire."

"The Darkness," I said. "Somebody's burning the place down from inside."

Before I could speak again, I heard a single gunshot report. Then there was something wet and sticky on my chest. Then I looked into Jack's eyes and knew what had just happened.

"Henry," Jack said, "what..."

Then the old man was flung backwards, a red rose blooming on his white shirt.

"Jack?" I said.

He looked as me as he fell, his eyes wide and fearful.

Then another gunshot sounded out, this one hitting the adjacent car, less than six inches from where I stood. We ducked for cover, waiting toe the firing to end. I stared at Jack, then quickly looked up to see who was shooting at us.

Eve Ramos was standing at the doorway, gun out, her face covered in blood and ash.

And then a barrage of gunfire like I'd never heard imagined tore the air apart, ripping Ramos apart in a hail of bullets and blood. Her body was flung through the air like a puppet, her gun firing wildly into the air, before she fell, lifeless, next to the burning building that housed her life's work.

I knelt down next to Jack, a knot in my throat as I hovered over him. A thin trickle of blood was streaming from his mouth.

"We need an ambulance!" I shouted as loud as I could. "Somebody help us!"

Two cops ran over, one of them carrying an orange kit. He placed it besides Jack, opening it, and began to work on my friend. My mentor. The man who was responsible for the person I'd become.

"You're gonna be fine, Jack," I said, holding his hand, praying for one squeeze.

Jack's eyes were open, and to my surprise he was actually smiling. That's when I felt that squeeze, the old, cracked palm in mine. The blood on my shirt from a man who'd lived a life that had seen more than I could ever hope to.

"It's ok Henry," he said, his voice weak, raspy. "I've told my story."

"No," I said, tears welling, as I squeezed his hand harder. "You can't. This is our story. You and me."

Jack smiled. Then he said, "I know. Butch and Sundance, Henry. Thank you for saving my life."

Then Jack O'Donnell closed his eyes for the last time.

Epilogue

Amanda held my hand through the entire funeral. I didn't cry once, and when the service was over, when the church had emptied, I hated myself for that. But then I realized that Jack had ended his life the way he wanted to, chasing that one big story, his name once again where it belonged. His final story.

Through the Darkness Comes the Dawn
by Jack O'Donnell and Henry Parker

Rex Malloy was dead. Eve Ramos was dead. Sevi Makhoulian was found less than an hour after Jack's death, hiding in a gas station in Queens. He was under indictment for enough crimes to keep him in prison until the rapture.

No less than a dozen people, ranging from accountants who handled the 718 assets to the Mayor himself, were under investigation. And I had no doubt that what they would find would end perhaps the largest drug conspiracy the city had ever seen.

And by investigators' estimates, nearly ten tons worth of narcotics had gone up in flames in that warehouse. Though he died to tell the story, Jack has saved hundreds, if not thousands of lives.

He would be remembered the way he deserved to be. A journalist who told the truth, a man who uncovered the greatest stories never told.

The day of the funeral, the Gazette ran a special edition with an insert that collected some of Jack's most famous pieces from his nearly fifty years on the job. Reading them on the subway to work reminded me of just what an amazing career he'd led. And just how rich a life had been lost.

When I got to my desk, there was a voicemail waiting for me. It was from Linda Veltre, the woman who'd edited Jack's book Through the Darkness nearly twenty years ago, chronicling the rise of the drug trade, the story where Jack had first learned of the Fury. Her publisher wanted to reissue Jack's book. And she wanted me to write the introduction.

Plus, she said, if I had any thoughts of writing my own book about the investigation of Eve Ramos and 718 Enterprises, she'd love to talk to me over lunch. Apparently she'd already received a call from Paulina Cole's literary agent expressing interest in writing a book about the story, but the editor felt mine was the right one to tell.

It was something to think about, but another day.

The day after Jack's funeral I walked into the offices of the New York Gazette, and immediately something felt different, off. I received several nods from my colleagues, the same ones who congratulated me with their eyes, but were afraid to speak because they knew what Jack had meant to me.

Sitting down, I looked out over Rockefeller Center at a city Jack had known better than most people know themselves. It was a city that pulsed with a million different veins, a million different stories. And those stories were still out there, waiting to be discovered.

Life would go on. Jack would have wanted it to.

From the corner of my eye I saw Wallace Langston making his way across the newsroom floor. There was somebody with him. I couldn't see who it was, but Jack was talking to him earnestly, pointing at things as they walked.

As they got closer, I could see that Wallace was leading around a young man. He looked to be twenty one or twenty two, a good looking kid with short black hair, sharp features, and an air of wonder about him. He was following Wallace's lead like a child experiencing a museum for the first time.

A new reporter. I smiled. The day Wallace had shown me the ropes didn't feel that long ago.

Jack was not introducing the new guy to anyone. That would come later.

Then Wallace took a detour and stopped by my desk. The new guy's cheeks were red, embarrassed, and he had trouble making eye contact.

"Henry," Wallace said. "This is Nicholas Barr. He's fresh out of J-school."

"Nice to meet you Nicholas," I said, offering my hand.

"Yeah, nice to meet me too. You. I mean meet you. Me, nice to meet you."

"Easy there Nicholas,' I said.

"You can call me Nick," he said, his voice shaking. "Or Nicholas. Nicky. Whatever you want."

"Nick it is."

"That's cool," he stammered. "I mean, ok."

"We'll catch up later Parker," Wallace said, and I felt the veteran editor's hand on my shoulder. Wallace would miss Jack as much as I would. It'd be good to tell stories of the old man. "Maybe you'll show this new kid the ropes some time."

"You got it."

And then, when Wallace and Nick Barr had left my desk, I heard the young reporter whisper enthusiastically to Wallace, "Dude, that was Henry Parker."

"He's a great reporter," Wallace said. "And actually, I think the two of you will get along quite well."

"Unreal," Barr said. "This whole place. Unreal."

I smiled, thinking about several years ago, my first day at the Gazette, when I swiped Jack O'Donnell's coat with his hand just to see if it was real. I remembered the pride and disbelief in knowing I'd be working just mere feet from a living legend.

Unreal. It had all seemed unreal.

Then I looked at Nick Barr, standing where I'd been just a few short years ago, and knew that Jack might be living on through me.

About the Author

Jason Pinter is the bestselling author of five novels in his Henry Parker thriller series, which have over one million copies in print worldwide and have been published in over a dozen countries, as well as the Middle Grade adventure novel Zeke Bartholomew: SuperSpy. He has been nominated for the Thriller Award, Strand Critics Award, Barry Award, RT Reviewers Choice Award, Shamus Award and Crime-Spree Award. Two of his books—The Fury and The Darkness—were chosen as Indie Next selections, and The Mark, The Stolen and The Fury were named to The Strand's Best Books of the Year list. The Mark and The Stolen both appeared on the 'Heatseekers' bestseller list in The Bookseller (UK). The Mark was optioned to be a feature film.

He is the Founder and Publisher of Polis Books, an independent publishing company he launched in 2013. He was named one of Publisher Weekly's inaugural Star Watch honorees, which "recognizes young publishing professionals who have distinguished themselves as future leaders of the industry." He has written for The New Republic, Entrepreneur, The Daily Beast, Medium and The Huffington Post, and been featured in Library Journal, Publishers Weekly, Mystery Scene and more.

He was named one of the top writers on Twitter (@JasonPinter) by Mashable and the Huffington Post, and his articles and essays have been covered in the New York Times, Los Angeles Times, CNN, The Atlantic, Boston Globe, New York Observer, Baltimore Sun, Salon and as far as Australia's Sydney Morning Herald. He was born in New York City and currently lives in New Jersey with his wife, their daughter, and their dog, Wilson.

Visit him online at www.JasonPinter.com a
nd on Twitter at @JasonPinter

CPSIA information can be obtained
at www.ICGtesting.com
Printed in the USA
LVHW021604040421
683400LV00013B/188

9 781947 993228